£2.

''Look, honey. Here's how it is. We work murder, not dope. I know what you're thinking. You give us the names of friends . . . and they're dopers . . . and the heat comes down on them. I'll level with you. We don't care about dope. You go ahead and give us the names of people to talk to. I guarantee you, if we walk in their pads and see a wheelbarrow of rock cocaine, we look the other way. We won't bust 'em for it and we won't run to the narcotics squad afterward and tell them who's holding. You can check on the streets about me. You won't find one person who will tell you I ever went back on my word. It's damn near all we have left in this business anymore.''

IN THE LINE OF DUTY

IN THE LINE OF DUTY

JACK MULLEN

AVON BOOKS ◆ NEW YORK

AVON BOOKS
A division of
The Hearst Corporation
1350 Avenue of the Americas
New York, New York 10019

Copyright © 1995 by Jack Mullen
Inside cover author photo by Mary Schamehorn
Published by arrangement with the author
Library of Congress Catalog Card Number: 95-94146
ISBN: 0-380-77614-6

First Avon Books Printing: December 1995

AVON TRADEMARK REG. U.S. PAT. OFF. AND IN OTHER COUNTRIES, MARCA REGISTRADA, HECHO EN U.S.A.

Printed in the U.S.A.

RA   10   9   8   7   6   5   4   3   2   1

To the men and women—past and present—
of the San Diego Police Department

But most of all, for Lynn,
whose mark is deepest

Acknowledgments

To Art Buchwald, for early encouragement; to my agent, Elizabeth Kaplan, and my editor, Tom Colgan, true professionals; with special thanks to writers Jean Jenkins, William Murray and Bill Mullen; and to ''The Padres'' writers' group of yesteryear.

Treasure up in your hearts these words: Be ashamed to die until you have won some victory for humanity.

—HORACE MANN
Commencement address, Antioch College

≋ One

"Is he dead yet?"

"If he ain't, he will be." The shorter man, solidly built, grabbed for the hunting knife when he said it. He grunted each time he rammed the blade home, and when he had grunted eleven times he stepped back to admire his work. "That'll do it," he said. He looked at the knife, then at his partner. "Guess we better take it with us, brother."

"Yeah. Guess we better." They both looked around.

"You take the bedroom. I'll start in here." He rubbed his hand against the arm of the sofa as he spoke, flip-flopping the fingers and transferring some of the blood onto the beige fabric. "It's gotta be here. And we ain't in no hurry now."

Vincent Dowling was not at all surprised that his day off was being interrupted. Perhaps it was because he was subject to being called to work at any time and couldn't relax anyway. Or perhaps he preferred death investigation to being at home. He wasn't sure which.

He brushed his teeth and wondered how long it would be before he'd have a chance to brush again. The telephone call from Central provided scant details, as always. A dead man in a ransacked house. Probably stabbed. And as usual, he ignored the information. What one patrolman considered ransacking could, in fact, be normal conditions for someone who lived like a pig.

1

What another thought were stab wounds could actually be bullet holes. The only thing that mattered was that somebody was dead. And he, San Diego Police Sergeant Vincent Dowling, and his homicide team were rolling.

He replaced the cap on the half-used tube of toothpaste, musing how neatly he had rolled it from the bottom. Helene had squeezed it from the middle. He would have to talk to her about it again.

His face had a twelve-hour stubble on it. Felt like sandpaper when he ran his fingers against the grain. That was clean enough. A stiff had never complained about five-o'clock shadow. Dowling had long since started shaving before going to bed on Friday and Saturday nights, in anticipation of a call-out. It seemed to him that more murders occurred on weekends than on weekdays. He'd never cared enough to total them up.

Dowling stood just under five feet eleven inches. His thick hair was short, an unruly red thatch that hung over a sloping forehead, diverting attention from a crooked part on the left side. Forty-nine summers had not yet diminished a handful of freckles on the cheeks. He placed both hands on his stomach and looked down. Waistline's not too bad, he told himself. Still a thirty-eight. A tight thirty-eight. Standing in front of the closet in underwear, dress shirt, socks and shoes, he went through the motions of selecting an appropriate suit. A Sunday. New Year's Eve day. Not much brass around the station. A dead guy in a messy house. He chose a brown suit that had seen better days. Fraying had begun near the top of the lapel. Once he would not have been allowed out of the house with that suit on.

When the telephone call came, he'd been struggling to reconcile the checkbook balance. He shoved the paper work aside and, from the desk drawer, removed handcuffs, his badge and a fresh notebook.

One dead body to a notebook, he taught his detectives. When you had those defense attorneys hurting in the courtroom and they were fondling your notebook, at least they couldn't start questioning you on some old case you weren't prepared to talk about. On the cover he wrote "Sgt. V. Dowling," and on the first page scribbled "Sun. Dec 31, 9:33 A.M. rec call at home ref 4399 Marlborough."

He grunted when he lifted the mattress and felt for his Smith & Wesson .38 revolver at the pillow end of the bed. Guns didn't do much good on the closet shelf when some midnight prowler was standing beside the bed with a butcher knife, he had explained to Helene twenty-six years ago. The five-inch barrel fit snugly into the shoulder holster, which he adjusted.

He was almost at the bedroom door when he patted his coat pockets, turned and walked briskly back to the desk, where he removed three packs of Camels from a drawer. Almost ready to see what was happening on Marlborough Avenue.

Dowling made a last stop at the kitchen counter, and was halfway through writing a note when Helene came through the front door. They met in the dining room and stared at each other.

"Call-out," he said.

"Jesus. That was predictable." She banged the grocery bag down on the oval table.

"I'm sorry, Helene. I don't plan these—"

"That's really lovely. You'll be gone until at least tomorrow; that's a given. You get to miss the New Year's Eve party at the Mayfields'."

"The Mayfields will understand. They know—"

"They know what?" She spun around and looked out of the window. Dark hair brushed her shoulder.

"So far," Dowling said, starting for the front door, "you haven't let me finish a sentence."

"Put me in San Quentin."

"And listen, Helene. I'm doing the bank statement. You wrote seven checks to the liquor store last month."

"Put me in Folsom."

He had the front door open. "I may make the party. It might be a quickie."

She raised her eyebrows. "You won't make it. Probably won't even try."

Dowling started down the porch steps, then looked

over his shoulder. Her arms were folded, her graceful figure framed by the doorway. Red blotches stood on both cheeks, and her hair needed brushing.

"After your fifth drink, Helene, you won't even know I'm gone."

A cluster of people had gathered in front of the two-story apartment complex when Dowling arrived at the Marlborough Avenue address. Some appeared sleepy-eyed, and a few were shirtless in unseasonably balmy weather.

Dowling drove up at precisely the same moment as his three detectives: Bones Boswell, Larry Shea and Speedy Montoya. Taking everything in with a glance, he estimated at least forty people were milling around. Rock music blared from a boom box in a parked car.

He eyed two TV vans parked across the street. A coroner's wagon with attendants in white pants and jackets was double-parked. A civilian photographer from the crime lab unloaded equipment from the police-department van.

"Welcome to Vincent Dowling's dog-and-pony show," he said to himself.

Two uniformed officers stood on the sidewalk. Dowling hoped one was a veteran. Pointing to them, the photographer and his three detectives, he gave his first order.

"Everybody over here."

Dowling walked to a spot on the sidewalk one house away from the action. This was always his first investigative step, taken before even looking at the body. He and his team would be briefed by the uniforms, out of earshot of those whom Dowling felt could wait for selected, filtered information.

He formed the seven of them into a tight circle, running his eyes over the tan uniforms and black gun belts. The shirt and trousers of the taller officer showed evidence of numerous dry cleanings. The small brass nameplate on his chest bore the name Cliff Edwards. The gun belt of the other officer was stiff, and the leather had not begun to crack from constant wear. Dowling looked at Edwards. "Lay it on us, officer."

Edwards thumbed through his pocket-sized notebook, then stuffed it into his rear pants pocket.

"The dead guy is a Roy Green. He's in the living room. Arms are in rigor. Lived here two years. A musician. Landlord lives in number one. Says he's a quiet, no-problem guy. The pad was really tossed. Married couple in number twenty-four saw him at 9:30 last night. Dead guy's girlfriend, a dumb-looking blond broad named Linda, was there. Number twenty-four took a Polaroid of them. He was checking out a new camera."

"Who found him?" Dowling asked.

"Number sixteen. Went in to return jumper cables he'd borrowed."

"Give me more."

"That's about it, Sarge. Krebs, here, did the door-knocking."

Six heads turned toward the recruit officer, who was standing stiffly, hands at his sides. Krebs glanced from Edwards to Dowling, then back to Edwards.

"You've got center stage, son," Dowling said softly. He saw the notebook tremble slightly.

"I knocked on all the doors, sir. Nobody heard anything."

"Jesus, did you forget about number eight already?" Edwards said.

"Oh, yes, sir. Number eight. Ah ... number eight woke up around 2:00 A.M. He heard a voice from the swimming-pool area call out, 'Let's go, Sammy.' But the landlord says nobody named Sammy lives here."

Dowling asked a few more questions; then he looked down at the four shiny black uniform shoes. "The photographer will photo the bottoms of your shoes. In case we find shoe impressions, we'll be able to tell which ones were left by the good guys and which ones were left by the killer. Then you can go back to work," Dowling said. "And by the way, Edwards. That was a pretty good job."

Dowling watched them walk away and breathed

deeply. For the last time that year he was about to begin his game of chess.

His detectives had their special strengths. After long hours of coaching, Speedy Montoya had become a meticulous crime-scene examiner. Larry Shea and Bones Boswell were skilled interviewers, with an ability to cut right through to things. They talked as easily with La Jolla stockbrokers as with downtown pimps and whores. Dowling himself would coordinate the investigation, evaluate the information and call the shots. If all went well, his homicide team would checkmate a killer.

They were physical contrasts as a team. Boswell and Shea were in their late thirties. Boswell, at six feet two inches, was extremely thin. His black hair, graying at the temples, framed heavy eyebrows and a lantern jaw, which made him appear several years older than Larry Shea. Shea was short and round and bald, with a cherubic face and twinkling eyes. Montoya, barely thirty, was dark-skinned and handsome, a product of Logan Heights, the Mexican-American barrio of San Diego. A champion sprinter in high school, Speedy Montoya still seemed to be in a race with the world around him.

"You gotta hustle in this world, Sarge," he had told Dowling once. "I hustled to get out of the barrio. I hustled to get out of uniform and into homicide. You can't stand still in this world."

"Except at crime scenes, Speedy."

"Yeah, Sarge." Speedy had grinned. "Except at crime scenes."

Dowling watched the patrol car drive away from the curb, then turned and looked at the door of apartment #21. He wrote in his notebook for a few minutes while his team waited.

"Shea and Bones. Talk to everybody again. Pin down that 'Let's go, Sammy' thing. Maybe we can do something with that."

Dowling looked at Speedy. "You do the crime scene after I do my thing. And remember, take your time. This guy's going to be dead for a long time. You burn three—"

"I know, Sarge," Speedy interrupted. "You burn three bridges in a homicide investigation. When you move the body, when you embalm it and when you bury or cremate it."

"Well, damn it, at least you've learned that much in a year, working with the big boys," Dowling growled.

He had a number of cardinal rules about death investigation. One was, never would there be more than two people inside the crime scene at a time. Evidence could be easily contaminated, and this was his way of cutting down the odds. Dowling's "thing" was to make a cursory inspection of apartment #21 to get a feel of what they were up against. He would go in with the photographer and supervise the picture-taking. The photographer had an array of equipment slung over his shoulder as he and Dowling stood in the doorway. Dowling's hands were deep inside his pockets.

"You playing with yourself again, Sarge?"

"Damn it. How many times do I have to tell you guys? When your hands are in your pockets you can't leave your prints at a scene. It would be embarrassing. Like a—"

"I know, Sarge. Like a surgeon leaving a sponge in a patient's belly."

Dowling ignored him and crouched in the doorway. Recognizing the obscure odor of death he had never been able to define, he stared across the cluttered room.

The body was in a kneeling position. The left side of the face lay flat against the top of a cylindrical upholstered stool. The left arm was draped over the top of the stool, and the right arm rested on the thigh of blood-stained Levis. Dried blood, both streaked and matted, covered most of the bare torso. The right biceps was unstained, and bore a tattoo of a fist with the middle finger extended. The eyes were not quite closed, and the mouth was not quite open.

"Start your distance shots. And take your time," Dowling said.

He waited a minute, then slowly and deliberately moved across the room, looking down at the carpet and studying each section where his foot would eventually land, looking for blood or dirt or fibers or any debris he might crush. Leaning over the body, he saw ugly lacerations on the fingers and hands. He knew they were defense wounds. Received by a person fighting for his life; hands upraised in an attempt to ward off a barrage of knife thrusts. Most of the defense wounds were on the outside and top of the left hand. Dowling guessed they were looking for a right-handed killer. Edwards had been right about the arms' being in rigor. Stiffening started in the face and worked downward, ultimately leaving in the same order. Judging by the rigor, the neighbor's statement and the flies in the room, he reasoned the murder had occurred around midnight.

Dowling noted the blood concentrated on the carpet in the area surrounding the stool.

"He didn't travel. Got hit right here," he told the photographer. He leaned forward to get a better look at the dark smears on the sofa. "Get me good close-ups of this."

Dowling's eyes ranged to a corkboard on the wall a few feet from him. He saw a Polaroid photograph of a smiling young man with shaggy brown hair, his left arm around a plain-looking blond girl wearing a yellow dress. The man was bare-chested and wore Levis. Dowling's glance returned to the blood-coated form slumped below him.

"Come on. Talk to me, you son of a bitch. Who did this to you?"

The photographer finished, and Speedy Montoya, sketch pad and measuring tape in hand, replaced him in the apartment. Dowling was aware of Speedy's voice speaking into a hand-held recorder.

"The nose is fourteen inches south of the north living room wall and sixty-five inches east of the west wall."

Dowling had seen what he needed to. He was about to leave the apartment, when Bones Boswell called to him from the doorway.

"Linda girlfriend just showed up, Sergeant. Somebody got the news to her."

Dowling recognized the girl on the sidewalk as the one in the photograph. She wore the same yellow dress. Probably the same underwear, too, he thought. He had already decided they were dealing with a low-class, doper crowd.

"Good morning, miss. I'm Sergeant Dowling. Sorry to meet you under these circumstances."

He opened the front door of the detective car for her, and gently took her arm to assist her in. Dowling would talk to her for a few minutes. The preliminary conversation would be light. Later, she would be interviewed extensively by Bones and Shea, but he needed to know a few things right away, and had some groundwork to lay.

"What was he dealing, Linda? Grass? Speed? Crack?" Dowling saw her stiffen. Her eyes were red and watery. He knew ordinarily they wouldn't have gotten the time of day from her and was thankful for the shock factor.

"Well . . . a little grass, I guess," she said. "But who would do a thing like this?"

Dowling offered her a Camel and lit it for her. "We rely on you and his friends to help us answer that. Who was closest to him? Besides you?"

"I really don't know." The girl tossed hair over her shoulder.

Dowling raised his hand and started his canned speech.

"Look, honey. Here's how it is. We work murder, not dope. I know what you're thinking. You give us the names of friends . . . and they're dopers . . . and heat comes down on them. I'll level with you. We don't care about dope. You go ahead and give us names of people to talk to. I guarantee you, if we walk in their pads and see a wheelbarrow of rock cocaine, we look the other way. We won't bust 'em for it and we won't run to the narcotics squad afterward and tell them who's holding. You can check on the streets about me. You won't find one person who will tell you I ever went back on my

word. It's damn near all we have left in this business
anymore.''

She searched his eyes, and Dowling continued.
"Now, in a little while, a couple of nice old detectives
are going to have a chat with you. You have a choice
to make, girl. You either lie to them and think you're
protecting a bunch of friends, or go right down the line
with them and let's see if we can't find out who made
a pincushion out of your boyfriend.''

Dowling drove away from Marlborough Avenue,
loosening his tie for the drive to the police station. This
one would be tough or easy, he thought. No in-between.
No gray area. They'd get a break or make one of their
own. However, he always tended to be an optimist in
the early stages of a case, no matter how bad it looked
or how few leads there were.

He was in the fast lane of traffic on Highway 163,
next to Balboa Park and the zoo, when his right rear tire
went flat. Cursing, wind blowing ashes in his face from
the cigarette dangling from his lips, he maneuvered the
unmarked detective car toward the shoulder, ignoring a
driver bearing down on him from behind with horn blar-
ing.

Now he was really glad he had worn the old suit. He
could have radioed in for the police garage rig to come
out and change the tire, but he knew that might take
hours. As he worked the jack into position he clicked
off the various motives in the case.

Burglary? Doubtful. The position of the body and no
forced entry into Roy Green's apartment discounted that.
Argument? Doubtful again. In spite of the tattoo message on his shoulder, Bones and Shea had learned Roy
Green was a passive individual. Not a likely victim of
a spur-of-the-moment stabbing.

Dowling grunted as he lifted the tire from the rim,
and feared he'd ripped the crotch of his pants.

A revenge killing by someone Green had cheated in
a dope deal? Always possible. But again, not consistent
with the person. Rip-off? A good chance of that. By

someone he knew. He'd been hit on the far side of the living room, well away from the door. Whoever it was would have known he was a dealer. They hadn't tossed the place looking for a fortune in rubies and pearls. If that was it, it was likely an ex-con. Dowling had counted forty stab wounds. At least forty. It was a brutal way to kill a guy.

The repair job completed, he continued south. To his right he saw the top of what had once been San Diego's landmark, the El Cortez Hotel, shut down for several years now, with the famous exterior glass elevator dismantled. He smiled, thinking of the days when he and Helene had showed off the city to visitors. She'd always squeezed his hand tightly in the glass elevator, afraid to look at the beautiful view of downtown and the city of Coronado to the southwest.

He thought about how Helene's drinking had become a problem in the past few years. He had no way of determining how much she was putting away. There was no talking to her about it anymore. No matter how gently he approached it, they always ended up in a shouting match.

The irony was that she had been almost a teetotaler when they'd met. A glass of wine with pizza had been an occasion. At a party, even a mild vodka tonic had made her screw up her face on the first sip. The vice-squad parties had come years later. That had been when she'd learned to drink. There'd been eighteen of them on the squad, and the old vice sergeant with emphysema had kept careful statistics. He'd said that pimps and hookers and trick rollers and fruit hustlers took a break on Sunday and Monday. So the vice squad did too. They'd been a tight-knit unit, and the Sunday-night parties had rotated from house to house. He and Helene would arrive home bleary-eyed and drunk, when the sun and the children were rising. But he had only been assigned to the vice squad for two years, and somehow they had lived through it.

He knew their close friends were aware of her drinking, and the children had to be. Matt was, what? Sev-

enteen? And Jenny two years younger. You couldn't
fool them at those ages. He had often thought of sitting
down with them, feeling them out, maybe being open
with them about it. But he had convinced himself that
he and Helene were products of a generation that didn't
discuss personal problems with their children.

The previous week he had picked up the name of a
woman psychologist who had helped a lieutenant in the
auto-theft detail. The stale joke around the squad room
was that the old lieutenant would have to cram for a
sobriety test. Dowling had figured the woman must be
good. He and Helene had been through a lot in twenty-
six years together, and he'd decided the counseling was
worth one more try. Helene had been to counseling, but
improvement had been short lived. Late the year before,
a series of hypnosis sessions had looked promising, until
Helene had stopped trusting the doctor. She'd come
home crying from the one AA meeting she had attended.
Humiliating was the word she'd kept using to describe
it, pointing out that the people at the meeting were too
weak to take control of their lives. They were therefore
incapable of helping her, and besides, she'd said, she
could stop if she really wanted to.

One of the psychiatrists had called Dowling in for a
session after Helene had seen him for three months. The
doctor had suggested, then urged, that Dowling transfer
from homicide to a forty-hour-a-week job like burglary
or juvenile. The doctor had said Helene considered him
an absentee father and husband who was more dedicated
to solving murders than to being part of a family unit.
The doctor had used words like *impact* and *analyzing
transactions* and *structured hunger* and *life patterns.*

Dowling had stopped for two quick drinks when he
left the psychiatrist's office. He was willing to do what
he could to help his wife with her problem, he thought,
but transferring out of homicide was unthinkable. He
had been in charge of a homicide team for thirteen years,
and, by Jesus, he would be in charge of a homicide team
until he pulled the pin. It was true he often worked
eighty- and one-hundred-hour weeks. That didn't mean

you had to stop being a husband and a father. Murders
were damn serious, and what Helene and that psychiatrist didn't—couldn't—understand was that a good
homicide team was the only thing standing between society and a bunch of caged animals. It was more than a
job; it was a . . . well, a calling of sorts. It was a pres-
tigious job. Homicide was the elite of the police department, and he enjoyed canceling cases that the other
detectives said "only Dowling could have solved."

A couple of years before, he had gone through a period when he had been terribly distracted. At one crime
scene he'd been trying to determine the angle of a blood-
stain and started thinking of Helene crying at home. Another time he'd interrogated a woman who had killed
her husband and three children with a hatchet while they
slept, and three times he'd called the woman Helene.

It had taken it all out of him. Standing in living rooms
and backyards and taverns and alleys and trolley cars,
staring at death. And trying to push Helene out of his
mind. It had been getting more and more difficult to do.
People always talked about how unhealthy it was to
bring work home with you. He was bringing home to
work with him. But after a stern talk with himself, he'd
begun pushing his personal problems out of his mind
when he left the house on a call-out.

Well, they would give this call-out their best shot. He
wanted to solve them all. But he was, above all, a realist.
He knew they'd eat a case from time to time. But not
because they'd sloughed off. Not because they didn't
think the case had enough class. True, he reflected, if
you could decide for yourself which cases *had* to go
unsolved, you'd prioritize them by the quality of the
victim. He was going to miss a New Year's Eve party,
and his whole team was going to lose a lot of sleep over
some pissy-ass, low-grade grass peddler. If you had to
eat a case, better Roy Green, or some pimp who'd gotten
shot by one of his whores he'd been kicking around, or
some hustler with shaved dice in his pocket who'd gotten beaten to death after a game. Better all of them than
some poor bastard standing on his feet behind a counter

forty hours a week getting waxed by a lousy stickup man who didn't want to leave a witness. Or a high-school girl getting raped and strangled in the bushes in front of her own house. Dowling had worked them all. But he knew he had to work them all the same way. Aggressively, methodically, and with a real desire to solve the case. Anything less and you became sloppy. Ordinary. You'd strike out on the quality case because your reach wouldn't exceed your grasp.

He thought about the mutilated body in the living room on Marlborough Avenue, and was stimulated by a rush of adrenaline. It was good to be back in the chase.

Two

They worked around the clock and into New Year's Day afternoon. At his desk, Dowling turned his attention to the yellow legal pad in front of him. The "things to do" list came easily and automatically. He scribbled silently, roughing it out in the time it took him to smoke a Camel.

He leaned back in the swivel chair and stared at a spot in the middle of the ceiling. They were trying to pluck a suspect out of a mass of people in a county almost as large, area-wise, as the state of Connecticut. He started to light another cigarette, but instead tossed it across his desk and watched it roll to a halt against the telephone. Twenty-eight hours had passed since he'd left his house. He had not spoken to Helene. Three times he had dialed and three times heard a busy signal. He reminded himself to check the cost of having a separate phone installed in Jenny's room, certain he had not spent as much time on the phone when he was fifteen.

He felt both frustrated and relieved about not being able to reach his wife. It was awkward to speak with her when he had been out all night. He knew she was no longer interested in hearing about his cases, and he had given up estimating for her when he might get home. Half the time he was wrong by several hours, and that made it worse. Plus, she would have a few drinks in her, and their conversation would turn ugly. One of them would hang up without saying good-bye.

Dowling directed his thoughts back to the things-to-do list. The property missing from Roy Green's apartment was inventoried in the margin of his yellow sheet.

   television set
   stereo
   Mossberg 12-gauge shotgun
   .22-caliber Derringer converted into a cigarette
     lighter

The Derringer particularly interested him. It was mounted on a brass stand. Whoever had that might become careless and pass it around. Dowling scanned the to-do list, checking off in red pencil things that had been done.

1. missing-property list sent to patrol lineups and property room
2. pawnshop detectives plugged for same
3. criminal-records check on all names in Green's address book
4. pawnshops—cover in person by Speedy
5. parole office—names of ex-cons recently paroled

He knew that recently paroled men usually had difficulty making an adjustment in the outside world.

6. interview all friends furnished by girlfriend
7. identity of anyone getting traffic ticket in area in last seven days

Daily critiques were another of Dowling's cardinal rules of homicide investigation. The entire team in one location, exchanging information, tying up loose ends; working as a unit instead of having one or two detectives branching out on some plan or theory not based on fact. With critiques, they might come across the one fact that, when woven together with what another knew, might break the case.

He stood and waited impatiently as the men assembled. Dowling conducted critiques standing near the chalkboard as his team sat around a table, holding notebooks. He looked at Speedy, then nodded toward Shea and Bones. "Guess where the Bobbsey Twins will be from midnight till 7:00 A.M., Speedy?"

"You don't even have to tell me, boss," Larry Shea said. "I know where I'll be. Sitting in a car outside Roy Green's apartment, with only shithead, here, to keep me warm."

It was customary for Dowling to send two men back to the scene during the "critical hours," the time frame in which the crime had occurred. They would stop everything that moved, looking not so much for a suspect as for a witness who might normally travel the area during those hours and have seen something worthwhile.

"How about the 'Let's go, Sammy' thing someone heard at 2:00 A.M.? Tell me something good about it, Bones."

"I can't, boss. Sammy's a fuckin' cocker spaniel, and his owner had him out looking for a fire hydrant after the late show."

That was the way it had gone in the early stages. Dowling leaned against the chalkboard and acquired a vacant stare. At least they had their motive. Speedy had found eight kilos of marijuana and six thousand dollars in tens and twenties hidden in a recessed square in the bedroom wall, covered by a knickknack shelf. The killer hadn't looked as hard as Speedy for Roy Green's stash and buy money.

Dowling hoped more than one person had been involved in the killing. The more suspects, the better the chance of obtaining helpful information when they caught them. The weak-link theory, he called it. One guy who hadn't taken part in the stabbing . . . who hadn't bargained for a killing . . . who had gotten in over his head . . . who wasn't con-wise, and could be coaxed or intimidated or scared into laying it all out for them. The more suspects the merrier. It occurred to him that there was a fair chance more than one guy was involved, considering the extent of the ransacking.

He always sent a detective to the morgue to view the autopsy. Dead men do tell tales, he knew, and a forensic pathologist could relate information about the size of the knife blade they were looking for, the angle of thrust, how long Roy Green could have lived and how far he could have traveled. If you didn't attend the autopsy and relied on the doctor's written report, Dowling felt you lost something in the translation.

"Bones. The autopsy starts in one hour and thirty-three minutes. Be there."

"Don't let them mistake you for a cadaver," Shea said as they filed out of the critique room.

"If they do," Speedy volunteered, "they'll save his old lady an embalming fee, what with all that booze stored up in his creaky old body."

They're still loose, thought Dowling, and that's good.

When he looked at his watch a few hours later it was 3:00 P.M., and nothing had broken. Dowling knew that if you didn't turn up something promising in the first twenty-four hours, you were usually in trouble with a murder case. They had been at it for thirty hours straight. To him, those were the most critical thirty hours. Homicide detectives couldn't sleep during that stage of the investigation, because time was their enemy. So many people to talk to. Roy Green's friends and acquaintances, more neighbors, family. If you didn't get at them right away you could miss out. People involved with the Roy Greens of the world had a tendency to forget things. Deliberately or otherwise. To make themselves hard to find for a few days because Dowling put so much heat on the streets. And blood evidence. Damn it. The guy who'd done that stabbing had to have gotten blood all over himself. On his clothing, in his hair, on the soles of his shoes and in the crevices between the soles and the stitching. And blood evidence was perishable. Easily washed away. Easily discarded.

The autopsy went the way he knew it would. Seventy-two stab wounds. About ten were fatal. A knife with a blade five to six inches long. He could have recited the cause of death without looking at the report.

Hemothorax, right, due to perforation, internal mammary artery and vein and heart due to stab wounds, chest.

Dowling leaned forward in the chair and cupped his chin in his hands. He didn't feel tired. But he knew the fatigue would set in if the members of the team didn't close their eyes. It was time to send them home for a while. His detectives were fighting a tendency to ease up a little at this point. He was reminded of it every time he went to a Padre or Charger game at the stadium in Mission Valley and saw people beginning to stir during the last line of the national anthem. So Shea, Bones and Speedy would go home, then come back fresh, and they'd make this case.

He would opt for a cot in the corner of the small critique room. It was his habit while working a case to sleep in the office. It gave him more time to arrange work assignments for his detectives, and was consistent with his sense of order. He sat on the edge of the cot and fluffed the pillow, then stood and grabbed his coat, knowing that his mind was not ready for the sleep his body craved.

He drove out of the underground police garage onto Fourteenth Street and glanced at the six-story glass-and-concrete central-headquarters building. Dowling had detested the place since the department had moved into it in 1986. He'd refused to condone something that looked more like a hotel than a police station. Instead of driving west on Broadway toward the harbor he made his way south for several blocks. It was a little out of the way, but at least he would be able to look at a real police station on his drive.

In less than five minutes he was parked at the curb across the street from the old building on Market Street. He sat in the car with the engine idling and looked long-

ingly at the red-tiled roof covering the Spanish-style
structure that had been built in 1938. Where he had reported, his first day on the job, in 1965. Sure, they had
outgrown it, and sure, it had been like trying to stuff ten
pounds of sand into a five-pound sack. But the beautiful
old building had character and charm, and it beat the
hell out of any hotel that doubled for a cop shop. The
place was abandoned now. His beloved hibiscus hedge,
which had once bordered the public sidewalk in front,
had been uprooted in favor of an impersonal chain link
fence. Sadly, he shook his head and drove on.

In less than three minutes he was in light traffic on
Harbor Drive. The view of the harbor relaxed him tem-
porarily, and he took time to savor the view of fishermen
mending their nets next to the large tuna seiners along
dockside. The late-afternoon sun from the west made the
blue water sparkle and accentuated the old County Op-
erations building on the waterfront.

He drove past the point just south of Hawthorn Street
where a wooden pier jutted into the bay. Fishermen,
young and old, clustered on the pier, alongside pleasure
craft and a few commercial fishing boats. A wide boardwalk followed the curve of Harbor Drive. The bay was
dotted by small craft anchored unattended.

Dowling spotted the Old Man just north of the pier,
and his foot eased off the accelerator. He made an illegal
U-turn, and cruised slowly toward where the Old Man
sat on a concrete bench next to the boardwalk. There
was a parking space nearby, but Dowling ignored it and
drove a full block further, parking next to one of the
many cars with out-of-state license plates belonging to
patrons of a popular seafood restaurant. He stood beside
the car and took off his jacket and tie, removed the gun,
handcuffs and bullet pouch from his belt, wrapped the
tools of his trade in his jacket and placed the package
on the front seat. After locking the car he unbuttoned
the top two buttons of his shirt and walked slowly north
on the boardwalk.

As a police officer he accepted the fact that new and
casual acquaintances tended to glorify his job. Everyone

had gotten a traffic ticket once that he didn't deserve, and that alone was usually good for a ten- or fifteen-minute harangue. He loved being a police officer, and he was proud to be one. But he and the Old Man knew zero about each other's life off the boardwalk, and Dowling liked it that way. If his reasoning was flawed he didn't care.

He passed an ice cream vendor and a group of Japanese tourists laden with camera equipment. The water lapping against the boats was dark and oily, with scraps of paper and wood fibers afloat. The pungent odor of the creosote-treated pilings was familiar and pleasant.

An old wooden fishing boat was tied up next to the boardwalk, and its crew of three ruddy-faced Portuguese men was laying equipment out on the narrow deck. Someone's radio told him Michigan was a few seconds away from defeating Washington in the Rose Bowl. The Old Man wore the same thick-knitted green woolen sweater. His ancient wide-brimmed black hat sat low on his forehead, exposing a clump of gray hair on the back of his head. He gazed straight ahead into the sun, toward the south tip of Harbor Island.

When Dowling stopped and stood beside him, the Old Man turned slightly toward him, and their eyes met for a moment. The eyes that looked at Dowling were dark, almost black, and the skin at the corners was deeply wrinkled.

Dowling looked to the water, oblivious of the people walking past them. A sea gull swooped and perched on a piling next to them. Dowling studied the bird carefully.

"That's the same species that landed on the same piling the last time I was here," Dowling said.

"It is the same bird," the Old Man said without looking at him.

Dowling studied the gull more carefully. He had looked at the one on the piling the week before and tried to find some characteristic, any characteristic, not common to the species.

"You're sure?" he said at last.

"I'm sure," the Old Man said.

The gull flew away, toward the end of the pier. Dowling watched it pose stationary in the air, occasionally moving its wings to adjust to an air current. The Ring-billed gull floated gently toward the surface of the water in slow spiral curves, lifting its wings skyward as it grazed the brine.

"Is he upset because he didn't catch a fish?" Dowling asked as a flock of other gulls flew in.

The Old Man's answer was covered by the roar of a city bus passing a few yards behind them.

"I couldn't hear you."

"Yes," the Old Man said again.

"Do the other gulls care whether he catches one or not?"

"No. The other gulls do not care."

"You're sure?"

"I am sure."

Dowling tried to focus on the Ring-bill, but it quickly merged with the flock, which as a group headed to the northwest. The salt air was pleasant, but he felt a chill. He looked at the Old Man. It was gratifying to have a link with someone who didn't draw from you. Who didn't need anything. Helene needed. Matt and Jenny needed. And so did Bones and Speedy and Larry Shea. And the captain of homicide. But the Old Man . . .

Turning, Dowling nodded good-bye and walked back to his car. The warmth of his jacket felt good. He headed for the station, passing the eleventh naval district headquarters at the foot of Broadway. He always felt better after seeing the Old Man.

Two years before, Dowling had been working a rape murder on the beach when the watch commander had called him in. Patrol had found Helene lying drunk on the sidewalk a block from home. The next day, Dowling had been sitting on the seawall, brooding, and noticed the Old Man for the first time, standing a few feet away. Two husky young men sauntered up to him, and Dowling overheard one of them say, "Loan me five dollars, old man."

He listened just long enough to insure the Old Man

did not know them, then got to his feet. "Hey, punks."

They turned their attention to Dowling.

"The Old Man's flat. Ya want to borrow a fin? I'll call the beat cop. Maybe he's got one." He started toward the phone booth, but the two were already moving rapidly away. Dowling yelled after them. "Stay off the boardwalk." The Old Man had simply waved his thanks.

Back at the station, Dowling crushed out a cigarette and laid a thin blanket from the storage locker on the army cot. He knew he'd go right to sleep if he could get his mind off the case. Calling home occurred to him, but that would have meant an argument. Rest was what he needed.

He stepped back into the squad room to put his gun and cuffs in his drawer and was startled to see Helene standing next to his desk. He could not remember the last time she had been to the station. From across the room she waved with her fingers. Dowling picked up the faint scent of cologne as he neared. She wore a pale pink dress he did not recall having seen before.

"I, ah . . . I tried to call earlier," he said.

She smiled. "Guess who's been tying up the phone."

"Yeah. I called to say I'm sorry about that crack I made when I left. It was a cheap shot. I'm—"

"As they say, sometimes the truth hurts." She smiled again. "You were thinking about your call-out and I was pressing you about the party. It's not important anymore." She put the paper bag she had been holding on his desk top. "What do you think's in there?"

"Time bomb?" He grinned when he said it.

"What is today?"

"Ah, Sunday. No, Monday."

"It's New Year's Day."

"Of course."

"What do I make on New Year's Day? What's the tradition?"

"Canoli," he said, reaching for the bag.

"Not as good as your baking, but you never seem to complain."

Dowling was biting into one when she finished the sentence.

"Good texture. This is very thoughtful of you, Helene. I—"

She interrupted him again. "You look tired." She touched his cheek softly.

"I was just getting ready to lie down."

She straightened his shirt collar and gave him a short hug. "Good luck. Be careful." Then she left without looking back.

He was almost at the door of the sleep room when he heard the squad-room door open. Helene stood with one hand on the doorknob. "I really do love you, Vincent," she said from across the room. Before he could answer she was gone again.

When he stretched out on the cot he know he'd go right to sleep if he could get his mind off the case. And Helene. He would have to remember to call her and thank her for the visit. It was encouraging, he kept telling himself.

His thoughts switched to the property list again. They had to have put that property in somebody's hands.

The cot was comfortable enough. He was getting drowsy. He wondered what the parents of Roy Green were feeling. Often he thought of the parents of victims, and the parents of men he had put in prison over the years. Most he had never seen; yet he'd touched their lives. He wondered what Green's parents looked like, as he drifted to sleep.

By late afternoon of the following day the team had made little progress. They had questioned, then released, two transients found sleeping in a van five blocks from the murder scene. Roy Green's girlfriend had supplied names of associates, and they were working their way through them. Dowling had sent his three detectives off in different directions and ordered them to check in by phone at 10:00 P.M. It surprised him to see Larry Shea walk into the squad room at five o'clock.

"If that killer walks into this office you'll catch him,

Shea. Why in hell aren't you out talking to people?''

"I need to talk to you for a minute, Sergeant."

"Talk."

"I was going to ask you about maybe getting off at five-thirty tonight. Or even six-thirty would be okay. It's our fifteenth anniversary. We made plans a long time ago. Dinner and a room at the Islandia. Valerie has a baby-sitter lined up for overnight. I hate to ask, but, ah . . . well . . ."

"I'm sorry, Larry. The answer's no. We're at a critical point." He saw the disappointment in Shea's face. "Sorry."

Shea turned suddenly and started to walk away, stopped, then spun around again and walked to where Dowling still stood.

"Yeah, it's really critical, all right. A dumb-shit doper gets murdered and the world stops. Maybe anniversaries never meant anything to you. Or maybe you just forgot."

Dowling's face reddened.

"Okay, Shea. Your choice. You go ahead and paint the old town red tonight. You want better hours? And weekends off? I'll see if I can't find you a nice slot in the records division. With the rest of the pussies. Your choice." They glared at each other for a moment.

"I'll work," Shea said softly. He picked up his notebook and headed for the door.

Dowling went to his desk, started to rummage through the interview reports the steno had just typed, but couldn't concentrate. He got up and walked hurriedly to the hallway. His pace quickened when he saw the elevator door opening for Shea. "Larry!" he yelled. "Larry, wait up."

Shea was holding the door open when Dowling reached him.

"Larry, look, I can't let you off tonight. It would mean four or five less people get interviewed before we knock off. One of them could turn it all around. I know how you feel about the anniversary, and all. I've been there, Larry. What can I say?"

Shea shrugged. "What the hell, Sarge. I'll have a few more anniversaries. The truth is, I probably wouldn't have enjoyed myself anyway . . . thinking about the case. I'm always thinking about the case. I'll be checking in with you."

The break came seven hours later. Following Dowling's orders, Speedy had canvased pawnshops, calling owners at home when necessary. In one shop he had seen what he'd first thought was a revolver. It had turned out to be a .22-caliber Derringer. Nonoperative. Converted to a cigarette lighter. Mounted on a brass stand.

Things had moved quickly then. A woman had pawned it. By 10:00 P.M. Bones and Speedy had caught up with her as she arrived home. An acne-faced man was with her. He had three baggies of crystal meth in his pocket. He was also a narcotics parolee.

Speedy and Bones had interviewed the pair separately. A man on the street had sold them the lighter. They had no idea where he could be found. Roy Green? Never heard of him.

Dowling liked it. It was going to turn out to be the right lighter. And whether the man and woman had done the job or not, they were on their way to cleaning this one up.

"Acne-face wants to deal with us on the bag of speed, Sarge," Speedy said. "He doesn't want to go back to the joint."

Dowling pointed toward the interrogation room. "Get back in there. Give him the standard pitch. Your sergeant is a hard-ass and doesn't make deals. I'll be in after a few minutes."

Dowling leaned back in his swivel chair and cupped his hands behind his head. He knew these kinds of guys like he knew the palm of his hand. They'd deal. But they'd try to give you just a little for a lot. Think they were getting you all excited. Feed you a crumb and hope it was enough. When in fact they had enough to just about do your whole case for you.

Dowling tried to act casual when he entered the interrogation room. In truth, he was nervous. He had long ago resigned himself to always being nervous when he was a minute away from matching wits with somebody over a murder case. It was due to what he considered the potential of a "terrible finality." If the information was there for the taking, and if he wasn't good enough, or lucky enough, or experienced enough, or intelligent enough, or thorough enough ... then they wouldn't get it. A case could go unsolved because on a given day he didn't have what it took during a showdown.

The man was smoking one of Bone's cigarettes and sipping a can of cola they had given him.

"He was at a party Saturday night, Sergeant," Bones said. "He remembers a couple of guys who were at the party that left for a while, and when they came back a couple of hours later they had a television set and a shotgun for sale. Thinks they may have sold the TV to a sailor who was at the party. But his memory is bad ... doesn't recall names of these two guys or anything about them."

Dowling's normal look was one that would convince most strangers it was safe to stop and assist him if his car was broken down on a dark road. When the hype looked up, he saw the game face. The jaw was set and the brown eyes were narrowed. Dowling snorted before he spoke.

"And that's what he wants to deal with? Wants to get out of going back to the joint by feeding us crap we'll find out for ourselves. Throw his ass in jail. For violation of parole. We just got the lighter positively identified as belonging to Roy Green."

Dowling started to open the door, then added, "Book him for suspicion of murder."

"Wait a minute, Sergeant. Wait a minute." The hype's eyes were wide open for the first time. "I just remembered something. I think they called one of the guys Bulldog. I think."

Dowling took a few steps and stood over him. "That's not my turnip truck you saw parked outside, asshole. Before you walk out of this place free, like you'd never been in here, I get names and places. And something to tie 'em to the job. So we know you aren't lying."

"If I give you all of that, I walk out of here?"

"That's the deal. Take it or leave it."

Dowling walked out. And hoped.

Thirty minutes later they pulled a twenty-five-year-old named Mack Slater out of bed, where he had been sleeping with a woman. Acne-face had pointed out the cheap, one-bedroom house in the Old Town area, a few miles north of downtown. A Mossberg 12-gauge shotgun was at the foot of the bed. Bloodstained clothing was in the closet. Dowling didn't have to wait for the lab report. He knew the blood would turn out to be group A, Roy Green's type. Slater screamed for a lawyer as they were handcuffing him. Dowling knew he didn't have to provide Slater with a lawyer; he just couldn't question him.

"Process him and book him, Speedy. The works. Photos, prints, hair samples, fingernail scrapings, blood. And Speedy, take your sweet time, for once. We need him under wraps while we're picking up the other guy."

The "other guy" named by the hype was Jimmie Bench. At 3:00 A.M. Dowling and Shea were in the records division, leafing through two thick folders.

"Jimmie Bench has been around the block," Shea said. "In and out of the can all his life. Youth Authority. Tracy. San Quentin." Shea turned a page. "Stickups, burglary, dope."

"How long has he been on the street?"

"Two months. Just got out of Q."

"Moniker?"

"Baby Blue. Must be the eyes, huh?"

Dowling looked at the photograph on the counter. The features were chiseled and well defined. There was almost a clean-cut look about the face. The eyes were pale blue. They seemed like sensitive eyes.

Dowling nodded. "A combination, Shea. Eyes, plus checking into Q when he was twenty-one. Takes a pretty good track record to go to that joint so young. The older cons gave him that name."

Dowling pored over the rap sheet of Mack Slater. The Bulldog. That fit, thought Dowling. Slater was short but powerfully built, with a fleshy face supporting thick lips that protruded and hung well below the normal lip line. He noted they were both members of the Aryan Brotherhood, a prison gang.

"Let's go grab Baby Blue, Sarge." Shea and Dowling were walking toward the squad room. They sidestepped a custodian swabbing the hallway with a strong-smelling cleaning solution. Dowling liked the odor. His early-morning odor.

"No, Shea. Not at 3:00 A.M. We'll wait till 8:30."

"I don't get it. I've never seen you worry about good manners when we're working a murder."

"We're not there yet. We need statements from this guy. Need 'em bad. We barge in there this time of morning he's going to know it's not routine. He'll know we got something."

Dowling had already decided they would use the old "we need help" approach. They would loosen up Baby Blue, then ease it to him.

Shea placed Jimmie Bench on a chair, across the wooden table from where Dowling sat. Shea took a seat at the end, to Dowling's right. An ashtray was the only item on the table, and the walls were bare. There were no windows.

Dowling didn't like the interrogation room any more than he liked the police building itself. It was sterile. It was in perfect repair. It was nothing like the interrogation rooms at the old building. Those rooms retained the odors from the smoke of thousands of cigarettes and the perspiration of thousands of bodies.

Jimmie Bench was attentive. Vigorous. His body language was crisp, and Dowling placed him way up there in the self-assurance category. He was perhaps an inch shorter than Dowling, well built, with square shoulders. His sandy hair was just a bit shaggy. The navy blue sweat shirt and denim pants were clean and well fitting.

"We need help, Baby Blue," Dowling began. "This

guy Roy Green gets knocked off at his pad and we're
hurting. For four days we've been talking with all of his
people. There's lots more to talk to down the line after
we talk to you.''

Dowling mulled over the formal advising of consti-
tutional rights. He needed to get the damn Miranda
warning past him. But not just yet. He could see the
wheels turning in his suspect's head. Asking himself if
these guys had anything. Or were they just fishing? Baby
Blue would think he'd look guilty if he didn't at least
have some sort of conversation with them. There was
more loosening up to do.

"So you see," Shea said quietly, "we need to find
out as much as we can about this guy Roy Green, and
people that knew him are the only ones that can help
us.''

Baby Blue was glancing at one detective, then at the
other. Dowling straightened his tie again. Damn Miranda. He had never forgiven the Warren Court for sad-
dling them with it in 1966. Actually, the Escobedo ruling
had done the real damage a few years before Miranda.
Miranda had just expanded on it a little, but since it had
come last, it was the one that had gotten the attention.
All this crap about the rulings making better cops out of
them, making them more professional, was just that.
Crap. Last month he and Shea had been in Tijuana working with the Mexican state police. The *Judicial.* Pulling
a San Diego killer out of a run-down hotel near the
bullfight ring. The *Judicial* had done the interrogating.
It was their country. The only Miranda they knew was
a third baseman for the Mexico City Red Sox. They had
gotten the confession out of the guy without even having
to get out the cattle prods.

"So anyway. I have to lay these rights on everybody
we talk to these days, so here goes.''

They didn't have to advise everybody. Only people
who were in custody and under some suspicion. If this
guy chose not to talk they'd have to let him go home.
But that was part of the psyche game. Make the Baby
Blues think everyone got advised. The tactic infuriated

Supreme Court justices. Dowling didn't care. He didn't work for them. He worked for the people of the state of California. Dowling pretended to read from a card but recited from memory.

"You have a right to remain silent during questioning, now or at any time. Anything you do say may be used in court against you. You have a right to have an attorney present during this or any conversation. Either an attorney of your own choosing, or, if you can't afford an attorney, one will be appointed for you prior to questioning, if you so desire."

Dowling looked at him. "Do you understand your rights as I have explained them to you?"

Baby Blue's face was expressionless. "Sure."

"Having in mind and understanding your rights, are you willing to talk to my partner and me?"

Baby Blue reached for a cigarette. Shea lit it for him while Dowling held his breath.

"Sure, I'll talk to you. I got nothin' to hide."

𝍌 Three

Dowling tried not to show his sense of relief. They did not ask any questions for a while. Baby Blue told them he had been looking for a job. Had a decent parole officer he checked in with once a week. Spent some time with his mother, taking her shopping and such. He'd met Roy Green through some guy whose name he had forgotten. Didn't know Green well, though. Hadn't seen the Bulldog for at least three weeks. He'd help Dowling and Shea any way he could, but he didn't know anything.

Dowling carefully studied Baby Blue. There wasn't much question that he had been in on it. After thousands of interrogations, he could tell when he was talking to the right guy. It wasn't anything he could put his finger on. Nothing he could testify to. Just a number of little things. Like the way a guilty guy would ramble on, talking about everything under the sun except what he was in there for.

Guys like that thought their willingness to speak gave them an air of innocence. They hoped Dowling would be deceived and wouldn't get back to an uncomfortable area of conversation they had just strayed from.

But an innocent guy—the innocent guy might be nervous, but he'd stick right to the point. He'd want to clear himself as quickly as possible.

Well, Baby Blue had been on the job, all right. Now to try and get him to admit it. Dowling lit his fourth cigarette.

"Tell us about the party Saturday night, Baby Blue."

His suspect looked up a little too quickly.

"Pardon, Sergeant?"

Dowling knew he'd heard him. Knew guys would ask you to repeat yourself when they needed a few seconds to recover and get their thoughts together.

"The party on Grand Avenue in Pacific Beach Friday night."

"Jeez. Grand Avenue. I don't remember ever being at a party there, Sergeant."

Dowling leaned back in his chair and thought for a full minute. Then he caught Shea's eye and motioned with his head toward the outer office. Shea got up and left, closing the door behind him.

Dowling was aware that he had to give a person a reason to be truthful. He couldn't tell him things would go easier, or that he'd talk to the judge for him. But if he was careful, he could imply it. Fuck the Supreme Court.

"You know, Baby Blue. A cop who's been around a while knows what it's like for a guy just getting out of the joint. They slip you some gate money—not much, though, huh?—a new pair of funky leather shoes and say, 'Go make an adjustment, boy.' You start feeling pressure from everybody. From your mother. From your relatives. From your parole officer. Get up early and read those want ads, boy. Telling all this to a guy who's just spent five years moving by the numbers. Getting locked down three times a day. Standing in line to eat, shit, shave and shower. Then . . . who in hell is going to hire you? 'Naw, we can't trust him, he's an ex-con.' So a guy starts to blame society. And he's about right to do that. Well, as a cop I'm a part of that society, but times like this I'm not proud of it. Not proud of it at all. I've just got a job to do."

The man across the table was paying strict attention. So far so good. Dowling got up and walked to the door.

"Come here. I want you to look at something."

"Look at what?"

"Just come here."

When they were side by side, Dowling opened the door a crack. Baby Blue peeked out. On the far side of the room Larry Shea stood next to the Bulldog, whose hands were cuffed behind his back. Dowling closed the door softly.

"There's your crime partner. The Bulldog's going back to the kennel. We pulled him out of bed six hours ago. Roy Green's shotgun was in the room, and the bloody clothing was stuffed in the closet."

The eyes have it, thought Dowling, and Baby Blue's eyes had grown soft and were staring at the floor. Shea reentered, and Dowling motioned them back to their chairs.

"We got it put together," Dowling said gently. "We didn't pick you out of the fuckin' phone book."

"What makes you so sure I was in on anything?"

"Come on, kid. I was a cop when you were messing your pants."

"What did the Bulldog have to say?"

"The Bulldog said it was just supposed to be—ah, hell. I'm not gonna do it. I'm not going to tell you what the Bulldog told us when we sat him down. I don't like that old game of playing one guy against the other, like some cops do. Just like I'm not going to tell him the things we talk about in private."

Dowling handed him a cigarette.

"See. I told you. We got it put together. You're bought and paid for. Now it's just a matter of locking you up and bringing the reports to the District Attorney. The D.A.'s going to ask us, 'What did the Bulldog say?' We'll tell the D.A. just what he said. Then the D.A. will say, 'What did this guy, Baby Blue, have to say?' Well, there are only two things we can tell the D.A. about that question. We can say, 'Baby Blue says, "Fuck you, prove it, cop." ' Or we can say, 'He was very truthful and laid it right out for us, Mr. District Attorney.' So, what's it going to be?"

Dowling could tell that one had hit home. A tiny bit of moisture started to form in the corner of the eyes, the robin's-egg-blue eyes of Jimmie Bench.

"Look. My partner and I aren't saying you went in there and did that to the guy. We don't think you bargained for the way it went down. You just got in over your head. Most everybody does once in a while. I have. Shea, here, has. But Jesus, we know you were there. Everybody's going to know you were there. We just want you to tell us your part in it. We don't want to hear it from the Bulldog. Just from you. Just your part."

Dowling could hear his own breathing. Baby Blue put his hands to the sides of his head and looked at the table. Dowling quickly reached into his pocket and removed a sheet of paper and a pencil. He drew a large circle. Across the circle he added four intersecting lines. Then he slid the paper across the table. The tip of the pencil was in the center of the circle when he began to talk.

"You see, this is a pie. It has eight slices. Now, all we want to know is how much of that pie is yours and how much is the Bulldog's. If it's half and half, if you and he did exactly the same thing in that apartment Saturday night, then I don't expect you to say anything. Anything at all. You just stay quiet. But if only a couple of pieces of this pie are yours, then I hope you'll tell us just your part in it. I'm not asking you to tell us the Bulldog's part. You don't look to Shea and me like the kind of guy that would snitch off a partner. We just want you to tell us what you did." Dowling put his hand gently on the other man's arm.

"Just what I did?" He was perspiring. "Just what I did?"

"That's all, son," Larry Shea said.

Baby Blue exhaled smoke, then looked down at the drawing.

"The Bulldog and I were in the living room with the guy. I went into the bedroom for a few minutes. When I came back the guy had been downed."

"Could you see where he'd been hit, or was there too much blood?" Dowling asked.

That was how you phrased it. Never say, "Was there blood?" and invite a "no" answer.

"There was too much blood. The guy was on his

knees, kind of leaning against that little stool.'' He
paused, then quickly added, ''But I didn't see the Bulldog do nothin'. I'm not saying he did nothin'. I'm just
telling you my part, Sergeant.''

''I understand.''

''One little thing,'' Shea said. ''It's been bothering
us. When you guys went into that apartment, were you
going to take all of the stuff you ended up taking? Or
were you just going for the dude's money?''

''Naw. We were just going for money. And dope if
we could find some.''

They questioned him in detail for another hour, then
processed and booked him. Dowling was tired. They had
missed three nights of sleep. It was time to head for
home. But they needed to wind down before hitting the
pillow. He passed another homicide sergeant's desk on
the way out of the squad room.

''We'll be across the street, getting the trail dust out
of our throats. If she calls, I'm still working. Right?''

The bar and grill near the police building was
crowded. They opted for a large table, circled by night
detectives off duty a few hours before. Puddles of spilled
beer covered the tabletop, and there were almost as
many pitchers as there were drinkers. A waitress was
refilling popcorn bowls, and Larry Shea was talking over
the din, providing a detailed account of how the Roy
Green case had been wrapped up.

''So at 3:00 A.M. we're sneaking up on this pad in
Old Town to pinch the Bulldog. We listen at the window
and can hear him snoring. Darker than hell. Kitchen
door's unlocked . . . we're soft-shoeing it into the bedroom and I flip the light switch just as Speedy is putting
the shotgun under the Bulldog's nose. The Sarge, here,
yanks the covers off. Says, 'Freeze, Bulldog, or we'll
blow your goddamn head off.' The Bulldog and the girl,
they freeze, all right. Lie there at attention. We get him
in the car for the trip to the squad room and I lay his
rights on him and he yells for a lawyer. So neither of
us is saying anything after that, and then the Bulldog

says—now, get this—says, 'If I'd known you guys were out there I'd have—' "

"Let me guess," a robbery detective interrupted. "Typical hard case talking big. 'If I'd known you guys were out there I'd have shot it out with you and taken a couple of cops with me.' "

Dowling's team laughed in unison.

"No, no. That's what I figured was coming," Shea said. "No, the Bulldog says, 'If I'd known you guys were out there I'd have gotten one last piece of ass.' "

Everyone laughed except One Beer Babcock, a forgery detective.

"The Bulldog knew he was going back to the joint," a chubby burglary detective said. "Figured it'd be the last piece he'd get for seven years."

"The last piece from a girl, anyway," a red-faced robbery detective added.

Another robbery detective drained his glass and reached for a pitcher. He wore a Marine Corps emblem in his lapel, and the bottom half of his tie was wet, because it had dipped into his glass when he sat down. He looked at Dowling and belched.

"Dowling's All-Stars do it again. No case too tough to crack, huh?"

Dowling shrugged. "We got a break."

"That team's damn good. Or else Dowling's got a rabbit's foot," a burglary detective said.

"That's a rabbit's foot he's wearing," another detective said, tugging on the lapel of Dowling's wrinkled brown suit. "And he's got his own rules. Never make the knot in your tie bigger than your head."

"So what, the guy's been looking like an unmade bed the last couple of years. He solves them murders," someone walking past the table volunteered.

An arm reached for the pitcher again. "And I'm sure his clothes are expensive. They only look cheap."

Dowling lit a Camel, trying not to laugh. He began filling glasses, automatically skipping One Beer Babcock's. Then he noted the chubby burglary detective's hand covering his glass.

"Oh, no. You dieting again, fat boy?"

"Not only dieting, my friend, but bicycle riding every day," he responded proudly.

"Must be the only bicycle in town with a Harley Davidson seat on it," Dowling said.

"Don't knock him, Sarge," someone else said. "I saw Chubby ride it. He really hauls ass."

"When Chubby hauls ass, he has to make two trips," Shea said.

One Beer Babcock got up to leave.

"Wait a minute, One Beer," an auto-theft detective called. "You can't go till I tell you guys what happened to my partner, here, last week when we were working day watch."

"I have to leave now," Babcock said, looking at his watch. "Well, make it quick."

The storyteller took a long swig of beer.

"My partner has a little something going on the side right after work, so he calls home and says he has to work a stakeout till midnight. But when he finishes romancing he falls asleep, and doesn't get home till six-thirty. It's just getting light out. His wife's asleep. He's tippy-toeing it, trying to get in there and get undressed and into bed without waking her. Now, you got to picture this. He's standing by the dresser—just pulling the knot in his tie down. She wakes up. 'What are you doing up so early, and where are you going?' she says. My partner never misses a beat. He slides the knot in his tie back up and says, 'Got to go to court. Gonna meet the D.A. for breakfast and go over testimony.' "

The chubby one had started to swallow beer, and when he began laughing it sprayed on the pant leg of One Beer Babcock, who was the only one not laughing.

"Come on, One Beer. Have another with us."

"You know I never have more than one." Babcock sniffed.

"Typical sailor," Bones said. "Afraid he can't get it up if he drinks more than one."

"One Beer's old lady thinks the saltpeter they gave him in boot camp is just starting to work," Shea said.

One Beer Babcock started for the door again. The robbery detective with the Marine Corps emblem called after him.

"I'd rather have a daughter in a whorehouse than a son in the Navy, One Beer." He got to his feet unsteadily, polishing the emblem with the dry half of his necktie. "Now, hear this." The bar quieted. "There are two kinds of people in this world. Marines—and those that wish they were Marines."

A loud voice rang out from the end of the bar, where off-duty patrol cops were drinking.

"There *are* two kinds of people in this world. Marines—and those that aren't queer."

Several hours later Dowling left the bar. He was relaxed, half drunk, sleepy and glad to have a jump on the afternoon rush-hour traffic. Humming happily and tapping the steering wheel, he pictured the captain of homicide briefing the command officers on the success of Dowling's team. Sure, they'd gotten a break. But damn it, what you did after you got the break separated a good team from a so-so team. That was what a lot of them didn't understand. It wasn't any accident Speedy'd been in that pawnshop and found the lighter. It was good, old-fashioned, get-out-on-the-bricks, wear-out-the-shoe-leather, talk-to-everybody-in-sight kind of police work.

It sure as hell didn't mean sitting in front of some computer monitor, waiting for a suspect's name to appear in bright lights. That was how some cops liked to work a case.

They'd gotten the break; then they'd had to drag the information out of that acne-faced hype. Finally, there was old Baby Blue. He had conned old Jimmie Bench out of his twenty-eight-year-old socks. He had made that nasty prick talk himself right back into prison. Made him go for a big piece of that pie he had laid out on the table. His team called it Mother Dowling's Folsomberry pie. Baked in sunny San Diego and guaranteed to cause indigestion from five years to life.

Dowling was pleased that he and Shea had wrapped

up Baby Blue without resorting to an out-and-out lie. They had tripped over the truth once or twice, but the job had gotten done. It was not that Dowling was opposed to lying, but he chose those instances carefully because of the burden that came wrapped around the lies. He did not enjoy the dual role of investigator and defendant.

One of his early cases was permanently lodged in his memory. A sixty-four-year-old waitress named Geraldine Carouthers had been locking up a tavern when a transient had murdered her and rifled the cash register. He had also taken her pack of Pall Mall cigarettes. When they'd brought the guy in for questioning the next morning they'd had a mild suspicion and no evidence, save a pack of Geraldine Carouther's brand of smokes.

An hour into the interrogation, Dowling had gotten "the feeling." The transient had kept smiling and shaking his head, and they'd been a few minutes from having to release him, when Dowling said, "I don't know why we're wasting time screwing around. We made you on prints five minutes ago."

The transient's smile had gotten wider when he said, "You ain't got my prints in that place, Slick."

"Who said anything about *your* prints?" Dowling asked him. "We lifted *her* prints off the cigarettes that were in your pocket."

When the man finished telling them what he had done to Geraldine Carouthers, he confessed to murders in Salt Lake City and Butte, Montana.

"You lied to him," the young prosecutor railed at Dowling the next day.

"He broke the pool cue in half and stuck one end up her ass and one end up her snatch," Dowling said.

"But there were no prints on the cigarettes."

"After he killed her he dragged her head to the corner pocket and jacked off in her mouth."

The prosecutor put his head in his hands. "Why did you have to tell me you lied to him?"

Dowling's jaw was tight when he said, "Because I only lie to the bad guys, never to the system."

Dowling had taken a pounding on cross examination. "I lied to obtain the truth," he'd said time and again, and the veteran defense attorney had hardly been able to contain his glee when he'd told the jury that homicide Sergeant Vincent Dowling was taking taxpayers' money to tell lies.

The jury had hung up, nine to three, for conviction. The second jury had decided the transient was more of a scoundrel than Dowling, and a first-degree murder conviction had been obtained.

Deceit was a part of the job that disturbed Dowling. He was afraid it spilled over into his personal life. Affected his relationship with Helene and their children. He was confident that the working life of a good detective was characterized by deception and guile. There was always an angle. A ploy. And it wasn't always used in an interrogation. There were lots of other times when he needed to use a ruse.

He was going to go home, and Matt would want to know all about the case. He knew Matt wouldn't settle for a general briefing. He'd want to know why Baby Blue had fried himself, and then it would all come out. Many times Dowling had tried to explain to his children why he did the things he did. They would look at him and nod. He wanted to grab them by the shoulders and shake them and tell them not to be like him, and that it wasn't a hocus-pocus world, and that he was an honest and respectable man, who was only trying to make the world a little nicer place to live in. But instead he would stammer, and by the time he'd decided what to say next, Matt would be bouncing a basketball in the backyard and Jenny would be dialing the telephone.

Sometimes he tried to think of one other job where an honest and respectable man would lie and scheme and connive to get his work done. He couldn't think of any, so he felt like a lone wolf.

Dowling could appreciate a good sting. He gave credit to a crook who used his wit instead of his muscle. Half the time the victims were looking to make a fast buck anyway. He smiled when he remembered his first lesson.

He was fourteen, and his family had driven from San Diego to Indiana to visit relatives. He'd gone to the county fair with his cousin Marvin. Marvin had been a big, sixteen-year-old farm boy, and they had anted up money to see the fat lady and the sword swallower and a pathetic midget with one ear. A line of men in soiled bib overalls had formed outside of a tent, and a barker'd promised real sex movies for seventy-five cents. Marvin hadn't been able to get his quarters up fast enough, and they'd gone in and seen a crackly black-and-white film of a Caesarean section.

Dowling looked at his watch when he reached the top of the Talbot Street hill. It was two o'clock, and he had not spoken to Helene since she'd left the police station. A street-corner vendor traded him a bouquet of yellow-and-white daisies for a five-dollar bill, passing the flowers to him through the open car window. If Helene was home, he hoped she would be sober, because he didn't feel like a confrontation. What he wanted was a hot shower and a three-hour snooze while his body ridded itself of the beer. Tired as he was, he planned to get up at dinnertime and spend the evening with her. Celebrate. If the mood was right, he would mention the woman psychologist. If she was gone, he decided to leave a note asking her to wake him. Perhaps then she wouldn't drink too much and they could talk meaningfully and maybe the mood would be right.

He remembered the night a month before when he'd felt closer to her than he had for a long while. He had been in the kitchen, holding the Pyrex measuring cup up to the light to insure that he was pouring exactly one third of a cup of water. To Dowling, the buttercream filling was the most significant preparation in his *bagatelle aux fraises*. The *génoise*, a spongy cake, allowed for the slightest margin of error. And the cake-soaking syrup that he would prepare last could be off a gram or two without attracting attention. But the filling had to be perfect, and he'd been attempting to make it so when Helene sneaked up behind him and snapped him on the rear with a dish towel. He lurched, knocking a carton of strawberries onto the floor. She began apologizing even as he spun around.

"Oh, I'm so sorry. I didn't mean to cause a mess."

She had taken him by surprise. In the old days she'd towel-snapped him at least once every time he baked. And when he baked he was so engrossed, he never remembered to be on guard for the sneak attacks.

"It's all right," he said. "No mess. I'll just rinse them off." He stooped to pick up the strawberries, and she helped, volunteering to wash and stem them. Dowling carefully selected large, even-sized ones for the outside of the bagatelle. He would trim the ends to achieve a uniform height.

They chatted while he boiled sugar and water in a heavy saucepan until it reached 250° F. on the candy thermometer. He measured Grand Marnier liqueur, then wiped the plastic open-ended cube he had devised to properly arrange the layers, while Helene made him repeat the stories she had not heard in years. How they had made a baker of him in the Navy, of his joining the police department before they'd met, and pestering the marvelous pastry chefs of the El Cortez Hotel and Lubach's when he worked the night watch, asking them scores of questions at 3:00 A.M. until he was finally invited in on nights off to watch them work. Of the blue ribbon he'd won at the Del Mar Fair for his Lindy's cheesecake, and his embarrassment when the other policemen had read about it in the newspaper and ragged him. Helene had laughed when he told her that, the way she'd used to laugh. He pushed the layer of *génoise* aside and took her hand.

"We ought to get out of this rat race," he said. She stopped smiling. "Go to New England. We could open a little bakeshop in New Hampshire or Vermont."

"We've never been there. We don't know anybody there," she said.

"So what? We don't need anybody else."

"Oh, Vincent. You don't mean it. I'd love it."

He looked toward the ceiling. "A small, specialty bakery. Just a few items each day. Croissants. Eclairs."

They fantasized until the telephone rang and he was called out because a woman had been found garroted in the bushes in Balboa Park. When he returned two days later, Helene asked him if he had been serious about moving to the East. A map of New England was on the table beside her. He had meant it when he said it, he tried to explain. Perhaps after he retired. She got drunk that night.

He stayed mad at himself for a week. It served him right for pretending they could step into the past as neatly as rewinding a reel of film, he thought. Too much had happened to go around holding memories up to the light. Still . . . when they had talked in the kitchen he'd thought he saw her eyes gleam when they decided they could tap a tree for syrup, and she'd giggled when he described how the snowman would look wearing his old uniform cap. For a moment she'd looked like a twenty-year-old girl, instead of a forty-seven-year-old woman. While he, with short, deft strokes, alternately brushed the second layer of *génoise* with syrup and kneaded the marzipan, Helene envisioned the narrow, tree-lined street on which they would live. He looked at her and smiled, sensing they would lie close that night and make love for the first time in a long while.

But, predictably, the phone had rung. The woman in the bushes had turned out to be a man in women's clothing who'd had anal sex with a seventeen-year-old sailor with yellow hair and freckles. When the sailor felt testicles he'd become ashamed and angry and strangled the transvestite.

So it hadn't turned out well for anybody. The sailor would spend the next ten years in prison, warding off homosexual attacks instead of plowing the family farm in southwest Missouri. Helene went on a five-day binge, and Dowling was racked with guilt because he had deceived her. To him, there was a difference between a pipe dream and deceit. But Helene had not seen it that way.

"Save your slick talk for your patsies at work," she'd cried. "I've got enough troubles."

The days had drifted by. Their conversation was functional and kept to a minimum. Once she'd asked if he ever intended to transfer out of homicide. He'd pretended not to hear. They were more civil than courteous to each other.

Matt was tearing into his studies, working part time at a service station and playing basketball. He would graduate from high school in June. That had surprised and embarrassed Dowling, who'd thought his son was in his junior year. When he discovered his error, he correctly reasoned that Jenny was in the tenth grade.

On a chilly December evening he had sat in the dark on the porch and asked himself if he loved his wife. He had trouble defining the word. A divorce had never entered his mind. The relationship had become stagnant, but that was because of her drinking. Helene had told him once that love was caring, sharing and sacrificing. He hated categorizing emotions but decided to try. He certainly cared for her. It was difficult to think of being married for twenty-six years and not caring. He did not spend much time on category number two. They shared a house, two children, an average number of bills and the morning paper.

When he asked himself the sacrificing question, he was not pleased with the answer. He had been remiss, and began compiling a mental list of ways to correct the situation. There wasn't much doubt he'd been stingy with his time because of work. He would volunteer to take her on long walks and promise her a movie once a week. At least once a day he would call her from work, no matter how busy he was. That was caring.

He sifted through other ideas until he got too cold and went into the house. Not once did he address the issue of transferring out of homicide.

December had crept toward the prospects of a new year. Then the telephone had rung again and Roy Green was on the floor with holes in his body. So Dowling had gone to work again.

As soon as he turned into the driveway he saw her car in the garage. He sat in his car for a moment, then walked past the hibiscus bushes in the back yard, taking time to admire the huge salmon-colored flowers.

The back door was locked, and he fumbled for his key. Their bedroom door was closed, and he could not see light under it. Helene had taken to long afternoon naps when she drank in the morning, so he used the light from the hallway to undress. She was lying on her side, with the blanket just below her shoulders. Her dark hair made the sheets seem whiter. He looked at her and sighed.

Dowling showered, brushed his teeth and put on pajama bottoms. He flicked the hall light off before he crawled onto his side of the bed. He lay on his back for a few minutes and conditioned himself to stop thinking of Roy Green and the Bulldog and Baby Blue, of stab wounds and blood and parole violators, and blond-haired girlfriends wearing dirty yellow dresses.

He turned on his side toward Helene and could smell the stale bourbon. He squeezed her hand. Then he leaped out of bed and turned the light on, because he knew she was dead. Helene's hand was ice-cold, and the fingers were stiff. He shook his head, and was still shaking it when he saw the whiskey bottle and empty container of Valium on the nightstand. The note was clutched in her hand, which hung over the edge of the bed. She was wearing her favorite cotton nightshirt, with roses and lollipops on it.

He felt chilled, and thought he was going to be sick ... started for the telephone ... turned back ... started for it again. As he picked up the receiver, he looked at Helene. Her eyes were closed, her lips forming a half smile. He put the receiver down and sat next to her. Instinctively, he touched her shoulder and leg. She was fully enveloped in rigor mortis, and the purplish discoloration of post-mortem lividity colored the underside of her pale arm.

He was shivering when he got up, sat down, then got up again. He pried the piece of light blue stationery from between her fingers and began to read. The first couple of lines were neatly written.

Thanks for letting me play the fool. It was some sleigh ride. Make Matt and Jenny understand somehow—if you have the guts.

There was a gap. The rest wavered badly.

You were the love of my life, Vincent. I wish it could have been different.

It was signed,

"till death us do part"

Helene

Dowling crumpled to his knees next to the bed and read the note again. When he finished, he tore it into tiny pieces, then stumbled into the bathroom and flushed them down the toilet. He returned to the bedroom and telephoned the police station; then he sat down on the floor in his pajama bottoms and cried.

❄ Four

Dowling wondered how long it had been since he'd held both of his children by the hand. Now Matt's hand was larger than his, and Jenny's was the grip of a young woman as he helped her into the limousine.

As they settled into the back seat, and after telling himself not to, Dowling glanced over his shoulder for a last look at the chapel. When he finally looked to the front, the uniformed chauffeur touched the wiper switch, and the light drizzle smeared the windshield. The hearse was directly in front of them. Dowling closed his eyes as they started to put her into it. Jenny began to sob, and her lips trembled. Long, dark hair hid her freckled cheeks. Dowling started to cry, felt nauseous, and wiped his tears with the back of his hand. Matt was staring straight ahead, running the palm of his hand across red hair that covered the collar of his navy blue suit.

Dowling was aware of wheels turning under him, and he calculated it would take less than five minutes for the procession to reach the burial plot. He stared at the back door of the hearse. His stomach knotted as he realized that, alive or dead, he would never see Helene's face again.

Vincent Dowling was accustomed to the sight of death but had alienated himself from the grieving process. He could recall being truly troubled only twice in the years he had been assigned to the homicide squad.

One case had involved an eleven-year-old boy accidentally shot by his older brother with an uncle's gun. Uncanny, Dowling had thought, carefully studying the body of the young victim. Almost a look-alike of his son. Same age, too. Dowling had sat on the edge of the bathtub, noticing the vacant brown eyes rapidly losing their luster, and withdrawn. He'd practiced treating children's bodies like department-store mannequins, because mannequins couldn't wake you in the middle of the night. When he'd arrived home later, he had felt a great sense of relief seeing Matt, warm and safe, playing dominoes in front of the fireplace.

The other case had been just as personal: patrol sergeant, a friend, shot to death by an armed robber. Dowling had attended the autopsy and received the three fatal bullets from the pathologist. Unlike some of the cops, he had remained distant and methodical throughout the investigation. A few months later, at home, nursing a bourbon and water, he'd begun to cry. When Helene had asked what was troubling him, he'd had difficulty getting the answer out. "Just Bennie. Seeing him lying there. His uniform still on . . . and his hair. When I walked in and saw him on the slab my first thought was, I didn't remember his hair having so much gray in it."

Scratch memories like that, and death remained clinical but interesting.

The limousine eased to a stop, and Dowling ushered his children out. Later, he could not remember the descent to the burial plot, on the slope of a grassy hillside. He and his children occupied the center seats in a row of ten folding chairs. The priest stood next to the coffin, and the mourners clustered around. As Father Behan prayed, Dowling studied the three-by-five leaflet in his hand. On the cover was a sketch of a church surrounded by trees. Below it was inscribed, "In remembrance." He opened the leaflet. The twenty-third psalm was printed on the left side, and the right side read simply:

HELENE DOUGLAS DOWLING
Native of California
Beloved Wife of Vincent

Mother of Matthew and Jennifer
We Will Always Love You

He read no further, and when the people around him began to move he got to his feet. He hesitated, took a step toward the coffin, then turned and began the climb back to the limousine.

He started as Matt nudged him and pointed back toward the burial plot, where Jenny still stood rigidly next to the coffin. Without a word, Dowling and his son returned to her side. He gently touched her arm.

"We're here, honey," he said. "Let's walk back together."

Jenny said nothing. Dowling could not distinguish her tears from the rainwater. They waited silently. "We have to go, Jenny," he said finally.

Angrily she wheeled toward him. "Oh, really. We have to go. Where, Daddy?"

"Jenny, I know how—"

"Or do you have to go to work?" she yelled, then clutched her face with both hands. "Oh, Daddy, I'm sorry. I'm so sorry."

Dowling put his arm around her, and she hugged him. "Why did it have to happen, Daddy? Why did it have to happen?"

Dowling shook his head and knew he couldn't answer.

The procession of mourners dispersed beyond the grounds of El Camino Memorial Park, and Dowling resigned himself to the fifteen-mile drive to Point Loma, the long peninsula that separated San Diego Bay from the blue waters of the Pacific Ocean. A handful of friends had been invited to the house, which annoyed him. His head ached, and he wanted to be alone.

The limousine rolled to a smooth stop in front of the modest, one-story white stucco house near Catalina, the street that bisects the peninsula, leading to Cabrillo National Monument and the Fort Rosecrans National Cemetery. The narrow driveway led past a small lawn surrounded by green junipers to a separate garage. Some of the houses on the street were showy, with homes like the Dowlings' sandwiched between.

Dowling saw Bones Boswell and captain of homicide Tom Stacy standing on the porch with drinks in their hands. He recognized most of the cars parked in front. His team would be there. That would help a little.

He gripped Matt and Jenny by the hand and said, "Let's do it."

Stephanie Mayfield, Helene's closest friend, had coordinated the arrangements. Dowling had agonized over the guest list before selecting twenty names, mostly couples. He had reluctantly agreed to Stephanie's urgings that they serve a buffet.

"Life goes on, Vincent," she'd said. "You and the kids can't come home to an empty house."

"It'll be empty when everyone leaves," he'd said, but the phone calls had been made.

Dowling handshaked and hugged his way through the living and dining rooms.

He went to the bathroom—their bathroom—and splashed cold water on his face. The toothpaste lay next to the brush holder. He stared at it. It would never be squeezed from the middle again. A lousy tube of toothpaste. A lousy flyspeck on the grand design of things. Shaking his head, he walked from the sink to the bathroom door. When he opened it, he was face to face with the framed paper napkin hanging on the hallway wall. The frame was oak, five by seven. Helene had inserted a bright red matting that bordered the napkin, upon which was printed "Angelo's, India & Grape."

Angelo's was where they had met twenty-seven years before, when he was completing his one-year probationary period. He'd joined the police department three months after being discharged from the Navy. Most of the first year had been spent alone, walking beats downtown and in Logan Heights and Southeast San Diego. Tough neighborhoods, where the courage and ingenuity of young cops was tested and evaluated. Occasionally he worked a car, filling in on sick and vacation reliefs.

But those were short term, and, like the other rookies, he did his year on the sidewalks.

His first regular car assignment was beat number two, which started a few blocks above downtown and extended north to Laurel Street, adjacent to Balboa Park. India Street divided the heart of the Italian sector, and that was where he met Angelo, a native of Sicily, who had opened the small restaurant on V-J day. Six of the twelve tables bordered the large glass windows. Family members waited tables, which were covered with red-and-white-checkered tablecloths. Angelo's was always filled with the aroma of freshly baked lasagna and manicotti.

Dowling brown-bagged on duty, because he likened eating in a restaurant in uniform to being in a fish bowl. But he usually went to Angelo's on one of his days off, enticed by the excellent food and friendly atmosphere. Angelo would not permit him to be presented with a check, because he was a policeman, so Dowling compensated by leaving the amount of the meal as a tip.

Twice he saw her having lunch with another woman. Blue eyes flashed when she smiled, and from his vantage point he could tell she was exceptionally polite to the waiters. Her complexion was smooth and creamy. Long, carefully brushed dark hair just touched the top of her chair. He noticed she did not wear a ring on her left hand.

A week later he stood talking to Angelo, next to the kitchen, when she entered alone. Winking at the restaurant owner, he grabbed a white towel and order pad. By the time he walked to her table the towel was draped over his left forearm. He stood slightly behind her, to her left.

"Good day, miss. Are you ready to order?"

"Yes, please," she said, closing the menu. "Antipasto and iced tea."

"We're out of antipasto."

"Oh. A slice of pizza, then."

"We're out of pizza."

"Out of pizza. Out of anti—" She looked at him. Her

eyes narrowed. "You're not a waiter. What is this?"

"I am too a waiter. It's my first day."

"Come on," she said, looking toward the rear at Angelo.

Dowling pulled out a chair and quickly sat down across from her. He put the towel around his neck and tied it into a cravat.

"You're right. I'm not a waiter. I should have known it wouldn't work."

"Look. I don't—what's going—"

"My name is Vincent Dowling. I'm a customer here. I've seen you before. I had to meet you."

"You had to meet—"

"Yes. I'm really very nice. Clean-cut. Single. Gainfully employed." He raised his upper lip with his fingers. "Good teeth. And honest to a fault."

"You're also crazy." She laughed a little.

Dowling waved Angelo to the table.

"Vouch for me, Angelo. Tell her I'm okay."

"He's a nice young man, miss," Angelo said with a thick Sicilian accent. "A little—how would you say—different. But a nice young man."

They talked for a few minutes while she waited for her food. Her name was Helene Douglas, and she worked for a dry cleaner in the next block. He was careful not to mention that he was a policeman, still having a rookie's paranoia about being accepted by civilians.

When her order arrived, he got up.

"It was nice meeting you, Helene. Maybe I'll see you again sometime."

"Maybe," she answered, tilting her head.

Dowling waited in the kitchen with Angelo on both of his days off the following week, but she did not come in. The next week she did. Alone. They had lunch together.

"I'm a police officer." He blurted it out.

"You are? That must be interesting."

He examined her for signs of disapproval and found none. The next week he met her at Angelo's and, this time, asked her out. They saw *The Sound of Music* at the Spreckels Theater. Neither of them had ever dated anyone else again.

Dowling removed the frame and put it in a dresser drawer. Tears ran down his cheeks. Someone was walking toward him, so he went back into the bathroom and washed his face again. Then he smoked another cigarette. It sizzled when he threw it in the toilet bowl, and he stared for a long moment at the water being flushed away.

When he left the bathroom he stood by himself in the living room doorway. Bones Boswell had his arm around Matt. Dowling could not see Jenny, so after checking the kitchen he went to her room. The door was closed, and he knocked softly, then opened it. She was sitting on her desk chair, her back to him. Her curly dark brown hair flowed to the shoulders of the navy blue dress.

"Go ahead on out there, Daddy. I'm not coming."

He walked to her side and kneeled next to her. "Honey, they're our friends. They're here to comfort us. They—"

"They can't comfort me." Her eyes were dry.

Dowling lowered his head. "You and I and Matt are—"

"Please leave, Daddy. I want to be alone."

He kissed her forehead and closed the door behind him.

The next two hours dragged by. He drank two bourbons.

"Take as much time off as you need," his boss, Tom Stacy, said.

"If I can do anything, Sarge. Anything at all," Speedy said.

"It was a lovely service," a woman friend said.

"If you and the kids want to use my folks' cabin," Shea said.

"You're a shit, Vincent Dowling," Stephanie Mayfield said. "You know it and I know it." They were standing alone next to the stove. "But don't worry, it will be our little secret." She slurred the last word, and some

Chablis spilled over the top of the goblet. "A *big, big* secret between me and my shit friend."

Dowling looked at the very short, very slight woman. "Have some coffee, Stephanie." He reached for the pot.

"I don't care what the coroner says, and I don't care what homicide says." She paused for a swallow of wine. "It was no accidental overdose." She wiggled her finger under Dowling's nose. "My best friend killed herself. Helene Douglas Dowling killed herself because she was a drunk. And she was a drunk because her husband is a shit."

Dowling turned and started for the dining room.

"Don't walk out on me, you son of a bitch." She grabbed his arm. "You'll listen to it here, or in the living room with everybody else. How do you want it, Mr. Murder Solver?"

Dowling put his drink down and folded his arms in front of him. He looked straight ahead, over her shoulder, at his baking utensils hanging across the kitchen.

"It's my job, Stephanie. I was gone a lot because of my job."

"Ha, ha and ha." She poured more wine. "All you cared about was the lousy police department. And lousy murders. And—"

"Damn it, she was drunk half of the time. I tried—"

Her finger was under his nose again. "She was drunk because you are a shit. Always gone. Solving one of your very important cases."

Matt took two steps into the kitchen, looked at them and walked away. Dowling started after him, but she blocked his path.

"Oh, don't worry," Stephanie said. "She never told them. They don't know. She covered for you. She always made them think you were Mister Wonderful. That's the kind of person my best friend was." She started to cry and hurried out of the kitchen.

Dowling tried to compose himself, made a fresh drink at the dining room table, spoke for a few minutes with a small group, then went into the bedroom and closed

the door. Since the day she'd died he had slept in the
den. He looked around the room, then ran his fingers
over the grainy surface of the large oak dresser. They
had refinished it the weekend they'd moved in, after
they'd painted the living room and tried unsuccessfully
to put a shower stall around the tub. He'd cut his finger,
and still bore the scar.

They'd moved in June, while an unseasonable Santa
Ana blew in from the mountains, and after trying for
years, Helene was pregnant with Matt. They had con-
firmed it the week before. They'd lost track of time, and
it had been after midnight when they finished the living
room ceiling. There was no food in the house, and they
had a dollar and a half in change. He was working in a
patrol car, and was paid once a month. They'd
scrounged through the car and through Helene's purse
and found two dollars more. He'd left to try to find a
hamburger stand, but everything had been closed in
Point Loma, and he couldn't drive downtown, because
the gas tank was nearly empty.

He'd found vending machines in a twenty-four-hour
laundromat, and she'd laughed when he came home with
cans of Pepsi-Cola and Tootsie Rolls. They'd feasted
over a napkin spread on top of an orange crate, then
made love on the living room floor.

When Dowling came out of the bedroom it was nearly
dark, and most of the guests had left. Stephanie Mayfield
was not to be seen, and he looked on the patio to be
sure she was gone. When he returned to the kitchen,
Captain Tom Stacy was standing by the sink alone.

"I'll be putting it up for sale next week, Tom."

Stacy put his arm around him. "Things will look better next week, Vince."

Dowling shook his head. "Things will never look better."

He looked out of the window at the shuffleboard court
he and Matt had painted on the driveway ten years before. The numerals were faded, and grass had started to
sprout next to the "ten off" square.

"It's all over, Tom. I'm a shit, and it's all over."

🖐 Five

Vincent Dowling sat in the darkness on his front porch, his stare alternating between the overflowing ashtray on the table and the outline of a magnolia tree in the center of his lawn. He was really not seeing anything. His plaid shirt was half tucked in, and his corduroy pants were dirty, and the same color as the cigarette ashes that clung to the lap of them. He did not smell the sweet aroma from a night-blooming jasmine nearby; nor did he feel the gentle breeze that was the late evening's answer to a warm April afternoon. Not a hint of light shone onto the porch from the living room window, because the house was totally dark. Dowling had been in the chair for seven hours without getting up. He should have been hungry and thirsty and stiff in his joints, but he was none of those things.

If he had been forced to assign feelings to each of the ninety days that had passed since his wife's death, he would have chosen words like *sullen* and *shock* and *grief* and *dejection* and *dismal* and *fear* and *horrid* and *guilt* and *rage* and *melancholy*. If his attention span had not dissolved he could have added more. *Blend* might have been another word he would have chosen, because the days were all the same.

Three times he got out of bed, dressed and drove halfway to work before realizing it was his day off. Once he actually reached his desk, and cursed his team for being late. Anyone who was in his presence for more

than five minutes knew about his attention span. The
District Attorney certainly knew about it. On a recent
day Dowling had taken the witness stand and during a
lull in questioning thought about Helene. He had asked
the defense attorney to repeat a question, and became
red-faced when everyone in the courtroom laughed, because all he had been asked was the spelling of his last
name.

Blur is the word he would have used to describe the
week following the funeral. The coroner had labeled the
death "accidental." Dealing with the mortuary over details and arrangements had been a nightmare. He had
forgotten about the life-insurance policy, until he found
an adjuster waiting for him on the front porch.

"Just a few questions, Mr. Dowling."

"Make it fast."

"You were married how long?"

"Twenty-six years."

"You discovered the body?"

"Yeah."

"We'll need a written statement of—"

"You got the coroner's report. You got the police
reports. My statements are on 'em."

"That's all very well, but we—"

"Go fuck yourself."

The twenty-thousand-dollar check had been sent, and
lay with the rest of the unopened mail on a living room
table. Dowling got out of the chair, slowly. Flipping the
crumpled Camel pack onto the table next to the ashtray,
he groped his way through the dark house and returned
to the porch with an unopened pack. His cigarette consumption had increased from a pack a day to almost two.

He wore a path between home and work. And isolated
himself. Most of the time he sat on the porch alone. If
his children were home he gave stern orders that he was
not accepting phone calls. If he was alone, he let the
phone ring. He had answered the phone that morning,
expecting a call from his daughter, who was staying
overnight with a friend. Instead he heard Stephanie Mayfield's voice. She urged him to come out of mourning.

"You just can't stay cooped up forever."

"Oh?"

"And Vincent, I'm so sorry about what I said in the kitchen."

Dowling said nothing.

"After the funeral."

"I remember. Good-bye, Stephanie." He hung up. He stood next to the phone and thought about the day Stephanie and her husband had talked him into letting them come over. At Dowling's request, Stephanie had removed Helene's clothing from the house. Then she'd talked him into allowing them to rearrange the furniture. The next day he'd moved it back.

He got up, smoked a last cigarette and went to bed with his clothes on.

Three weeks passed, and to Dowling, no changes of substance occurred in his life. His obsession with Helene's death made him incapable of separating the phases of grief he had been enduring. The shock had come first. For days after the funeral he'd been numb and cold and distant. There was a tightness in his throat, accompanied by constant diarrhea, which surprised him, because he ate little.

When the numbness wore off he became aware of how great his loss was. She'd been a part of him, the love that gave substance and meaning to his life. Fatigue took over, and he alternated between sleeping and crying. Depression struck him like a sledgehammer to the head, and he was sure he was drowning in a sea of emotions he could feel but not express.

Tom Stacy forced him to take time off. "A week, two weeks, Vince. As long as you need. Forget this place and get well."

In truth, there was little difference in his train of thought at work or home. He went through his murder investigations by rote. Or tried to. Stacy reminded, then chided him about late, and about incomplete reports, errors of omission and indifference. Dowling had not made notes on his yellow sheets since the Roy Green case, though several murders had crossed his desk.

Historically meticulous in the preservation of evidence, he neglected to impound bloodstained evidence in one case. A husband had suspected his wife of seeing another man and obtained an address through a private detective. The husband had entered the empty apartment by jimmying a window, and lay quietly under the bed with a butcher knife until the other two points of the triangle arrived. When the room was dark and the bedsprings were creaking, he slithered out. The wife was on top with her head back and eyes closed when he began to carve her. The boyfriend dove through the window, and told Bones Boswell, "I thought she was yelling because I was such a good lay."

"A mattress cover, Dowling, a fuckin' mattress cover. How could you forget to grab it?"

"I just forgot, Tom." He shrugged.

Dowling's responses to his children contained no more depth than his responses to Tom Stacy. He was only marginally aware that Jenny had been morose since the day of the funeral and largely withdrew to her room when he was home. He never saw her cry. Their few conversations always ended the same way.

"It's just all my fault, Daddy. My room was always messy. It made my mother so upset. That's one thing that made her drink."

"Jenny, that doesn't make any sense at all, you—"

"And I'd wait until the last minute to study, Daddy, not like Matt. She got so angry at me."

"Jenny, stop it. Please, stop it."

"If I hadn't upset her, she wouldn't have drunk so much and the accident wouldn't have happened. It was me. It was nothing you did wrong. You were never here to do anything wrong."

When he was not at home, Jenny cleaned and cooked and washed and straightened before retreating to her room. "The woman-of-the-house syndrome. Not uncommon in these cases," Dowling would be told by someone later. She even adopted some of her mother's habits. Reading the newspaper standing on the porch, and sleeping without a pillow.

When either of the children approached him with questions or problems, he gave them short replies. He lacked the ability to care, and he exploded when Matt, the spokesman, asked for details of Helene's final moments.

"How much can you say about an accidental overdose of booze and pills?" he shouted.

The scholarship application forms for the University of Redlands were in Helene's desk. Matt stopped asking his father to complete them in time for the fall term. Then he halted all conversation about college.

Dowling didn't feel like sitting, so he stood, leaning against the wall of Tom Stacy's office. He had been summoned so many times in recent weeks he was no longer nervous or curious.

Stacy was a big man with white hair and sagging shoulders. He wore suspenders with metal clips, and drank from a milk carton on his desk. They went way back. Stacy had been the captain of homicide forever, and Dowling's boss for thirteen years. Dowling remembered Stacy's bouts with gastric ulcers, which had led to stomach surgery. Stacy took a drink of milk. "How's Matt doing on the new job?"

"What new job?"

Stacy banged his fist into his palm. "See, damn it. There you are, Dowling. Your kid gets a job in a gas station and you have to hear about it from someone else."

Dowling shrugged and folded his arms across his chest.

"You have to talk to them, Vince. You're still their father."

"I talk to them, Tom."

"You have to talk to them about their mother. You have to talk to them about their mother's death. Kids—they don't get emotional support from their friends like adults do. Like adults could if they'd accept it."

"They're kids, Tom. They heal quick."

"Horseshit, Dowling. People think kids don't grieve

like adults. They do. They hurt just as much. Their guts tumble around and their hearts ache, and they look to you, you dumb bastard, to tell them what to do. To tell them how to feel better and make the hurt go away. They want you to put your arms around them and squeeze them and let the tears run down your face. Let 'em know it's okay to be upset. It's okay to cry and scream and miss her.''

Dowling said nothing.

Stacy threw his arms in the air. "They're watching you. Tell them the truth."

"I am telling them the truth. Are you calling me a liar?"

Stacy held his hand up as if he were stopping traffic. "Tell them the truth about how you feel. Give Matt and Jenny a chance to talk to you. That's all I'm saying, Vince.'' He walked to Dowling and put his arm on his shoulder. "We all need to talk to someone sometime. I should order you to see a shrink. If you want to talk— if you need a friend, try me."

"Thanks, Tom. But I'm doing okay. And there's really nothing to say." He started for the door, but Stacy blocked his path.

"One last thing. Putting on my captain's hat now. You can't be like a wounded animal and go lie down and bleed. You could use a haircut. And a new blade in your razor. Start showing me something. Your cases leave a lot to be desired. I got a business to run."

Dowling walked out of Stacy's office and never thought about the conversation again.

Hardly a night passed that he did not wake up perspiring, and once, at his desk, he fantasized that she was away on a trip. He dwelled on their talk about the bakeshop in New England. She was sober and laughing and dreamy-eyed and caring, and she had believed in him.

He dwelled on other things. The cruel words he had spoken to her.

After your fifth drink, Helene, you won't even know I'm gone.

It wasn't supposed to end like that. He reasoned he'd

said those words because she was a drunk. Then he got angry with her for being a drunk. Then he got angry at himself for being angry with a dead person, and the wheel kept spinning.

She had been the love of his life, and he'd traded her for a sorrowful bunch of confused priorities. He'd traded her love for the opportunity to be a hero. He'd cheated the one who had loved and nursed and consoled and forgiven him until there was nothing left. In the end, her life had been reduced to a bottle of whiskey, a vial of pills and scribbled words on a piece of paper.

He remembered all of the times the team had worked around the clock and held their critiques and he'd filled the yellow pages, then let them rest. They'd washed the blood off their hands and gone home. And Helene had been there to hug him and turn the covers back and be his wife.

He kept reliving the day he'd come home tired and frustrated and Helene had wanted to talk about their "communication problem."

"Come on," he'd yelled. "I'm tired. I've been working on this case for seventeen days."

She had been standing by the mantel, and pounded it so violently, the brass candle holders shook. When she'd wheeled on him her eyes had been wild and watery. "I've been working on this marriage for seventeen years," she'd screamed.

He sat on the porch and thought about the other cops saying that Helene Dowling had gotten her nose so far into the bottle she'd suffocated. He felt like climbing to his rooftop and screaming to the world that all she had wanted to do was purge her soul of the devil who had red hair and carried a badge in his pocket. Instead of climbing to the rooftop, he went to the waterfront to see the Old Man.

Dowling found him and wanted the magic to work again. They stood together on the boardwalk while the sun went down and sea water lapped against the pilings.

Dowling lifted his head to the crimson sky and took a deep breath.

"I'm a police officer. A detective. Right here in San Diego." He thought it sounded foolish. A flock of gulls squawked in the distance.

The Old Man did not turn to him, but he nodded. Dowling paused, waiting—hoping the Old Man would say something. Then:

"How did you learn so much about gulls?" Dowling asked.

"I was a fisherman."

"You don't fish anymore?"

"Not anymore."

"I never did." He licked his lips and tasted salt spray. "Sometimes I wish I'd never come to San Diego."

The Old Man looked at him.

"Indiana. That's where I was born. Near South Bend. Do you know where that is?" He felt foolish again.

"Football," the Old Man said.

"Sure, that's it. Football. The Golden Dome. I'd probably still be there, except my mother was never well, and the doctor said get her to Arizona. My father took a wrong turn and we ended up here, and that was that."

A family of tourists walked behind them. The smallest child, a girl, held a double cone, and rivulets of strawberry ice cream covered both of her hands. Dowling ran his fingers over the piling and felt the pits and gouge marks.

"My name is Vincent Dowling. My wife is dead." He fired the words out. "I don't know your name."

"My name is Vito. I lost my wife too." The Old Man kept looking into the bay.

"I didn't lose mine. I gave her away. I was wrong. Dumb. It's a long story."

The Old Man turned toward him. "I have lots of time."

Dowling looked into the black eyes and could read nothing. "Yes," he said. "Perhaps . . . sometime."

As he drove away he was convinced he had talked

too much. Telling his troubles to others wasn't going to make the pain go away.

Four Dowlings had made the trip from Indiana. His brother was ten years older. Dowling fondly recalled the two of them, racing with their father's lunch to catch the trolley he drove in east San Diego, eventually jumping off at the waterfront, where the minor league Padres played in a rickety wooden ballpark. His brother had died with a lot of other Marines at Heartbreak Ridge in Korea, a place Dowling had had to find on a map. When he turned fifteen his mother, who was forty-nine, had died of tuberculosis. She'd been deeply religious, and had told him when death was near that it was God's will. He'd had difficulty with that.

He had more difficulty when his father's widowed sister came to live with them. He didn't want a surrogate mother, and he got into fights at school until the system transferred him to Snyder Continuation, downtown. He showed them what he thought of that by getting a tattoo in a crummy parlor full of drunk sailors on West Broadway. Eventually he settled down, received an honorable discharge from the Navy and joined the police department. When he had been a policeman for nine years his father retired and returned to Indiana. Running away from memories, thought Dowling, when he took his father to the airport. And bad timing, at that. A closeness of sorts had been beginning to form between them, and he recently thought of many things he wished he had said.

A week after seeing the Old Man, Dowling found himself seated in a psychiatrist's office. At a homicide seminar once, he had heard Dr. Leonard Boudreaux simplify it all.

"The county pays me good money to have a chat with your suspects between booking and arraignment. Before they get a lawyer. Are they sane? Can they form an intent to kill? If they can, I tell it to the judge."

Dowling figured Boudreaux to be about sixty. He was overweight, red-faced, a chain smoker, with a bulbous nose that supported half-rim glasses, which teetered on the downward slope. Dowling liked the man but was puzzled by the command visit.

"How come you need to see me on this one, Doc? The son of a bitch is going to cop a plea."

"Stacy thought we ought to tighten it up a little, just in case. So anyway, he formed the intent when he cocked the automatic. Looks pure and simple." Boudreaux put his glasses on the crowded desk top. "How has your life been going, Sergeant?"

"How has my life been going?"

"I've got to get that echo eliminated in here." Boudreaux smiled.

Dowling was putting on his sport coat. "My life's all right, Doc. I got my problems. Like everybody else." He pulled up the knot in his tie. "It was good seeing you again. Look for you in court."

"I hear your wife passed away."

"Four months ago."

"How are you handling it?"

"Rough at times. But I'm handling it."

"You have children, don't you?"

"Stacy must have briefed you on that too. Boy and a girl. Seventeen and fifteen."

"Are they adjusting?"

"They're doing fine. Now. It was tough for them at first. Kids bounce back."

"Um-hm."

"What else did Stacy tell you?"

"Sergeant, don't ever short sell the value of a pal."

"What else did he tell you?"

"Pals who care about each other. Can't put a price on that."

"I think it's also called sticking a nose into other people's business."

"Come on," Boudreaux said. "Sit down and let me poke at you a little bit." Dowling looked out the window, put his hands on his hips, then looked at Boudreaux and sat down.

"I'll summarize it, Doc. Accidental overdose of booze

and pills. She was a rummy. Twenty-six years of marriage. Down the drain, like that.'' He snapped his fingers. ''Life goes on, so me and the kids have been going on.''

''Have you been this angry for four months, Sergeant?''

''Angry?''

''Yeah, angry.''

Dowling sank deeper into the leather armchair. ''I've been everything I think for four months, Doc. It just won't go away. I can't make it go away. I hear a song. I see a picture. Yesterday, I saw a woman on the street, walking away from me. . . . I ran to catch up. I knew it couldn't be Helene, but . . .''

''It's called selective memory,'' Boudreaux said. ''Can't do anything about that. Shouldn't try to. Memories are important.''

Dowling nodded. ''I miss her so much. Hard to think of going on sometimes.''

Boudreaux got up and sat on the edge of his desk, closer to Dowling. ''I had an old girl in here not too long ago. Lost her husband. Fifty-seven years they'd been together. I told her about the empty-chair dialogue. It worked for her.''

''Empty-chair dialogue?''

''Sure. Easier than stepping in dog shit. Take two chairs and face 'em together. You sit in one. Pretend your wife, Helene, is in the other. Talk to her, Sarge. Say some of the things that have been eating at you. Get a little anger out. You'll know what to do.''

Dowling said nothing.

''When's her birthday?''

''It's in October. The third.''

''Celebrate it.''

''Huh?''

''Celebrate it. Don't pretend it's an ordinary day. It was her day. It's a reminder to you and the kids that you got hit hard and survived it. Anniversaries, same thing. You'll see.'' They talked for two more hours.

Five days later, Dowling faced two dining room chairs

together. He ended up throwing one across the living room.

A few days later Dowling investigated a barroom murder and arrested a man. The wrong man.

They did their crime scene and found a sober witness, and everything pointed to a heavy-drinking ex-lumberjack living in a run-down hotel. They caught up with him two days later, and Larry Shea found a gun under the mattress. The man had a long record of assault.

The test-fire bullets were under a microscope when Bones discovered patrol had been checking the guy into detox when the shots were being fired in the bar. The squad room became uncomfortably quiet, because nothing like that had ever happened to Sergeant Vincent Dowling.

"Jeez, Sarge," Speedy said. "If we'd of just checked his rap sheet closer . . . I never figured—"

Dowling shrugged. "Tomorrow we'll go through the neighborhood again. Find the right guy."

They arrested a man in another run-down hotel and obtained a confession. Dowling was not with them when they fished the gun out of the water in the boat basin behind Seaport Village. He was standing behind a closed door in Tom Stacy's office.

﹌ Six

"*Transferred!*" Dowling screamed it. "Transferred out of homicide. Jesus, Tom. Jesus!"

Stacy paced the width of his cluttered office. "If you'll let me finish what I was—"

"Transferred? You can't do that to me. I'm a homicide copper."

"Vince, listen to me. I've agonized over this. You won't hear it now, but it's best for you too. You see, you—"

"You can't transfer me, Tom. This is where I work." He pointed at his chest and drummed his index finger until it made a hollow sound. "Tom, this is me."

"I'm sending you to the relief pool. Nine to five. Weekends off. This is your last chance to get yourself together."

"It's that son of a bitch I threw in the can for the barroom job, wasn't it, Tom? One mistake. One lousy mistake in fifteen years of working dead bodies."

"Come on, Vince. That's not it, and everybody around here except you sees it. You were the best. Look at you now. For Chrissake, I tried to talk to you."

"What's the matter with me? A little grief-stricken, maybe." His face was red. "I'm sorry I grieved, Stacy. Sorry it interfered with business."

"Oh, spare me, Dowling. Your team's been carrying you for four months. Those guys care about you. So do I. But now I have to be a company man."

"I'll change. I'll do whatever you say. Don't can me."

Stacy walked to him. He put both hands on Dowling's shoulders. "All I want is for you to get a handle on your life. Then we'll talk about work. Go home and take care of yourself."

"Don't do it, Tom. I'm getting better. I did the empty-chair dialogue again. And it worked. I talked to her, Tom."

"Talked to who?"

"I talked to Helene. Last night."

"You have to go see Boudreaux again, Vince. You have to go see Boudreaux."

"Am I still transferred, Tom?"

"You're transferred."

"Well, fuck you, and fuck Boudreaux, and fuck this whole place."

Stacy was pointing at him. "Go ahead, you miserable bastard. Blame the rest of the world. Then look at yourself. When's the last time you got a haircut? When's the last time you brushed your teeth twice in the same day? When's the last time you baked a damn pastry? When's the last—" He stopped, and shook his head. "Ah, the hell with it."

Dowling was at the door. "Don't be sorry. I'm a cop. I still follow orders. You want me to be yesterday's news, I'm yesterday's news. So long, Stacy."

He ran across the parking lot to his car. He needed badly to see the Old Man. When he reached the boardwalk the man wasn't there. Dowling cursed, then ran a red light and wondered why horns were honking.

He drove wildly, staring straight ahead. He couldn't believe they'd kicked him out of homicide. Over fifteen years. Just out—like that. All he'd given them. All that dedication. The long, crazy hours had wrecked his life. They'd killed the marriage. Jesus. That was a bad word. They had *ruined* the marriage.

And what did he have to show for it? Who really cared that he had sent a couple of hundred killers to prison? Well, he knew what he had to show for it. A good wife turned stewbum; a job of being mother and father to two kids; and a kick in the ass from the department, which had just shoveled him away, like a dog turd on the lawn, from the only job he wanted to hold down there. His head ached. He thought about putting his gun to it and blowing away what few brains he had left. But the kids. Jesus. They were going to face some crises down the line. He didn't want them to remember how badly their old man had handled his problems, and, lord, they still didn't know how their mother had died.

He double-parked in front of a liquor store and bought a bottle of gin. He couldn't live and he couldn't die. As the car chugged up the hill, two blocks from his house he reached for the bag on the seat next to him. Placing it between his legs, he fumbled with the cap on the pint of Gilbey's. As he slowed to make a right-hand turn, he took two long swallows.

✿ Seven

Cliff Edwards shifted his weight from side to side as the patrol car made its way through heavy morning traffic. Next month, June, would be worse, thanks to the tourist trade. He hated working with a recruit officer. Having one behind the wheel was worse yet. Someone had to train the recruits, but he was thankful that he was rarely called upon. He suspected his sergeant thought he was too hard on them, or set a bad example by not being "professional" enough.

This recruit looked like a high-school student who had never seen a square meal. Edwards stared at the long, scrawny neck and decided he looked like Ichabod Crane.

"*Slow it down.* You're a police officer, not a fire fighter." The recruit jammed on the brake. Edwards lurched forward, and caught himself with one hand on the dashboard. Oh, sweet Jesus. This was the most dangerous part of police work.

"Pull it over to the curb, Ichabod," he shouted.

"Who? The car ahead of us? What did he do?"

"No, damn it. This car."

The recruit looked dejected. "What's the matter? And why did you call me Ichabod?"

Edwards got out, and in long strides walked around the car to the driver's side.

"That's two questions. And you haven't been on the department long enough to ask one. Move over. I'm driving."

The recruit tried to slide to the passenger side but was held in place by his seat belt. The long face reddened as he moved the traffic-citation booklet, first-aid kit and other paraphernalia that separated them.

Cliff Edwards slid behind the wheel of the black-and-white Ford. People often mistook him for being taller than six feet three inches, their estimate based on his lean, rangy frame and long arms. The hair that grazed the interior roof was very blond and barely regulation. It did not quite touch the top of his ears or the top of his collar. His brown eyes were neither hard nor soft. Friends said he had a radio announcer's voice.

Edwards didn't fasten his seat belt, but it wasn't because he'd forgotten to. For three years he had been a San Diego police officer. At first he'd worn the seat belt religiously. Then he'd learned what the recruit had just learned. Seat belts were supposed to keep you inside the car. When he pulled someone over for running a red light, he wanted to be outside. Fast. With his hand resting on the butt of his gun. So he could get the drop on some fugitive lying in the back seat who was reaching into his waistband for a pistol. That way, the pathologist wouldn't be making the Y incision in his chest at the same moment that some cluck from administration was checking the "yes" box next to the question: "Seat belt fastened as required?"

"Here's the way it is, rookie. I'm the wheel man for the rest of the day. And tomorrow, too, if I'm still stuck with you. Meanwhile, you better watch me and learn how to drive this son of a bitch. 'Cause if you don't, one of your classmates who can is going to take your job away from you. You're not out for a drive with your wife and kids. You 10-4, rookie?"

"10-4." The recruit sighed. "But this whole thing, the whole job. It isn't what I thought it was going to be. You're the third training officer I've been with. The other two said I was doing okay. But with you, most of what I do seems to be wrong. Even when I'm following procedure."

Cliff Edwards maneuvered the car in and out of traffic

with ease. It seemed to glide instead of roll, yet he appeared to be looking everywhere but at the road ahead. In the space of three blocks he glanced inside of two liquor stores, a deli, and had studied a number of pedestrians on the sidewalks, in addition to the occupants of cars driving in the opposite direction. If an all-units description of crime suspects were to be broadcast, he wanted to know who had just gone by.

"Procedure, huh?" Edwards said. "Some of the procedure they teach you in the police academy is valid, and you should use it all the time. Some is useful once in a while. And a lot of it you should shit-can. Like these damn seat belts."

"I forgot to buckle my seat belt last week and an officer marked me low in safety precautions."

"Then he had to be a traffic-division officer, Ichabod. Seat belts are real big things with traffic officers. But they wouldn't recognize a burglar if one sat on the hood of their car."

The recruit sighed and opened his notebook. "Is there anything I can do at home over the weekend to improve myself, Officer Edwards?"

"Yeah. You might start with the fuckin' want ads."

By noon the armpits of Edwards's uniform shirt were soaked with perspiration and he had a headache.

"How many tickets have we written today?"

"None, sir."

"That's the first question you've answered right. Start looking."

By 2:00 P.M. they had taken two reports of break-ins at fast-food restaurants. Edwards had taken several others recently.

"The night-watch guys must be sitting on their asses in the coffee shops again. Have you worked the night watch yet, Ichabod?"

"Yes, sir. Five times so far."

"Well, here's something they won't teach you in the academy. If you make your probation, which I doubt, and get a beat of your own, do what I do." He looked to make sure the recruit was paying attention. "Bring your coffee in a thermos. Drink it on the move. While you're warm and dry, bullshitting with the coffee-shop commandos, some burglar will be walking away with a sackful of your beat.''

Cliff Edwards made a sharp distinction between day and night police work. On the night watch you caught the crooks in the act. But the day watch was where you found out who was stealing from you after dark. A lot of lazy cops thought they were on vacation on day watch.

"When you work days, Ichabod, get out of your car and talk to people.''

"Talk to who, sir?''

"To café owners. Pool-hall people. Everybody. They drop little bits of information without even knowing it. Like who's been on the streets. With who. And, just as important, who hasn't been around. The 'who hasn't' may be laying low after a good burglary score or a stickup.''

The recruit shook his head. "I don't know if I'll ever learn all of this.''

"Tell me, Ichabod. Say a car blows a stop sign and we hit him with the red light and right away he pulls into the driveway of a house. What are you thinking?''

"I don't know. I guess I'd figure he runs that stop sign all the time because it's a few doors down from his house.''

"How about he pulled a stickup three blocks away and figures we don't know about it yet and he's pulling into that driveway to relax us?''

"I don't know if I'll ever learn all of this,'' the recruit said again.

"You won't if you keep thinking like a Sunday-school boy. You'll be lying on that front lawn, full of holes, with your ticket book in your hand, while he's off running another stop sign.'' He paused. "Get used to looking for evil, Ichabod.''

Cliff Edwards cruised slowly along University Avenue. He watched the street people stroll by, and glanced at others leaning against the building fronts in small

groups. He knew all of them. Their names were in the
green tin box on the seat next to him. "The Edwards
Files." He was proud of them. The box contained not
only their names, but their birth dates and addresses as
well. Car descriptions, license numbers, criminal records
and associates were all cross-referenced. Gang members
carried red asterisks next to their names. The longer he
worked the beat, the fewer names were added, because
he knew everybody worth knowing. He worked a dozen
hours a week at home keeping the files updated. When
somebody went to jail, he moved into the "OOCB"
section. "Out of Circulation, Brother."

He did not know the tall man wearing the red shirt,
standing next to the bus stop. The man was lighting a
cigarette, and when he saw the police car he looked
away quickly. Edwards pulled the car into the service-
station lot behind him and stopped.

"Find out who that guy is, Ichabod. 'Red shirt,' over
there."

The recruit looked at the man, then at Edwards. "Do
we have probable cause?"

"Screw the probable cause."

Later, Edwards said, "That's one of the ways you
keep your beat clean, Ichabod." He wrote the man's
name on a card and put it in the green box. "You kick
him off your beat and onto the next one." Edwards
smiled. "I got a drone working the beat next to me. I'll
lay you five to one that right now he's in a coffee shop
or out chasing pussy. So I send these transients over
there and let them steal from him."

Cliff Edwards was romantically involved with the al-
lure of his beat. He considered it his piece of ground,
and laid claim to it as surely as if it had been recorded
in his name in the county assessor's office. He loved the
excitement—never knowing at ten o'clock what was going to happen at five minutes after. A person couldn't
have asked for more independence. The sergeant had ten
officers working for him and couldn't be everywhere at
once. So Edwards made his own decisions and worked
the beat his way. He felt powerful. He took his job se-

riously and had never been in real trouble. Not the
booze-drinking, girl-chasing trouble that some cops got
in the grease over. There had been heat over the "white
killer duck" caper, but he could laugh about that now.

Four months before, he had picked up a white duck-
ling that was scampering about in the middle of a busy
intersection. He'd collared it after a great deal of effort,
and intended to take it straight to the Humane Society.
But en route, he'd covered a disturbance call and wound
up arresting some wild-eyed creep who was all doped
up.

He'd handcuffed him after a struggle and put him in
the back seat with the duck. The guy was yelling and
carrying on something awful, until Edwards turned and
shouted, "Listen, buddy. Shut the fuck up, so I don't
have to turn him onto you."

"Go to hell. Turn who onto me?"

"My killer duck. The department won't put a dog in
every car, so we use white killer ducks, and they go for
the goddamn eyes."

The duck had chosen that precise moment to leap onto
the guy's lap and stare at him. The creep had made the
rest of the trip sitting like a statue, without uttering a
word.

That would have been the end of it, except when he
got to jail and came off his high he uttered a lot of words
about it. As tends to happen, the story had gotten back
to the department brass. Edwards had received a written
reprimand for poor judgment and conduct unbecoming.
However, the chief's office had been more amused than
upset.

Edwards and Ichabod moved on, handling routine radio calls and helping find a lost child as the sun moved
toward the west.

"Those detectives must be awfully smart," the rookie
said.

"Why do you say that?" Edwards slowed for a signal
light.

"Well, in the academy they showed us a lot of the

crime cancellation statistics, and how many arrests the detectives made.''

Edwards snorted. ''It's not that the detectives are so smart, Ichabod. It's that the crooks are so dumb.''

''They are?''

''Sure. They taught you about M.O. in the academy, didn't they?''

''We're just getting into that. That's 'method of operation,' isn't it?''

''Yeah. And it covers a whole lot of things. Like method of entry. Some crooks will always use a half-inch pry on the door of a business. And another burglar will only pick on corner houses. Wants two streets to choose from if he gets caught in the act and has to split.''

The recruit nodded. ''One of the instructors told us about a robber who always brought a bottle of aspirin and a loaf of bread to the counter before he put the gun on the clerk.''

''Yeah, yeah. That's all M.O. But you see, Ichabod, the thing that ends up getting the crook caught is that he gets predictable. That's their biggest mistake. That's how I caught the kissing bandit. You probably heard about that pinch.''

''No. The kissing bandit? Are you serious?''

''Sure. This wacko was pulling stickups. Picking on small businesses with pretty girls working there. After he got the dough he'd make 'em give him a kiss.''

''How did you catch him?''

''M.O., Ichabod.'' Edwards pulled the car to the curb and stopped in a red zone. He drew an imaginary map on the seat with his finger. ''He'd only been hitting on Wednesdays and Fridays. He'd made a half circle. From Market Street up to my beat. I scoped out the three best-looking girls working my area. A laundry, a doughnut shop and a travel agency . . . and just kept checking them. Caught him in the act at the doughnut shop.''

''All by yourself?''

''Sure, all by myself. Waited till he got out the door. Put my shotgun in his face and made him open his mouth. Stuck the muzzle right in there. Said, 'Here. French-kiss this, you crazy peckerhead.' ''

"Jesus. You're some kind of cop. What did the guy do?"

"He pissed in his pants, Ichabod. Right in the parking lot."

Edwards pulled away from the curb and blended into traffic. "Another way crooks are dumb is that they go nickel-dime. Liquor stores. Mom-and-pop markets. Like the wacko. Takes a lot of jobs to make dough that way. Way too much risk. If I was a crook I'd go first class or not at all."

"With everything you know, I bet you'd be one heck of a crook."

"I'll tell you one thing. If I was, I'd always be on guard for a detective slipping an informant onto me."

"They do that? Is it legal?"

"Yes to both. Hell, informants are their bread and butter. They make detectives look good. A smart crook looks at anybody he doesn't know as an informant. Then he doesn't get burned."

Edwards swung onto a market parking lot, told the recruit to buy two Cokes and began organizing their paper work. He proofread the traffic citations and burglary reports, made entries in his daily journal and spent a few minutes arranging index cards in his green box. There were parking places on either side of the police car, and he noticed that other motorists chose not to use them.

"I heard you were an All-American basketball player," the rookie said as he slid back into the car.

Edwards looked up and grinned. He was beginning to like the recruit. In fact, he had been honorable mention All-American.

"Yeah, that's right. The other cops talk about that a lot, huh?"

"I heard it in the coffee shop. Some sergeant was saying you had school records for field-goal percentage shooting."

"And assists. And—I'm proud of this one—fewest personal fouls over a three-year period."

"Wow. I played some basketball," the recruit said. "It's tough to score a lot and not foul much."

"It's discipline and planning, Ichabod. There are ways you can foul and not get caught." He looked at the paper work left to be completed. "Anyway, quit bullshitting and get to work."

Edwards had been a basketball player, all right. At Hoover High School he'd been all-everything, and people said there had never been a player like him in San Diego. His scoring records still stood. He had been romanced by most of the college basketball factories and felt pampered and wanted.

An assistant coach from one of the North Carolina schools had swayed him. "The town is shaped like a basketball," he drawled, "and the whole place is full a' gold and glitter." He hadn't been far wrong.

Edwards had gone there for a look. The field house was awesome, the athletic dormitories lavish. Ten other high-school prospects were on the same tour. On the second night, one of the senior forwards threw a party. They lined him up with a buxomy blond sorority girl, and she had his pants unbuttoned before he'd finished his second beer.

He'd been a starting guard his last three years of college. At six three, though, he was small for a college player, so he changed his style and became a playmaker instead of a scorer. None of the starters wanted for anything. Friendly alumni businessmen provided clothing and cars and cash. For a while he fell behind badly in class, but a coach told him not to worry. To "concentrate on the X's and O's." At the end of the year, Edwards was not surprised to find straight B's on his transcripts.

He was all-conference in his junior and senior years. They went to the NCAA finals, and had it won until their opponents rattled off twelve unanswered points in the final three minutes to take the trophy.

Edwards was certain he would go high in the draft and have a lucrative pro career. It was destined. Salaries had rocketed, and he'd planned to invest his wisely, then hang it up at the age of thirty and spend the rest of his life on golf courses and luxury cruises. But he didn't get drafted. The NBA scouting book on him read: "Great playmaker—good leader; lack of size and lateral movement equals poor risk." It had been a terrible jolt, and he'd gone to free-agent and try out camps with the Celtics, Lakers and 76'ers. The book had been accurate, however, and he'd gone into a period of depression.

He needed twelve units for a degree, but considered himself a failure and was too embarrassed to return to the campus. For a year, he'd kicked around, working odd jobs, until an ex-high-school friend introduced him to police work. He'd taken the job as a lark, thinking it would be glamorous. Then the beat had hooked him.

The recruit drained the last of his cola and bent the can. "How come you're not playing pro ball now? Getting rich."

"The travel, Ichabod. They couldn't pay me enough to live out of a suitcase." He started the engine and pointed the car toward the station. "This is my whole life now."

The statement was nearly accurate. His waking hours were consumed by the job. If he was not working, he was in court or updating his files. He hated taking the time to serve as the treasurer of the kids' football league, but it was politically wise. The chief's office encouraged officers to become involved in community affairs, so being treasurer and all of his hard work were a means toward an end. Toward a promotion to the detective bureau.

In the last year he had made more felony arrests than any patrolman in his sector. His supervisors knew it, and the detectives had to know it. He had cleaned up a lot of burglaries and robberies for them. They were constantly coming to him for information on who was who. With his green tin box and computer memory, he never disappointed them. With one enormous failure behind him, the future looked nothing but bright.

*   *   *

Dowling moped and sulked and went through the motions of being a police officer. Two weeks had elapsed since Stacy had transferred him. Dowling had not spoken to Stacy after that. Had not spoken to him, and had seen him only twice. From a distance. That was not an accident. Dowling took circuitous routes in and around the police station. He traveled in stairwells instead of elevators. The whole scheme was designed to allow him to go from point A to point B and be seen by the fewest number of people. To avoid morning hellos and evening good-byes and middle-of-the-day gossip sessions.

He was still angry about the transfer. Angry and embarrassed.

A young lieutenant with styled hair and a three-piece suit gave him assignments in the Management Services Unit.

"Juvenile division. Stationery usage up 22½ percent over second quarter last year. Case load only up 17 percent. Think about it, Sergeant. Then find out why."

Or: "These are invoices, Sergeant." The lieutenant shuffled them like a deck of oversized playing cards. "Toilet-paper invoices. We're paying what they're billing us, and I've just established we're by God receiving what we ordered." He sliced the air with his forefinger. "But when you examine the storeroom shelves, you'll, by God, discover it isn't all there. Think about it, Sergeant. Then find out why."

The same admonishment followed each assignment.

"I know this job isn't glamorous, Sergeant. But it's, by God, important. We don't catch killers and we don't save lives and we don't put offenders behind bars. But the eyes of fiscal management and the chief's office are upon us. We are an important spoke in the wheel of justice. Think about it, Sergeant."

It was hot in the office. Dowling suspected the air conditioning was working in the chief's suite. His collar stuck to his neck, and his shirt stuck to the back of the chair and his cigarette tasted hot and stale. The lieutenant was on the phone, talking to a lieutenant in the Research and Analysis Division. The language was foreign to Dowling. The lieutenant reached for an ivory cigarette holder. Dowling had never seen a cop use one. It occurred to him that within five years the cigarette holder would be on top of an assistant chief's desk. The lieutenant was that kind of specimen.

He tuned the conversation out and dwelled on questions that had been nagging him since the transfer. For the first time, he wondered who he was, and if he stood for anything. The questions went unanswered. That disturbed him. He was used to putting neat investigative packages together. Packages with a beginning and a middle and an end. He was a forty-nine-year-old ex-package wrapper with nowhere to go. A man was supposed to be the most productive in his forties and fifties. He leaned back in his chair and thought about cops.

Cops make their mark in their twenties and their thirties. They're ripsnorters with hard, athletic bodies. They climb fences and kick in doors and carry crying babies out of smoke-filled houses. They wrestle in gutters with boisterous drunks and painted whores who gouge and bite and kick and scratch and scream. Then they gather in saloons and tell their stories.

"And then, I get her cuffed, this bitch with one arm. She says—she says, 'Your time will come, you dirty bastard. You wear your prick on your hip. Your time will come. . . .' "

Their time sneaks up on them. Like comfortable shoes they grow old overnight. At fifty they are through. They look ten years older. Their faces sag and their stomachs pooch, and their eyes are hollow and sad. They retire and guard banks and racetracks and convention centers in ill-fitting uniforms; or walk the aisles of discount department stores, wearing Hawaiian shirts and denim pants, and huff and puff and risk coronaries, chasing youthful shoplifters through crowded parking lots.

Dowling wondered if it was a form of punishment for all the years of indulging in gallows humor or black humor or squad-room humor or sick humor or whatever kind of label the sociologists wanted to put on it. They

sat around and drank and laughed and ridiculed all of
the human weaknesses that spawned the evil that allowed them to draw a paycheck. If it wasn't sordid, it
wasn't funny. And the more sordid the better.

Dowling wondered who he was.

The lieutenant was off the phone. "You mean you've
never investigated a cop?"

"I was a detective, not a headhunter."

"I'll pretend I didn't hear that, Sergeant. Because this
one came from the chief's office." He looked smug.
"Seems Internal Affairs is overworked." He handed
Dowling a manila folder. "Looks like we may have a
bad cop, Sergeant. A young patrol officer. Volunteer
treasurer of the Pop Warner Football Association. The
complaint comes from the association president. Seems
the president reviewed the books. Seems the president
found some rather, ah, rather extraordinary—"

"How about just sticking to facts?" Dowling said.

"Yes, well, missing checks. Marked-up reconciliation
statements. Questionable ledger entries for petty-cash
expenditures. Vague and evasive answers by the officer
when the president questioned him. And"—the lieutenant smiled—"here's the clincher. Look at the officer's
file. A couple of reprimands in it. One for conduct unbecoming. I'm always suspicious of cops who have reprimands in their file."

Dowling was always suspicious of cops who did not
have reprimands in their file. They were the do-nothings.
The wait-for-trouble-to-find-them types. They had per-
sonalities like toilet seats. They ended up with styled
hair and three-piece suits.

"He also has a commendation or two, Sergeant. One
little attaboy from you, as a matter of fact. Seems he did
a respectable job, protecting a murder scene and taking
charge until you arrived."

Dowling looked at the name on the file. Patrol officer
Cliff Edwards. Dowling glanced at his memo. The Roy
Green case. It had to be the Roy Green case. The case
he couldn't make go away.

"It's a serious allegation, Sergeant. A serious allegation. The eyes of the chief's office are upon us. I want you—"

Dowling held up his hand and headed for the door. "I know, Lieutenant. Think about it, and find out why."

⧸⧸⧸ Eight

Jimmie "Baby Blue" Bench was feeling the effects of the twelve-hour bus ride. They were on the last leg of the trip, a stretch of Interstate 80, east of Sacramento. The windows of the bus were barred, and the thirty-seven prisoners on board were chained, with their hands just far enough apart to permit them to smoke. A heavy metal screen separated them from the driver and an officer riding shotgun. The bus smelled like peanut butter, because seventy-four sandwiches had been doled out south of Fresno. Baby Blue was sitting next to a one-eyed Mexican from Los Angeles, and they had run out of things to talk about before the driver had shifted into high gear.

With stiff legs and aching shoulders, he leaned back in the seat and thought about the chain of events that had made him a passenger. Only a few months ago he'd had grass under his feet. On parole, but at least free. How could he have screwed up so badly? So quickly? He'd been at a party with the Bulldog and a bunch of others. A couple were ex-cons too, and he remembered being worried about that. If his parole officer found out about his "associating," he would have been violated. Sent back to the joint. Well, he hadn't gotten violated. It was worse than that.

He'd knocked off a pint of vodka and a couple of Quaaludes and quit worrying about his parole officer. Then the Bulldog had told him about an easy score over on Marlborough Avenue. Some weed dealer named Roy kept money in his pad. The guy would be easy. They could intimidate him. Muscle him for it. The guy wouldn't be able to run to the cops and cry about his stash money being ripped off.

But the Bulldog had had to waste the guy. Stabbed him a bunch of times, then held the knife out for Baby Blue. He remembered the look in the Bulldog's eyes. And they were partners. So he'd taken the knife and stabbed the guy. Roy had jerked a couple of times, like a long-haired puppet on a string. Then the Bulldog did the guy some more. The rest was history.

After the arraignment, the court-appointed lawyer had said the D.A. would probably consider a plea to second degree. The lawyer had said it sounded reasonable to him. They could fight it all the way, try to prove there'd been no "intent to murder" when Roy had let them in. But there was a better-than-fair chance a jury would come in with a verdict of first degree.

Baby Blue had agreed. Quickly. There was no doubt in his mind it was better to cop the plea and cut his time down. He'd been around long enough to know that the plea would look better someday down the line when they were considering kicking him out. He could tell them what they needed to hear—he had been remorseful right after they'd done the job. Hadn't even wanted to waste the taxpayers' dough messing with preliminary hearings and motions and trials. He could tell them that rehabilitation and all that crap had started immediately.

In his mind, this never-plead-guilty business was overrated. When they had you all sewed up, all the F. Lee Baileys and Johnnie Cochrans in the world couldn't get you off.

After he'd entered the plea they'd sent him to Chino, the processing center near Los Angeles. He'd spent a dreary week there being interviewed by psychologists and taking the Rorschach and a number of other tests. While he was drawing trees and sticking pegs in holes, the Department of Corrections was deciding which of twelve state prisons his mail would be sent to. He'd daydreamed about being sent to a conservation center at Sonora, or Susanville up in the Sierras. They were prisons, sure, but minimum security, and full of a lot of first timers.

But he knew it would be Folsom or San Quentin. He'd done time at Q already, and they sure weren't going to send him back to kindergarten. He also knew he wouldn't be seeing the Bulldog, because the state separated crime partners in murder cases.

His thoughts were interrupted when the bus driver braked abruptly for a red sports car weaving through traffic. He looked at the wild flowers blooming on the green hills and wondered when he'd see them again. Then he wondered who he would know at the prison. The cons there would know the name of everybody on the bus and what they were coming up on. He knew all about the grapevine, and the trustees who pulled duty in the administration building would already have passed the information along to sixteen hundred listeners.

They were well past McClellan Air Force Base when the driver turned and yelled, "It won't be long now."

"It won't be long, my ass," someone called from the rear. "Thirty years if I'm lucky." Nobody laughed.

The bus cruised into Folsom city and the talking stopped.

The town was nestled on the side of a Sierra Nevada foothill. It had been a tent-city mining camp in 1848, thriving and bustling, as had neighboring camps with colorful names like Prairie City, Mormon Island, Adler Creek and Negro Bar. Those towns had disappeared, but Folsom had survived.

"Where the west came and stayed" was what the old-timers said.

"The end of the world" was what the inmates said.

The prison was perched on a grassy knoll three-quarters of a mile from Mercy Hospital. Convicts had constructed the prison with gray granite in 1880 while townspeople splashed along the banks of the American River and stared at them.

The bus stopped at the outer gate, then rolled slowly

for one hundred and fifty yards to the main gate, past the gift shop on the left. The prisoners' names were checked off, and they were herded into an assembly hall next to the administration building. A bus bearing prisoners from northern California jurisdictions had already unloaded. A correctional officer in a green uniform with lieutenant's bars was at the podium. Another officer stood a few feet away, and Baby Blue recognized him. Robert Burns MacIntosh. He had been at San Quentin.

He tried to catch MacIntosh's eye. At San Quentin, Baby Blue's mother had driven up to visit him several times. He'd always worried about her making the long haul alone. She'd been in her early sixties then, had arthritis and became easily fatigued. His mother had to count her pennies, and the thousand-mile round trip cost at least fifty dollars for gas, plus a motel room to rest in before starting the drive back to San Diego.

Once, looking at her through the glass in the visitor's area, he'd sensed she was upset. Sobbing, she'd told him about having to replace the water pump near Bakersfield. She had spent the motel money and would have to drive home that night. The worry, anger and frustration had welled up in him, and he'd punched a black faggot in the chow line after she left. A few days later he'd received a letter from her. Robert Burns MacIntosh had escorted her to the main gate and, learning of her problem, lined her up with the prison chaplain. His mother had shared dinner and spent the night with the chaplain and his wife, and had sent the couple some jars of her peach preserves.

Baby Blue had thanked the guard, and little by little, a friendship of sorts had formed.

MacIntosh had been born and raised in Jedburgh, Scotland, a small town on the English border. He'd come to the United States, obtained citizenship and, at the suggestion of a friend, taken the California State Civil Service examination. MacIntosh had been living in San Francisco, and the friend had told him, "Maybe you can get a job at San Quentin."

"At the time I didn't know what a San Quentin was,"

MacIntosh told Baby Blue in his Scottish brogue. His first night on the job he'd received a two-day suspension for "counting a dummy" while making a head count in the cells. The inmate who'd placed the "dummy" there was discovered on the prison grounds, attempting to escape.

" 'Twas a good dummy, though," MacIntosh told him, and "from that day on I became the best counter in the whole blasted prison system." MacIntosh sometimes sang softly while making his rounds, and Baby Blue and some of the others would sing in unison when they knew he was approaching.

> You'll take the high road
> And I'll take the low road,
> And I'll be in Scotland before you.

MacIntosh would grin broadly and inquire why lads of such good taste in songs were doing a stretch at Q. Baby Blue had learned the song in the fifth grade but had never been able to make sense of the words, until MacIntosh explained that the song had been written by a Scotsman condemned to hang in England. The song had been composed the evening before he went to the gallows, and was dedicated to his true love. The author would be dead when she received the poem; thus he would travel the "low road" to the banks of Loch Lomand. Tears had formed in MacIntosh's eyes as he related the story.

The voice of the lieutenant at the podium jarred Baby Blue back to the present.

"It's hardly appropriate to say, 'Welcome to Folsom,' but as long as you're here I'm going to lay out some ground rules. I see a few familiar faces."

The lieutenant shuffled some papers.

"We have five housing units. Buildings one, two, three and five are general population. Number four is the 'seg' unit. Maximum security. The hole. All of you are assigned to general population. We don't care what kind of a beef you're in here for." He looked at the papers again. "We got cop killers in this class, and stickup artists, and some guys who can't keep their pants zipped up. But everybody starts off on the same footing. We have to live together. Behave yourself and you stay in general. That gives you yard privileges most of the day. We have lock-downs and counts after breakfast and in the evening."

The lieutenant moved to the side of the podium and scanned his audience. Some were looking back at him. Most had their heads down.

"If you stir the shit or give the officers a bad time, you go to the seg unit. This is a heavy joint. Most of the guys here are thirty years or older. They're pretty much just doing their time. You won't have young punks getting in your face, trying to make a name for themselves." The lieutenant folded his arms and did not speak for over a minute.

"Another thing. We've never lost a prisoner from inside of these walls. Get this fixed in your heads. We don't negotiate if you decide to take an officer. There is no such thing as a hostage situation, in our eyes. You're not going anywhere. We'll come in and get our man even if you've already killed him. And when we come in—it's gonna rain all over your asses."

He droned on for another fifteen minutes, covering rules and regulations. When they filed out, MacIntosh was standing by the door.

"Was hoping you wouldn't be back, Baby Blue."

"I was kind of hoping that too, Mr. MacIntosh."

The moustache looked bushier than he'd remembered. MacIntosh stood every bit of six feet tall, with light brown hair now turning gray. Baby Blue calculated he was in his early forties. He had muscular forearms, and the ever-present pipe was protruding from his uniform-shirt pocket.

"How's your mother, lad?"

He shrugged. "Disappointed. Like always."

"For what it's worth, I've been picking up talk since

yesterday. About your putting the Bulldog in a bad way.''

''Thanks for telling me, but that flat ain't so.''

He was concerned but not surprised that the news had traveled so fast. He hadn't really snitched off the Bulldog. Not in the usual sense. They'd have convicted the Bulldog even if he hadn't let that Dowling bullshit him. They had the shotgun and the bloody clothes. He'd have to work his way—talk his way—out of this one.

In methodical fashion, he and the others were photographed, fingerprinted and issued two pairs of stiff blue denims and toilet articles. Just when he wondered if he would ever be able to lie down again, they were placed in transit cells for the night.

The next morning regular cell assignments were made. Baby Blue got onto the empty bunk, rolled over onto his stomach and looked at the gear spread out on the other bunk. Most of the cells at Folsom housed one inmate, and he was disgusted to find he would be sharing his cell. When he saw a narrow multicolored bandanna hanging from an end rail he raised his head and peered at it.

A black! He was bunking with a black. It had to be. The chump had two dew-rags, and right now he was jiving in the yard with the other one wrapped around his funky black head. Jesus. That was the pits. Maybe MacIntosh could get him transferred to another tier, he thought. With another loser. Who was white.

Then he lay back and wondered if it really mattered. He'd spent time in Juvenile Hall, starting when he was thirteen, for the things he'd been caught on. That did not include stealing or prowling over one hundred cars. Or stealing and selling the ring he'd copped from his mother's jewelry box—which had belonged to her dead mother. Or gang-mugging drunk sailors on the streets south of Broadway.

Living in a Navy town had kept his pockets jingling. All those gullible young white hats pouring off giant aircraft carriers with money in their socks. Certain that Broadway, from Kettner to 16th Street, was all there was of San Diego. His challenge had been to get into their wallets before the other hustlers on the west end of the avenue. The young girls with tight asses and tighter jeans swaying back and forth in front of the photo shops, luring them inside for the deluxe package that included a framed eleven-by-fourteen, with extras in wallet size. Or the pimply-faced guys with shiny suits behind the glass counters. Skinning them good. Convincing them to shell out big bucks on junk jewelry for girlfriends baking them cookies in Nashville and Sandusky and Galveston.

When Baby Blue and his cronies could get them into a pool hall it was all over. Playing down to someone the first couple of games, when the ante was small, then watching the guy's face when all the tough bank shots started dropping in. And if Baby Blue and his pals did stumble onto a good stick, some street-smart shooter who knew the difference between the eight ball and the five ball, they'd waylay him while he was heading for the ship. Pound him into the grimy downtown gutter and get their money back and then some.

The next five years had held a few commitments to road camp through the Youth Authority. Baby Blue always smiled when he thought of his first acid trip—in the San Diego County jail. When he went to state prison for the first time, at nineteen, it was almost a lark. Until he got to the Deuel Vocational Institute at Tracy. A bunch of young punks, like himself, showing each other how bad they were.

He'd gone for liquor-store stickups. Caught on his second job by two cops on a stakeout team hiding in the beer cooler, expecting someone else. They'd nailed him, shoved him into a patrol car, gone back to the cooler. Twenty minutes later the fool they'd been waiting for showed up, and they took him down too.

There were a lot of beefs at Tracy, sure, but you hardly ever saw a shiv. If some dude got into your face you duked it out with him. Whether you whipped him or not didn't really matter. You showed you had balls enough to fight. If you didn't fight they'd hang a sissy jacket on you, turn you out, and you'd spend the rest of your time with your pants down, getting fucked in the ass.

But at least you didn't have to put up with the gangs
so much then. He'd done a couple of years at Tracy, got
lucky and stayed out for a year. Then he'd gotten caught
holding burglary loot, and got sent to San Quentin. Q
was heavy, but with older cons you didn't have the constant fighting you had at Tracy. Not at first, anyway. The
last of the old con bosses had run the joint, and if you
played by their rules you didn't get walked over.

MacIntosh had told him once it was probably the
Vietnam deal that had gotten it going. The freaky,
weirdo students coming over from Cal Berkeley yelling
about prison reform. Radical white lawyers coming in
to visit black militants and stirring everything up.

"The outside world moving in on the prisons with all
of their frustrations." That was what MacIntosh had
said. "Turning the prisons into ideological battlefields."
All those visiting lawyers making these guys think they
weren't lawbreakers, but "political prisoners of an op-
pressive society."

And the blacks had eaten that up. Well, they sure
weren't political prisoners. They were just punks who'd
screwed up and gotten caught. Just like him.

He closed his eyes and clenched his fists. Above all,
the gangs were what made life in the joint so miserable.
He had heard all the stories of how they'd formed. The
Mexican Mafia first. All those *cholos* from the barrios
of East Los Angeles. Trying to run the whole prison.
Controlling the narcotics and loan-sharking, extorting
you for your smokes and stabbing anybody who got in
the way. It wasn't enough to have one gang of Mexicans.
The pukes from the farming communities of central California had gotten tired of being pushed around by the
Mafia, so they'd named themselves the *Nueva Familia*—
New Family—and stabbed twenty-two of the L.A. Mexicans in three days.

The crazy whites had figured they couldn't stand
around and be sitting ducks, so some dumb Nazi had
dreamed up the name Aryan Brotherhood, and that made
three gangs. And all the ABs really were a bunch

of outlaw bikers and white supremacists and losers like himself who needed some protection.

· Of course everything had gotten fancy then. Charters were written up, and membership councils appointed leaders, and it flowed over to the streets outside the walls.

As bad as that made it, things got worse when the blacks decided to get into the act. A bunch of psycho revolutionaries who tagged themselves the Black Guerilla Family and once in a while teamed up with the *Nueva Familia* to fight the whites. And just when it seemed like the lines were all drawn nice and neatlike, one gang would carry out a contract for another gang and snuff some poor son of a bitch who couldn't be looking all directions at once.

The Black Guerilla Family was down to a few old has-beens, so more blacks, the Bloods and Crips, came charging in. The gangs made the tension so thick you could cut it with a homemade shiv. Constant fear and pressure. The days were gone when you could sit in a corner of the yard minding your own business and doing your time. Now every time somebody got stabbed, the first thing you thought about was how it affected you down the line somewhere. Used to be you could relax in the yard. Almost like a Sunday-afternoon picnic. Now everybody looked like a bunch of caged animals out there. The MMs all grouped together on one side and the NFs here, and the Crips somewhere and the Bloods somewhere and the ABs trying to protect their backs.

And Jeez, the Asians. He'd forgotten about the Asians. When he'd first gotten to Q there'd been only a few of those skinny-ass shits running around the yard. Then the Cambodians had formed up the Oriental Boy Soldiers. And the Laotians had answered back with the Oriental Killers. He could hardly keep track anymore.

Well, to hell with it all. He'd do the best he could. Get a little gig going to make a buck. Try to get in on brewing up some applejack and trade it off for smokes. Something lightweight. He sure didn't want to end up in the seg unit . . . the bucket. Talk about isolation. His nerves got shot when he couldn't kick it with any of the brothers. Single cells, and taking meals sitting on your damn bunk. *Maybe* a half-hour of exercise in the postage stamp of a yard.

He'd spent a month in the bucket at Q while the Department of Corrections investigators were trying to solve a murder. Some white dude was in for child molesting, and a bunch of them sitting around one day had gotten bored and decided to hit him. The guy had started using cocaine, and one of the ABs, Bugger Red, had told the guy he could get him a snort in the showers. The guy had gotten all happy and showed up right on time, and Baby Blue had been the point man, or lookout. He'd stood by the washbasin, and he'd never heard anything when Bugger Red had stuck the guy. He'd just seen the blood mixed in with shower water. They'd put him and Red and four or five others in the bucket while they tried to sort it out. But, like always, when it happened inside the walls, nothing ever came of it. What he'd come out of there knowing was, he could never handle another stretch in isolation.

Baby Blue walked into the yard from an exterior door of Building One and shaded his eyes from the sunlight. The yard he saw was part grass, part concrete and composition dirt. A wooden wall used for handball was on one side, and a softball diamond was on the other. Next to some basketball hoops, several domino tables were anchored to the ground. He saw two gun towers. One was just inside the wall and reminded him of an overly tall, disjointed lifeguard stand. The second one rested on top of the building he had just exited. The correctional officers, with rifles and shotguns, seemed to be looking back at him. He stood for a moment, then recognized an AB from San Quentin standing with a group of other whites.

"Hey, brother. What's happening?"

"Hey, Baby Blue. Nothing shakin' but fat girls' hips. We heard you was coming up with that busload of fish yesterday."

"Yeah. Came on up here because I missed you dudes. What are you up on now?"

"Robbery," the man said. "But I'm a short timer, brother. They gave me a date last week. Ninety-four more days. That's the good news."

"What's the bad?"

"I owe motherfuckin' Michigan ten years."

"For robbery?"

"What else? Let me intro you to some brothers."

Baby Blue met several members of the Aryan Brotherhood. Most were heavily muscled, from long hours of weight lifting. Their body odors offended him.

"What kind of joint is this?" he asked.

"Heavy. Like Q," said one.

"MMs and NFs ain't as strong here. Got a lot of 'em split up between Q and Soledad," added another.

"Watch out for a bull named Pennington," said the first man. "He's old Folsom. Been here thirty years. Works nights and on weekends. You look at him wrong—he'll get a couple of others. They'll work your ass over but good."

"Pennington, huh?" Baby Blue said. "I'll remember that name. What's he look like?"

"Built like a fireplug. Face like a hat full of assholes."

"How long was you out before you fell?" asked a man with a shaved head.

"Couple of months."

"Murder beef, huh?"

"Yeah."

"San Diego?"

"Yeah."

"The Bulldog dropped too."

"Yeah. We both pled out. He's at Q."

"We know."

Baby Blue took the first man aside, and they sat down by the backstop of the softball diamond.

"Who's the man here, brother?" he asked.

"Boston Joe Garvey. You know him?"

"No. I heard of him when he was at Soledad."

"A good dude. Got it together."

"Is he from Boston?"

The man laughed. "Shit, no. Hardly ever been out of the joint in California. He's thirty-five years old. Done over fifteen years hard time."

"What kind of beef this time?" Baby Blue asked.

"Big casino. He'd been out of Soledad two days and cut some dude's head off in San Francisco. He had the ABs at Soledad."

"I know."

"Your buddy MacIntosh is working here now."

"Yeah. I saw him when I checked in, brother."

The chow whistle sounded, and they got up to take their place on the numbers. He picked at his dinner, and was alone in the cell waiting for the lock-down and head count. A very short, very slender black man walked into the cell. They looked at each other.

"My name is Xavier X," the black man said finally. "You are Mr. Bench."

"They call me Baby Blue. What's the X stand for?"

"Xavier X is my entire name." The black man did five deep-knee bends. "You are a member of the Aryan Brotherhood, are you not?"

"Yeah."

"Emotionally and philosophically, how do you feel about bunking with a black?"

"I ain't wild about it. How about you?"

"I am not wild about it either."

Xavier X removed a black bandanna from around his head. "You are serving time for murder." It was not a question.

"Yeah. You?"

"The same."

"How long you been locked up, Xavier?"

"Twenty-one years."

Xavier X was very dark-skinned. High cheekbones and deep-set brown eyes accented a smooth face. His head was shaved. He never looked into Baby Blue's eyes when he spoke.

"Why are you a member of the Aryan Brotherhood, Mr. Bench?"

"That's a hell of a question. The same reason you're either a Blood or a Crip. Got to be in a tip to stay alive in this place."

The black man was doing push-ups. "You have made a presumption, Mr. Bench. An erroneous one, at that. I am not associated with either of the two organizations you mentioned." He was doing push-ups furiously now, and spoke with no shortness of breath. "The Crips and the Bloods are young savages whose motives for killing are fashioned by avarice and misguided direction. They understand not the value of austerity, obedience and abstinence from drugs and alcohol. It amuses them that I fast four days a week to practice internal discipline and to rid my body of impurities."

"How come you ain't in a tip?"

"I am. The Black Guerilla Family. What do you know about the Black Guerilla Family, Mr. Bench?"

He wondered why the black man kept calling him that, and it irritated him. "What's to know? A bunch of nig—bunch of blacks sticking together."

Xavier X stopped doing push-ups, got to his feet and shook his head slowly.

"No, it is much more involved. Much more complex. The BGF was a Maoist group founded by the late George Jackson. I shall relate more, but first there is some history you must absorb."

Tomorrow he would definitely talk to MacIntosh about this weird nigger. This stir-crazy son of a bitch.

Xavier X lay on his bunk and began isometric exercises with his fingers and biceps.

"My father was a Black Muslim in Detroit in the 1930s when the cult was formed. He learned that Christianity was manufactured by European whites who used the religion to enslave the Negro in North America. I became a Muslim in New York City and studied at Columbia. When Martin Luther King's Civil Rights movement failed we were not surprised. America had robbed the black man of his language and his land and his religion and his past and was attempting to rob him of his future."

Baby Blue was getting drowsy.

"Every avenue we journeyed to better ourselves we were thwarted by white roadblocks. The white race is impure, and integration was undesirable to us . . . teachings of Elijah Muhammad . . . became a Black Panther . . . insufficiently militant, so . . . formed the Black Liberation Army . . ."

Baby Blue was falling asleep, and Xavier X's voice was cutting in and out.

". . . took it upon ourselves to assassinate the white pigs who wore blue uniforms and badges and gun belts and were the symbol of white oppressionists . . ."

Baby Blue heard what followed, and his eyes opened wide.

"In Oakland I executed two white policemen with a shotgun. We lured them into a housing project on a bogus disturbance call. I was arrested. Convicted. By an all-white jury, incidentally, and sentenced to death. When the state supreme court ruled the death penalty unconstitutional I was removed from the row at San Quentin and transferred here. My reprieve from the gas chamber reinforced our belief that it is proper to take a life for a righteous cause. Never for greed, Mr. Bench. Only for pure and noble motives."

He stopped talking, and Baby Blue sat up.

"Hey, Xavier."

"Yes."

"What do you call that stuff, man, when you can't sleep?"

"That stuff is called insomnia."

"Yeah. That's it. Insomnia. If I could bottle you up and sell you to people who had insomnia, I could make a bundle."

The black man threw his head back and laughed. "You know. You may turn out to be all right after all. For a honky."

*   *   *

Baby Blue struggled through his readjustment to prison life for the next few days. Then he received word that it was time to meet the leader of the Aryan Brotherhood. He located Boston Joe Garvey sitting on a domino table in the yard. Garvey's face was thin and pockmarked. Black hair combed straight back glistened through a layer of pomade. Two brothers were sitting next to him, but Garvey waved them away as Baby Blue approached. They did not shake hands.

"Glad to—glad to meet you, brother."

"Good meeting you, Baby Blue. You hangin' in?"

"Yeah, Boston Joe. Having brothers here helps."

Garvey looked at him. "I got word that brothers at Q want you hit."

"Want me hit? You've got to be jiving, brother."

"Ain't a man here ever heard Boston Joe Garvey jive. They said you snitched off a brother in San Diego. The Bulldog. Said you was fall partners."

Baby Blue was aware of his palms perspiring. He shook his head, looked up at the gun tower, then turned back to Garvey.

"I never snitched anybody off. Would never snitch off a brother."

"How did it go down?" Garvey demanded.

"We got hung up for wasting a grass dealer. I told the cops my part in it. Only my part, Boston Joe. Never did a number on the Bulldog."

"Did you testify?"

"Never testified. We both pled out to second."

Garvey placed snuff between his teeth and lower lip. "I can live with a brother riding his own beef. The way word came out of Q was more like you set the Bulldog up."

"No, sir. No way."

"Well, it didn't figure. The brothers here who know you tell me you're a stand-up guy."

Baby Blue nodded and watched a spray of dark juice dart from Garvey's crooked teeth to the dirt at their feet.

"I'm gonna send back word that I looked into it. And that for now, I'm satisfied."

"That's cool, Boston Joe. That's righteous."

"But. Me and all the brothers would feel better if you did a little job for us. Sort of prove yourself, you understand? You'd probably feel better too, huh?"

"Yeah. I'd feel better. A lot better."

Boston Joe Garvey forced a grin. "Save us from cutting your cock off and stuffing it down your throat." The grin vanished.

"Anything, Boston Joe. Anything," Baby Blue muttered.

"Tomorrow—under this table. There'll be a shiv with an eight-inch blade. I want you to hit somebody."

"Sure. Who?"

"I want you should hit a bull."

"Sure. Sure. A bull. Who? Old Folsom Pennington?"

"No," Boston Joe Garvey said. "Not Pennington. Another one. Robert Burns MacIntosh."

⑨ Nine

Four days had passed since Garvey had given him the order to kill MacIntosh. Baby Blue had gathered a group of brothers around the domino table. On the pretense of chasing a stray handball, he'd retrieved the homemade weapon and secreted it under his dungaree jacket.

In the privacy of his cell, he measured the shiv from the tip of his fingers to a point about three inches past his wrist. The balance and workmanship surprised him. At San Quentin, the few that he'd seen close up had been crude. This one was well shaped, well honed and thickly wrapped at one end with black electrical tape. He curled his fingers around it and gripped tightly. If he could divert MacIntosh for just an instant, make his first several thrusts into the chest . . .

Physically, the job would not be difficult to carry out. All of the correctional officers on the staff, save those in the gun towers, roamed the grounds unarmed. They were seldom in pairs, and MacIntosh, who was assigned to Baby Blue's housing building, was usually stationed on a chair at the end of the catwalk on the first tier. From time to time, MacIntosh would make his rounds on foot, but he was never segregated from the inmates by a protective barrier. There were bound to be a couple of witnesses, but they wouldn't talk. They'd be killed if they did. The worst that could happen if one did snitch would be a murder charge by the D.A. in Sacramento. If that happened the prisoners would start running

things. One of his brothers, some lifer who had gotten
a reprieve from death row, with no hope of ever being
sprung, would come forward and take the rap. The lifer
would swear that he'd killed MacIntosh. Faced with the
denial by Baby Blue and the other guy's confession, a
jury would acquit him. He knew juries had little concern
for what went on behind the walls of Folsom Prison.

If he didn't do the job on MacIntosh, well, they'd kill
him for sure. Death was the automatic penalty for refusing a contract, and it would just be a matter of time.
He knew the ABs had nothing against MacIntosh. It occurred to him why Boston Joe Garvey was the man. He
knew how to put a person to the severest of tests.

For three days he slept poorly. He became depressed.
His troubles became magnified. He tried to think of one
person in his life who loved him, or had stood by him,
whom he had not wronged. And he could not. A spinster
English teacher in the eighth grade had taken a liking to
him. She had discouraged the boy's vice principal from
expelling him for fighting and playing hooky. He had
rewarded her by stealing a camera from her car and selling it to a ninth grader.

Only once had he ever thought about trying to turn
his life around. It was at San Quentin, when he received
a discharge date. He'd gotten pumped up, and on his
mother's last visit, had promised her he was in jail for
the last time. When he got out, he'd stayed with her,
and they'd talked seriously and deeply for the first time.
His mother lived alone, and he'd spent days sifting
through his old belongings and sitting in the kitchen
while she cooked and told him about his father.

"He left the police department when you were little,"
she explained. "He'd only been on for about five years,
and the pressures were getting to him awful, and he began drinking. Once he got caught with a bottle in his
patrol car, so they fired him. It hurt him terribly, because
he loved being a policeman." She sighed, and stopped
peeling carrots. "I could never get him to stop drinking.
Then . . . let's see . . . he had all kinds of odd jobs. He
repaired bicycles at a shop over in Mission Beach, and

delivered furniture, and he tried to get a job as a gardener with the city, but they wouldn't hire him. They thought he might have a drinking problem.'' She shook her head and turned to face him. ''You were only seven when he died. He had colitis and sclerosis of the liver, and he just died.''

Baby Blue wondered if the old woman felt pain. Her voice was even, and he suspected she had often had this talk with herself. ''A lot of his police buddies came to the house after the funeral and told me and your aunts how brave he had been. Once, he climbed out onto the Laurel Street bridge in Balboa Park and grabbed a woman who was trying to jump, and they both almost went flying, but he saved her.''

She dug out old photographs and showed him one of his father in front of the police station.

''He loved you and your brother, and right after you learned to walk he took you down there to show you off. He was a good man, James, just like you're a good man.''

His mother had worked two jobs to support him and his older brother, David. He remembered coming home with David after school and having to telephone his mother at work and check in. Then they would watch television until she returned and fixed dinner. His brother had joined the Navy as soon as he turned seventeen, and was still a radioman on a destroyer somewhere. Baby Blue had received frequent letters from him in San Quentin but never replied.

It was time to do something.

When the sun was directly overhead, Baby Blue walked slowly into the prison yard. Some Mexicans were playing softball, and a noisy group had gathered to watch. Boston Joe Garvey was at the fringe of the crowd, on the third-base foul line. Baby Blue walked to his side. Garvey continued watching the game.

''It's been four days, Baby Blue.''

''I know, brother. I been doping it out. Now's the time.''

Garvey said nothing, but nodded and twisted his lower lip.

Half an hour later Baby Blue saw MacIntosh strolling on the third tier. He was alone, so Baby Blue climbed the stairwell, after making certain the other catwalks were empty. He undid one button on his jacket and made sure the knife was not causing a bulge. When he reached the third tier, MacIntosh had stopped walking and was looking into an empty cell. His back was to Baby Blue, who came up softly behind him.

"I'm supposed to kill you, Mr. MacIntosh."

MacIntosh turned quickly. Baby Blue saw the color drain from the guard's long face.

"Why, lad?" MacIntosh looked over his own shoulder. "What's behind it?"

"It's all connected to the Bulldog thing." Baby Blue was looking everywhere. His hand moved across the front of his jacket. "I don't think anybody's got a hard-on for you. It's just the way it is. But watch yourself, Mr. MacIntosh."

"When did you—"

"I have to go. Have the night shift make a shake-down. The shiv will be in the crapper."

He hurried down the stairwell and went to his cell. He lay down on his back and folded his arms under his head. And waited.

The shakedown took place just before the 10:00 P.M. lock-down. The knife was found taped under a sink in the bathroom, and the usual amount of narcotics and contraband turned up in the cells. The occupants went to the bucket. Word was passed that Building Number One would be locked down for at least three days.

"Isn't this some shit? What got this going?" Xavier X asked. "Three motherfuckin' days in this mother-fuckin' crib."

"Yeah," Baby Blue muttered, and quickly fell asleep.

By the third day of the lockdown, Xavier X and his isometric exercises were grating on Baby Blue's nerves. The two men had spoken little. Their food was cold and tasteless by the time it reached the cell. Baby Blue had started several letters to his mother and his brother but had torn them up.

There were things to think about. Things to plan. The ABs were going to try and get him, and he guessed they wouldn't farm the job out to one of the Mexican gangs. It was a personal thing with them now.

The lock-down ended the following morning, and he spent the day alone in the yard, under the gun tower. Toward late afternoon he spoke with MacIntosh near the entrance to Building One.

"Well, I'm scheduled, Mr. MacIntosh."

"You're sure, lad?"

"Ain't no doubt about it. None of the brothers are talking to me. They're afraid they'll get hurt if they're standing next to me when it comes down. And they think Boston Joe will figure they're warning me."

"You were right. Dammit. I'm going to get you put in the seg unit."

"No. That's no good. I go crazy in there. Besides, I'd have to come out sometime."

"I laid it all out to the associate warden. He'll transfer you to Soledad. Or the special-housing unit at Pelican Bay."

"It ain't no good, Mr. MacIntosh. There's brothers at every joint. I can't hide. Who knows? I may work my way out of this."

"I'll respect your wanting to handle this your way, lad. Don't be going to the movies, now; you'd be a sitting duck in there. You're a tough 'un. You'll be hard to kill. It will take two of them. We'll be watching."

Fear gripped Baby Blue for the next three days. It was a feeling that was remarkably unfamiliar. He had capered with guns and knives and clubs and fists all of his life, and the flow of adrenaline had always been a buffer to fright. Now he was the hunted, and he no longer slept, even in the security of his cell.

Days, he spent in the yard, sitting alone, getting to his feet if anyone came near. He ate only one meal a day, to avoid the danger of the crowded mess hall. When he did eat, he was aware of an officer loitering near his table.

He began regretting the decision not to kill Mac-Intosh. Anything would have been better than waiting to be killed himself. He wondered what he would do when they came after him. In the end it would hardly matter, because they were all a pitiful bunch of losers. Folsom Prison had been built for the lot of them, and anyone who got released would come back if his heart was still beating. Baby Blue had never associated with anyone who had gotten out and gone straight.

He tried to recall how much he had learned about prison murders over the years. They could stab you or strangle you or beat you. Or drown you. He'd once seen an informant's head submerged in a vat of split-pea soup at San Quentin. He had never seen a gun in prison. The element of surprise was what they craved. The shower room was a favorite spot, but any place you stood in line was satisfactory. The yard was probably out, because the guards in the towers knew. He hoped Mac-Intosh would not push the transfer idea.

He had seen inmates commit suicide while waiting to be hit, but decided he lacked the courage. He wished he had someone to talk to.

The next night, before lock-down, he sat on the edge of his bunk while his cell mate drafted a letter to an attorney on a lined legal pad. Baby Blue got up and stepped onto the catwalk in front of the cell. The corridor was empty, and an officer was going down the steps. Pausing, Baby Blue took three steps to his right and looked into an unoccupied cell. He waved to a man in the cell next to it, who was standing in the doorway. He was starting to turn when he felt what he thought was a punch in the lower back. It was only when he turned completely that he saw Xavier X in a flurry of motion pummeling him in the chest and stomach with his right hand. The black man's left forearm was under his chin, forcing his head upward, and it was not until he dropped to his knees that he realized he was being knifed. He put his right hand on the floor to steady himself and attempt to rise, but his hand slipped in a pool of blood. He tried to cover his head with his hands and crawl while he was being stabbed in the back, when he saw his guts protrude through a slash in his denim jacket near his navel. He tried to scream, but blood gushed from his mouth. He barely heard the voice of Xavier X while he was being slashed again.

"For a noble purpose, Mr. Bench. Only for a noble purpose."

He was unconscious when the officer found him lying alone on the catwalk. Blood that had spilled from the edge of the catwalk to the tier below was on the officer's hair and face. Baby Blue was carried on a gurney to the prison hospital, where a physician with alcoholic breath seemed to be probing his abdominal cavity with bare hands. Regaining consciousness, he saw Old Folsom Pennington's face a few inches from his.

"Who got ya, Baby Blue? Who got ya?"

He was on his way out again when he whispered, "Don't know. Never got a look at the dude." In his forced reverie, he was in his mother's kitchen.

⚡ Ten

The street was dark and quiet. A dog was barking in the distance. Dowling noticed a watering can at the edge of the porch. When he nudged it with his foot and discovered water in it he decided to empty it into the wooden planter filled with geraniums. He stood for a while, and when he couldn't put it off any longer, went into the living room. Sitting in his armchair, he attacked a month of unopened mail. He paid bills, spent a frustrating hour deciphering Matt's scholarship forms and was caught off-guard by a two-line note from Tom Stacy and his wife, declaring that they were thinking of him and his children.

During the first week of June, he was reflecting on it when he spied something in a stack of junk mail he'd been about to toss. A handwritten envelope with his father's return address on it surprised him. The letter was dated May twenty-second.

Dear Vincent,

As I was fishing out something to write on I wondered when I last wrote. The phone has been doing the talking since I came back to Indiana. What I have to say does not come easy for me.

You and I, sadly, have at least one thing in common. We lost our wives when they and we were far too young. I got angry and let it affect my

110

outlook on the world. I am sorry to say I neglected you and your brother, bless him. This will sound pretty deep, but a friend of mine told me at the time that I must ''reduce the obscenity'' of her death. If I did nothing it would ''result in the ultimate triumph of obscenity'' over your mother. I wish I had listened to my friend.

I feel lucky I got to know Helene. She had a softness I had seen long before in another woman. I wish you could have known your mother better.

I must confess I scratched my head when you decided to become a policeman. Maybe I had become too cozy, perched on the driver's seat of my trolleys and buses, warm and dry, and with no more purpose than to be a good fellow to my fares and get them safely to the end of the line. When I saw you in your uniform for the first time, my chest swelled. I have followed your career more closely than you probably know. While I am rolling here, I will tell you something else. When you were a baby I would hold you and kiss you and tell you how much I loved you. You would coo, and I pretended you were saying you loved me back. I wish I had not quit telling you that.

It is nearly midnight, so I will sign this off. I am looking at something that belonged to your mother. I want you to have it and will mail it soon. As for me, I am feeling old and tired, and frankly, I am more than ready to see your mother again. Do not make the same mistake I did.

I love you,
Dad

Dowling wiped his eyes and went back out onto the porch. The cool air felt good, and after a few minutes he walked to his daughter's room. Jenny was sitting on the edge of her bed. Two dusty cartons from a garage shelf were on the floor next to her. The hem of her terrycloth bathrobe rested on one of the cartons. He smelled bath powder.

"Good night, Daddy," she said, without looking up.

"Can I come in without a warrant?"

"You can come in."

He stood with his hands in his pockets, looking at the old decal-covered toy box she refused to relinquish. He whistled softly and straightened the edge of an oval throw rug with his toe.

"What are you doing?"

"Going through pictures."

"What kind of pictures?"

"Pictures of my mother."

He saw a large corkboard she had leaned against the far side of her bed. Dozens of photos were scattered on the hardwood floor.

"That's one of the rainy-day jobs we used to talk about doing someday." He felt awkward. "Sorting pictures." He took a few steps and looked at the board plastered with pictures. "May I, Jenny?"

Her look told him it was all right, so he picked up the board and carried it closer to the light. Some of the pictures were in color: most were not. Jenny had arranged them chronologically. The first one was of him and Helene and Angelo in front of the restaurant. The last one had been taken the Christmas before she'd died. Helene was lighting a candle on the mantel. Her face was soft, almost reverent. The two photos spanned twenty-seven years, and his eyes recorded the changes.

"Were you wounded in this one, Daddy? Had you been shot?" She pointed to a photo of Dowling in the back yard, with one leg in a cast.

He smiled a little. "No, I've never been shot. I'd broken my leg. Running."

"Running?"

"Well, running away. That is, someone was chasing me. I tried to jump over a little fence and landed wrong."

"Who was chasing you? A criminal?"

"Jenny. Criminals don't chase cops. Tom Stacy was chasing me."

"Mr. Stacy? The captain of homicide? How could he chase anyone?"

Dowling laughed. "We were at the police picnic. There was an egg-tossing contest. With fresh eggs, of course. I substituted a hard-boiled one for Stacy so, naturally, he and his partner won. Then, when the judges checked his egg, it looked like he'd cheated. That's when he came after me."

"How did he know you'd done it?"

"He just knew. I guess that's why he's captain of homicide."

"Was I there?"

Dowling studied the photo. "No. This was before you were born. I always figured I could have cleared that fence, but I was carrying a quart of beer, and . . ." He put the photo down. "There's something I want to tell you. It's hard for me to talk about. Your mother's death."

"We don't have to talk about it, Daddy."

"I do, Jenny."

He walked to the window and stared at his reflection. "Let me say this, and please listen carefully. Your mother did not drink because of you. Your room not being clean . . . your waiting until the last minute to study . . . these are things that all mothers put up with. I don't mean 'put up with' in a bad way, but it's part of family life. And when I think of you blaming yourself, it's all so untrue. Does that make sense?"

She was looking down.

"Look at me, please. Does that make sense, Jenny?"

"If that's true, why didn't you tell me when I said it?"

"I couldn't then. Now I can." He sat on the toy box. "You told me she didn't drink because of anything I did, since I was never here . . . that I was always gone. Well, you see, that's why she drank."

"Thanks for trying to make me feel better," she said. "But that couldn't have been the reason."

"Why not?"

"Because if that was really it you would have done something about it. You would have quit homicide and worked something where you would have been home with us."

Dowling got up, sat next to her and held her. "You'll learn as the years go by that people put things off. Like sorting pictures. People like me get caught up in something and begin to believe it's more important than it really is." He let go of her and got up. "We'll talk about it again, huh?"

"If you want." She kept sorting photos.

He stood in the middle of the kitchen and looked at his baking utensils. The bronze two-and-a-half-quart heavy-bottomed saucepan hung from an overhead beam, grazing the springform pan and his favorite rolling pin. The heavy-bottomed pan was what he used for *pâte à choux,* the cream-puff pastry. It was the last thing he had baked before Helene had died. He remembered being dissatisfied with the chocolate sauce. It had turned out slightly too rich. What had concerned him was the amount of egg. A droplet too much or too little ruined the texture, in his opinion. The pastry had been fine. But not the chocolate. He went to the cupboard and rooted through folders and envelopes until he found it. Ten typewritten pages on how to melt chocolate. Making a pastry was not such a big deal, but understanding why you had problems—that was what made a pastry chef. He thumbed through the pages, took the data to the living room and sat in his chair for an hour.

Much later he tiptoed into Jenny's room when he was certain she was asleep. He picked up the corkboard and took it to the hallway light. There was one picture he was looking for. When he found it he put it in his shirt pocket. Then he put his father's letter with it and went to bed.

Dowling sat at his desk in the Management Services Unit and looked at the checks and ledgers. His investigation had been perfunctory. The evidence against Cliff

Edwards, police officer, badge #6773, was substantial. He had embezzled money from the association, and Dowling was curious about the "why," not the "how." The paper trail had been simple to follow, and Dowling wondered how Edwards would respond when he interviewed him. As it turned out, Edwards acted mildly surprised.

"I haven't done anything wrong, Sarge. I'll help you any way I can to straighten this thing out."

Dowling opened the attaché kit he had borrowed and removed the photocopies of the missing checks the bank had furnished. He spread them out facing Edwards. Most were written to "Cash," in amounts ranging from fifty to two hundred dollars. One was to a Firestone tire center, and another to a hotel in Palm Springs.

"Firestone. Yeah. Tires for my car. I reimbursed them."

"There's no evidence of reimbursement."

"Well, maybe that one wasn't a reimbursement. They said to pay myself back for incidentals."

"Come on, Cliff. Five hundred bucks for tires and three hundred bucks to horse around in Palm Springs isn't 'incidentals.' " They talked and looked at receipts and ledgers, and Dowling made notes.

"Tell me. Why the sloppy bookkeeping? I know about your patrol files, and you were organized as hell on that murder I caught on Marlborough Avenue."

"Sarge, honest to God. I wasn't looking at this as a big deal. When I was playing ball in college this kind of stuff was, you know . . ."

"But this isn't college. And I'm not the NCAA."

Cliff Edwards leaned back and extended his long legs. "Okay. I'll pay it all back, take a five-day suspension, and someone else can be the treasurer. It was a grind anyway."

"Cliff, this isn't like calling in sick for work and going to the beach. It's a little more serious than that."

"How much more serious?"

"Like complete-restitution-and-resign serious."

"From the association."

"From the department."

Edwards jumped to his feet, striking the underside of the table with his knee. "Resign? Over this? This is bullshit."

"Let me give you—"

"I've seen cops get shit-faced and shoot at aircraft carriers from the Broadway pier and get suspended. I've seen 'em suspended for screwing in police cars in the police parking lot. Resign, bullshit."

"Cops don't steal, Cliff."

"I'll never resign. This job is my life. My whole life."

"No, you think it's your whole life." Dowling got up and came close to him. "You have to walk away from it now."

He stopped talking and waited. Edwards put his head in his hands. When he spoke, he did not look up, and Dowling had difficulty hearing him.

"I can't. I'm the best cop out there. This isn't right."

Dowling put his arm around the man. "Go for a new line of work. Tell them you got tired of lousy hours and lousy court decisions. You got a lot going for you. You're a college guy. Apply all the energies you put into that green file box of yours into a new career." He paused. "Otherwise, you go to jail."

They looked at each other, and neither one spoke. A minute later Dowling said, "Give me an answer tomorrow. Don't make me lock you up."

The next day Dowling locked him up. That evening he walked past a newspaper rack where headlines announced, ROGUE COP BOOKED IN THEFT. A sidebar story was titled, ALL-AMERICAN STEALS FROM KIDS' FUND. There was a file photograph of Cliff Edwards driving the lane in the NCAA finals. Dowling stood in place and looked through the Plexiglas at the young basketball star. He remembered what an old-timer had told him once. "A copper in jail is akin to a badly wounded lion surrounded by a pack of wolves."

*   *   *

Dowling lost five pounds in the next two and a half months. After constant prodding by Matt about an exercise program, he consented to experimental walks in the evening, and had stretched them from two blocks to twelve. Jenny harped about his smoking, and he gradually reduced his consumption to a pack a day.

"They didn't have a course in nagging when I went to high school," he told them, pretending to be stern.

He was still not sleeping well.

Telling himself it was for the benefit of his children, he arranged a consultation with Leonard Boudreaux. The three of them went to the first session, then individual meetings followed. Dowling tallied them as stressful ordeals. He saw Boudreaux fashioning the sessions as instruments of expressing the truth and feelings and he was ready to express neither. When Matt and Jenny held conversations about their therapy, he stayed well on the fringes.

Nothing changed for him at work. The cases he drew became more demeaning in his eyes. Over the years, he had seen the department use selective work assignments to coerce deadbeats into resigning or retiring. They kept the pressure on until the beleaguered bastard pulled the pin. He did not really believe such was the case with him, and he was becoming more confused and less angry. He was even starting to tolerate his new lieutenant.

Cliff Edwards had quickly pleaded guilty to one felony-theft count and received probation. Dowling approved when the court considered the officer's background and history of community service.

He ate Mexican food twice at Chuey's in Logan Heights, a few minutes from the police building. Bones and Shea and Speedy stacked beer bottles next to plates of *chile rellenos* and *enchiladas* dripping with sour cream. Their company invigorated him, but he extended his walks on those evenings. A veteran sergeant from the sex-crimes detail had taken Dowling's place, and the team was in the process of adapting to the wishes and procedures of a new leader.

Although their conversations were brief, he had quit

running from Tom Stacy when they bumped into each other. Stacy eventually coaxed him to dinner, and Dowling X-ed out the August 17 page on his desk calendar before he drove to Stacy's house.

After dinner, they sat in front of a patio fireplace and sipped brandy. Dowling blew smoke rings from a long cigar and listened to the fire crackle. He was glad he had accepted the invitation.

"French apple pie coming up," Irene Stacy said, getting up. She put both hands on Dowling's shoulders from behind. "I should have bought it. Baking for you always makes me nervous."

"Well," Dowling said, after she'd gone inside, "what's next? Boudreaux going to come down the chimney?"

Stacy winced and put another piece of avocado wood on the fire. They sat in silence for a while.

"Got a bad series starting up," Stacy said. "Stickups. Big, mean mother with a sawed-off shotgun."

Dowling yawned.

"Two jobs in the last ten days. A restaurant right after closing and a house in Mission Hills with the family watching TV."

Dowling flicked an ash from his cigar. "What's the M.O?"

"Wears a ski mask. Tied the family up."

"Who's dead?"

"Nobody yet."

"Then how come homicide's working it, and not robbery?"

"He put a restaurant employee in the hospital. Clubbed his face in with the butt of the shotgun."

"So?"

"The parents of the victim live next door to the chief."

"Oh."

"I hope he's a transient. Moves the hell on to L.A. or Phoenix."

Later, Dowling drained his snifter and reached for a forkful of pie. "What did he tie the family up with?"

"Brought his own rope."

"He's not a transient, then," Dowling said.

"I hope you're wrong. He's going to kill somebody."

"What's your pleasure, my love?" Curtis Graham asked his wife over the drone of a television commercial. "The news, or read in bed?"

The woman fingered the curved handle of the cane leaning against her chair. "If I thought I could watch the news without hearing about council redistricting or airport relocation. Oh, let's read."

Curtis Graham pushed himself out of his chair with a grunt. "Stay there while I get your medicine. Don't try to get up by yourself."

He walked into a large kitchen, opened a cabinet and searched an eye-level shelf for the prescription containers he wanted. Then he looked out of the garden window above the sink at the lights of La Jolla sparkling below. As he reached for the light switch, he heard a scream. Curtis Graham hurried to the living room. "I'm coming, Marjorie. I told you not to—"

He was surprised to see her still in the chair when he reached the doorway. Her hand was over her mouth. He heard the voice an instant before he saw the figure standing just inside the sliding-glass patio door.

"On the floor, goddamn it. *Now.*"

Curtis Graham stared at the eyeholes in the navy blue ski mask. Yellow piping on the bottom of the mask touched the turned-up collar of a bulky dungaree jacket. Then he saw the shotgun held at waist level by gloved hands.

"I said, on the floor *now.*"

"I . . . I have to help her. She's arthritic. We'll do whatever you say."

Moving to his wife's side, he placed trembling hands under her elbows. "We have to do what he says, dear. Then he won't hurt us." With great difficulty he got her up. Minus the cane, she took a cautious step as her husband clutched her forearm. Her leg buckled, and she almost fell.

The masked figure moved for the first time. He put his foot in the small of Marjorie Graham's back and shoved. The woman's feet dragged along the plush nylon carpet, then followed her torso into a heap fifteen feet away.

Curtis Graham turned quickly. "You can't—"

The gunman broke Curtis Graham's cheekbone with the butt of the sawed-off shotgun, and blood squirted onto the glass-top coffee table as he fell next to it.

"Don't ever move like that again, old man, or I'll blow your fuckin' head off."

Curtis Graham thought he was going to throw up. He crawled to his wife's side and put his arm around her. He stroked her heaving shoulders until his hands were jerked behind him and tied together. The laces of the gunman's black boots were inches from his face. The ringing telephone bewildered him, and he was more bewildered when their assailant answered it.

"Yeah. Yeah. Yeah. No." Almost grunts instead of words. Click.

"The combination to the safe, old man. Give me it."

"Dear God. Let me think. It's fourteen–twenty-six . . . oh, my God. I know it. Please."

"While you're stalling, I'll be standing in the middle of this old blister's back."

Curtis Graham clenched his teeth. Beads of perspiration rolled down his forehead and into his eyes. Blood soaked the carpet under his chin, and he heard his wife's bones crack.

"It's seventeen, that's it. Fourteen–twenty-six–seventeen. I swear it."

"You better be right, old man." Adhesive tape was placed over his mouth, then wound around the back of his head and around his mouth again. His wife's gray hair was next to his face.

As a strip of tape was being torn he heard her mumble: "And David said unto God, I am in a great strait; let us fall into the hand of the Lord; for his mercy is great; but let me not fall into the hand of man."

*   *   *

Dowling felt rested. He had spent a great deal of the Labor Day weekend with Matt and Jenny. They'd barbecued, rented video movies and cleaned the garage. The scale informed him that he had dropped another pound. He was dictating a report when a receptionist approached his desk.

"There's a Mr. Bench here to see you, Sergeant."

"Mr. Bench? Who the hell is he?"

"He said you'd remember him by another name. Baby Blue."

⚈ Eleven

Dowling was startled. Everything kept coming back to the Roy Green case. Helene was probably sitting on the edge of a fluffy white cloud, laughing at him. Sending one of Roy Green's killers back to haunt him. Somehow she had managed to spring him in just eight months, and even today, even in weird California, that was a pretty good trick. If the court of appeals had seen something Baby Blue's way and ordered a new trial, he wouldn't have been on the street. He'd have been sitting a few blocks away in the county jail, waiting for his lawyer to pick a jury. Dowling was curious but walked cautiously around the partition to the public area.

"Hi, Sarge. Remember me?" He got out of a chair with difficulty and extended his hand.

"I remember." Dowling shook his hand and considered the possibility that Baby Blue's motive was revenge. When he'd been a rookie, a parolee had walked calmly into the burglary squad room and shot four detectives. He ran his eyes over Baby Blue's clothing. He had lost weight. The eyes seemed deeper set, and the face was drawn. A polo shirt hung loosely over the shoulders, and clean-wash pants accentuated narrow hips.

"If you tunneled your way out, you didn't get very dirty."

"Huh? Aw, Sarge." He laughed. "That's the first time I ever heard you say anything funny." His hand shook when he reached for a cigarette. "Heck, Sarge. I found a fast way out. Better than all them fancy writs and high-priced lawyers." He fumbled with the hem of his shirt, then yanked it up to neck level. His chest and stomach were covered with raw, diffused scars. Dowling recognized some of the longer ones as surgical incisions.

"Jesus."

"Pretty bad, huh, Sarge?"

"Yeah, pretty bad. Who didn't like you?"

"My cell mate."

"Because?"

"Nothing, really. Nothing between him and me."

Dowling gestured toward the other side of the partition. "Come into my office and sit down." He took a Camel from the pack, then put it back. "So what are you doing out so soon?"

Baby Blue lowered himself carefully into a chair. "Turned out I became quite a problem for the warden. Medical problem, he says, and a security problem. It's a long story. Anyhow, I been home a week, is all." He looked at the papers on Dowling's desk. "How come you ain't in homicide? I went there first."

"That's my long story. Where are you hanging your hat?"

"With my mom."

"Just the two of you?"

"Yeah. She's trying to fatten me up. Says, 'You have to get your strength back, James.' She calls me James, Sarge."

"If you'd listened to your mother when you were a squirt you wouldn't be sitting here with a chest full of holes."

"I know. But I'm listening to her now. If I don't get a job soon I may go to South Dakota to live with a relative of hers."

"South Dakota?"

"Yeah. It's up near North Dakota. Workin' on a farm. Milking cows and all of that."

Dowling rubbed his chin. "You probably know a lot about cows."

"Aw, Sarge. What's to know? Grab 'em by the tit and start pulling." Baby Blue put a hand on the desk to steady himself, then shifted in the chair and grimaced.

"Hurts, huh?"

"Some."

"You got wheels?"

"Naw. I came down on the bus."

Dowling looked at his watch. "It's close enough to quitting time. I'll give you a lift. We'll drink a couple of cold ones and you can tell me your long story."

They sat in Dowling's car on the G Street pier, looking alternately at the downtown skyline and portions of the curving Coronado bridge. It was not a pier in the real sense, although once it had been. It was a narrow strip of concrete and grass and parking meters, with a lone restaurant on the end blocking their view of lumbering aircraft carriers docked alongside the North Island Naval Air Station. The pier contributed a few yards toward San Diego's shoreline count of seventeen and a half miles.

They sipped beer and smoked, and Baby Blue told Dowling about Boston Joe Garvey and Robert Burns MacIntosh and Xavier X.

"They gave me the last rites, Sarge, but I didn't know it." He told Dowling about the emergency surgery at a Sacramento hospital, the brief stay at San Quentin's hospital ward and the quick, unexpected parole.

"So you didn't stick this guy MacIntosh because you considered him a friend, huh?"

"You got it, Sarge. Some things even I can't do."

Dowling watched two young women jog in front of his car toward the concrete boardwalk that led to the Spanish Village Landing a few miles to the north. The "medical and security problem" was its formal language, but gratitude was what the state was showing Baby Blue. At great risk, he saved a guard's life by not killing him. Inmates at twelve prisons were receiving a subtle message from Baby Blue's "pardon."

"Of course old Baby Blue ain't out of the forest yet, Sarge. There's brothers on the streets here." He held up an empty can. "But I'll be looking over my shoulder."

"Did the D.A. go after this Xavier X?"

"Naw. I didn't snitch him off." He opened a second beer. "I been doing all the talking. How come you ain't in homicide?"

"Oh, it was a lot of things," Dowling said, refusing another beer.

"I figure it must be burn-out, then. Lookin' at them stiffs all the time and chasin' down dumb shits like me." He wiped his mouth with his hand and dropped a potato chip on the seat. "A lot of guys at Folsom know you. They said you're nobody to mess with."

Baby Blue gave him names, and they talked about murder cases. Dowling started the car, and asked, "What were you saying earlier about a doctor?"

"Oh, they told me before I left the joint to go to a doc after I got home. For some kind of repair stuff. My mom's been after me about that. Says, 'James, you must take care of your health.' "

Dowling pulled onto Harbor Drive and headed for East San Diego.

"I got me a girl friend already, Sarge."

"Your parole officer would probably rather you had a job."

"You want to know her name?"

"Can't wait."

"Aggie." He looked pleased. "I met her a couple of times before you sent me away, Sarge. Only she wouldn't have nothin' to do with me then, 'cause I was popping pills and messin' up. She's real straight. She goes to college, too, Sarge."

"College?" Dowling said, trying not to show surprise.

"Out there on the mesa. San Diego State."

"What's she studying?"

"Aw, Sarge. I don't know." Dowling eased into heavy traffic on Interstate 5 north and stayed to his right to catch the I-8 ramp. He slowed for a car with surfboards on top that was broken down on the shoulder.

"Guess I'm kinda on parole with her too, huh, Sarge?

This time I'm gonna do it. Stay straight. I got people pulling for me. I want to do it this time.''

"Why did you look me up?"

"It was just one of those . . . what do you call them . . . impulsives. You're the only guy I know in this town who's not a crook.''

That satisfied Dowling. Cons had dropped in on him a few times with no apparent motive. "I was just curious what it would be like shooting the shit with you when I wasn't heading for the joint," one had told him.

When Dowling reached the curb in front of Baby Blue's apartment complex he put the car in neutral. "You shouldn't pick just any doctor, Baby Blue. I know a pretty good one. I'll give him a call and get back to you. We'll see about a job when you're patched up.''

Baby Blue got out, then leaned through the open window. "Thanks, Sarge." He started to walk away, stopped and called, "Do you think I can do it this time? Go straight?''

"Sure," Dowling lied. "Sure, I think you can do it.''

🦢 Twelve

Thirty minutes later Dowling was at the waterfront. The Old Man was not there. He sniffed the salt air and watched a piece of wood float into a tiny oil slick on the water. Then he reached into his coat pocket and found his father's letter. Water lapped against the seawall as he read it. When he looked up, the Old Man was standing next to him.

"Hello, Vincente."

"Hello, Vito." He put the letter in his pocket.

His back was to the Old Man when he said, "Did you ever get yourself into a bind you couldn't get out of?"

"A bind?"

"A situation." Dowling turned and faced him. "Something happened. Something bad. I lied. Made people think something else happened."

Dowling turned his attention to the crimson ball of sun resting on the horizon. "Strange, isn't it?"

"What?"

"I spend my life searching for the truth." A gull landed nearby and pecked at the ground. "Someone who loves me is very proud of me. That makes me feel guilty. I feel like I'm made of glass. Someone makes a remark about something, anything, and I think they know what I did." He kicked an ice cream stick into the water.

"What did you lie about?" the Old Man asked quietly, putting his hand on Dowling's shoulder.

Dowling sat down on the seawall. His body slumped

before he took a deep breath, then made his confession.

Driving home, it occurred to him that he might have made a mistake talking to the Old Man. Once a person started jabbering a little, he often ended up baring his soul. That was what he relied on in his business. Get them talking just a little. Then you could sit back and listen and watch and plan and poke in little feeler phrases here and there and direct things your way, and pretty soon they were telling it all and—my God—he was not only guilty; he was paranoid. The Old Man hadn't interrogated him. The Old Man wasn't trying to get him to stand on the boardwalk and shout to the world that he was the one who had made Helene Dowling's pack so heavy, she had chosen to lay it down instead of buckle under the weight any longer.

The Old Man had told him he could make things right.

But he was a killer, just like Baby Blue, and maybe that was why it had been comfortable in the car on the G Street pier. There wouldn't be many of those sessions, though. He would give Baby Blue six months. Then some cop would be air-mailing him to Q or Folsom. The guy had big plans now. But wait until he'd gotten his first bad break. Wait until his first boss had fired him for loafing, or that new girl friend had thrown his bedroll out on the lawn. Then those big plans would become as improbable as a city boy milking cows.

He wished he hadn't made the commitment about the doctor and the job. He had enough to think about. Two of the things he had to think about were waiting at home, and he suspected he would feel better if he put a good meal on the table for them.

When he came out of the market, three large porter-house steaks were at the bottom of the bag and a twisted loaf of sourdough bread stuck out of the top.

Matt and Jenny were not home, but he started the barbecue, changed his clothes and went to work on a bottle of beer. He felt its effect quickly, a nice, warm glow, which made it easier to prepare the salad and sprinkle the bread with garlic powder.

They arrived two minutes apart, through different

doors. Matt unbuttoned a grease-stained work shirt as he stuck his head into the kitchen.

"I have to hustle. Mark has tickets to the Sports Arena. Meeting him there."

"But I've got—"

"Concert, Dad. Big time." He headed toward the bathroom.

"What about dinner?"

"I'll grab a hot dog there."

Dowling walked through the dining room as Jenny came in. She looked so young and fresh and pretty that he squeezed her and held her an extra moment.

"I'm cooking tonight, kid."

"I'm on my way out, Daddy." She snatched a pile of books from the floor.

"You just got in."

"Every Tuesday. Study seminar." She sang it. "I'm working very hard. My mother would be proud of me."

"Yeah, well, I'm barbecuing steaks." He was looking at her back as she put distance between them.

"Steaks. That's big-time cholesterol, Daddy." She blew him a kiss.

He went slowly to the kitchen and rewrapped the meat. The salad went into a large plastic container. He lit a cigarette, opened another bottle of beer and went to his chair on the porch. Matt took the steps in one great leap.

"Hey! I finished the scholarship paper work," Dowling shouted.

"The what papers?" Stringy red hair stuck out below the Padres cap.

"Remember? Redlands. University of."

"Oh, yeah. I don't know, Dad. The boss is talking raise." He was getting into his car as he finished the sentence.

Dowling and Baby Blue sat in the examining room of Dr. Emery Marcus, an abdominal and thoracic surgeon at Scripps Clinic. Chest X rays, an upper G.I. series and a barium enema had been completed.

"You were smart to come in, Mr. Bench. There's a little patchwork left to be done on you. You have a diaphragmatic hernia." He wrote on a chart, and continued. "Your diaphragm is a musculofibrous septum. It separates the thorax from the abdomen. In other words, it forms the floor of your chest and the roof of your stomach. You need a diaphragm that's working right to breathe properly."

"I'm breathing pretty good right now, Doc," Baby Blue said, rubbing his palms together.

"I know you are. Right now. The doctors in Sacramento did a good job on you. You got stabbed . . . sixteen times. Fractions of an inch made the difference between living and dying. Your diaphragm got cut badly. The emergency surgery saved your life. But sometimes, due to the trauma, a small hole in the diaphragm is missed. In time it gets bigger. That's what has happened here. It has to be sutured. Sewed up. Plus, your intestines got shoved up into the chest cavity, so we have to resect."

"What's that, Doc?"

"Repair the diaphragm and put the rest of the intestines back in your abdomen, where they belong."

"Can't all of this stuff wait awhile?"

"Sergeant Dowling told me you were anxious to be fixed up and find a job and get on with your life. We should do it within a week for medical reasons."

"Will I be okay, Doc?"

The doctor smiled. "I've done it a few times. You'll be fine."

The day before Baby Blue was to be operated on, Dowling received a gold medallion in the mail. It was the size of a silver dollar, and the edge was engraved with laurel leaves. In a circle radiating out from the center to the leaves were words too small to read. Dowling went to his desk for a magnifying glass and read: "Treasure up in your hearts these words: Be ashamed to die until you have won some victory for humanity."

There was a note in the package with the medallion.

"I don't know where your mother got this. I just know she had it as long as I knew her. Good luck. Dad."

He had never owned anything belonging to his mother. She had been dead for thirty-five years, and he almost never thought about her. His mother had not known Helene or his children, and time had dimmed his memory of her. He recalled a slender woman with graying hair and a solemn face. It occurred to him that she'd read a lot and recited verses from the Bible to him and his brother.

He read the inscription again, rubbed it gently and put it in his pocket. The next morning he took it to work. When he arrived, he also had the photo from the corkboard. It was of Helene and him, standing next to each other at the shore, arms entwined, like two old chums. Lifting his blotter, he slipped the picture under it. In twenty-eight years he had never kept a picture at work.

A few days later he was reading the morning paper when a story caught his eye. A ski-masked gunman had entered a house and tied up the residents, then raped a sixteen-year-old girl in the kitchen. A cache of gold coins and antique jewelry had been stolen. "Homicide Captain Tom Stacy admits the suspect is probably responsible for three previous crimes, including the vicious beating of an elderly couple in the La Jolla Muirlands."

The story went on to relate that the homicide sergeant in charge of the case had been admitted to the hospital with chest pains while conducting the crime-scene investigation.

The following day Dowling was waiting in Stacy's office when he arrived.

"Tom, I want the series."

"What series?"

"This series." He tossed the newspaper on the desk. "I want to work it. I'll solve it."

"Whoa, Vince. Look, this is too—"

"Tom, listen to me. I need this series. I'm starting to . . . I'm going to do something. About things. About my life. There's things I have to learn. Being a father and a mother and . . .'' He threw his arms in the air. "I don't know how to do it, but I've got to get better. The job. The job is something I know how to do. It'll all follow the job, Tom. I'll make it follow.''

"Vince, this is too quick. Too quick to come back to homicide. It takes too much out of a healthy guy, and you don't have that much to give. Not now. Wait awhile. Maybe next year.''

"Please, Tom. I've got to reduce the obscenity. I don't have until next year. I don't even have until next week.''

"It's just too soon.''

"Look at me. Look at this fuckin' suit, Tom. It's brand-new. I bought three of them. I won't let you down. That guy has to be caught, and I have to get well. Please, Tom.''

Stacy turned his back to Dowling and touched the corner of his eye.

"Tomorrow. Let me sleep on it. We'll talk tomorrow.''

⁂ Thirteen

For the second consecutive morning, Dowling beat Tom Stacy to his office. Two armchairs flanked the desk, and he sat in one, looking across stacks of crime reports and briefing memos. The walls, unlike those of most commanders' offices, were devoid of plaques and certificates of achievement. Dowling knew the history of the memorabilia on the bookcase shelves. An elaborately hand-tooled beer stein had been a gift from Stacy's counterpart in Munich, and the handcuffs had belonged to his first partner, killed in a gun battle.

"You're a tenacious son of a bitch," Stacy said from the doorway. His jacket was slung over his shoulder. He hung it on an old-fashioned clothes rack, glanced at his desk top and stretched. Then he looked down and patted his paunch. "Jeez, I got to start doing some sit-ups. Look at that." He sat down, put on his glasses and picked up a memo.

"Well?" Dowling said.

"Well what?"

Dowling rolled his eyes. "Am I coming back or not?"

"Oh, that." Stacy didn't look up. "Yeah, you're coming back." Dowling took a deep breath and exhaled.

"I'm reluctant about this move, and that bothers me." Stacy got up and started pacing. "I've been a cop for forty years. Get my facts, make my decisions and don't look back. But I must be getting old. Since you were in here yesterday I've made up my mind three times and

changed it twice. Irene and I talked at breakfast. She's
one of your fans.''

"I won't let you down, Tom."

"I hope you don't let yourself down, either."

He handed Dowling a thick folder. "You've got four
cases. A restaurant and three residences. Nobody can
make his face because of the ski mask. No fingerprints
because of the gloves. Lot of problems.''

"The last one was a sheriff's case," Dowling said.

"That's another thing. He does three in the city, then
jumps to Rancho Santa Fe. All the sheriff's reports are
in that folder.''

Stacy paced some more. "You and I have seen some
bad actors in our time, Vince. This guy's one of 'em,
and he's progressing. Job number one at the restaurant,
he smashes a kid's face in. Then, number three, the elderly couple in the Muirlands. Kicks her across the
room. Breaks his jaw. They lay there for twenty-four
hours till the daughter got worried because they weren't
answering the phone. Both still in the hospital.''

"Then the last one," Dowling said.

Stacy's eyes narrowed. "He tied up the mother and
father; then he raped their sixteen-year-old daughter.
With them watching." He lit a cigarette, unaware that
he had one burning, and banged his fist on the desk. "I
want these motherfuckers locked up.''

"More than one suspect?"

"There's two. Read the reports. Then we'll talk."

"Okay Tom. About your decision. I want to thank
you for—"

Stacy pointed to the door. "Never mind the speeches.
The one you gave me yesterday will last for a while."

"You're going back to homicide, Daddy? Why?"
Jenny stood in the middle of the kitchen with dinner
dishes in her hands.

"Because I—"

"I don't understand. I don't understand this at all."
She was shaking her head. "You won't be home anymore. It'll be like it used to be."

"No, no, Jenny. It won't be like it used to. It will never be like it used to. I can do both."

"What's both?" Matt sponged the sideboard.

"Both is being a homicide cop and a father. I've given this a lot of thought."

"But you just found out today. How could you have given it a lot of thought, Daddy?"

"I've—uh, I've thought about it a lot today. I'll get the broom." He hurried to the laundry room, adjacent the kitchen.

"Why didn't you tell them you didn't want to?" Jenny called to him. Dowling put his palms on the washing machine and let his shoulders droop. She asked it again.

"Because I'm a police officer and I follow orders."

He returned with the broom and dust pan. "Come on, clear out of here so I can sweep."

"Who ordered you?" she said.

"The department ordered me."

"Well, that's the end of curfew," Matt said.

Dowling was grateful for the change of subject. "No, that's not the end of curfew. For one thing, I'm gonna be here most nights. And for another, I trust you. We have to trust—"

"Trust what, Daddy?"

He had trouble getting the words out. "We have to trust each other."

Jenny kept to herself until mid-evening, when, at Dowling's urging, she made sundaes with the ice cream he and Matt had gone to buy.

"You make the best sundaes, Jenny," he said.

"My mother made the best sundaes." She plopped a cherry on each mound of ice cream.

"Hey, Dad. Where did you get that medallion?"

"What medallion?" Jenny asked.

"The one I saw at Baskin-Robbins."

Dowling dug into his pocket, separated the gold piece from his change and handed it to Matt. "It belonged to my mother."

"I never saw it before," Matt said.

"Grandpa just sent it to me."

"Hey, there's writing on it. 'Treasure up in your hearts these words: Be ashamed to die until you have won some victory for humanity.' That's cool. Who said that?"

"I don't know, son. How did you read that without a magnifying glass?"

Jenny disappeared for a few minutes, returned to the living room and announced that she would be working in her room for the rest of the evening. "Good night, everybody," she said from the doorway. "And by the way, Horace Mann, an educator, said that."

"How do you know?" Matt asked.

"Some of us study." She was partway down the hall when she added, "Besides, that's what the *Dictionary of Quotations* says."

There was no question in Dowling's mind that he would be met with a verbal barrage when he reported to his old desk in the squad room. That was the way it worked, the way policemen responded to misfortune and blew tension out of the air. What he had not prepared himself for was the silent treatment. No one acknowledged him when he entered the office, and after he had arranged the desk top to his liking, he decided to move things along.

"All right. Get it over with. Fire your best shots."

An armed-robbery sergeant looked over the top of his glasses. "It's Dowling. I didn't recognize him, because he's wearing a decent suit."

"And look at him. He's lost weight, too," someone from another homicide team yelled.

"He hasn't lost it," said a sex-crimes detective with sad eyes. "It's in his ass."

This, for Dowling, was the easy and wonderful part of returning. It was as if he had never worked for a young lieutenant in a three-piece suit. Feigning displeasure, he asked, "Are you finished?"

"We were surprised they transferred him back here," volunteered another homicide sergeant. "With his sunny disposition we figured he'd go to Community Relations.''

"No," the first robbery sergeant said, "the smart money was on his being sent to sex crimes. Dowling can read the overnight reports, get a hard-on and not have anybody notice it when he stands up."

After the roasting someone asked him how it felt to be back.

"Fine, just fine," he answered. In truth, it was far from fine. Comfortable, maybe, because he had his old desk and his old team. Scary, maybe, because he might have been rusty after a layoff. He had looked at dead bodies for thirteen years before the transfer. And that was another thing that made it not so fine at all. The series didn't even involve dead bodies. Just a couple of tough hoods knocking people around and walking off with a sackful of money or jewelry. It had been a long time since he'd worked armed robberies and assaults.

He kept asking himself why he had not found the courage to be truthful with his children about the return to homicide. That was the unfinest thing of all. Maybe they would have understood. Supported him.

The voice of Larry Shea interrupted his thoughts. "Well, what's our first step, boss? I've been watching you sitting there juggling it all around. Just like old times."

"The first step, Larry, is for me to read these investigative reports." He thumped the foot-high stack with the palm of his hand. "Then we'll see where we are. Like old times."

In fact, he had read them the night before, at home. The piece of paper on top of the pile listed the four cases, with his notations.

August 9, Thursday—restaurant—Reuben E. Lee
August 15, Wednesday—house—Mission Hills—
    Faulkner
August 28, Tuesday—house—La Jolla—Graham
    (arthritis)

September 18, Tuesday—house—Rancho Santa
   Fe—Bond (rape)
Always takes victim's car

The cases were definitely related, so he would not
have to waste time establishing that. The thing that puzzled him most was how the residences had been selected.
Each home had a safe. How did the crooks know about
the safes? There was no other visible common thread
between the three families. He would have to find one.

It had taken him five hours to read the reports. What
had jumped out at him was the careful planning and
skillful execution of each robbery. Brutal but skillful.

Clues were scarce. The gunman was probably a white
man, because, in two cases, a witness had seen blue
eyes. The robber always abandoned the car on a dark
street, less than one mile away from where it had been
stolen. There was no evidence that the cars had been
wiped down, so the gunman must have kept his gloves
on to drive. Lots of prints had been lifted and accounted
for. The phone call had to be from an accomplice, who
was probably stationed nearby and calling to find out
whether help was needed. It bothered Dowling that the
first case had been at a restaurant, followed by the three
residences. That was unusual. Criminals usually stuck to
the same method of operation. But method of operation
included a common type of victim.

He went back to the top sheet and looked at the dates
again. The time span between cases was: six days, thirteen days, twenty-one days.

He paused and wondered what the robbers were doing
while he was looking at reports. They weren't lurking
in the shadows, with turned-up collars and darting, evil
eyes. They were pushing a cart down the aisle of a supermarket, or watching their kids on the swing sets at
the beach, or sitting in a dentist's chair. Crooks were
like everybody else. They had shopping lists and children and cavities. Whatever they were doing, he hoped
they would continue doing it for a few more days. He
needed time.

* * *

The woman standing next to Dowling had jet-black hair. They were both looking out of the ninth-floor hospital-room window, toward east San Diego. She was shorter than average, slender, with a button nose and deep green eyes. He guessed she was in her early thirties. When they introduced themselves she had not smiled.

"He's told me about you, Aggie."

"He's told me about you, too," she said without expression.

It seemed to him she was one of those women who became more attractive as she aged. She explained that Baby Blue had been taken "for tests for preop, something or other." They talked uneasily for a while about Baby Blue, his impending surgery and the difficulty of finding visitor parking.

Dowling kept glancing at the door, until she said, "Do you wonder why I see him?"

He did wonder. He knew a lot of women who hobnobbed with ex-cons and outlaw bikers, but Aggie Pride simply did not fit the profile.

"I try not to poke my nose in other people's business," he said.

"That's not much of an answer, Sergeant."

"You're a pretty good interrogator, Aggie." He rubbed his chin out of nervousness and looked at her. The green eyes were still looking at him. "When he told me, I figured you picked up strays. But meeting you, talking to you . . ." He shrugged.

She smiled a little for the first time. "There's something about him that's very likeable. I know he's done . . . rotten things. I guess he must have. Being in prison, and all. He was a kind of hero, you know, in prison. They wanted him to kill a guard but he wouldn't do it, so they went after him. Anyway, he's very kind to me."

Dowling said nothing.

"I met him once or twice just before he went to prison this last time. There were always other people around.

And the guys he hung out with were bums. Macho bums. You know, undressing you with their eyes, and all. Talking garbage. But he . . . well, like I said. He was kind.'' She smiled a little. ''And those blue eyes.'' Then she looked down and rubbed two fingernails together. ''I don't think it'll amount to anything,'' she said. ''I think one of these days I'll turn around and find a detective at the door.''

''Is that what you think?''

It was her turn to shrug. ''Color me pessimistic, Sergeant. I followed a sailor to San Diego. A few days after I convinced him to marry me, he went to sea. I was very faithful. He came back from the Philippines with two presents for me. An embroidered pillow and a dose of clap.'' She folded her arms. ''I ran back to Nebraska, hardly unpacked and ran back to San Diego.'' She gave Dowling a hard look. ''Why are you being nice to him?''

''Huh?''

''I didn't think that was such a hard question to answer. Why are you being nice to him?''

''I'm not sure. He caught me by surprise. Walked in on me. But as you say, he can be very likeable.''

''And that's it?'' She was still staring at him.

''That's it.''

''What do you want from him, Sergeant?''

''Want from him?''

''Yeah, want. W-A-N-T.'' She spit the letters out.

''Jeez, Aggie. You sure turned on me in a hurry. One minute we're solving the hospital's parking problem, and then—can't I just be his friend?''

She laughed. ''Come on, Sergeant. You're a cop, not a sociologist. You've got better things to do with your time than nursemaid ex-cons.''

Dowling smiled at her. ''You're the one should've been a cop. You'd be suspicious of Monday following Sunday.''

''Bullshit. I'm just looking out for him. I've heard about cops like you. You're going to screw him around somehow.''

"Look, lady." Dowling loosened his tie and pointed his finger at her. "You got a couple of tough breaks between here and Podunk, Nebraska, and it gave you a hell of a crust. It's too bad somebody along the line didn't teach you it's okay to be nice to somebody just for the sake of being nice." He headed for the door, then pivoted. "Maybe someday you'll sort your life out. Meanwhile, I like it better in the hallway."

He took a few steps but stopped abruptly at the door. Turning, he pointed his finger at her again.

"People like you make me want to puke. Think you got cops all figured out. If I can pick 'em up and toss 'em in prison, I can break their fall when they come out. Maybe I can drink a beer with someone who's killed a guy, but I wouldn't be caught dead saying hello to some crumb who stole an old lady's purse. End of speech. This time I'm really gonna wait in the hallway." He turned and collided with a rolling gurney, pushed by an orderly and carrying a grinning Baby Blue.

"Hey, Sarge. You gotta signal before you change lanes." Before Dowling could respond he said, "I see you met Aggie."

"We met."

"And Aggie's on her way to the cafeteria for coffee," she said. "So I don't hog all of your visiting time." She brushed by Dowling and pinched Baby Blue's cheek. "I'll see you in a bit."

Baby Blue reached for her, but she was past him and into the hallway. "What do you think of her, Sarge? She's something, huh?"

"She is something."

"After the operation, maybe I'll move in with her for a week or two. The doc says I gotta have full-time care after they spring me. And my mom works. So Aggie volunteered her place." The orderly transferred him to the bed, covered him with the blanket and cranked up the head section. "Course, it'll only be for a while. My mom's one of those old-fashioned types. Figures me and Aggie—under the same roof and all. Says, 'James, I suppose it's necessary, for a few days.' "

An anesthesiologist entered, and Dowling waited in the hall, hoping Aggie Pride would not return.

"Chow's good in here," Baby Blue said a few minutes later. "Can't smoke, though. Kind of like being in lock-down, Sarge."

Dowling pointed to a book on the nightstand. "Greek mythology," he said.

"Belongs to my cell mate." Baby Blue motioned toward the empty bed. "He's got walking-around privileges." His voice lowered. "They took a bunch of cancer outta his belly. The guy's a college professor. Reads books all the time, I guess. Says he's read that one three times. So I borrowed it."

"Got it committed to memory yet?"

"Aw, Sarge. I can't even understand it. Hey." He opened the book and thumbed his way toward the end. "You ever hear of a dude named Charon?"

Dowling shook his head.

"Seems this Charon was a ferryman. Takes your soul to Hades. That's hell, ain't it?"

Dowling nodded.

"Takes your soul to Hades on his ferryboat after you die. That's heavy. Do you think that could be true, Sarge?"

Dowling looked at the book. "Anything's possible."

"Sarge." He held the book to his chest. "If anything goes wrong tomorrow. Not that I'm worried or anything. But if it should. Would you talk to my Mom? Tell her— aw, Sarge. You'll know what to say."

"I have a better idea. You tell her yourself. Tonight."

"I can't. I just can't."

"I think you can. But nothing's going to happen to you. The ornery ones don't die, Baby Blue."

"My professor friend ain't ornery."

Dowling got up and went to the window. "You can see your neighborhood from here. In a couple of weeks you'll be back in it. And your professor friend will be teaching a bunch of freshmen the difference between a Roman and a Greek." He talked for a few more minutes with his back to the bed. When he turned around Baby

Blue was asleep. Dowling turned off the lamp and walked out.

Years of habit helped Dowling locate the receiver before the telephone rang a second time. He could not focus on the illuminated dials of the alarm clock.

"Lieutenant Blake in the watch commander's office, Dowling. Your boy hit again."

"Where?"

"Cafe Del Rey Moro. Shot a busboy."

"Condition?" Dowling's feet were on the floor.

"He's alive."

"I'm rolling. Hey. What time is it?"

"12:30 A.M. Why? Were you asleep?"

🎇 Fourteen

Helene had once timed him reacting to a call-out. In fourteen minutes he had reached the front door. The sub-categories were: wet shave, two and a half minutes; shower, one minute, forty seconds; drying body and tooth-brushing simultaneously, two minutes, ten seconds; dressing, three minutes, twenty seconds; finding car keys, four minutes.

He was startled when the front door opened just as he reached for the doorknob.

"Jenny. What are you doing? Do you know what time—Where have you been?"

"Daddy." She grinned. "You asked me three questions."

"You're damned right I did. I thought you were home. Where have you been?"

"To a movie."

"They don't serve beer at movies. You've been drinking. I can smell it all over you."

"I had one little beer." She made a tiny space between her thumb and forefinger.

"You are fifteen years old, young lady. You don't drink beer. All right, this is it. I'm on my way to work. You be here in the morning. We'll get to the bottom of this."

"Daddy, I go to church in the morning."

"You be home immediately after church."

"After church I have softball practice."

"Right after practice, Jenny. This is serious."

"I go to work after practice."

"Go to bed, Jenny. Go right to bed and sleep it off."

He was halfway to his car when he halted abruptly and looked straight ahead. Three seconds later he wheeled and ran back into the house. At the same time that he pushed open the door to Matt's room he fumbled for the light switch on the wall. The face under the rumpled hair looked at him curiously, sleepily.

"Dad?"

"Yes, Matt."

"What's the matter?"

"The matter? Why, nothing's the matter. Good night, Matt."

During the drive from Point Loma, he thought more about his children than about his case. As he slowed under the two stone arches that signaled the entrance to the west side of Balboa Park he remembered other Sunday mornings. When Matt and Jenny were very young he used to let Helene sleep in. He would scrounge up a quick breakfast, usher the kids to the car and head for the park. They had a favorite picnic area near the Spreckels Organ Pavilion, and he would let them romp on the wet grass and kick a beach ball. It occurred to him that his business was quite different this morning. There would be blood on the floor of the popular restaurant in the park.

Bones Boswell was using the radio in a patrol car parked in the Prado area. As soon as he saw Dowling, he asked, "What's the matter, boss?"

"Why do you say that?"

"It's written all over your face."

"I have a crisis at home." He shook his head slowly.

"Jesus, boss. Can I help? What is it?"

"Nothing I care to talk about now." He reached for his notebook. "They'll break your heart, Bones. They'll break your heart."

"Who?"

"Kids, Bones. Kids."

They walked toward the Spanish courtyard that bor-

dered the Del Rey Moro. There were no sounds except
the clicking of their heels on the red-tiled surface.

"All the customers had left when he came in," Bones
said. "Bright red ski mask this time. Put the shotgun on
everybody. A busboy near the door thought he could
sneak out, and the guy blasted him. Right in the back.
Patrol says he was alive when the paramedics started for
Sharp Memorial with him."

Dowling walked into the dining room through a glass
door. His hands were in his pockets. Through a huge
window he saw a colorful explosion of carnations, roses
and chrysanthemums in the floodlit garden. Upturned
chairs occupied the tabletops, and he stepped around a
bucket of water and a mop. The manager was talking to
a patrolman in excited tones, waving her arms.

"He was so big. Six foot five. Six foot six, maybe.
And he didn't have to shoot him. He could have yelled,
'Stop.' Clarence would have stopped."

The woman was no more than five feet tall, so Dowling subtracted a few inches from the height, because the
suspect would have looked like a giant to her.

"How much did they get, ma'am?"

"I don't know yet. Thousands." She started pointing
in different directions. "We had a big dinner crowd from
the Old Globe. And two weddings in the garden. And a
bachelor party in the bar and—my God—did they find
my car?"

"Not yet."

She sank into a chair. "If the police officer hadn't
come in to use the phone, we'd still be tied up and poor
Clarence would be lying there bleeding. This is awful.
When will you know more, Sergeant?"

"As soon as we talk to the doctor, ma'am."

"About my car, I mean."

Later, Dowling stood next to his car and looked up at
the California Tower through the eucalyptus trees. They
had not waited five or six days between jobs this time.
Only forty-eight hours. Restaurant-house-house-house-
restaurant. In the sixth-largest city in the country there
were plenty of both to choose from. When he returned

to the restaurant he ordered Speedy to do a neighborhood check on the Sixth Avenue side of the park.

"I don't care if it is three-thirty in the morning. Knock on doors, Speedy. These bastards don't live by the clock. We can't either. Find somebody who saw something. Get lucky. And Speedy, don't make me tell you again. Hands in your pockets at a crime scene."

"Okay, Sarge, okay. But speaking of crime scenes . . ."

"What?"

"It seemed like we went through it pretty fast tonight. Faster than we used to. I just wondered."

Dowling hooked his thumbs in his waistband. "When you get a badge that says 'sergeant' on it, then you can start wondering. Now, get going."

They had obtained photos and measurements and interviewed witnesses and had an all-units out for the manager's car. On the other hand, they had only given the wooden floor a cursory inspection for shoe impressions. And a shoe impression would have looked good to Dowling now. With a distinctive wear mark, perhaps. Any piece of physical would have looked good to him at that moment. Speedy was right. He shuffled back into the restaurant to look again.

It was nearly 5:00 A.M. when he drove out of the park. Speedy was standing in front of a three-story Victorian converted to a rooming house, waiting for him.

"I didn't do any good door-knocking, but I got something for you."

Dowling was curious, and stepped out of the car.

"Some old-timer wants to see you."

"Who is he?"

"I don't know. Couldn't make out his name."

"Drunk?"

"Yeah. Says, 'You're a cop, huh?' Says, 'Who you work for?' I says, 'Sergeant Dowling.' The old guy laughs. Says, 'Sergeant, is it? Get him up here. I got to see him.' "

"Well, let's go, then," Dowling said.

"You really want to see him?"

"Sure. Maybe he owes me money."

They started up the steps of the outside stairway when Speedy asked, "How's the busboy?"

"He took one in the spine. The doc says he may walk again, but he'll never ice-skate."

"Ice-skate?"

"He's been training for the Olympic tryouts."

"And sometimes I think I got troubles," Speedy said softly.

Dowling was puffing when they reached the third floor. Long ago he had learned to be accessible. To take telephone calls without having them screened, and sit down with anyone who asked for him. He wasted a lot of time that way. He also solved a lot of cases.

Dowling reeled from the stench when they walked into the room. Yellow, urine-stained sheets hung over the edge of a bed, and roaches crawled on an opened can of corned-beef hash next to a hot plate. The one window in the room was packed with cardboard. Empty beer cans and wine bottles were strewn about. A toilet in the corner with the seat up had fecal matter on the rim of the bowl. Cigarettes had burned themselves out on top of an old wooden dresser. The man sat in a torn leather chair. He was unshaven. His hair was gray and rumpled, and a dirty shirt did not reach the top of soiled, unzipped pants.

"Is that you, Dowling? The old eyes don't see so good anymore." The voice was slurred and raspy. Dowling peered in, squinting, trying to adjust to the dim light.

"It's me, Mac."

"The kid said you were in the park on a job. Is old Charlie McCord on the desk tonight?"

"Charlie's been dead about five years, Mac." He turned toward Speedy, who straddled the doorway. "Speedy. I want you to meet one of the finest cops that ever pounded a beat. This is retired patrolman McNamara M. McNamara."

Speedy half-waved.

"What kinda job, Dowling? Have a drink."

"No, thanks, Mac. Some stickup men are eating us up. Just knocked off the Del Rey Moro."

"The Del Rey, huh? Check out the Hardesty brothers, Dowling. They used to hang around the park. Want a drink?"

"McNamara broke me in, Speedy. Taught me more in a couple of months than anybody else taught me in a year."

The old man grinned. "Those were the days. Sure you won't have a drink?"

Dowling walked to him and clasped a gnarled, blue-veined hand. "We have to go, Mac." The odor was getting to him.

"Wait a minute. Before you go. Tell the rookie here a story."

"Mac, it's five-thirty in the morning."

"Tell him about Thirty-second and G Street, Dowling. That's a good one."

Dowling cupped his chin in his hand and shook his head. "Well, Speedy. The first thing you have to know is that any time you went on a call with McNamara, after you got there, he'd give a fuckin' speech. It didn't matter if there were two or fifty-two people there to listen to it." He walked to the door to get a breath of air. "Anyway, this day . . . we get a disturbance call at Thirty-second and G. I guess it was a disturbance. It was a damn pier-six brawl. About ten women. Gals that live around there, all down on their luck, fighting over something stupid. They're swinging broom handles and garden hoses and anything they can get their hands on. So we pull up and plow into the middle and get 'em separated, and then, of course, McNamara has to give them a speech." Dowling walked to the center of the room, folded his arms and looked at McNamara, who was smiling and nodding. "McNamara raises both hands in the air, Speedy. Says, 'I am ashamed of all of you. I can tell merely by looking that all of you ladies were raised better than this. You are probably college women. Brought up with a keen appreciation of human dignity. I want this stopped immediately. I want you to return to

your homes and write letters to loved ones, or sew.' By
now, Speedy, he's really got their attention. You could
hear a pin drop. They're hanging on his next word.
Then. *Then.* McNamara blows a fart you could have
heard in Kansas City and that should have ripped out
the seat of his uniform pants. I'm just standing there next
to him. McNamara points his finger right at me. Says,
'Officer Dowling. What a disgraceful thing to do in the
presence of these ladies. Go to the car.' ''

Speedy Montoya doubled over and held his stomach.
''What did . . . what did you do?'' He could hardly get
the words out.

''I didn't know what the hell to do. So I went and
got in the car.''

''Who are the Hardesty brothers, Sarge?'' Speedy
asked as they navigated the rickety stairs again.

''Stickup men from the sixties. One got the gas chamber and the other one died in a car accident.''

''Is he senile?''

''A little, maybe. Mostly just a rummy who's out of
touch.''

''He's a slob, Sarge. A damn slob. How can anyone
live like that?''

Dowling looked at him. Clean-shaven. Ramrod
straight. Alert. Poised.

''How much are you knocking down a year,
Speedy?''

''About thirty-three grand.''

''That old cop is drawing four hundred a month. You
could get by on that, couldn't you, Speedy?''

Speedy said nothing.

''The city doesn't scale up his pension year after year,
like the Feds. Mac retired in 1966.''

When Speedy had left, Dowling sat in his car and
wondered how long McNamara had been alone.
Someday the rent collector would find him on the floor.
McNamara's liver would give out or one of his cigarettes
would ignite the bed. He remembered an old, retired
sergeant he'd found in patrol, who had pinned his badge

to his T-shirt before he blew a hole in his head with his service revolver.

Dowling had never thought of it before, but now it hit him like a mallet blow to the temple. Where would *he* be in twenty years? Long retired, with Matt and Jenny gone. Rattling around in the house. Cornering some poor patrol officer and spewing out his version of the Hardesty brothers. The thump of a newspaper being delivered from a slow-moving car startled him. He faced some hard decisions about his life, and he knew he'd better start confronting them.

It was starting to get light, but he could not get Mc-Namara out of his mind. McNamara had taught him more than anyone else.

"When you're flushing out a burglar, Dowling, hold your flashlight way out to the side. Not in front of you, like a shit-eatin' bull's eye."

"You never write a ticket to a cop or a cop's family, Dowling. Friendship first. Morality second."

"When we go on a family beef call, remember, the man is the dick-head 99 percent of the time."

Dowling smiled, recalling McNamara's routine the first day with any rookie. McNamara in a crowded diner, with his sleeves rolled up, shouting to the waitress.

"My usual, Edith. A nice tongue sandwich. The rookie, here, says he won't eat nothing that comes out of an animal's mouth. He wants a platter of scrambled eggs." The diner crowd would break up, even those catching McNamara's performance for the second or third time.

Dowling swung the car door open and hurried up the steps.

"Is that you again, Dowling?"

"It's me, Mac. I came back to thank you."

"What the hell for? You didn't take a drink."

✿ Fifteen

Dowling was laboring. When he'd begged Stacy to give him his job back, there were a number of things he had not considered. The amount of concentration necessary, for one. He found himself drifting in the middle of composing a "to do" list, in the middle of a critique; once, even, in the middle of a sentence. Matt and Jenny would leap to mind. Or Helene. Or his father. Or the medallion in his pocket. He had not thought about how time-consuming working the series would be. Little by little he was arriving home later and later.

Matt had said nothing, but Jenny complained twice. "You said it wouldn't be like it used to, Daddy. You promised."

Fatigue was another addition to his forgotten list. He wasn't bouncing back the way he'd used to after being up all night. The day after the Cafe Del Rey Moro case he'd actually dozed at his desk. Another thing wrong—missing—was the intensity. He wanted those guys in jail, all right, but he was going through the investigative steps methodically, without attacking. Being methodical was one of his trademarks. Being passive was not.

Returning to homicide had seemed like the thing to do. It had seemed secure, perhaps a sign that nothing had changed so drastically. Perhaps he had begged because he'd hoped it would make Helene's death seem less isolated. It crossed his mind to admit to Stacy that he'd made a mistake. That Stacy was right. What was it he'd said?

"This is too quick, Vincent. It takes too much out of a guy." After making his decision Stacy had grinned and said, "I hope you don't pull a Sailor Holmquist."

Sailor Holmquist. Stacy had arrested the man when he was a homicide sergeant, in the fifties. A toothless transient who'd cut the throats of runaway teenagers in the freight yard near the waterfront. Stacy had gone north and witnessed his first execution, but not before Sailor Holmquist had requested to see him.

"When I heard you wuz on the guest list, Mr. Stacy, I wanted to tell you I ain't sore at you. The old sailor is finally at peace with hisself. I done bad. I'm ready to sniff that gas tomorrow and let the Lord decide where he'll billet me. My mind's made up, and I ain't changing it."

Fourteen hours later Sailor Holmquist had charted a different course. He had contemptuously ordered dog food for his last meal, bodily thrown the priest out of his cell and, strapped to the throne of death, stuck his tongue out at Stacy through the window of the green gas chamber at San Quentin. Stacy and Dowling had made reference to the story many times over the years.

Dowling looked at the "to do" list, then thumbed through the stack of reports. He wouldn't change his mind, like Sailor Holmquist. Not just yet.

On one yellow sheet, clipped to the top of the file folder, Dowling scratched "M.O. and Physical." Under it, in short sentences, he wrote:

Restaurant-house-house-house-restaurant
—phone call to suspect at scene
—blue eyes; 6'0" to 6'3", husky
—takes victim's car   July 22
—drops car mile away   July 28
—doesn't wipe car down   August 10
—safes; diff dealers, makes   August 31
—ski mask   Sept 2
—sawed off shotgun

—violent
—ties victims

He had seen most of it before, but the phone call from the outside accomplice was unique. That was why he'd directed bulletins to all armed-robbery details in the western states. The information outlined method of operation, descriptions, types of establishments robbed, the exact words used by the gunman and the telephone-call routine. He hoped a detective in a distant city would have worked an identical series. That would have given him another avenue of investigation. And detectives remembered. That was what robbery work was all about. Names, faces and M.O. He hoped an attentive detective in, say, Seattle, would tell him he had not only worked the series, but arrested suspects, later paroled. Then he would have names to work with. Seattle would have gift-wrapped his case for him. But no significant responses were received.

Recent robbery parolees to the San Diego area were investigated, but Dowling saw nothing that excited him. Past and present employees of the two restaurants were being looked at by his team, but he held little hope there. He was not disturbed that the ski mask eliminated facial identification. Nor did he care that the chances of solving the case with physical evidence were minimal.

Fragments of wadding accompanied shotgun pellets leaving the muzzle, and at least the wadding came with a clue. Usually the brand of shell could be determined.

Matt constantly pressed him for scientific details.

"So the lab can tell the make of shotgun, huh, Dad?"

"No, Matt."

"If you get their shotgun, you'll be able to tell it fired those shots."

"Nope. Shotguns have smooth barrels. Handgun barrels have markings the lab uses to identify bullets the gun fired."

Dowling had been confronted with those problems in the past. The cases had been canceled by carefully studying the location pattern and determining where to put undercover teams on stakeout to catch them in the act. Unless they learned something very revealing, there would be no stakeouts on this series. There was no location pattern. Fifteen miles spanned the homes, and by design or accident, both San Diego police and the sheriffs' homicide unit were involved. He hated that. The sheriffs were a good outfit, but it was difficult enough to communicate with a detective in the next squad room. Or sometimes, even, at the next desk.

There was another thing he knew about his suspects. Neither was a safecracker. Unless you hauled a safe away and butchered it, the thing had to be torched or punched or peeled at the scene. His pair could not do that, or they would have burglarized the places without sticking a gun in people's faces. Without adding time to their sentence. Their entry was basic. Unlocked doors or windows, usually. In the rape case the guy had broken a window in the back of the house, so no one had heard him enter.

But how were the residential victims being selected? How did they know there were safes in those homes? The members of the team were still banging their heads against the wall on that one. He looked at his notes again.

SAFES—different makers   diff models
diff dealers   diff insurance co's

That frustration jarred him into thinking about another fact that made him confident they were dealing with well-schooled professionals. The clothing worn by the gunman. Usually, a good composite clothing description was theirs by the time five jobs had been pulled. But this suspect apparently wore a different set of clothes for each job. A different ski mask. A different bulky jacket. A different pair of wash pants. A different pair of shoes. They were obtaining new gear for each crime, then disposing of it. That was unusual. And clever. This way, a shoe impression found at a crime scene could never be

compared, and fibers found clinging to a victim's doorjamb would not match any garment his suspects had in
their possession. They were shrewd businessmen, putting some of the profits back into the company to insure
future successes.

The team settled in the critique room, and Dowling
took his customary spot next to the blackboard. Between
puffs on his cigarette, he chalked statistical information
on the black slate and invited comment.

"So what can we say about our boy?"

"Big sucker with blue eyes," Bones Boswell said.

"Violent," Larry Shea added. "Garbage mouth."

Speedy Montoya nodded. "Knows exactly what he's
doing."

Dowling coughed and rolled up his sleeves. "OK. Report."

The detectives looked at their notebooks and took
turns speaking. Dowling paced the length of the small
room.

"Lab confirms the shotgun is a 12-gauge. Fired a
Remington."

"Vice and Narcotics snitches aren't picking up any
talk."

"The tire impressions the sheriffs hoped was from the
suspect car turned out to belong to a neighbor."

"That's it?" Dowling turned his palms upward.

"Oh. Bones and I sat outside those two restaurants at
closing time," Speedy said. "Our guys didn't need any
inside help. We could see the employees' routines.
Where they park. Everything."

Dowling sighed and looked at his "to do" list.

"Bones. Take a good look at those three houses. I
want to know if they're on corners. Mid-block? Freeway
access? One-story, two-story? Escape routes. What do
you see from the street? You know what I want." He
looked at Speedy. "Get to the newspapers and TV stu-
dios. Start a file on everything that's been printed or
taped about those five jobs."

"Sure, Sarge. Why?"

"A few reasons. I want to know what our suspects

have been told. And if some would-be informant starts whispering stuff in our ear it helps us to validate his info.''

"Helps if we get false confessions, too, huh?''

"You're learning, Speedy. And you, Shea. Call all of the LAPD geographical divisions. Run the M.O. by 'em. Maybe they missed the mailing. Tell them we're hurting.'' He looked at his list again. "Then get me a good up-to-date list on the jewelry that's been taken. We gotta keep on top of the pawnshops.'' He stretched. "That's it. Get to work. And remember. Treat this like a homicide.'' He was reaching for the doorknob when Bones said, "You forgot about the round table, Sarge.''

"Huh?''

"The round table. Remember? You told me in the squad room we were going to do one. You just forgot to write it down.''

Dowling nodded. The round table was his name for calling all of the residential victims and their families to the police station at the same time. He would place them around a large conference table and ply them with coffee and sandwiches. He was searching for the common denominator that would lead him to his suspects. He would list categories on the blackboard:

gardeners	grocery stores	hairdressers
service stations	dry cleaners	insurance agents

He would sit back and request that they visit among themselves, discussing habits and life-styles and friends. It had worked for him before.

Dowling had not mentioned the round table to Bones. He had just forgotten. He looked at the loyal detective, who had not wanted to embarrass him in front of the others. "Thank you, Old Bones,'' he said softly.

"Can we sit a few more minutes, Sarge?'' Bones asked. "Something's been gnawing at me.''

When they had reassembled, the tallest detective leaned back in his chair. "Let's look at the M.O. again,'' he said, closing his eyes and massaging his forehead with long, hairy fingers. "Who in hell would be that slick? Dumping clothing and going from city to county and . . . the phone calls. We're talking big-league unique, here. We're talking . . . talking either a goddamn master criminal"—his voice trailed off—"or a law-enforcement type."

Dowling leaned against the bulletin board with arms folded, in a room turned silent.

"What's the punch line, Bones?" Larry Shea asked.

"Huh?"

"Every joke's got a punch line."

"Open mind, Shea. Always keep an open mind. It could be a cop," Bones replied.

"I got your open mind right here. A bunch of words on a shittin' blackboard and you're ready to point to a cop. That's bullshit. I thought I knew you, Bones?"

"Hey, Shea. Why don't you take your act out in the waiting area with the rest of the citizens? This room's for detectives only," Bones said.

Shea slid his chair back, and it slammed against the wall as he jumped to his feet. "When's the last time you got knocked on your ass, Bones."

"I dunno. When's the last time I was home?"

"I agree with Bones," Speedy said. "We have to—"

"Fuck you too, Montoya. It figures you'd agree with him. What the hell do you know about cops? You hop-scotched over to this office without paying your dues, and now you're a fuckin' expert." Shea was warming to it. "Me? I put in ten years in a car and five years on the bricks in burglary detail. Me and my partners against the scum bags in the rest of this fucked-up world." He paced the small room. "A bunch of uniforms out there right now climbing into those black and whites with a peanut butter fuckin' sandwich in a bag trying to make this city a better place. And you're sitting in here talking this crap. I thought I knew you guys."

"Enough, already," Dowling shouted, raising both arms. "Sit down, Shea." They stared at each other, and

Dowling pointed to the chair. "Sit down, Shea. I've got the floor now."

"We get heated up like this because we've got pride in who we are and what we do. And when a cop does mess up we go after him hard and we get sick about it but we do what has to be done, and that's what separates being a cop from being damn near anything else." He paused for breath. "And Bones is right, and if I had my head screwed on right I'd have seen it too." He looked at Shea. "Bones isn't saying our crook is a cop. He's saying we have to consider it. But I'll bet my ass that our inside guy is not the mastermind. Because he wouldn't have done that rape. Nope. Our mastermind is the outside guy, insulating himself and sending that animal in to do the scut work."

They talked for another twenty minutes, and when they broke Larry Shea lingered, with his head down. Bones patted him on the shoulder when he passed, and Speedy paused in the doorway. "Come on, Shea. I'm thirsty, and I'm buying," Speedy said.

Dowling sat at his desk and tuned out the hum of activity in the squad room. Message slips were stacked at the edge of his blotter. He was annoyed that Baby Blue had called again, because he was trying to phase out the relationship. The surgery had gone well enough, and Aggie Pride was caring for him. It would be more than fine, Dowling thought, if he never saw her again. It was good, though, that he'd spent a little time with Baby Blue. You could never tell about cons with rap sheets like his. It was better to drink a couple of beers with them than to have them standing outside your living room window in the dark, lining up your occipital bone in the cross hairs of a rifle. He'd told Baby Blue during a recent call that he was involved in a case and would be calling him less frequently. Then the hideous gift had arrived in the mail. A souvenir ashtray covered with logos from the zoo and the waterfront and La Jolla Cove. Dowling had put it in the back of a cluttered drawer in the kitchen, and his heart had not been in the thank-you call.

"I figured you'd like it, Sarge. For your desk."

"The chief won't let us have anything that—that decorative in the squad room. I've got it at home."

The fact that Baby Blue's eyes were the same color as the gunman's had not escaped Dowling, but the gunman was taller and huskier than the ex-convict. And Baby Blue had been in the hospital when the Cafe Del Rey Moro had been robbed. Wanting to be thorough, Dowling had telephoned the state and verified that Baby Blue had still been in custody when the first crime had occurred. He told himself he was grasping at straws. They would keep it to themselves, this business of considering a cop as their suspect. After all, nothing really pointed that way, and the whole department would be stirred up if it leaked.

Dowling sighed heavily when he picked up the next message slip. Jenny had called, and he knew what that was about. He'd placed her on seven days of house restriction over the beer-drinking incident, and it had not been well received. He took a deep breath and dialed.

"I drink one little beer and get put on restriction," she cried. "Last year Matt goes into a bar—with a phony ID—gets in a big brawl, and nothing happens to him."

Dowling shifted in his chair. "That's not exactly true, Jenny. I had a long talk with him. And he did get taken down to the police station."

"Yeah. And got cut loose as soon as they found out who his father was."

"Matt's a boy," Dowling said weakly.

"Oh, wow. Chauv-in-is-tic. I'm not saying I wanted Matt to get in trouble. I'm saying if he didn't, I shouldn't. Equal rights, Daddy, equal rights."

"Jenny, the decision stands." He put his hand to his forehead. "Now, in this case, I think the punishment fits the crime. If your attitude seems to—well—I may cut a day or two off of it—for good time."

Jenny played in a softball tournament the following day.

The Saturday-night poker game had become a ritual for Dominic Bonelli and his five selected guests. It started late, and usually continued until the first rays of morning sun cast a sheen on the waters of the harbor. Bonelli had owned the Captain's Table restaurant for twenty years, and he catered to patrons whose discriminating taste in seafood overcame their concern about exorbitant menu prices.

The game took place in the owner's oak-paneled office. Thick cocoa-brown carpet accentuated the wood. Eyes of stuffed big game looked down at the casino-style card table. The room was huge, like Dominic Bonelli. Drinks and food were brought in by employees until 3:00 A.M. Then Bonelli, quick and nimble for a giant of a man, would assume the dual role of part-time waiter and ardent poker player. His ground rules were simple. Five-card stud only. Fifty-dollar limit. Three raises. No markers. "Good, old-fashioned poker, hey, boys?" he was fond of saying.

Seated around the felt-topped table with him were a dentist, a contractor, a real-estate broker and two car dealers.

"I'll check," the dentist said. A queen and a jack covered his down card.

"Twenty bucks." The contractor flipped the money to the center.

One car dealer called. Then Bonelli called through a cloud of cigar smoke.

"Twenty more," the other car dealer said.

The dentist folded, then leaned back in his chair and sipped gin. "Shit-house cards," he said. "Nothing but shit-house cards."

"Tomorrow you'll fill a cavity and recover," Bonelli said.

"Excuse me, Mr. Bonelli. I need to see you for a minute. Out here, sir." The night manager spoke from a partially opened door separating Bonelli's office from a darkened corridor.

Bonelli excused himself and walked toward the door. By the time he reached it the manager had stepped back out of sight.

"I thought you'd left, Herman." Bonelli took a few steps into the corridor. "Where the hell are you?" He squinted into the darkness.

"Not one sound, you bastard," the man in the ski mask whispered. He grabbed Bonelli's dark, oily hair. "This is a shotgun I'm stickin' in your eye."

Bonelli's foot struck the arm of the manager, who was lying face down on the floor.

"Close your office door real slow, now. That's it. Now get on the floor with him." The owner's chest heaved as he sank to the floor, using the walls to guide him. The gunman leaned over them and said softly, "Now crawl to the foyer and open the safe." He put the muzzle of the shotgun under Bonelli's testicles, then raised it briskly. "You try anything I don't like, I'll blow your fuckin' balls off." He looked at the manager. "You too. Now, get movin'."

When the currency was in his bag, the gunman herded the two men back toward the office. The poker players' heads turned simultaneously when the door crashed open and Bonelli and the manager were hurled into the room. The sawed-off shotgun was leveled at them. The masked figure crouched slightly and stepped to within a few feet of the table.

"Hands on the goddamn table. *Now!*" He removed another canvas bag from his jacket pocket and threw it on the table. "Get the money in the bag. First one that moves gets blown away."

While the contractor carefully swept the bills into the bag, the gunman slowly circled the table. His head darted from side to side, and he stole glances at the open door, then at Bonelli and the manager, lying against the wall. Ten hands were palms down on the table. The dentist's eyes were closed, and his head was down.

"Rings and wristwatches too. Hurry up."

The telephone seemed to startle him when it rang, and he hurried to Bonelli's desk and picked up the receiver. "Yep. Yep. Yep. Um-hum." With one yank he pulled the cord from the wall.

"Toss the bag on the floor," he told the contractor. "Then hands back on the table. Nice and easy."

"Now," he said, holding both bags in one hand and moving the weapon with the other, "everybody's hands up."

The dentist's hands were the last to be raised. The gold ring under them was conspicuous on the green felt.

"One smart boy, huh?"

"Please. It was my father's. And his father's."

"In the bag, smart boy."

"It's not worth anything. Not worth much money. Please."

"In the bag." The muzzle was under the dentist's chin.

The dentist picked the ring up and stared at it. "I don't think you'll kill me for this ring. You made a big haul. I'm going to put it in my pocket. Slowly." His hand was almost to his shirt when the explosion occurred. The flash from the barrel was a lighter hue than the blood that gushed onto the tabletop. Part of the dentist's brain plastered itself on the face of an elk mounted on the wall.

Dowling parked his car on the street and cursed when he saw the coroner's wagon in the parking lot next to the restaurant door. He would raise hell with patrol about that. It was unnecessary. Stupid. They could have driven over evidence. Smashed cartridge cases. Smeared bloodstains.

"Why don't we just sell tickets and get a few more cars in here?" he shouted. "It's only a homicide scene."

When he walked inside he found himself face to face with Tom Stacy. He could not remember the last time the captain of homicide had rolled in in the middle of the night.

"What in hell are you doing here?" Dowling asked.

Stacy folded his arms. "You've been around. You know how phones have a habit of ringing when people get murdered."

"But why your phone?"

"Oh, that. Our chief of police is a predictable guy. He always calls me when the mayor's brother is the dead man."

"The mayor's brother? Our mayor?"

"Yes, Sergeant. Our mayor." He looked at his watch, then turned toward a light to read it. "It's 4:00 A.M. Be in my office in two hours. And bring some answers with you."

The hallway outside Stacy's office was deserted. Dowling carried coffee in a Styrofoam cup, and some of it splashed onto the carpeting. He thought better of bringing it into the office, and the two quick gulps he took burned his tongue.

On the drive to the station from the restaurant he had made the decision. He was in over his head. Somebody else—anybody else—could step in and do a better job. Stacy had been right. It was too soon. He had children to raise. That was a full-time job. Probably the Management Services Unit *was* the right spot for him. Somebody had to tally rolls of toilet paper.

He straightened his tie, squared his shoulders and silently rehearsed his opening line. Then he opened the door. Stacy was standing behind his desk, one hand clutching the back of his head.

"I got a bitch of a headache," Stacy said before Dowling could speak. "I just went into the john and made the mistake of looking at myself in the mirror. You know what I saw, Dowling?" Stacy sighed. "I saw a sixty-four-year-old fart with tired eyes, with an ulcer, with a scowl on his face, and with twenty-six officer-involved shootings this year. With three good coppers dead and two coppers wounded. Sixteen times we killed the bad guy." He sat down and swiveled in his chair. "While you were in that restaurant, a patrolman killed a guy coming at him with a hatchet." Stacy got up again and paced. "By the time the sun goes down tonight, a bunch of people will be screaming that we should have shot it out of his hand like Matt Dillon or John Wayne." He straightened a row of books on a shelf. "Easy to get tired in this fuckin' business, isn't it? Look at us. We're one hundred and thirteen years old, total. Ought to be home in bed." He ran his fingers through white hair. "I swore in on this job in 1949. San Diego was a sleepy old Navy town with about three hundred cops and all two-man cars, and half of 'em slept in the cemetery on night shift. I was making two hundred and fifty bucks a month. Now I'm knocking down about sixty-eight thousand a year and we got two thousand cops in one-person cars and I got the mayor's brother lying on a slab, and you know what, Dowling? I wish I was back sleeping in the cemetery with my two hundred and fifty a month." He stopped for a breath, and added, "I can't tell you how much it means, having you back. You're going to make these guys."

Dowling walked to the window and saw sparse traffic on the downtown streets below. "The shit's going to hit the fan tomorrow morning, Tom. The council will have the chief on the carpet at 8:00 A.M. I'll get you a head start."

"You're thinking right. Give me a memo on everything. Everything we've done on this series since day one." He removed his glasses and rubbed his eyes. "The sad thing is, these politicos haven't paid any attention to the first five jobs. Nothing in it for them. But I can hear them now. 'You mean maniacs have been running around shooting people? What do we have a police department for?' " He opened a folder. "Why did that son of a bitch have to play poker last night?"

"I'm out of here. We're working," Dowling said.

"They'll want to know if we're operating stakeouts."

Dowling stopped at the door. "Hell, no. Nothing close to a pattern."

"Get stakeouts going."

"Tom, we have over a million people and over two thousand restaurants. There aren't enough cops—"

"We have to put on a show, Vince. I have to tell the media about our commitment. Pick some places. Thirty or forty of them. Manpower was a problem yesterday. It won't be tomorrow."

Dowling was actually past the door when Stacy called him back again. "Your favorite deputy chief called just before you got here. He's proposing a task force. Feds. D.A. Sheriff."

"That dumb son of a bitch can't wipe his ass without getting it on his fingers, Tom. I'd rather take a whipping than be part of any politically motivated horseshit committee. Why, if my team can't catch a couple of punk stickup men, you may as well stick us in uniform and have us walk Pacific Beach looking for space invaders." He put his fist in the air. "Please fight it, Tom. Stall 'em. A task force will ruin this investigation."

"I'll try. But you better get your ass cracking."

Dowling hurried out the door. He didn't see Stacy smiling.

That evening, in his kitchen, he put on a pot of coffee. He changed into an old sweater, comfortable sweatpants and slippers with holes in them. He had to make two trips to the car to carry in the stacks of crime reports, file memos, records and yellow sheets. Dowling placed them around the perimeter of the dining room table. He cleaned his reading glasses and watched a tree branch brush the window. It was starting to rain. That meant he had to build a fire. There was plenty of wood, and he was glad. He decided he would be there for a long time. Twice he had gone over all of the data. He must have missed something.

%% Sixteen

Six hours later, the fire had reduced itself to a heap of glowing coals. Rain pelted the side of the house near his window, and a cup of cold coffee sat dangerously close to the edge of the table. Dowling was exhausted. His throat was raw from smoking, and a sour taste had burned its way to the pit of his stomach.

He had digested thousands of words and hundreds of disjointed facts; read and reread about arthritic Marjorie Graham and Clarence the iceskating busboy; about the young rape victim and how the mayor's brother had been belted to eternity with a hole where his face had been. He had pored over photographs and measurements and laboratory reports and memos of work completed and work not completed; studied bulletins and newspaper articles and the arrest records of scores of men.

If the answer or a workable clue was there, he had missed it. Fatigue finally made him indifferent, and he leaned back in the chair and stared at the ceiling. Two hours had been spent reviewing the notes of the sergeant he had replaced. The sergeant had been making notes in a police car when the heart attack had disabled him.

Most of the symbols and abbreviations eventually made sense to Dowling. There was, however, one notation that particularly puzzled him. It appeared to be a name; "CE Groma." In the center of the page, under a heading titled "Suspects," several names had been entered. Each had been crossed out with a brief explanation

next to the name. "In custody," "alibi checks out,"
"no good." Groma was scribbled off to the side, con-
spicuously alone. There was no criminal record for anyone by that name.

The sergeant had been released from the hospital, and
Dowling visited him the next morning.

"Groma. Groma. I don't remember that name.
'Course, I couldn't remember my own name for a few
days after my ticker went south on me." He patted his
pajama pocket. "No more smokes, Dowling. But you
know what? I don't miss 'em." He lowered his voice,
because his wife was in the next room. "You know what
I miss? A couple of shooters of good gin and *chiles
rellenos.*"

"Groma doesn't do anything for you?"

"The cardiologist says in a few weeks I can have
three ounces of wine a night. Fuck that."

"Here. Look at your notes again," Dowling said impatiently. "Right there. CE Groma."

The man picked up his glasses. He was pale and
needed a shave. "Naw. That's not a name. See, it's
spaced wrong for a name. When I write like that I'm
putting the first letter instead of the whole word. Like,
'for old times' sake' would be FOTS. He looked closer.
The 'CE' would probably be the initials of the person
who said it."

"For Chrissakes, who said what?"

"That's what I can't remember. Five words, though.
Whatever it was, he said five words. G-R-O-M-A." He
ran his fingers through thinning gray hair. "It didn't turn
out to be anything important or I wouldn't have let it
alone."

Dowling picked up the piece of paper. "Well, it was
just a loose end. You know I'm hurting or I wouldn't
be here bothering you. I'll get out of here. You're supposed to be resting." He got to his feet and stuffed the
paperwork into a worn manila folder.

"It isn't that important to me anymore, Dowling.
Slow it down or I'll be visiting you." They looked at
each other. "Ah, hell. Let me see that again." He stud-

ied the data for another fifteen minutes. "Let's see I
wrote this when I was in the lab. And this. I wrote this
at the records counter. See the SDPD number right
there?" He ran his finger up the margin. "I was sitting
on the crapper when I made those arrows. Wait a minute.
Now I remember. GROMA. Get robbery off my ass.
G-R-O-M-A."

"What in hell are you talking about?" Dowling
asked.

"Some ex-cop thought we were doing a car surveillance on him. But we weren't. He made that statement
to his old patrol partner. Said to his old partner, 'Get
robbery off my ass. I'm not doing anything.' His old
partner told robbery."

"Who was the ex-cop?"

"I forget the kid's name. His initials are C.E., though.
See. Right in front of the GROMA. Hell, you busted
him, Dowling."

"For what?"

"For stealing from that Pop Warner football league."

Dowling eased into the chair slowly. C.E. Cliff Edwards. The basketball player. It seemed like a decade
ago.

"Like I said, it didn't turn out to be anything. I elim-
inated him, but I don't remember how. Tell you what.
See Noah Greentree over in Narcotics. He'll remember.
He didn't have a fuckin' heart attack."

"I barely got the gist of what he was saying, Noah,"
Dowling said, filling their beer glasses from the pitcher.
"Let me have it from your end."

Narcotics detective Noah Greentree and Dowling had
gone through the police academy together. Greentree
wore a bulky sweater and Levis, and they covered a
physique Dowling compared to a Charger linebacker. He
was a medium-complexioned black man.

The two detectives turned their backs on a group of
noisy off-duty patrol officers at the next table.

"Here's how it went down," Noah Greentree said.
"We were doing a surveillance on a coke dealer. Tailed

him all over town. Didn't see anything good. End of the day he goes into this pool hall. Talks to a big blond guy. I played a hunch. Decided to tail the blond guy.'' Greentree tossed down the beer. "It was a bad hunch. He made the tail in five minutes. Looked right at us and waved, so we backed off.'' He slid his glass toward Dowling, who poured. "This talking makes me thirsty.'' After he swallowed he continued. "Next day we find out the blond guy is an ex-cop, this Cliff Edwards. Runs the pool hall. He doesn't have any narcotics involvement. It was a bad hunch, like I say. Nothing ventured, nothing gained, type of deal.''

Dowling made circles with his glass. "There's more than that, Noah. Cliff Edwards yells to someone about it.''

"Oh, yeah. He runs to his old partner. Tells him robbery detail's been following him. Say's he's not doing robberies. The ex-partner, he's all cop. Runs over to the detective division with the news. That's it. It was all a big nothing.''

Dowling pushed his chair back. "I have to go, Noah. My kids will be home in a few minutes. But tell me, why would a guy think robbery was chasing him if they weren't?''

Noah Greentree looked at him. "I know what you're thinking, but they checked him out on your series, and I know how they eliminated him.''

"How?''

"What color eyes does your stickup man have?''

"Blue.''

"Then this Cliff Edwards dude has brown eyes. Whatever color your stickup man has, he's got different.''

Dowling spent portions of the next three days trying to get Cliff Edwards out of his thoughts. Records-division files proved Noah Greentree right. Edwards had brown eyes. He was not the gunman, and the outside accomplice had never been seen. Years of homicide experience were cautioning him about spending valuable time on Edwards. It was a flimsy lead, and he had seen too many detectives get sidetracked out of desperation. It would be foolish to pursue it now. Perhaps later. If nothing developed.

Three hours after he determined it was foolish, Dowling checked with a source of his in a card room. He learned that an old man who was phasing himself out of the business had hired an ex-cop to run Luckie's pool hall.

"He's a little pushy, Sarge. But hell, it ain't a Sunday school he's running."

"How's he come across to you?"

"Gets some mileage out of being an ex-cop. Likes to talk sports. Sees every goddamn thing goes on in the joint."

"Who's he tight with?"

"Nobody but hisself, Sarge. Nobody but hisself."

It occurred to Dowling that he had learned little about Cliff Edwards before arresting him in late May. Dowling had been lumbering around in a fog then. Edwards had acted as if he deserved no more than a scolding for blatantly stealing money. What had bothered him most was that Edwards had been such a competent patrolman. He hated to see those kind leave police work. San Diego cops did not steal. When they resigned or got fired it was because they could not cut it, or because they were drinking, or girl chasing on the job, or because their wives pressured them to work normal hours around normal people. Edwards was a little salty, but the department usually mellowed those young guys out of the Wyatt Earp syndrome, and then their considerable talents were well focused.

It also occurred to Dowling that running a pool hall was an unusual occupation for an ex-cop in the nineties. Perhaps it was a stopgap until Edwards could adjust to the trauma of the arrest. Probation with no time served could hinder him in the job market for a while.

He told himself not to consider Edwards a suspect. There was a lot of difference between pocketing a few bucks that had been entrusted to you and blowing people off the face of the earth because they didn't want to cough up some silly ring. It was stupid to run in circles, when the guy you really wanted was out there somewhere. Still, he wished he could think of a simple way to eliminate Edwards.

That was the investigative method he liked best. Elimination. There was nothing tricky about it. You merely went after the guy with the intention of proving he had not committed the crime. And sometimes, the harder you worked to eliminate him, the more factual and incriminating evidence kept jumping out at you. Mediocre detectives developed a theory, then tried to make the facts fit the theory. It was supposed to be the other way around. He promised himself he would keep an open mind about his old friend Cliff Edwards.

"Why do you want to tell me the post-op instructions?" Dowling was on the telephone. "Why not tell him?"

"Because you're the one he'll listen to," Dr. Marcus said.

"I'm busy as hell, Doc."

"This Baby Blue is an interesting patient, Sergeant. Very strong constitution. A surgeon appreciates that. But I get the feeling he'll only take me seriously for a little while. Until he feels better. Then he could get into trouble."

"All right," Dowling said, shaking his head.

"Lots of rest. Proper diet to combat disease. Infection is a hazard. A big hazard."

"That can hurt him, huh, Doc?"

"That can kill him. So don't let him get feisty. In a few weeks he'll be up and about and feeling better each day."

"Hallelujah."

"Another thing. No smoking. If he starts coughing the hernia can reoccur. The intestines come back up. The hernia strangulates and his blood supply gets knocked off. He could go in a day, so watch him carefully." Dr. Marcus paused. "That's what you get for being a Good

Samaritan. Good luck on whatever it is you're working on.''

Luck. He played with the word after hanging up. Branch Rickey had said luck was the residue of design. Vincent Dowling had never subscribed to that in full. A significant number of cases had been solved for him over the years by pure, simple, dumb luck. He smiled, remembering the stickup man hit by a bus as he was running from a jewelry store. Another time, a prisoner on a high floor of the federal jail had looked out the narrow window and seen a sailor throw a woman off the sixth-floor fire escape of a downtown hotel. A prison guard had called the police, and Dowling had arrived while the sailor was on the telephone reporting that the woman had committed suicide.

Dowling loved luck, and he wanted some badly.

"So where are we?'' Dowling asked. "Where in hell are we? I'll answer my own question. We're nowhere.''

He was propped against the wall in the critique room, exhaling smoke from his nose and mouth. Bones and Shea and Speedy looked tired and dejected. Loud laughter from the squad room rumbled through the closed door and broke his concentration. He yanked the door open and yelled to everyone in sight, "Does anybody care that we're trying to solve a murder in here?'' His carotid artery bulged, and his face was red. The room quieted instantly. He closed the door and walked the length of the small room.

"Like working in a zoo.'' Circling the table, he looked over their shoulders. "We just have to keep plugging. Stay on the bricks. The answer's out there unless these bastards are from out of town. And history says they're local.''

He went back to leaning against the blackboard. "Somebody say something brilliant. Pull a rabbit out of the hat, Bones.''

"The way we're going, I'd pull out a handful of rabbit shit.''

They sat quietly for several minutes, each reviewing his folder and shuffling papers.

"Sarge. What do you say we take a look at this Cliff Edwards?" Speedy said.

"Oh?"

"It's been sticking in my craw." Speedy cleared his throat. "That 'get robbery off my ass' thing."

Dowling looked at Shea and Bones, who were looking down at their notebooks as Speedy searched for an invisible piece of lint on the sleeve of his jacket.

"Did you say craw or craws?" Dowling asked.

The detectives looked at one another.

"We had a couple pitchers of beer yesterday and got talking about him," Shea said. "There are some similarities. Of course, we figured you'd already thought of them but, like you just said, Sarge, we're nowhere."

Bones reached into his pocket. "We put some stuff down on a napkin, boss, if I can still read it." He squinted, and unfolded it on the table. "It got a little wet."

"See, the thing is, Sarge, if we were going to take a look at this guy, we'd do it on our own time if you wanted us to," Speedy volunteered.

Dowling looked around the table. They had been putting in twelve- and fourteen-hour days. One of the newspaper articles had named the members of his team, and a television editorial had made it sound like they were standing still.

"Well, Mr. Montoya, you seem to be the spokesman. Perhaps you'd be kind enough to come up to the blackboard and translate from your parchment."

Bones quickly slid the napkin across the tabletop, but Speedy hesitated. "Come on, put it on the board," Dowling said.

Speedy divided the board into a right side and a left side, then wrote:

SUSPECT	CLIFF EDWARDS
big guy	big guy
clever—well planned	could qualify
	cannot eliminate

"No fingerprints and no face ID," Speedy said.

mask—gloves   would know to do

"If he's as good a cop as they say he was, he'd be a hell of a crook, too, Sarge." Speedy wrote more.

varies location—all over   would know to do
varies target—house,
   restaurant

Speedy took his seat like a nervous schoolboy. Dowling picked up the chalk and added. "Motive."

"All right. You guys started this. Give me motives."

"Money," Shea said.

"He was pretty sore at the department about getting booked. Could be getting back at us," Bones said.

Dowling picked up the chalk again and wrote "Money-Revenge."

"He has an ego as big as this squad room," Dowling said. "His ex-partner said he didn't play pro basketball because he flat wasn't good enough. But Edwards put out a different reason. Says he didn't want to play in the NBA."

They all looked at the board. "How are you going to get around those blue eyes our killer has?" Dowling asked. Nobody spoke. Near the bottom of the board he wrote:

NEGATIVES
big city=lots of crooks to draw from
Edwards=no history of violence
Edwards=brown eyes
suspect=blue eyes

Dowling sat down at the head of the table. "Listen carefully, now. Let me tell you why you can shuck the big-guy category. The killer has blue eyes. I'm not buying any far-out stuff like Edwards' changing eye color with contact lenses. Not right now, I'm not. You show me more on him, I'll reevaluate.''

He got up and drew a line through "big guy." "So we have zero on Cliff Edwards. But I like the way you teamed up on this. Some good work gets done in gin mills. We'll get this case put together.''

He was about to dismiss them when Bones said, "Boss. We were talking about that 'get robbery off my ass.' Shea said something interesting. Tell him, Larry.''

"Say a kid in school is cheating on a test. Has the answers up his sleeve, and the teacher comes and stands next to his desk. The kid figures the teacher's suspicious.''

"Sure," Speedy said. "And if some woman's cheating on her old man and she sees him sitting in his car on the street four doors away, she thinks he's wise. Even if, in fact, he just has car trouble.''

"We don't know anything about his life-style. Or who his friends are. Or his financial picture," Dowling said.

"We'd find out if we tailed him, Sarge," Speedy burst out. "Stick to that son of a bitch like mustard on meat and get those answers.''

"Noah Greentree's narcs got burned in five minutes, trying to stay with him," Dowling said.

"This isn't Noah Greentree's narcs," Bones said. "This is Vincent Dowling's homicide team. The varsity.''

"We won't lose him. The Mexican-ass bandito will be riding in his hip pocket," Speedy offered.

"It would mean more time away from your families. And girl friends, Speedy. You're gone most of the time now.''

"You're telling me," Larry Shea said. "I've been away from home so much that my kids don't recognize me and the dog bites me. And some guy has my phone number mixed up with the weather bureau. Always calling, wanting to know if the coast is clear.''

"Come on, Shea. That one has whiskers," Bones said.

"A surveillance, huh? I'll tell you what. I'm not sold

yet. I'll decide about a surveillance after I have a talk with that son of a bitch," Dowling said.

"Have a talk with him!" They all said it at once.

"Yeah," Dowling said. "An accidentally-on-purpose kind of meeting. See where his head is. See what my guts tell me."

"Jeez, Sarge. You told me when I first came over here to be careful about gut feelings. To stick to facts." Speedy moaned. "You're making me crazy."

"That serves you right for memorizing all the shit I hand out," Dowling said. "Some old geezer I talked to the other day said Edwards grabs lunches quite a bit at a Taco Bell around the corner from his joint." He rubbed his stomach. "A couple of beef burritos would probably go pretty good right now."

The truth was, Dowling reminded himself, there were three or four places to go for a really stellar burrito. Bea's came to mind. And El Indio and Chuey's and a little hole in the wall in Normal Heights whose name he could never remember. The fast-food restaurant whose lot he was parked in was not one of them.

His patience was rewarded on the third day when he watched Cliff Edwards stroll into the brown-and-yellow-stucco building. Dowling got out of his car and intercepted Edwards when he exited with a bag in each hand. Dowling did his best to act surprised.

"Hey, Cliff." Dowling extended his hand.

Edwards smiled. His blond hair hung slightly over the collar of his shirt, and he stood on the high end of a gradual slope, towering over Dowling. Edwards shuffled the bags and shook hands.

"Sergeant Dowling." He exaggerated each word. "I'm doing good. Real good. How about yourself?"

"I'm well enough."

"I heard you're back in homicide, Sarge."

"That's a fact, Cliff. That other job wasn't me." Behind him, two boys on skate boards leaped a curb in the parking lot, and it startled him. "Jesus, more dangerous than the freeway." He lit a cigarette. "I'm glad I ran into you. Was kind of wondering how you were doing. How you were looking at things.''

"What do you mean, Sarge?"

"How you feel about what happened? About me and the bust and all.''

"Oh, that. No hard feelings. No hard feelings at all.''

He was still smiling when Dowling said, "You were pretty mad last time I saw you. In court.''

"Well, that was then and this is now. But I'm kind of puzzled. How come a big-time homicide cop with a heavy case load would waste any time worrying about how *I* feel? You got something else on your mind?''

"What else would I have on my mind, Cliff?''

"How would I know? You're the hotshot detective. I'm just a cop gone bad. Remember?''

Edwards broke the short silence. "But you know what? Turns out you did me a favor. I don't miss that job at all. Spending all day fucking over people and working lousy hours and going to court on my middle-of-the-week days off and getting second-guessed by everybody in town. You really did do me a favor. Do you believe that, Sarge?''

It was Dowling's turn to smile. "Sure, I believe you, Cliff.''

⚡ Seventeen

"The best thing about surveillance is, I get to wear grubby clothes," Larry Shea said. "The worst thing is, I'll have to take a leak just as our boy starts to move."

"Take it in *your* thermos," Dowling said, and put the transistor radio closer to his ear. "Jeez, we don't play good on the road. Ten–nothing Steelers already."

Dowling tried to take some weight off his left buttock, because his leg was going to sleep. The Toyota Corolla had been his choice of cars from the undercover pool, because there were so many of them on the road they would be less conspicuous. He got himself adjusted, reached down to push his lunch sack aside and discovered he had stepped on it and crushed the banana Jenny had packed. No matter. Shea would keep it from going to waste. The police radio, concealed in the glove compartment, was turned low, so it would not attract attention from pedestrians walking near the car.

Luckie's pool hall on Euclid Avenue was in midblock, so Dowling had positioned their car on the first side street north of it. They could not see the pool hall, but had a clear view of traffic on Euclid, and had located Cliff Edward's dark green pickup truck in the parking lot next to the establishment. Dowling had positioned Bones and Speedy in a supermarket parking lot at the first intersection south of them.

"I told you guys about the Taco Bell meeting, but it's gnawing at me, Larry. He's lying. He's got to be lying.

He was a hell of a cop, and it's in his blood, and he's got to miss it every day of his life. But he says I did him a favor.'' Dowling blew a crude smoke ring toward the window. "And I don't know if he lied to me because he's a crook, or if he's just too angry still to admit it. But it's enough to make me take a look at him.''

"It would be sweet if he was our suspect, Sarge.''

"Yeah.'' Dowling glanced into darkness in the rear-view mirror. "My source says he doesn't flash money or jewelry. Says he's still single. Pickup truck's the only thing he's seen him in.''

"How do you figure him wrecking a career, tapping that till?''

"How do you ever figure people? He got greedy, Shea. Used to having things given to him. Done for him.''

"Temptation's right in front of you on this job. He couldn't have lasted long.''

Dowling yawned. "Once when I was a sergeant in patrol, I found a door of a business unlocked. It was two nights before Christmas. Helene and I had bought the kids about five or six one-dollar presents because we didn't have anything. Anyway, I go inside to check this place out and there's a safe. Door standing wide open. And money. I can't begin to tell you how much, but it was all stacked up with bands around it. I remember this like it was yesterday.''

A patrol car cruised by their position, slowed and made a U-turn. Larry Shea badged him off.

"Anyway,'' Dowling continued, "I stood there look-ing at all the dough. Thinking of Matt and Jenny Christ-mas morning. And Helene wanting a washer and dryer. And then I went over to this desk and found the owner's home phone number and called him. I can hear noise in the background, and you know what the turd says? Says, 'What are you bothering me for? I'm having a party.' Lock the goddamn safe and get the hell out of there.''

Shea whistled, and Dowling went on. "So I took one last look at Fort Knox and closed the joint. I woke Helene up when I got home, and told her about it.

She says, 'That's you. That's one of the reasons I love you.' "

"How do you figure people?" Shea said.

"I think I got some lovin' that night."

"You miss her, huh, Sarge?"

"I miss hell out of her, Larry. I'd give anything to be able to do it over."

They talked while Pittsburgh put another field goal on the scoreboard. A man in his sixties, clothing disheveled and clutching a brown paper bag with a bottle protruding from it, weaved toward the car. Both elbows were pointed to his sides, and the shoulders took turns sagging.

"He looks like he's surprised every time his foot touches the sidewalk," Shea said. The man's head was down. "Probably a retired homicide sergeant. Notice his eyes never leave the ground. Looking for evidence."

"Probably walked away from a funny farm," Dowling said. "Probably had a team like the one I've got."

Dowling had not told Tom Stacy about the surveillance. Stacy would have felt obligated to pass the information up the chain of command, and that meant it would have come to rest in city hall. Except it would not have rested there for long. Within twenty-four hours a city council-person's aide would have leaked it to the media. Everything would have gone downhill then.

Dowling had hurried to Noah Greentree with a flurry of questions after meeting Edwards. He'd wanted to know more about the dope dealer Greentree's squad had seen talking to Cliff Edwards.

"Was he a big guy, Noah?"

"Hell, yes, he was big."

"A violent guy, by chance?"

"Nastier than a hat full of snakes, Dowling."

"Where's he living now? I might want to take a look at him."

"He moved to the bay area. San Quentin."

The traffic on Euclid Avenue had thinned out somewhat by 7:00 P.M. Shea wadded a sandwich wrap-

per, then tore the end piece from two packaged cup-
cakes.

"How do you eat that crap?" Dowling asked.

"I have to. You don't bring in your baked stuff anymore. Like that chocolate cake you made that time."
Shea put his hand on his stomach and made a circular
motion.

"That wasn't 'chocolate cake.' That was layered *génoise* and biscuit with a cream filling."

"The filling made me cry, Sarge. What was it?"

"Cream, white chocolate, unsalted butter and dark
rum."

"Jesus. I'd marry you if I didn't have to sleep with
you."

The white Honda Civic that Bones and Speedy occupied was wedged into the second row of the parking
lot, with a chain of shopping carts next to it. Nothing
obstructed their path to the driveway.

"Quick. Quick. The one with tight pants, bending
over. Putting her groceries in the trunk," Speedy said,
tugging at Bones's arm. "Aw, you missed it."

"You'll find another one."

"You got to be quick, Bones. Her pants were so tight
that if she farted she'd have blown her shoes off."

"Just don't embarrass me and use the binoculars."

"Do you think Edwards is our guy?"

"The answer's 'E.' Insufficient data to tell." Bones
peeled the wrapper from a meat-loaf sandwich.

"How in hell can you relax on a surveillance?"

"I've worked a lot of them."

"How much time you got on, Bones?"

"Eighteen years."

"Boy, I'm the rookie. The boss has twenty-eight.
Shea's got sixteen. Ten for me. I'll never make it."

"You'll make it if you get married and quit fuckin'
yourself to death."

Speedy pointed to a second brown paper bag next to
Bones. "You brought two lunches?"

"That's dog food."

"Dog food?"

"Always bring dog food on a job like this. Dowling taught me that. Sometimes a car tail turns into a foot tail. And a foot tail ends up in backyards and next to garages and under windows and you walk smack into a big shepherd snarling at you. You'll wish you'd brought him dinner."

Speedy's eyes followed a blond woman wearing shorts. "I sure learn a lot from that guy. From all of you. When I listen."

"He makes us better cops. Like this street-scramble thing, to confuse Edwards in case he's listening on a scanner." Speedy studied the piece of paper on his lap. "I've about got it memorized. If we mean 'north,' we say 'west.' And if we mean 'south' we say 'east.'"

"You got it. And remember, instead of the six main streets in this part of town, we're using Grand and Garnet and those other four. If Edwards is listening he figures it's a surveillance out in the beach area."

"He'll never shake this tail, Bones. I guarantee it."

At ten minutes to midnight, Dowling drained the last of his coffee from the thermos. "We can't come back from behind anymore, Larry. Balanced offense but not many points. Not like Air Coryell days. We play the next two at home. Maybe—"

"*He's northbound Ingraham,*" Shea shouted, starting the engine.

Dowling groped for the microphone. "*El jefe* to Mexico. He left the nest. Northbound Ingraham and we got him. Go a block west and parallel us."

Shea maneuvered the car into the traffic lane so that two cars separated them and Edwards's truck. "He's catching the green at Garnet and ... turning *west*. Coming your way, Mexico. Let me know when you have the eyeball, then take him."

When the other car acknowledged the message, Shea raced to another street paralleling Edwards and turned in the same direction.

"We're on him from a block back," Bones advised. "He's still going west. Passing Fanuel ... passing Dawes ... passing Cass ... *No.* He's turning south on

Cass. *No*. He straightened out again, still going west.
Aw . . . I don't know what he's doing."

Shea reached forty-five miles per hour trying to stay
even.

"He's the first car stopped for the red light at Mission
Boulevard," Bones called. "We're still a block back.
There's four cars between us and—*He ran the goddamn
light*. Can you pick him up? It'll be obvious if we run
the light behind him."

Shea cut sharply to the left, swerving to avoid a truck
coming onto the street from an alley.

"Forgot it, *el jefe*. He's history," Bones blared into
the radio. "He turned left after he ran the light. When
we looked down the street he was gone."

Dowling triggered the key on the mike. "OK. Back
off. He's hinky. Forget him and get out of sight."

"10-4, *el jefe*. He just vanished. Now there's only us
and one car coming our way and . . . aw, hell. It's him.
He just passed us going the other way."

"Get the hell out of there and meet us at Balboa and
Genesee," Dowling ordered.

When they were parked next to each other in front of
a liquor store, Dowling asked, "Are you sure that was
him, and not another pickup, that came back at you?"

"It was him, boss." Bones sighed. "Speedy ducked
down in the seat, and I got a look at him. The prick
waved at us and smiled."

Dowling threw his notebook against the dashboard
and walked away from the car. He returned with a six
pack of Budweiser.

"Everybody shut up and suck on your beer. I want to
reconstruct this." Dowling drank half of the can on his
first pull before placing it between his legs. Finally, he
said, "Were you ever closer than a block to him when
you were going the same direction, Bones?"

"No."

"There were always cars between you and him?"

"Always."

"Shea and I were only on him for two blocks. And

there were always cars between us.'' He took another drink. "He didn't make us tonight.''

"But why drive like that if he didn't make us?'' Speedy asked.

"I worked a bookmaker in vice who drove like that going to get a loaf of bread,'' Dowling told them. "He drove like that everywhere he went. It was his routine. Like we have our routines at crime scenes. To stay sharp. Edwards had his reasons. He didn't want anybody following him. But he didn't make us.''

"But he waved at Bones,'' Speedy said.

"He probably waved at every car he passed on the way back. Figured if it was a cop he'd screw over their mind.''

"Where are we, Sarge?'' Shea asked. They all looked at him.

Dowling shook his head. "He's too tough to tail. But why is he driving like that? Is he into dope? Gambling? Is he our suspect?'' He put an empty can into the large bag. "I don't know. And I don't know what to do.''

✹ Eighteen

Two days later, pacing the hallway outside of the squad room, Dowling was wasting time fretting about California's no-wiretap ruling. The most populous state in the Union, with the most crime and . . . A New York cop would have had a court-authorized tap on every phone that Cliff Edwards came near and would have heard *something*. Something that would tell him, "Is he or isn't he?" It was one thing having a suspect you *knew* was working you over and it couldn't be proved. It was quite another to wear a collar of question marks around your neck.

When he returned from the men's room he was surprised and happy to see Kewpie Clemons swiveling in his chair behind the desk.

"Make yourself right at home, you old goat," Dowling said. They hugged each other, and Dowling waved him back to the swivel, seating himself in a hard-backed visitor's chair.

"Thought I'd see what it's like where the air is rare," the other man said. Pretending awe, he looked around the squad room. Then he stared at Dowling. "I don't know what to say about Helene, except I'm sorry." He sighed. "I was at the river when it happened. Didn't know about it till after . . . after the services and all."

"I know," Dowling said. "I got your card. It meant a lot." He cupped his hands behind his head. "You're

186

a long way from Northern Division, Kewpie. What's going on?''

''First time in over a year I've been downtown. But here's what's going on, Vince. We threw a couple of guys in jail last night. I wanted to tell you about them.''

Dowling leaned forward.

''We got a fight call. At the Marine Room, of all places. If we get a call there it's usually about a stolen Rolls or Mercedes. Anyway, a couple of guys are shit-faced, and challenging everybody in the joint, and the big guy does a job on the bartender, who's trying to keep the cops from being called.''

Kewpie Clemons ran his hand through graying hair. ''Right away we see these guys aren't La Jolla, Vince. And the big guy was a real shagnasty. We had to thump him. Once we got there the little guy just kinda stood aside till it was over; then he puts his hands behind his back, like he's used to it.''

Dowling nodded.

''So I figure it's just another ass-hole full of booze and full of fight. But they're carrying a couple of grand in their pockets. Driving a big, cherry-red Caddy.''

''Dope?'' Dowling asked.

''Maybe. But I covered the residential job in the Muir-lands. Where the guy stood on the old woman's back?''

''The Graham case.''

''Yeh. And I woke up this morning, thinking. Big guy. Mean. Lot of dough. In the area. And I'm still a cop, you know,'' he said, smiling.

''How big, Kewpie?''

''Six three, six four. Two and a quarter, anyway.''

Dowling reached for paper.

''Alvin and Jason Ketchell. Alvin's the big one. Wouldn't give us an address. Here's a copy of the arrest report. Felony assault. Figured that would hold them awhile. They're out of Wyoming, if you can believe their ID.''

''Jeez, I appreciate it, Kewpie. Gives me someone to look at. Stacy can tell the mayor we're not standing still.''

"Well, I don't take these jobs personally anymore,
Vince. But those old folks . . ." He got out of the chair.
"I'm history, partner."

"Hey. You taking the sergeant's test anymore, Kewpie?"

The other man shook his head. "When I said hello to
this place all those years ago, being a beat cop was good
enough for me. It still is, Vince."

"Do you still get worked up out there? All that crap."

"Nah. Not anymore. I let the young lions get excited.
They can learn to pop the bicarbs and antacids. You
know what I get upset about? When I drop a line in the
water and all those trout have gone to Harvard Business
School. See, if I let it get to me and have the big one,
a year from now they'll be saying, 'Kewpie who?' Nah.
All I want to do is to be a good guy, treat people right
and grab a paycheck and a pension." He waved. "This
time I really am outta here. Good luck, Vince. Watch
your ass."

The odor from within the trash-dumpster enclosure
was pungent. To Dowling, the location of the critique
was secondary. Having two to three of them a day was
the important thing. The quiet of the squad room area,
with chairs to sprawl out on and a blackboard to stare
at, was preferable, but it didn't make logistical sense that
evening, because he had scattered his team throughout
east San Diego. Actually, he had paired them with gang-
detail cops, and most of the day they had been one step
behind their quarry, Chongo Calderon. Two years before, Chongo had emptied his 9mm automatic from the
window of a moving car, missing his target but killing
a twelve-year-old boy on a bicycle a block away. They'd
slapped his name on a warrant while Chongo was heading for Ensenada, sixty miles south of the border. This
morning, a relative of the victim's had gotten wind of
Chongo's return.

So Dowling had opted to hold the meeting at the rear
of a convenience store, and they stood in the early-
evening dark with a dinner of soft drinks and beef jerky

from the plastic containers next to the cash register.

"Chongo will drop for us by accident," Dowling told them. "I gotta tell you boys about the Ketchell brothers."

When he finished, he held up four fingers, then touched the end of each of them with his thumb from the same hand as he ticked off each fact. "Number one, Alvin's a big, big guy with blue eyes. Number two, they got a mean streak. Number three, cash in their pocket. Number four, they're in La Jolla, near the Grahams'."

He made a face and moved away from the dumpster. "I know, Bones," he said, anticipating the objection. "Where do a couple of Wyoming cowboys learn about a safe in a house in San Diego?" He shrugged. "Step at a time, huh?"

"Let's get at 'em," Shea said between bites of a steaming rolled tacito that had been frozen a few minutes before.

"Here we go," Dowling muttered, holding his pen and notebook toward a light mounted on the wall of the building. "I'll run record checks. Bones, you and Shea get on their car. Speedy, you go through their jail property. Copy everything in their wallets and—" He interrupted himself. "Forget it, Speedy. I'll handle the jail stuff. You get back with the gang squad. Find Chongo. Everybody call in in two hours; let's see where we are."

They were walking to their cars when Speedy said, "Hey, Sarge. Where did that uniform guy get the name 'Kewpie'?"

"He and I were patrol partners in the sixties," Dowling said. The others closed in next to Dowling's car. "We got a disturbance call about a gin mill at Thirtieth and Adams. Soon as we took a step inside we were looking at the disturbance. An old blister with a foul mouth perched on a barstool. Jeez, she could cuss." He smiled at the memory. "So Clemons—Stanley Clemons, it is—he figures we'll tell her to pipe down and we'll go back in service. He's just opening his mouth, when she looks us over, points at me and says, 'You look old enough to be a cop.' She draws a bead on Clemons, says, 'And you, you look like a fucking Kewpie doll.' " Dowling stopped while his detectives laughed. "So he's been Kewpie Clemons to the whole department since."

"What'd you do with her, Sarge?" Speedy asked.

"Well, that's the hell of it. She's gotta go to jail for drunk and disorderly, and we tell her to get off the stool, and she says, 'Go piss up a rope.' So I look at Clemons and he looks at me and we each put an arm under her shoulder and jerk her off the goddamn stool and head for the door. We take about five, six steps and stop, cause she's rockin' between us like a backyard swing set. We look down. She hasn't got any legs."

Nobody could stop laughing for a few minutes, until Bones got a sentence out. "So what did you do with her?"

"We put her in jail."

"No, you didn't," they all said.

"Well, what else could we do? We couldn't take her back in there. And she wouldn't tell us where she lived. What the hell were we supposed to do? Leave her on a bus bench?"

A few hours later, Dowling sat at his desk, watching the hands of the clock close in on midnight. Bones and Shea had located the Ketchell brothers' car in the parking lot of the Marine Room. A big, flashy Cadillac with Utah registration and a zipped-up satchel on the back seat.

"The only thing we could see from the outside was the satchel," Bones had told Dowling over the phone. "Since it would have been an illegal search, we called a tow rig and made a police impound. Utah says it's registered to Jason Ketchell, but they can't get us details on the sale until morning."

Dowling had sent them home, and lingered over the list of jail property he had compiled. Big Alvin Ketchell had no wallet, and had been booked wearing expensive-looking cowboy dress wear and a pair of red boots. Jason had been wearing a navy blue suit with faint pinstripes and black cowboy boots. They had twenty-eight hundred dollars and change between them.

Jason's wallet interested Dowling, though there was little in it. A Wyoming driver's license, a slip of paper with a telephone number on it and a motel receipt. He played with the receipt, dated July 10, from the San Diego Hilton on Interstate 5. From hotel security he learned they had checked out on July 14, after paying cash on a day-to-day basis.

July 10 was exactly thirty days before the series had started, at the Reuben E. Lee restaurant. Was there a sawed-off shotgun in the trunk of the Cadillac? Where had they been staying when Kewpie Clemons had pinched them? Was there a motel key in the car? What was in the satchel? Who the hell were these guys?

Dowling had made a cursory telephone call to the state police in Cheyenne and learned of a number of misdemeanor arrests by the Laramie County Sheriff's Department. A felony detention in Casper during May stimulated him, and he vowed to pursue it in the morning.

When Speedy notified him that Chongo Calderon was in UCSD Medical Center with internal injuries and a police guard, Dowling headed home.

"He spun out, Sarge, and took the telephone pole head on after going full fuckin' circle. He wasn't as good a driver as the patrol officer chasing him."

"You're talking to the right man if you want to know something about the Ketchell boys," Hoss Wilkie said into the telephone. "They were in knee pants when I was a young deputy, and we kinda wore each other out."

"Are they bad actors?" Dowling asked.

"Well, now, Alvin, he grew up mean. We used to kick his ass on Saturday nights and throw him in the pokey for fightin' and drinkin'. And Alvin didn't care who he'd fight. Kick lady folks around, if he took a notion."

"How about Jason?"

"Now, Jason. I always figured if it wasn't for Alvin, ol' Jason'd be sitting at a workbench somewhere, figuring out what makes one of those computers tick. He's got that kind of mind if you talk to him long enough. Sometimes I figure Alvin's responsible for 'em both going wrong, and other times I figure it's the other way around. Beats hell out of me, Sarge. But it's sorta like Alvin's carrying some kind of magnet and ol' Jason just comes humming on in. But what it comes down to is they're just a couple of thieves."

"Do you know about this arrest in Casper for armed robbery?" Dowling asked. "That's in another county, isn't it?"

"Yes to both. We got a cozy state here, Sarge. They stuck up a rancher's house and made a pretty good haul, but the law couldn't prove it."

"How do you know they did it, Hoss?"

"Well, there just wasn't anybody else around there *to* do it."

"What was the M.O.?"

"Well, Alvin put a stocking over his face and put a shotgun to the old boy and tied him up with some drapery cord and cleaned him out."

"What'd they get?"

"A lot of cash. The old boy won't say exactly how much, 'cept he'll say it's over ten grand. Hell, could be fifty grand."

"Why won't he tell you?"

"Don't know. Could be he's running scared of the IRS or he just plain don't want any other crooks to get wind of it."

"So they just beat you on it?" Dowling asked.

"Well, yes and no. Thing is, in Wyoming we either lock 'em up or run 'em outta the state. See, we don't have the same-type problems you city fellas have. We don't have to keep lookin' at boys we don't like."

They talked for half an hour longer, and Dowling filled yellow sheets as he listened.

"You're ever up our way, Sarge, you stop on in and we'll have a couple and talk shop. Meanwhile, you ever need anything in Wyoming you tell those sheriffs you're a pal of Hoss Wilkie. You hear?''

An hour later, after filling out a request slip, Dowling and Speedy Montoya checked their sidearms in the gun locker at the county jail on West C Street.

"How come you're starting with Jason, Sarge? You told me always start with the dumb one."

"The dumb one is talking to a lawyer right now. They haven't appointed one for Jason yet." They sat on a bench in the narrow hallway near the interview rooms. Indistinguishable commands from booking deputies echoed from a hundred feet away, and a procession of trustees paraded denim-clad prisoners to and from the rooms.

"What brings you to San Diego, Jason?" Dowling asked, after he had introduced himself and Speedy and received a Miranda waiver.

"The good weather, Lieutenant. And all those TV shows about beaches and . . . what do you call 'em, bikinis.''

He was thirty years old, and short and very slight. His black hair was parted and slicked down on a white forehead above blue eyes. A pair of eyeglasses protruded from his jacket pocket.

"Hard to believe inmates can't smoke in your jailhouse, Lieutenant."

"I'm a sergeant, and we're pretty clean livers here, Jason."

"Where else have you had your fingers in the ink?" Speedy asked.

"Back home, is all."

"What for?" Speedy said.

"Oh, drinking and fighting and a little stealing up in Cody once. Broke into a house and took some jewelry and stuff."

"Who was in the house when you went in?" Speedy asked.

"Nobody." He acted surprised. "They was all at rodeo."

"Tell us about the bust in Casper," Dowling said.

"Casper?"

"Yeh. The armed job of a house."

"Oh, that was a misunderstanding, Lieutenant. A bad misunderstanding. A case of mistaken identity, is all."

"What hotel are you checked into now?" Dowling said.

Jason Ketchell smiled. "I think I'll pass on that one." He looked at Dowling. "I'm a very private person."

"What would Hoss Wilkie do if you told him a whopper like that?" Dowling asked.

"Hoss Wilkie? Ain't he died of meanness yet?"

Speedy turned a page in his notebook and said, "Where did you come up with the thirty grand to buy the Caddy in Salt Lake City?"

"I won it shooting dice. Do you shoot dice, Lieutenant?"

"I don't know anything about gambling," Dowling said.

"Well, that's how I make my dough. Get into a backroom game and hustle 'em."

"You must know all the angles," Dowling said. "All the odds."

"I do, I do. That's the secret."

Dowling turned sideways in his chair and crossed his legs. "Tell me, Jason. How many ways to make a seven?

"Ah . . . I'd, ah . . . I'd have to figure it."

"You may have a lot of time to do that," Dowling said, getting up and starting for the door. "Thanks for the company."

"Hey! You can't talk to Alvin, you know. He's got a lawyer."

When they were out on the sidewalk, Speedy took a breath of fresh air and said, "He only told us what he knew we'd find out anyway."

They waited as the red, German-made, electrically powered Tijuana Trolley passed them, then crossed to the parking lot on Union Street.

"You do know craps, huh, Sarge?"

"I never had the dough to play much, but the game—

and the odds—interest me.'' He turned to Speedy when they were in the car. "Listen carefully, now. Tell Bones and Shea to start packing. Tell them to call Hoss Wilkie and let him know they're coming. That son of a bitch doesn't want us nosing around his hotel room, and he's got a reason for it.'' He paused. "Like Stacy says, money's no object on this one. Bones and Shea are going to have to rework that Casper job with them, based on what we know about our series.'' He got out of the car and walked around to the driver's side. "I'm going in and take a look at Alvin; then I'm going to the D.A.'s office. I want you to—''

"I know, Sarge. Phone security in every good hotel in town and find out where they're hanging their hat. I'll get 'em.''

"And be sure you check every—''

"Every last name that starts with "K," because crooks using an alias like to use the same letter, and check anybody who lists a Wyoming address and . . . don't worry. They're mine.''

A few minutes later, Dowling sat at the interview-room table and watched Alvin Ketchell being ushered in.

"You can't talk to me. I got a lawyer,'' the big man said.

"You're still a prisoner, so I can *look* at you. Sit the fuck down,'' Dowling ordered.

Alvin did, slowly, looking to Dowling like a man who had never won an argument with a Wyoming jailer. At least six three, and every bit of two forty or two hundred fifty pounds. With eyes as blue as his brother's and wild, bushy hair. The face was crude. Jack Palance on a bad day, Dowling told himself.

For the first few minutes, Alvin Ketchell tried to stare Dowling down. When he tired of it, he looked away and fidgeted. Dowling's mind was racing, and he tried to slow it down.

Was he looking at his killer? It made more sense than an ex-cop orchestrating a violence binge to get simple revenge. There was nothing distinctive about the voice.

A lineup could be held. He could put Alvin in a row of six pug-uglies and make them all say the same words: "Don't ever move like that again, old man, or I'll blow your fuckin' head off."

He could clad them all in ski masks and dungaree jackets while they were giving their speech. "Rings and wristwatches, too. Hurry up."

But Dowling's lineup history was checkered. More than once, a lineup subject who had already confessed was ignored by the witnesses; and some dumb bastard in jail for nonsupport when the murder went down had been singled out as the killer. He decided to forget the lineup. For now.

But it reminded him. Did Alvin freely toss the word *motherfucker* around? He would check with Hoss Wilkie about that.

"Put your hands in the middle of the table," Dowling said. They were big and meaty and swollen, with cuts collected at the Marine Room forty hours before. But were they the hands that had pulled the trigger and caused Dominic Bonelli to repaint his wall? Were they the hands that had ripped the shorts and panties off the crying teenaged girl in Rancho Santa Fe and traumatized so many decent people over the past two months?

And if they were, how *did* the brothers know about the safes? True, they'd hit town a month before the jobs had begun, but that was moving pretty fast. And Jason would have had to be the composer, because the hulk sitting across from him couldn't have poured piss out of a boot if the instructions were written on the heel.

Dowling had hoped to get a gut feeling, but he hadn't. The answer was still "E," insufficient data. But if it was the Ketchells who'd done the jobs, at least he wasn't chasing a ghost anymore.

The search-warrant affidavit was going to be a little thin, which was why Dowling had coerced Melissa Hamilton into drafting it for him. She had been preparing for a preliminary hearing, and peered at him from behind a stack of paper on her desk.

"Come on, Dowling, the duty deputy can handle that."

"Not as good as you can handle it, Melissa. You're the best."

"Bullshit."

"It's the mayor's-brother series."

"I'm a prosecutor, not a politico. Get somebody else."

"A teenaged girl got raped in front of her mother and father."

Three hours later, it was done, and Dowling and Melissa Hamilton sat in the chambers of municipal court judge Alton Freeman, who sucked on an unlighted pipe and sipped coffee from a red-and-white Stanford mug.

"Well, what are you trying to slip by me this time?" Freeman asked as he started to silently peruse the four-page document on legal-sized paper. Dowling read it to himself as they waited.

Personally appeared before me on this 12th day of October, 1993, the affiant, Vincent Dowling, a peace officer, who on oath, makes complaint, and deposes and says that he has and there is probable cause to . . . search of a vehicle described as a Cadillac . . . a gray canvas satchel on the seat . . . the following property, to wit: a sawed-off shotgun, a ski mask or masks, strands of rope or cord, a motel key or evidence of motel registration . . . things which consist of evidence which tend to show that a felony has been committed, or tend to show that a particular person has committed a felony.

Your affiant says that the facts in support of the issuance of the search warrant are as follows:

Your affiant is investigating a series of crimes that commenced on August 9th of this year, the method of operation of which is . . .

Your affiant was advised on October 10th by police patrol officer Stanley "Kewpie" Clemons that Clemons arrested . . .

Your affiant has noted the size of Alvin Ketchell, and has been advised by Laramie County Deputy Sheriff Hoss Wilkie of a propensity for violence over . . .

Your affiant examined the wallet of Jason Ketchell and found a telephone number. The subscriber of that phone number, Ms. Irma Blankenship, told your affiant she met Jason and Alvin Ketchell in a country-western bar in San Diego on Sunday, September 23rd, one day following an armed robbery and shooting at the Cafe Del Rey Moro. Ms. Blankenship advised affiant that Jason Ketchell displayed "thousands of dollars" and told her he was an investment banker. On this date, after waiving Miranda rights, Jason Ketchell advised your affiant he paid cash for a new Cadillac in Salt Lake City with gambling profits. Jason Ketchell bragged that he knew "all the odds" related to dice games. When your affiant asked Ketchell the number of possible combinations in which a "7" could be rolled, Ketchell could not answer.

Your affiant commenced the actual physical mechanics of preparing this affidavit and attached search warrant today . . . locating and consulting with Deputy District Attorney Melissa C. Hamilton . . . based on the aforementioned information, facts and . . .

Your affiant prays that a search warrant be issued . . . for the seizure of said property . . . same be brought before this magistrate . . . pursuant to Section 1536 of the Penal Code.

Dowling watched anxiously while Freeman scanned the pages a second time.

"Okay. You've brought me better ones, Sergeant, but I'll give you your warrant. It's here," Freeman said finally.

Dowling and Melissa Hamilton were at the door when

Freeman said, "Hey, affiant. The answer is eleven to one. What's the question?"

Dowling, who had turned to listen, started for the door again and answered over his shoulder,

"What are the odds of getting a four or a ten on one roll? Jeez, Judge. A first-year law student would know that one."

"*Nothing!* Fucking *nothing!*" Dowling screamed, throwing the satchel against the wire fence of the police impound area. "Empty satchel. Empty trunk. Nothing in the . . . Jesus!" He lit a cigarette and inhaled twice before he spoke again. "I don't know, Speedy. If you'd told me—"

"Are you okay, Sarge?" Two uniformed officers were watching behind the enclosure.

"Oh, yeah. I'm just great," Dowling said.

Exactly two hours later he screamed again when Speedy phoned him at his desk.

"The cowboys made bail, Sarge. They flat bailed."

🎞 Nineteen

Dowling slammed his car door shut, then stood in the parking lot looking at the 320-foot-high observation needle pointed into the night sky. He did not have the faintest idea of what he would do when he walked through the gate of Sea World. The telephone call had been only a few seconds old when he felt the apprehension setting in.

"Another one . . . ski mask . . . lot of money . . ."

He had dressed slowly, then sat in the car for ten minutes before starting it. Instead of driving straight to the aquatic amusement park, he veered through the rolling streets of Point Loma. If he stalled long enough, Speedy would beat him there and Speedy would know what to do. Dowling had done it for thirteen years, and he just did not want to do it anymore.

He had been careless again, and it was costing. He should have asked the jail to alert him if his suspects were being bailed. After all, the process took hours, not minutes. Plenty of time to set up a surveillance on them. Plenty of time to find out just who was putting up the dough. Plenty of time to . . . the steering wheel vibrated when he pounded it. This was *great*. The goddamn cowboys were who knows where. Shea and Bones were in Wyoming, wiping barbecue sauce off their chins, and he and Speedy Montoya were staring at job number seven. Shorthanded and helpless and knowing for certain that job number seven was going to fan the media fires and light this town up but good. This wasn't some fancy restaurant or affluent residence. He wished it were. This was goddamn Sea World, and goddamn Dan Rather and Peter Jennings and Tom Brokaw knew all about Sea World.

"He had to have been hiding right next to our building, or else the girl closing up the concession stand would have seen him walking in here." Dowling stood behind Speedy and forced himself to listen. The night manager mopped his face with a handkerchief as he spoke, but beads of perspiration escaped and ran down fleshy jowls onto his collar. His bald head shone from the floodlight on the roof.

"I know you've been over it once with the uniformed officers," Speedy said, "but I need to hear it again. Please."

The manager stuffed himself into a wicker chair and closed his eyes.

"All right, Detective. We use this office as our counting room. All the monies come in from the concession stands, too. The park had closed." He loosened his tie and dabbed at his Adam's apple with his handkerchief. "I was standing by the desk. I can show you." He started to get up.

"Not just yet," Speedy said. "The lab is looking for evidence in there."

"Oh, Lord. Where was I?"

"Standing by the desk."

"I was by the desk and in he came, Detective. A huge man with a terrible-looking ski mask. He started yelling for everyone but me to get on the floor. I thought it was some kind of joke. Then he took the guard's gun from him. Right out of his holster. I'm a wreck. Where was I?"

"Security guard's gun."

"I still thought it could be a horrible joke. Then he pointed this tremendous gun or rifle, I don't know what it was. Pointed it right at me and made me open my mouth. He put it right in my mouth and said, 'Is everybody in here that's coming in here?' I couldn't talk. I nodded. He said, 'If you're lying to me, motherfucker, I'll blow your head off.' I almost passed out. He took my car keys from my pocket. Then he made me open the safe. Tied all of us up with adhesive tape. Then he was gone."

The security guard stood a few yards away. His shoulders slumped and his head was down. Dowling guessed he was in his sixties. Reading the nameplate on the uniform shirt, he said softly, "Don't feel bad about losing your gun, Mr. Casper. You were overmatched."

Fear was still in the guard's eyes when he looked up. "I never ran into anything like this on a job, Sergeant. I'm retired Navy. I just didn't know what to do."

"I'm glad nobody got hurt. Did you, by chance, see his eyes?" Dowling's hands were in his pockets.

"Oh, yes. That's something I was trained to do. Looked at everything I could. His eyes were blue. No doubt about it." The guard put his hand in the empty holster. "I wish my wife didn't have to learn about this. She worries so much anyway."

They worked until 2.00 A.M. Speedy's young eyes had spied the guard's gun near a fence in the parking lot. Dowling had expected them to toss it. They hadn't made any mistakes yet.

"A different twist on the phone call," Speedy told him. "Alvin made a call out. Dialed seven digits. Local call. The old guard counted them. Jason was probably at a phone booth in the sports-arena area."

The manager's car was recovered by patrol, in a hotel parking lot a mile away. The take would be calculated in the morning, but Dowling knew it would be substantial. Sea World admission cost over twenty dollars per person. The retail value of jewelry stolen from the residences was in the neighborhood of a quarter of a million dollars. Dowling was confident that the loot was either cooling off or being fenced out of town.

If they weren't moving the stuff, where in the devil were they keeping it? In a motel room? In a safe-deposit box? Nothing sounded good to him. And if they were taking it out of town, where was it going? Not to Wyoming. Too far away. And Hoss Wilkie knew everything that went on in those parts.

But those answers were all "nice to know," and what Dowling needed now was to put his hands on Jason and Alvin. Once he did that the rest would follow. He'd make it follow.

"I found the Ketchell boys, Sarge," Speedy declared the next morning, saying the words on the move toward Dowling's desk. Dowling looked up, startled. The look told him he wasn't being kidded. In front of him was a full "to do" list, every item tailored to start the painstaking task of locating the Ketchells in a county of over two million people. Only five hours before, he had sent Speedy home, with an admonition to sleep four hours and return prepared to work around the clock.

"Where and how and . . . you got that look on your face," Dowling said.

"I stepped out of the shower, grabbed my coffee mug and got thinking about what kind of day we were looking at. Then, while I was making myself pretty, I remembered something an old red-haired homicide sergeant taught me when I first came over here."

"Where the fuck are they, Speedy?"

"The old red-haired sergeant said, 'Before you spend time turning this town upside down for anybody, always—"

Dowling interrupted him. He looked forlorn. "Always check the jailhouse."

"Yeah. I called from home, Sarge. They're in there. Got booked about an hour before our Sea World job went down. They're in for—"

Dowling interrupted a second time. "They're in for drinking and fighting." He sighed, wadded the "to do" list into a crude ball and threw it in the vicinity of the wastebasket.

"Yeah. They'd only been out about six hours. Tried to drink up all the booze in Mission Valley. Jason said something to some guy's girl friend. The guy gets in Jason's face. Then Alvin turns the guy upside down and kicks him in the head, and . . . Anyway, a lady police officer ended up parting Alvin's hair with her night-stick.''

Dowling was facing the wall, rocking in his chair.

"They must have gone back to their hotel after they got out," Speedy continued. " 'Cause they had credit cards on them that patrol ran through NCIC. Ties 'em into burglaries up the coast.''

Dowling nodded, still facing the wall.

"I was so sure," Speedy said. "It looked so good."

"Maybe we wanted it too badly," Dowling said finally. "Call Hoss Wilkie. Tell him to put Bones and Speedy on a plane. You go get some breakfast. I'm gonna go jump off the fuckin' Coronado Bridge.''

Dowling didn't jump off the bridge. Not quite. He did corner Tom Stacy for the better part of an hour, however. "I'm going crazy, Tom. Just going crazy." He shook his head. "And I don't ever want to see another cowboy. None of the loot is . . . ah, I've been over this a hundred times.''

"The case will go down for you, Vince. If you work it hard enough and catch a break. If that loot was being shown around locally, word would have made its way to the streets. Somebody's informant would have picked up talk.''

An informant was what Speedy Montoya wanted to talk to Dowling about when he beckoned him into the hallway a few minutes after Dowling had left Stacy's office. Dowling had seen the woman Speedy had ushered in moments before. She was young, with flowing brown hair that reached the shoulders. He had not gotten a good look at her face, but had paid attention to the tight white blouse with buttons straining over her breasts. She wore clean faded Levis and leather high heels.

"She's the one, Sarge. She's just the one." Speedy rubbed his palms together. "What do you think?''

"I'm sure she has a world of talent, Speedy. What are you and I doing out in the hallway?''

His voice lowered. "Sarge. She's one of my sources." He said it very deliberately.

"Marvelous." Dowling leaned over for a cold drink from the water cooler.

"Sarge. Don't you see? Cliff Edwards."

"What's he got to do with her?"

"Nothing yet." Speedy looked over his shoulder and lowered his voice. "This one is going to get us the answers on Edwards. She's going to get next to him, and we'll know more about him than his mama. All we have to do is—"

"Speedy. Listen carefully. Cliff Edwards is not a suspect. We don't duke informants onto people who aren't bona fide suspects."

"Sarge. Remember the case last year when I first came to homicide? The cabbie in the alley. She's the one who turned it. She picked up some talk and told a source of mine, and we went from there. Remember?"

Dowling remembered. He was not slipping quite that badly. They had obtained the knife and confession from a skinny black man the day after the murder.

He put his arm around Speedy. "You get an attaboy for thinking big, but Cliff Edwards hasn't shown us anything."

"He hasn't shown us anything because we can't look at him," Speedy protested. "We can't tail the son of a bitch. We don't know what our crooks look like. We don't know where our loot is going. We've eliminated the cowboys. We can—"

"No, we have to—"

"Please, Sarge, listen to me." Speedy grabbed Dowling's arm. "You told me once, said, 'Speedy, there are three kinds of cops. Those who make things happen. Those who watch things happen. And those who say, "What happened?" ' We've been watching things happen. I got it figured."

Dowling saw the intensity in the brown eyes. Speedy's handsome face was drawn. "Go on."

"The timing is perfect. The job went down last night. It's twelve noon now. We move her into the pool hall with a wire on her, and who knows what we'll hear? Who knows what she'll see? Edwards could be bragging about the job. Or flashing big bucks. Or meeting someone who turns out to be his crime partner. This is the time, Sarge. When Bones and Shea step off that plane, we may have something good to tell 'em. This is the *time*.''

"Who is she?" Dowling asked wearily.

"She works in a photo shop on West Broadway. She's been around. If Edwards doesn't talk to her in the pool hall, she'll get him under the covers and fuck his eyeballs out. He'll talk to her, Sarge."

Dowling hushed him when two women officers passed and looked at them strangely. "Any informant that ever lived can roll over on you. And pretty girl informants have been known to fall in love. Especially with big, good-looking blond cops and ex-cops."

"Not this one, Sarge. Give her a try. One shot."

Dowling took a deep breath. "I'll talk to her. In the interrogation room."

"Where's home, Cookie?" Dowling asked, through the aroma of cheap cologne. She had "downtown" written all over the pretty face. Large feathered earrings swung each time her head moved.

"Bowling Green, Ohio. Twenty-five miles from Toledo."

"Does everybody in Bowling Green have dimples?" She blushed and did not answer.

"Family?" Dowling asked.

"An All-American family. Daddy dear is a surgeon. Mommy dear teaches at the university."

"Brothers? Sisters?"

"Two brothers. One's in med school. One's a bum. My Phi Beta Kappa sister is going for her master's. You ask a lot of questions. This must be a pretty big caper."

"How old are you?"

"Twenty-three."

"How old?"

"Twenty-one. Almost."

"Why San Diego, kid?"

Speedy lit a cigarette for her. She was full of confidence, and smiled at Dowling. "Oh, warm weather. And a long, long way from Bowling Green.'' She inhaled deeply and blew smoke to the side. ''As soon as I turned eighteen I jumped on a Greyhound. Got a waitress job. That didn't last long, because I couldn't carry more than two plates. Got into the escort service for a while. Money was good, but . . . I like it better pulling sailors off the sidewalk at the photo shop.''

''Tell the sarge about Mr. Bushes, Cookie,'' Speedy said.

''I don't know.'' She wrinkled her face.

''Naw. It's OK, come on.''

She tossed her head back and laughed. ''Oh, boy. He's the only customer I kept from the escort service. Once a week—God, tomorrow night's the night. Once a week I borrow a car. Drive to his house. Park directly in front. Always have to wear a dress. That's part of the rules. Turn out the lights and shut off the engine. Then I take my panties off and lay them on the seat. Get out of the car. Walk up to the door. Knock, knock, knock.'' She demonstrated with a closed fist. ''I know he won't answer. Turn around and head down the path to the sidewalk. When I'm just about to the end, he jumps out of the bushes and yells. Goes *Agggghhhgh*' . . . His face gets all screwed up. I walk to the car and drive away.''

''That's it?'' Dowling asked, laughing.

''That's it. Two days later I get a hundred-dollar bill in the mail. I've never met the guy.''

They talked for a while, then Dowling said, ''What has Speedy told you?''

''That I may be taking a look at a guy. That there's a buck in it.''

Dowling got up and motioned Speedy to the squad room. ''I'm reluctant, but what the hell. Go ahead and brief her.'' He looked at his wristwatch. ''Get a female detective to wire her. Let's get her in the pool hall by 2:00 P.M. I want to be home by 5:00 today.''

Dowling sat at a desk in a small real-estate office across the street and two doors down from Luckie's. The desk was next to a window and afforded him a view of the pool-hall entrance. The real-estate broker provided

Dowling with coffee and a dictating machine for special effects when Dowling explained they were targeting dope dealers on the sidewalks.

"It's a good feeling, being part of a police operation, Sergeant. You boys don't get paid enough, dangerous as your work is."

Feeling conspicuous, Dowling shuffled papers and pretended to glance at pamphlets as he trained his vision on Luckie's. The window he was looking out of bordered the sidewalk, and a passerby would occasionally nod hello. Speedy had briefed Cookie, then rushed off to testify in a preliminary hearing. Dowling wished someone else had been available to handle the cover.

The on-body recorder he had selected was self-contained, and the live conversation could not be monitored. They would have to listen to it later. Cookie had been instructed to meet Dowling at a large parking lot fifteen blocks away if she left Luckie's by herself. If Cliff Edwards was with her, she would phone Speedy at the first opportunity. To make her less conspicuous, they had arranged for a girl friend to enter with her. If and when Cookie signaled, the girl friend would leave alone.

Dowling was pessimistic about the chances for success. He had long been mindful of the inherent problems in police-informant relationships, and tended to minimize the use of informants. By necessity they were either criminals or people who lived on the fringes. As a whole, they were unreliable, and often committed crimes while in police "employ." It was time-consuming, tremendously time-consuming, to control and direct them. Often, it was like raising another child.

Dowling placed informants into three categories. The first type worked for cash on the old barrelhead, like Cookie. The information they supplied was suspect, because they were anxious to please and would embellish or distort the facts. Group two consisted of people who had been charged with a crime and were cooperating with the police in hopes of obtaining leniency from the justice system. "Working off a beef," they said on the streets. Dowling saw little difference between them and the first group.

It was the third category that occasionally interested him. People who from time to time provided information because they liked a particular cop. They were not adverse to accepting money after the information was tested, but they did not walk around with their hand out. Some who refused payment felt they had the right to commit a "free crime." He did not have much of a quarrel with that concept, depending on the crimes involved. He had harped once to a young prosecutor, "If a guy solves a murder for us and gets grabbed later for a burglary, we have to go to bat for him. The system owes the guy something."

He drained his coffee cup and noted that Cookie had been in the pool hall for an hour. A few minutes later he saw the girl friend leave by herself. A twinge of excitement shot through him. There was a chance that Cookie was at least talking to Cliff Edwards.

Another type of twinge had startled him earlier. Cookie's friend had worn a peasant blouse, and twice she had leaned over, exposing flesh and cleavage. He had felt a stirring in his groin, and realized he had not thought of sex since Helene's death. Their sex life had diminished in frequency and quality in the final two years of their marriage. He was unable to remember the last time they had made love. He was trying to pinpoint it when he saw Cookie walk out of Luckie's alone and walk to the bus stop on the corner. Dowling headed for the meeting place.

"I got it. I got it," she said, sliding into the car seat, next to Dowling. They were parked in a row of cars behind a discount drug store. "It must be him. Wait until you hear what he said about yesterday." She smiled broadly, and white teeth flashed. "I think this tape is worth a hundred bucks, not just fifty, Sarge."

"What did he say? Give me the tape." He held out his hand.

"I like this kind of work. It's a lot more fun than being in Ohio. And he's cute. Too bad he's a robber."

"What did he say?" Dowling asked again, putting the cassette into the recorder. He closed the window halfway, reducing outside noise and aromas from a drive-through doughnut shop.

"He said he'd taken a big chance yesterday to make a lot of money. He was talking quietly when he said it, Sergeant, and looking all around. Tomorrow night he wants me to go out with him. Will you arrest him before then?"

"Let's listen to the tape, Cookie." They both lit cigarettes. He was stimulated.

"I'm pretty sure he likes me. He looked me over real good. I flashed some boob for him, and his eyes got big." She smiled again and wiggled her shoulders. "He said hello to us a little while after we got there. We were goofing around, trying to play a game. I made sure he heard me tell Rusty to take a hike, so he figured I was interested in him, too. Pretty good, huh?"

"Cookie." He had his finger on the control. "Let's listen to the tape."

He pressed the button and picked up the sound of balls clicking on table tops. A television set droned in the background, and he heard the low hum of men's voices. There was some meaningless conversation between Cookie and Rusty, until Dowling recognized the voice of Cliff Edwards.

"Hey, pretty girls. How come we're so lucky today?"

"Time on our hands, mister." It was Cookie talking. "We just want to play by ourselves. If you don't mind."

"This isn't any hustle. I'm the boss here. What's your name, Red?"

"Rusty."

"Mine's Cliff. How about you, Time On Your Hands?"

"What does it **matter**?" **Dowling** heard Cookie say sharply.

"Aw, come on. I just try to get to know the customers. I won't bite. What's your name? I'll close my eyes while you tell me."

Dowling heard her laugh. "Cookie. That's my name.

And if you say anything about looking good enough to eat I'll whack you with this . . . what is it, anyway?''

Cliff Edwards laughed. ''You're OK; shoot the next game on the house.''

Dowling wet his lips and lit another Camel with the one he had been smoking.

''He leaves for quite a while, Sergeant. Then he comes back and leaves again.''

They listened for thirty more minutes; then Dowling heard Cookie say, ''You look tired, Rusty. I think I'll hang around awhile. Call me tomorrow.''

''Where you from, Time On Your Hands?'' Dowling heard Edwards say.

''What difference does it make? Damn. How come that one didn't go in? This is a rip-off.''

They talked for several more minutes; then Edwards left.

''Next time, I think,'' Cookie told Dowling. ''When he comes back out. Listen good.''

''How about you and I going out sometime? Like tomorrow night,'' Edwards asked.

''I don't think so.''

''Ah, come on. You got to be a better date than you are a pool shooter. We could have some fun. How about it?''

''N-o.''

''Let's see. You're in love with some dippy white hat on an aircraft carrier. Promised him you'd be true blue.''

''White hat, my fanny. Look, pal. This town is full of guys like you. Trying to get in my pants for a hamburger and a beer. I don't need it, see. So you toddle off and run your business and I'll concentrate on getting this damn ball in the pocket.''

''You got an attitude, girl. This town isn't full of guys like me. I wasn't figuring on a hamburger and a beer. I was thinking about a nice quiet dinner at the Marine Room. That's in La Jolla. On the beach. Waves come right up to the window. Floodlights on the sand. Candles on the table flashing on beautiful faces like yours. Bottle of Chardonnay. How about it?''

There was a long pause before she answered. "I know
your type. Takes a girl out to a cool place the first date.
Then it all goes downhill. You run a pool hall, not a
bank."

"I make more dough than the rest of the chumps who
run pool halls."

"That's what they all say."

"Yeah. Well, I mean it. I make more dough because
I take chances."

"What kind of chances?"

Dowling held the recorder closer to his ear.

"Big chances. Like yesterday. Yesterday I took a
chance everybody else would be afraid to take. But I
took it. And it means big money, baby. Big money."
His voice got lower. "You stick around me. We'll have
some fun."

"We'll see. Maybe I'll drop by tomorrow."

"You do that. Drop on by tomorrow."

"He walks away then," Cookie told Dowling. "I shot
a few more balls, then split. Played it cool. Didn't even
wave good-bye to him." She looked pleased. "Worth
an extra fifty bucks, huh, Sarge? How do you like it?"

Dowling liked it fine. He had heard a lot of on-body
recordings where otherwise clever crooks had gotten
careless. The day before, his suspects had scored heavily
at Sea World. They'd collected big money. He wished
Speedy were there to share this moment. By God, 'get
robbery off my ass' had meant something after all.

Cliff Edwards would have known precisely how to
execute those jobs. Great pains had been taken. Then . . .
then he'd gotten careless, like so many of the rest. Taken
in by a pretty face. Dowling smiled to himself. Cookie
would drop by Luckie's again the next day, all right.
And the next day, and the day after that and . . . She
would probably have Edwards confessing it all on the
tape. At the very least, even if he was closemouthed
about the crimes, she would see evidence of preparation
for the next one. The chances were fair that she would
meet the guy with the ski mask. Maybe she wouldn't
know it was he, but Dowling and his team would know.

He was visualizing the mechanics of an arrest and was startled by the voice to his left, at the half-opened car window.

"Why, Sergeant Dowling. What a surprise running into you here."

Dowling didn't have to look up. He recognized the voice. For thirty minutes he had been listening to it. Closing his eyes for a split second, he fumbled for the "Off" button on the recorder. When he raised his head, Cliff Edwards was standing a few feet from the car. Legs apart. Hands on hips like a referee indicating an offside penalty. Dowling allowed himself a quick look at Cookie. Her mouth was wide open.

Edwards moved closer, so that his head was nearly in the car. Strands of his blond hair fluttered in the October breeze, and his forced grin was too forced.

"And look who's here with Sergeant Dowling. It's old Time On Her Hands. What a small world."

He looked at Dowling's lap. There had been no use trying to conceal the recording unit. Dowling could hardly look at him.

"I'm sure you don't know this, Sarge, but Time On Her Hands dropped into my pool hall. She's a hell of a player. Once she figured out which one was the cue ball, she shot a mean stick."

Dowling was feeling sick to his stomach.

"I'd have been here sooner, Sarge, but it took a while to follow that bus. Makes a lot of stops, you know."

He thought he might throw up.

"We had a swell talk. I told her all about what a big chance I took yesterday to make some money." Edwards reached into his shirt pocket and pulled out a large piece of paper. "Yesterday I ordered a big, oversized table, Sarge. Here's the invoice. Dated yesterday. Take a look at it, Sarge. Take a good look at it."

He summoned the strength to speak. "Okay, Edwards—"

"Oh, I'm not through yet. See, all the other chumps in the pool-hall business are too cheap to buy this big table. So I'm going to make big money with it, 'cause

I'll lure their customers to my joint. Yeah. I sure took a big chance yesterday, but it'll pay off. Smart. Huh, Sarge?''

Dowling leaned back in the seat and shook his head slowly. He tried to tell himself it was not happening.

"You sure went to a lot of trouble, Sarge. Somebody must have snitched to you about the pinochle game in the back room. Heck, I know I broke the law. We were playing penny a point. I should have known I couldn't outsmart you.''

Dowling was numb all over.

"Hey, honey. Get the police department to buy you a new blouse. Those top two buttons keep coming undone on that one.''

Cookie began to cry.

"You won't find any of my prints on those tits, Sarge. No, sir.'' Cliff Edwards suddenly stopped grinning. "You sent a little girl to do a big girl's job, Dowling. Better luck next time.''

Edwards vanished as quickly as he had appeared.

❦ Twenty

Dowling was in an emotional fog. Minutes after Cliff
Edwards had walked into the night, he'd still thought he
might lose his stomach's sour contents. Cookie had
sobbed and asked him questions, but he had not heard
them. Fumbling for bills in his jacket pocket, he'd
pointed her toward a taxi stand at the corner of the lot.
Then he'd headed for the security of home.

He could not have devised a worse predicament. Several times, he told himself he had experienced a bad
dream. He had not really eaten doughnuts in a cluttered
real-estate office and sat in an undercover car with an
ill-adjusted young woman from the Midwest and been
made a fool of.

He had been ripped to shreds by a kid in his twenties
who'd only had a cup of coffee with the same police
department Dowling had devoted his life to. Cliff Edwards had set him up like Dowling had set up so many
others. With planning and savvy and daring, and a sixth
sense about Cookie. Everything Cliff had told her could
have been presented to a jury, and Edwards would have
laughed his way out of the courtroom. Indeed, the case
never would have been issued, because the D.A. would
have laughed Dowling out of his office.

A few blocks from home, Dowling recalled how Edwards had managed his patrol beat. How he had utilized
intelligence and hard work to make felony arrests and
reduce crime, and how he'd roved the streets with his

green metal box, which contained the "Edwards Files," into which he'd placed the names of criminals and street people. Dowling wondered whether the ski-masked gunman had been selected from those files.

By the time he parked in front of his garage, it had all come together for him. He understood why the crime locations had been selected with a view toward preventing stakeouts, why different clothing was worn each time, why faces and hands were covered and why a phone call was received by the demented son of a bitch clutching the sawed-off shotgun. Cliff Edwards was lurking nearby, and he wanted to be sure his crime partner had not met with misfortune. The kind of misfortune that could cause Edwards to end up with his hands cuffed behind his back. Dowling was certain that Cliff Edwards was orchestrating the crime series.

He was reeling as he unlocked the back door and groped his way across the dark kitchen. Before he reached the light switch, his arm brushed against the handle of an empty frying pan, and it crashed to the floor from the stove top. He picked it up and hurled it against the wall, not seeing the chips of plaster floating to the tabletop. The front door opened as he entered the living room.

"Hi, Daddy. Good-bye, Daddy. Photo shop closes in fifteen minutes. Have to pick up a picture. An enlargement. Of my mother." She was heading for the hallway, toward her room.

"*Jenny.*" He yelled it, and she stopped in her tracks. "What in hell do you mean, 'my mother'? Why do you always say 'my mother'? Why don't you say 'Mother' or 'our mother' or 'Mom' or any other damn thing?"

"I don't know."

"What kind of answer is that?"

"I have to go, Daddy." She started toward her room again, but he intercepted her.

"Not until you answer my question."

"I just answered it."

"Oh, no, you didn't. You answered it like some mug

on the street answers me. Why don't you say 'Mom,'
like you used to?''

"Because . . ." She took a step backward. "Because
things aren't like they used to be.''

"And just what is that supposed to mean?'' he yelled.

"*Please*, Daddy. Let me by. I want to go by.'' She
tried to sidestep him, but he moved with her.

"You act like someone who cared a hell of a lot more
for your mother than your father, young lady.''

"Haven't you been listening to anything I've said in
the last nine months?''

Dowling stepped back. "That's good, Jenny. Now I
don't listen to my daughter, huh? That's real good.''

Tears formed in her dark eyes. "You were gone a lot,
Daddy.''

"I was gone a lot. Oh, that's really good. Go ahead
and air it all out, Jenny. Kick me when I'm down.''

"I'm not trying to kick—''

"I was gone, all right. I was out trying to make a
living. Getting rained on and spit on and hit with bricks.
Trying to put a couple of meals on that table right
there.'' He pounded on it three times. Jenny turned and
stepped toward the front door, but he grabbed her arm
and stopped her abruptly.

"No, no. You started this. Now you're going to hear
me out. Nobody wants to hear my side of it. They figure
they know it all. Figure they know everything.''

She was crying. "What is there to know, Daddy?''

"Go on and act innocent, Jenny. I know what you've
been thinking. I know what everybody's been thinking.
You and Matt and Stacy and Stephanie Mayfield . . .
goddamn her.''

"What are you talking about?''

"All the resident experts look at old Vincent Dowling
and call him an uncaring, coldhearted son of a bitch. I
bet they have big times when they get together to talk
about me. They think I didn't love her. Didn't love your
mother.''

"Matt said you loved her, but you loved your work
more.''

"Matt what?" He stepped toward her. "Loved my work more? Don't you ever say that again. I ought to slap your face across this room." Dowling brought back his right hand and swung the open palm toward her.

The arm stopped in midair when he was jerked forcibly backwards. Matt's face loomed over him. Matt held on with both hands, but Dowling shook himself loose and, in the same motion, hit Matt with his closed fist. Blood squirted from his son's split lip, and Dowling's forward motion carried them together against the wall. Jenny screamed, and raced to them, tried to pry them apart. Father and son lost their balance. Jenny fell to the floor with them. Dowling moved his head, because Jenny was screaming into his ear; then he saw blood roll down Matt's chin.

"I'm sorry," he cried. "Oh, God, I'm sorry." He tried to wipe the blood away with his hand. "I'm sorry." Then they were grasping each other, knees and feet shuffling, trying to rise.

"It's okay," he heard Matt say. "It's okay, Dad."

"I'm sorry, I'm sorry, I'm sorry."

"No big deal, Dad. I'm all right."

"I'm sorry I lied. I loved her."

Dowling began to cry, but Jenny cried louder. Matt slipped under Dowling's weight, and they fell to the carpet again. Dowling tried to hug them both. Tears streamed down his cheeks.

"All I am is a liar. I lie about everything. I told you I got sent back to homicide. I lied. I asked to go back. I even lied to you about that. It was the only place I felt safe."

They hugged him. Four young arms fought for territory, and when they had a grip, they squeezed, and he felt their strength.

"We love you, Dad," Matt said.

Jenny could not control her crying.

"I loved her. I loved her so much. I never meant to hurt her." He buried his head in Matt's chest. "The night I . . ." He choked on the words. "The night I asked her to marry me. I said forever. Told her we'd be together forever, and she's gone. I loved her.''

Dowling was crying so hard, the children strained to hear. "We were going to grow old together. Even when I was here, I was gone." They struggled to a sitting position and ended up in a circle. "When she was telling me her troubles I wasn't listening. I was wondering whether the lousy lab would be able to lift a print from a lousy piece of cellophane. When she was telling me what the dentist said about your braces, I was deciding how I was going to snooker some suspect into telling me why he'd slit somebody's throat." They hugged one another more tightly.

"Once . . . once I found a bottle of booze in the laundry hamper and I gave her hell and she cried, and when she tried to tell me why, the damn phone rang and I went out and looked at a dead body." Dowling could hardly see through his tears.

"Dad." Matt's head was pressed to his. "It's okay."

"It's okay." Jenny nuzzled her way in. "We love you, Daddy."

"There's more," he said, sobbing. "You won't love me when I tell you more." He pried his arms loose and put his head in his hands. "She killed herself. My Helene. She killed herself. Suicide. *Suicide.*" His voice rang throughout the house. "*Suicide.*"

"No, Daddy," Jenny screamed. "No, no, no."

"*Suicide,*" he yelled.

Matt got to his feet. "But you said . . . they said—"

"*Lies.* All lies. I live a lie."

"That can't be," Matt said, shaking his head.

"She left a note. I tore it up. I tore it up like I tore her life up. Oh, God. I loved her and I love you and I've destroyed it all." He couldn't stop crying and he couldn't talk anymore. His voice quavered, and Matt and Jenny took him under his arms and led him to the sofa, and they sat down together. Jenny stopped crying, and the room was quiet. Dowling looked into their faces and saw compassion and caring and all the things he could not have hoped for. He still saw it when they covered him with a blanket and put a pillow under his head.

"Get some rest, Dad," Matt said bravely. "Then we'll talk some more. We love you."

When he opened his eyes, he was not sure if he had slept. It took him a while to re-create what had happened. A ray from the porch light allowed him to read 8:00 P.M. on the clock. The house looked dark, but when he pulled himself to a sitting position he saw light from the kitchen. He was tempted to lie back down or tiptoe into his bedroom. It had all been blurted out, and he wondered what Matt and Jenny were thinking. Feeling. Perhaps the shock had worn off and they despised him. Rubbing a hand through his hair, he decided to find out.

They were seated at the small table, a carton of milk and graham crackers between them. Dowling sniffed the aroma of fresh coffee and knocked gently on the doorjamb.

"It's me."

He could not read their faces. "May I?" He motioned toward the third chair. Matt pulled it out for him, and he sat down slowly. Jenny poured coffee for him, and he patted her arm.

"Is everybody OK?" he asked.

Matt nodded. Dowling touched Jenny's arm again, and she nodded as well. The coffee tasted marvelous, and he cradled the cup in his hands. Matt went through the motions of wiping crumbs with a paper napkin.

"It's great coffee. Thank you." He wondered whether he should have stayed on the sofa. Matt's lip was swollen and starting to discolor. "Maybe you should put some ice on your mouth."

"It'll be all right." There was resentment in his voice.

Jenny looked at him and looked away. She had donned a sweat shirt with a hood and a blue-and-gold Charger logo.

"There are better ways to say what I said out there," he said, taking another sip.

"The main thing is we know," Matt said flatly.

"The main thing is you know," Dowling repeated.

"I never thought that," Jenny whispered.

"Me neither." Matt took a deep breath. "You said there was a note. What did it say?"

He had recited it to himself scores of times. "It said, 'Thanks for letting me play the fool. It was some sleigh ride. Make the kids . . . Make Matt and Jenny . . .'"

His voice broke. Reaching for a piece of paper on the counter, he told them, "I'll write the rest out."

Make Matt and Jenny understand somehow—if you have the guts. You were the

He felt tears forming again.

love of my life, Vincent. I wish it could have been different.

Pushing the paper toward them, he said, "She signed it, 'till death do us part.'"

They read it slowly and continued staring at it. "Why did you tear it up?" Jenny asked.

"For a lot of reasons, I suppose. Guilt. Not enough guts to make the two of you understand. Shock. I'm not sure."

"Does anybody else know?" Matt asked.

"No."

Nobody spoke for a while. Dowling poured a second cup of coffee and sneaked glances at them. "I'd like to talk about this more. From time to time. If it's OK with both of you."

They both nodded again. He went to the bathroom to urinate, and on the way back to the kitchen picked up the hall telephone on the first ring. Nothing could have prepared him for the message from the watch commander's office.

"Your boys just took Sea World."

"That was last night."

"There was a shooting this time, Vince."

"Is this a joke?" He remembered Cliff Edwards's face at his car window.

"I wish it were. Are you rolling?"

🎵 Twenty-one

When he hung up he paced for a moment, then walked slowly to the kitchen. Standing behind his children, he put a hand on each one's shoulder.

"I need to ask you to trust me about something." They looked up. "The phone was for me. A call-out." He saw Jenny tense. "This will sound strange. Telling you I have to go out. Especially after saying in the living room about . . . about the night Mom needed me home and I went anyway. I know I need to be here tonight. But this is different. Please trust me."

"What's different?" Jenny said. "Just go to work. Go on."

"If he says it's different, it's different," Matt said.

"I don't deserve to be trusted. But I'm going to earn it. This call-out is very important, too. Very different. I love you both. I'm lucky to have you." He headed for the bedroom. "I'll be out all night. I have to do whatever it takes on this one."

When he arrived at Sea World he parked in the same spot as the night before. It seemed as if a week had gone by, instead of a day. Stacy's car sat near the entrance. In twenty-eight years Dowling had known series suspects to hit two nights in a row. He had known them to hit the same victim more than once. He had never known them to hit the same victim on consecutive nights. "This afternoon he showed me up, and tonight he's farting in my face," he said to himself.

"Are you all right? You look terrible," Stacy said. He moved closer to Dowling. "Are you drunk?"

"No, Tom. Stone sober." Over Stacy's shoulder he saw the night manager in the identical location where he had been the night before.

"It's a coroner's case," Stacy said. "Young girl. Employee. Walked in when the job was going down."

Dowling saw the body in a pool of blood near the office door. The lab photographer circled it, hunched over. Shea was writing in his notebook, and Dowling moved closer to listen. The manager was wiping his face again. His eyes closed periodically as he spoke.

"He—he came bursting in again. The same man. We just couldn't believe our eyes. He called me fat ass. He said, 'We're going to play the same tune we played last night, fat ass.' " The manager looked past Shea toward Dowling. "It was just terrifying. Then he took the gun from the guard again."

Dowling looked toward the fringe of the group. A different guard stood with his head slightly bowed. This guard was in his late twenties or early thirties, tall and square-shouldered.

"Then he said, 'Just like last night'—oh, God . . . that's the trouble, you see. He said, 'Is everybody in here that's coming in here?' And, oh, Jesus, help me." The man began to cry, and touched his eyes with a tissue. "Jesus help me, I forgot about her." He looked in the direction of the body and quickly looked away. "It was her first day on the job. She sells hot dogs. And I was so stressed . . . so upset . . . I just forgot about her. That's why I told him everybody was accounted for." He began sobbing uncontrollably.

The guard stepped forward. Dowling guessed he was a moonlighting marine from Camp Pendleton or the Recruit Depot.

"He was just making us lie down on the floor, sir. That's when the young lady opened the door. She was carrying her change bank and, well, sir . . ." The guard had a southern accent. "The guy with the shotgun just plain wheeled around and fired. He never gave her a chance. Just wheeled and fired, sir. He was almost point blank. The impact lifted her right up. He grabbed the money from the safe and ran like hell.''

Dowling walked around the patrol officer guarding the body. The photographer was still taking pictures. Blood had soaked into the pink-and-white-striped dress and apron. The metal box lay next to her, its top open, coins and currency mingled in the blood. The left breast was gone, and long black hair had fallen across her face.

Dowling stepped back and saw Speedy Montoya sitting on a concrete wall next to a planter box. A frail Mexican man sat next to Speedy, his head in his hands. Bushes blocked their view of the body.

"This is Mr. Martinez, Sergeant. Rita's father." The man looked up and met Dowling's eyes. "This is Sergeant Dowling, Señor Martinez. He's in charge.''

The man's dark eyes were wet and his brown skin was deeply wrinkled.

"She was our baby. Our *niña*. Our Rita. She come long after her brothers and sisters, Sargento. This was her first night to the work. I come to pick her up.''

Speedy told the rest. The man worked for National Steel and Shipbuilding. For thirty-five years, he had packed his lunches and sweated in the boiler rooms, and his daughter had received a scholarship from the school of veterinary medicine at the University of California at Davis, beginning in the spring semester. The next day the family was to have held a party in her honor. A new dress was in the back seat of the car.

"I see my Rita now, Sargento?''

"Not just yet, señor," Speedy said, putting his arm around the man's shoulder, holding him back.

Dowling returned to the body. He looked down again, into the face of death. A look he decided long ago could not be faked. The hem of the dress rested high above her knees.

"Are you through shooting?'' he asked the photographer.

"I'm through.''

Dowling knelt, his right knee in the pool of blood,

and after gently raising her hips, tugged until the skirt was lowered far enough to cover the firm thighs. He carefully moved silken hair out of her face, and for a moment touched her soft brown hand. Then he whispered, *"Buenas noches, niña dulce."* He was still looking down when he got to his feet. Stacy stood next to him.

"I had a lot of things left to do when I was seventeen, Tom." His jaw set and his eyes narrowed, the crow's feet next to them becoming more pronounced. A line for every victim, Helene had once said.

"So these cock suckers want to play hardball?" His teeth stayed clenched, and he nodded. "Well, we'll play hardball."

"I've seen that look before," Stacy would tell his wife the next morning over breakfast. "But not in a long time. This is going to get interesting."

It was 11:00 P.M. when they left Sea World and went to the homicide squad room. Dowling was pleased to find it quiet. A night team was in one corner, shuffling papers. He ushered his team into the critique room. They each carried a Styrofoam cup of coffee, and Larry Shea was taking huge bites from packaged oatmeal cookies.

"When we leave this room, we're going home," Dowling said. They all looked at him curiously. "This is the first time in thirteen years I've ever sent a team home right after a murder. I have two reasons. One, I have to go home. It's a personal thing. But secondly, I want you to go catch eight or ten hours of good sleep, because when you report back here at noon tomorrow, you may not get home for a while." He took a gulp of hot coffee and lit a cigarette. "Cliff Edwards is one of our suspects. I haven't had a chance to tell you what happened this afternoon."

He told them the story.

"So now we all know. It was my fault. I sent that kid into the pool hall and she was overmatched from the start. It wasn't planned well. I just blew it. Period." He lowered his voice. "I don't want to hear the name Cliff

Edwards repeated outside of this critique room. It has to be kept secret. Understand?''

They nodded.

''Somehow, we're going to catch that son of a bitch. We're going to need luck and hard work. City Hall is getting daily briefings. If I tell Stacy about Edwards, he has to pass it up the line. And those numb nuts politicos will have it all over town in fifteen minutes. This is extrasensitive because Edwards still has friends down here. Nobody would intentionally help him, but he can poke 'em around for general info and they won't even know why he's asking. Speedy. You can keep Cookie shut up?''

''It's done, Sarge. She's embarrassed.''

''I'm embarrassed too,'' Dowling said. ''Very embarrassed. You guys have been carrying me. I needed to be carried. What we're going to do after you come back all rested up is take our knowns and work hell out of them. We've had a lot of jewelry taken. We've got good descriptions of it. Even some photos from insurance files.'' He grabbed his yellow pad and a pencil.

''Bones. Remember the LAPD sergeant we solved the kidnapping-murder for?''

''Can't ever forget that one, boss.''

''Well, you're going to be seeing a lot of him. Pack your toothbrush, because you'll be in L.A., and I don't want to see you back here until you've checked every pawnshop in Tinseltown.''

Dowling pointed at Speedy. ''You're going to hand search every traffic stop made in this city on these eight nights.'' He pointed to the dates of the crimes, which were scribbled on the bulletin board. ''You check every traffic ticket. Every traffic warning. Every traffic accident. Look for Cliff Edwards, of course. That's the easy part. And every time you find paper work on a guy who's six two and bigger and a couple of hundred pounds, you run that guy through criminal records and see what you come up with. Use your good instincts. Maybe we'll get lucky. Those bastards have to drive to and from a crime scene.''

"That stuff's all in the computer, Sarge. I can do it in no time."

"Listen carefully, Speedy. I said hand search. Computers have glitches. Make mistakes. Good detectives on a hand search don't. I don't care how long it takes. Find us something."

Dowling yawned, stretched, rubbed the back of his neck and reached into his pocket. He slid a key across the table to Larry Shea. "This gets you into my house. You're going to be there for the next few days using my phone. I want you to make a list of every store in town that sells ski masks. Then make a contact with every damn one of them. As careful as these guys've been, you'll probably strike out. But we have to try. I don't want you making the calls from here in case Cliff Edwards's name comes up."

He got up and walked around the table. "That son of a bitch humiliated me. We can spend all night trying to figure out why, but the fact is right now it doesn't matter. What matters is that we catch him." Dowling smashed his fist into his palm. "God, it was awful. Sitting in that car with Cookie and listening to him. Knowing he'd done a job on me. But big deal, huh? Sticks and stones and all of that. I'm a big boy." His face tightened, and he banged his fist on the table. "But that little Rita Martinez . . ." His voice lowered. "He didn't have any beef with that little girl. We're going to make him pay for that."

A few days later Dowling stormed into Tom Stacy's office and proclaimed, "Helene committed suicide. Pills and booze. She left a note. I read it. Then I tore it up."

Stacy put down some photographs he had been looking at. "I can understand how a man would do that," he said calmly.

Dowling was flabbergasted. "Did you know, Tom? Did you suspect?"

"No."

"The death certificate has to be changed. And the investigative reports have to be corrected."

"I'll handle that. I am the captain of homicide." He moved to Dowling's side and put his arm around him. "It's good to see you back, old pal."

The day after he told Stacy, he told his team.

"Shit happens," Bones said.

They shook his hand and went back to their assignments. An hour later Dowling walked to the traffic division, where Speedy was laboring over a couple of thousand traffic-related contacts.

"Come on, Speedy. Take a break. I'm going to call in a marker, and you may need to play a role in it." They used the stairwell to travel up two flights. "We're going to the Special Enforcement Detail. They're a new unit. Do you know what they do?"

"Sort of a goon squad, aren't they?"

Dowling smiled. "They do stakeouts and surveillances. Try to surprise bad asses they get info on. Lot of action."

"I hand-picked sixteen top-drawer detectives, Dowling," Lieutenant Elmer Mendoza said. "All gutsy, hardworking, stand-up guys. Hell, we've been involved in five shootings our first three weeks of operation."

"No coppers hurt though, huh, Elmer?"

"Nah." He blew a cloud of foul, dark cigar smoke. "We got the advantage of knowing who we're doing business with. Not like those poor bastards in patrol."

Lieutenant Elmer Mendoza was short, with a barrel chest and receding black hair. The square face looked in need of a closer shave. He was a few years older than Dowling.

"Did you want this job, Elmer?"

"Ha. That's the funny thing." Mendoza leaned forward on both elbows. "I'm running burglary detail and the boss runs this job by me, and I tell him, 'Sure, I'm interested.' Few days later he tells me I got an appointment with a shrink."

"A psychiatrist?" Speedy asked.

"Sure. I was as surprised as you are. I find out he's going to take me on, plus four other lieutenants. Most of 'em are book guys. That guy over in juvenile's one of 'em. He's going for a master's, or something, you know. And that guy you worked for, Dowling. The one with the cigarette holder.'' Elmer Mendoza leaned back and put both hands behind his head, juggling the cigar in his mouth.

"So I keep the appointment. Big, fancy office in La Jolla. The guy sits me down, nice enough guy, first question out of the fuckin' barrel, 'What do you think about violence, Lieutenant Mendoza?' I says, 'Good violence or bad violence?' The doc looks at me kind of funny. Says, 'Is there a difference?' Wants me to explain it.'' Mendoza paused to draw on the cigar. "So I tell him. Good violence is when freedom fighters kill invaders who've been raping and pillaging their village, or when some guy whacks an intruder over the head who he catches butt-fucking his nine-year-old daughter, or a cop has to shoot a guy who's drawing down on him.'' Mendoza blew his nose with a large red-and-green handkerchief. "Bad violence is people getting killed in dumb wars, or a young girl jumping off the Coronado Bridge because her boyfriend just dumped her and she thinks she's too skinny, or a cop roughing a guy up just for practice when he makes an arrest.'' He folded the handkerchief carefully before he put it back in his pocket. "It's supposed to be an hour appointment. Me and the doc shoot the shit for almost three hours. Next day they tell me, 'You got the job.' Here I am, Dowling.''

"How busy are you, Elmer?"

"Busy as hell. All our work comes directly from the chief's office. After the requests have been screened and approved. Big-time stuff, huh?''

"Yeah.'' Dowling smiled weakly. "I need some help, Elmer. Tailing a suspect. Narcotics tried. My team tried. Nobody can stay with the guy. I know the fly boys could get the job done, but they need paper work to do an air surveillance. I figured your crew could do the job for me.''

"We're pretty good at it, Dowling. Send a memo to the chief's office and I'll get somebody on it.''

"Ah, that's one of my problems. I can't memo it right now. That's why I can't ask the Air Support Unit. I'm keeping a lid on my suspect info. It's the mayor's-brother caper, Elmer." He gave a sorrowful look. "It's real important to me. I thought on a slow night you could take a look at him for me."

Mendoza got up and walked around his desk. "I don't have any slow nights, Dowling. And even if I did I have to have front-office approval; I have to follow orders. Rules are rules. Sorry."

Dowling got up. "Come on, Speedy. The lieutenant's a busy man, and we're wasting his time."

"Look, Dowling. I'd help you if I could. I just—"

"Funny isn't it, Speedy?" Dowling had reached the door. "You save a guy's career for him. Really put your ass on the line for him. And then, when you need something, it's 'Oh, I'm too busy. Rules are rules.'" He started to open the door. "Just when you think you've got people figured."

"Whose career did you save?" Speedy asked in a loud voice.

"Well, Speedy. Twenty years ago Mendoza and I were vice-squad partners. He was a swell guy then. Always following the head of his dick around, but a damn good partner. One night—on duty, of course—he wants to make a quick stop and see a girl friend."

"Wasn't that against the rules then, too?" Speedy asked.

"Yeah. It was. So old faithful Dowling, I wait down the street in the car. The vice-squad car. Half an hour later—"

"Aw, come on, Vince. That was a long—"

"Half an hour later, I see this figure running toward me. Balls-ass naked except for shoes and socks. Carrying the rest of his clothes. Leg bleeding from a big laceration under the knee. He flies into the car. His little round pink and brown body all out of breath; says, 'Get going, partner. Her old man just came home.' He'd cut his leg, Speedy, tumbling out of the bedroom window.

We get a block away; he says, 'Oh, shit. My badge and gun are on the living-room table' "

"Whew." Speedy whistled. "What did you do?"

"What did we do? Well, Speedy. Your sergeant was in pretty good shape in those days, so I go back for it alone. I mean, what's a friend for? What's a partner for?"

"Did you get the badge and gun?"

"Oh, yeah. I got it back. I knock on the door, and the husband opens it, and there's no question in his mind I'm the Romeo. The guy's bigger than the doorway, but I can see the badge holder and gun on the table. The guy obviously hasn't spotted them yet. I'll tell you, Speedy. I've been in some pretty good fights on this job, but that big son of a bitch and I went round and round and round. I'm on my last legs. Face all bloody and one eye closed, but I manage to knee him in the balls, grab Lieutenant Mendoza's property and make it back to the car. Without that stuff the husband's out of luck, so we never hear anything about it."

"Gee, Sarge," Speedy said, "you're some guy."

"Like I said, Speedy. What are friends for?"

Dowling opened the door and stepped into the hallway; then Mendoza yelled, "Get back in here, Dowling."

"Pardon?"

"Get back in here, you prick."

"What do you mean, Lieutenant?"

"Just sit down and tell me about the guy you want tailed."

By week's end, Speedy, Bones and Shea had completed their assignments. They had learned nothing of value, and Dowling alternated between trying to think of new ideas and secretly hoping Cliff Edwards would hit again. He did not want anybody killed or injured, but if Edwards had called a halt to his crime spree, Dowling knew they would never make the case. When he thought about the consequences to potential victims, he examined himself, as he had done so many times over the years.

He was a law-enforcement officer. A minion of justice. A gatekeeper. The last bastion separating good and evil. Yet he was hoping a violent criminal would act again, so he could have the satisfaction of arresting him. He did not think his ego was involved. Perhaps, he kept saying to himself, it was purely and simply the thrill of the chase that made him feel that way. Whatever it was, his attitude disgusted him, and he had difficulty keeping his mind on business.

Then Elmer Mendoza gave him more bad news.

"Sorry, Dowling. We can't stay with Cliff Edwards. He's too cagey. Too slippery. He's too good for us."

"I didn't have high hopes," Dowling said softly.

Mendoza put his hand on Dowling's shoulder. "Maybe a little later we could have another go at him."

"Maybe," Dowling said, shaking his head.

Three hours later, Dowling was the only one in the squad room. It was totally dark out, and he stood by the window, staring at the lights of the city. The phone at his desk rang, and he would not have answered it but for Matt and Jenny.

"Sergeant Dowling."

"It's me."

"Who's me?"

"Aw Sarge. Me. Baby Blue."

He wished he had let it ring.

"I'm feelin' good, Sarge. Aggie's taking good care of me."

"What does the doctor say?"

"Says no smoking, no drinking, lot of rest." He laughed. "Says lots of lovin', though."

"Hmph."

"I need to see you, Sarge."

"I'm too busy."

"See, Aggie lost her part-time job, and, ah . . . we need rent money. I was wondering if . . . you know . . . do you have anything? Anything I could do?"

"Hang on a minute." Dowling put the phone down

and walked back to the window. Several minutes passed before he picked up the receiver and said slowly, "Give me a call Monday morning. Don't come down here; just call me." He paused. "I may think of a little something for you to do."

⚅ Twenty-two

From his vantage point, the morning haze obscured Point Loma and blanketed the gray waters of San Diego bay. After some thought, Dowling had decided to check out an undercover car for the meeting on the G Street pier. When he turned onto the pier from Harbor Drive, parking spaces were plentiful, and he chose one at the end next to the restaurant. He mounted the steps leading to the raised concrete oval that provided a view of the giant aircraft carrier docked at North Island.

Sitting on one of the benches he pondered another of his cardinal rules. If an ex-con was staying straight, Dowling never proposed an informant's role. Being an informant meant being on the street, and being on the street meant being back in the breech. If Baby Blue or anyone else was going to end up back in the joint, he would have to accomplish it without Dowling's help. It simply had to be the other guy's idea.

Turning to the east, he watched the sun glimmering on the top of downtown buildings. Then his eyes followed the path of an old Toyota sedan with a broken windshield as it veered toward a parking space. As he got into its front seat, Dowling noticed the weight loss immediately. Baby Blue's features were more pronounced, but the eyes and smile were unaffected. The polo shirt and corduroy pants hung loosely on his lean frame.

"How's your health?" Dowling asked as they shook hands.

"Pretty good. I'm eating better."

"Are you sleeping all right? The doc said it might be uncomfortable."

"Aw, Sarge. Aggie makes me take lots of naps. Got me on a schedule. Like being back at Folsom. Everything by the darn numbers."

"Count your blessings."

"This is her car. 'Course, she don't know I'm meeting you."

"We can both count our blessings. What about this money problem you got?"

They watched a city employee empty parking meters, carefully sliding coins into a sack. Baby Blue shifted his weight.

"Aggie got laid off of her part-time job. Some big contract went to that other airplane place in Seattle. She's home, going through the want ads. Rent's due. She ain't got many bills, but we got to live."

"How much will straighten you out?"

"Four or five hundred bucks."

Dowling said nothing.

"I've never snitched before. 'Course, I could always find a hustle before."

Dowling said nothing.

"Anyhow. I knew a few dope dealers in Ocean Beach. Some of 'em ought to still be around. I could duke some undercover narc into 'em."

Dowling got out of the car and walked to the center island housing the row of meters. He leaned on one and watched a Chinese man sweeping the sidewalk in front of the restaurant. A delivery man unloaded produce from a truck at the end of the building. Odors from the kitchen were indistinguishable to Dowling. He took a cigarette from his pocket, seemed to study it, then flipped it up and down in his hand. When he got back into the car he sat with one foot against the dashboard.

"Somebody told me you were a pool shooter," he said.

"Yep."

"How good are you?"

"Good enough to hustle the chumps. Not good enough to play with the big boys."

Dowling looked at him. "How do you think you'll feel, doing this kind of thing?"

"I got to eat, Sarge. And I don't want to steal nothin'."

"You didn't answer my question."

"I'll feel okay because this is business. And I can't get a job just yet."

Dowling took a wad of tens and twenties from his coat pocket. Stacy had issued the money to him from the informants' fund, a budgeted allotment that made its way from the city treasurer to the chief's office. He handed the currency to Baby Blue.

"Here's four bills. Put your initials right here." He handed him a voucher. "No, wait. Don't put your initials. Put . . . put O.G. In case somebody other than the auditors get into our books. Like defense attorneys." He fished out more money. "Here's fifty for expenses."

Baby Blue stammered, "Ah, Sarge. I don't want to ever have to testify against anybody. I couldn't do that."

"No testimony. Just information." Dowling had expected him to say that.

"Promise?"

"You got my word."

"That's cool," Baby Blue said. "I'll get on out to the beach right now. Used to be a dude named Ozzie moving coke out of a pad on Narragansett Avenue. I knew his brother in Q."

"Forget him and forget the beach." Dowling said. "Here's what I want you to do. There's three pool halls out in your part of town. The Eight Ball on El Cajon, Luckie's on Euclid, and Chalk 'n' Stick on University. You go in all of them. Shoot some pool, look around. Get to know some people. When you—"

"What am I looking for, Sarge?"

Dowling turned toward him again and set his jaw. "Why don't you, let me finish?"

"Sorry, Sarge."

"Now, anybody asks who you are, tell them. You're Baby Blue. Just got out of the can. That's all you need to give them. Anybody starts pressing you, go on the attack. 'Who the hell wants to know?' Got that?"

"I got it, Sarge. The guy you're after must hang around all three places, huh? Who is he? What kind of gig?"

Dowling put his hand on the younger man's shoulder and could feel the sharp edges of his shoulder blade.

"Rule number one is, forget all the bullshit talks you've had with guys who snitched. Rule number two is, listen. I'll tell you what I want you to know. Now, if—"

"But I gotta know what I'm after."

"Rule number three is, don't fuckin' interrupt me. Who's running this show?"

"You are, Sarge," he answered, looking down.

"Who does the listening and follows orders?"

"Me."

"Good," Dowling said. "We're making progress. Couple of more rules, then that's it for today. Listen very carefully. Never, never phone me from anyplace but a pay phone. I don't care how safe it seems at the time. Savvy?"

"Yes, sir."

"And if a cop ever stops you—for anything. Questioning. Suspicion. Even if he's going to throw you in jail. Never mention my name. Don't be one of these piss-ant informants who coughs it right up." Dowling mimicked a falsetto. " 'Oh, I'm out here working for Sergeant Dowling in homicide.' You dummy up and go along. I'll handle things the next day. Got that?"

"Got it, Sarge."

Dowling tapped on the roof of the car with the fingers of his right hand.

"This may be the most important thing I talk about. If you were pulling jobs and some cop slipped in a snitch, how would you discover it?"

"Aw, I don't know, Sarge."

"Think about it for a minute."

"I guess if a guy was too nosy."

"What do you mean by nosy?"

"Aw, Sarge. A guy who asks too many questions."

"*Exactly.* And the way to guard against asking too many questions is, don't ask any questions."

"Boy, that's pretty hard to do. I'd probably forget."

"So you train yourself. When you were capering, you'd give a lot of thought to pulling a burglary, right? Same thing here. When you start to open your mouth, think first about what you want to say. If you're going to do a job, do it right."

Dowling put his hand out. "Give me your wallet."

"Huh?"

"Give me your wallet. I know, that's your line, but give it to me."

Dowling laid it out on the seat between them and carefully sifted through every photograph, ID card and shred of paper. He started a pile of discards, beginning with a piece of paper on which Baby Blue had written the phone number of the homicide office. Then he added a bus schedule for the route from east San Diego to the police station. Satisfied that there was nothing left to compromise him, he handed the wallet back.

"Well, what are you sitting on your ass for? Go earn your money." As the Toyota drove away Dowling called after him, "And get your windshield fixed, so you don't get a ticket."

That evening Dowling took Matt and Jenny to the Chicken Pie Shop on El Cajon Boulevard. For years, it had been in Hillcrest, and they had frequented it because it was inexpensive and the food was tasty. It seemed strange, seeing three menus on the table instead of four. Dowling thought the pastry was especially good, maintaining its texture amidst the hot gravy and chunks of white meat. Steam filtered through the crevice he created with his fork. He started to say something, but was startled to see a red welt next to Matt's eye.

"Hey, I just noticed your eye. Did I do that the other night? I'm sorry."

Matt shook his head.

"He got in a fight," Jenny said.

"Jesus Christ, Jenny. Thanks," Matt said.

"Watch your language." Dowling raised his voice, then quickly lowered it. "What fight? When?" He leaned forward to get a better look at the wound.

Matt sighed. "The next day. An argument over a parking spot. The guy pushed me. Sort of. He was a big guy. A lot bigger than me. I clipped him good. Lots of times. I was pretty mad."

"Who were you mad at, him or me?" Dowling asked softly.

"Everybody, I guess." Matt looked at his plate and picked at the chicken pie. "You and him. I kept hitting him. I—it was like I was hitting you." He looked at his father. "I was mad at everybody. Mom too."

"Mom?" Jenny cried.

"Sure. I was mad at her for—for killing herself. Because I loved her. And I didn't care how much she drank. I mean, I did, but I loved her and I wanted her here, and—when I finished hitting the guy I think I was crying."

"And you were mad at me because?"

"Jeez, Dad. Don't you know? 'Cause of what you did. You lied to us." Matt's face was taut.

"Are you still mad, son?"

"I guess I am. Do you know how many times I thought about Mom all these months? How many times I thought maybe if I'd come home from school earlier that day, I might have been able to save her? Get an ambulance? 'Cause I thought it was a big accident."

"I never realized you might feel any blame," Dowling said.

"Lots and lots of times, Dad."

"I'm sorry. Very sorry."

"I'd be working over on the full-serve side. The guy might have said ten bucks' worth. I'd be pumping away, thinking of Mom lying in that bed, needing help. Dying.

And I'd look up and I'd have fifteen dollars' worth in the tank.''

Jenny touched her brother's arm.

"Sometimes the guy would say, 'Ah, I'll pay the extra five, kid.' The other times it was on me. Heck, Dad. A couple of weeks ago I almost worked for nothing, it cost me so much.''

Dowling put his hand on Matt's arm, next to Jenny's. A waitress poured more coffee. When she left, he said, "What are you feeling right now, Jenny?''

"I feel sorry for Matt. I didn't know he felt guilty too. I was busy blaming myself.''

"God, I'm sorry. I had no idea that you two thought it was your fault. It was my fault, not yours.''

They sat in silence, and the cash register near the door rang constantly. Dowling kept crossing his feet. He lowered his head and spoke softly into his coffee cup.

"God, I wish she was here.''

Dowling received daily phone calls in the next several days.

"I think I got what you're after, Sarge. A punk who hangs around The Eight Ball wants me to drive a load of guns to Mexico for him. Three hundred bucks in it for me.''

"Tell him no. Tell him it's too hot for you. You're just getting used to being out.''

"There's fifty guns, Sarge.''

"I don't care if there's a thousand guns. What's going on at the Chalk 'n' Stick?''

"They ain't doing much business. Hey, the guy who runs it went to school with me.''

"Small world. What about Luckie's?''

"Played some nine ball with the owner. Big dude named Cliff. He asked my name, and all. I gave him the rundown.''

"All right. Move around and keep your eyes open. And listen. Make sure everybody knows you're hanging around all three joints. That's very important.''

The following day, Dowling made a phone call to

Stephanie Mayfield. He had spoken to her only once since she'd dressed him down in the kitchen after the funeral.

"You were right, Stephanie. She committed suicide."

"I heard from another cop's wife. It's all over the police station."

"I know it is. That's OK."

"Thank you, though. For calling me."

"There was a note, too. I tore it up."

"I heard that, too."

"Yes, well. It's no secret. Not anymore."

Before he hung up, he said, "I'm very sorry, Stephanie. For many things. You and she were so close. I want to thank you for being such a good friend to her. A true, loyal friend throughout her—ordeal. She loved you, Stephanie."

"We loved each other, Vincent."

"I know."

"We'd love to see you. Come on over one of these days. Soon."

"I'll do that, Stephanie. I'll just do that."

He continued to be surprised at the way people were receiving the news. It got easier with each telling, because his guilt was lessening, and he suspected it was because people were not turning on him, as he had thought they would.

Never before had he felt such a sense of duty and responsibility toward his children. They were far more important than Cliff Edwards and crime victims and his team and anything else he could think of. "There is a balance, Dowling," he told himself again and again. He was beginning to believe he could achieve it.

His team was delighted when he announced that Baby Blue was on an intelligence-gathering mission, and that he'd sent him in right behind Cookie.

"It may be risky," Dowling told them, "but Cliff Edwards shocked us, nailing Sea World twice in twenty-four hours. Sometimes the unexpected works best."

"Did you lay it all out for him, Sarge?" Speedy asked.

"No. He doesn't know anything. Whatever he gives us about Edwards ought to be believable."

"If he doesn't know anything, he can't make a slip and blow it. Or get himself hurt, huh, boss?"

"Or lie to us very easily."

The telephone calls came regularly, and the background noise satisfied Dowling that Baby Blue was using a pay phone.

"This time I got it, Sarge. Yeah, boy."

"Let's have it."

"That Chalk 'n' Stick is a doggone pharmacy. Big dealing. Coke. Horse. Grass. It's all there. Get this!" Baby Blue sounded excited. "A dude from L.A. wants me to go with him on a big buy. For protection."

"Ho-hum," Dowling said.

"What?"

"Tell the L.A. guy thanks, but no thanks. You're doing a hell of a good job, Baby Blue. You're doing just what I told you to do. Keep circulating."

"Darn, Sarge. This is crazy. But you're the boss."

Two days later they met on the G Street pier for what Dowling decided would be the last meeting at that location.

"Luckie's is doing a fair business. Mostly evenings and weekends. Last couple of days he didn't charge me to play."

They got out of the car and walked to the boardwalk. Three young black boys were fishing with drop lines.

"What's this guy like, Baby Blue? The guy that runs Luckie's."

"Cliff? Pretty good dude. Talks like he's got some street smarts."

"You said he asked your name. Did you tell him you were an ex-con?"

"Sure. He wanted to know what kinda beef. I told him we cut some guy up over a misunderstanding." He lit a cigarette. "First one today, Sarge."

Dowling was skeptical. "Go on," he said.

"Yesterday some guy Cliff had been talking to came over and started shooting with me. Name's Gypsy. He'd done some Youth Authority time. We started cutting it up about the joint. Little while later Cliff tells me, 'Gypsy says you got a pretty good pedigree.' I tell Cliff, 'Maybe so, but I don't have to prove nothing to that punk.' "

"What does this Gypsy look like?" Dowling asked it quickly.

"Little, scrawny guy. Comes up to my shoulder." Dowling sighed and changed the subject. The chill from the bay made them retreat to the car.

"I want you staying in and resting in the mornings. Only time you have to be in these pool halls is middle afternoon and early evening. And that doctor will have your ass if he catches you smoking." Before there could be a response he added, "And you have to be damn careful you don't go wandering off with these pecker heads you've been running into. Your parole officer will be locking you up for consorting."

"You're supposed to tell my P.O., Sarge."

"I know I am. But I didn't. Five people know, and that's plenty. If there's heat, I'll ride it."

They talked for a while, then shook hands before Dowling climbed out of the car.

"Forgot something," Baby Blue yelled to him. "That guy Cliff from Luckie's wants me to drop by Friday night about 7:00 P.M."

"Why?"

"Didn't say."

"Stand him up."

"Huh?"

"Stand him up. Stay out of there for a few days."

"Jeez, Sarge. It could be something. How am I going to get next to anybody? I had the gun deal to Tijuana. You didn't care about that. The dope deal at the Chalk 'n' Stick. I think I ought to show Friday night and see—"

"Do you remember when I handed you four hundred scoots and we agreed I was running this show?"

"Yeah, I remember. I just—"

"Well, nothing's changed since then. Stay out of that

place. Now, get on home before Aggie puts out an all-units for you.''

Dowling started to walk away again, then said, ''Start hitting the other two around dinnertime, Luckie's from seven until ten. You're doing a good job, Baby Blue.''

Three nights later Dowling sat in his quiet kitchen in a quiet house on a quiet Saturday night, trying to get his mind off Cliff Edwards. He had spent the afternoon doing household chores and wondering why Edwards had wanted to see Baby Blue the night before. When he'd finished wondering about that, he wondered what Edwards's reaction had been when the informant had failed to show. If he'd even had a reaction.

It occurred to him what must be done in order to stop thinking about the case. Gulping the last swallow of coffee he threw open his spice cabinet and rummaged for a bag of pecans. If he could find some, they would end up atop rolls as wide as saucers and two inches high. The pecans would stick to a bed of brown-sugar-and-honey glaze. Historically, the more upset he was the more he baked.

Whenever he had a string of unsolved murders, all available kitchen space became cluttered with pies and cakes and rolls and cream puffs and a variety of breads. Helene had packed the treats in cartons to be carried to the police-station parking lot. Dowling would distribute them to officers who rode patrol cars in the depressed areas of Logan Heights and Southeast San Diego. ''This is for the kids on your beat. Shut up about where it came from,'' he would admonish, ''or you'll never get a transfer to detectives.''

He bit into one of the pecans, decided they would do, then grabbed an apron after washing his hands.

''Did the guy at Luckie's—what's his name, Cliff?—did he say anything about your not showing Friday?'' Dowling asked into the phone.

''Yeah, Cliff is his name. After I'd been in about half an hour he says, 'Where were you Friday?' I played dumb, said to him, 'Huh? Friday?' He says, 'Yeah, I told you to come on in Friday night.' I says, 'Oh, I got hung up.' Then he let it alone.''

Dowling heard him coughing. ''You're smoking, aren't you?''

''Aw, Sarge. Just a couple.'' He coughed again. ''Anyway, Cliff ain't sore about Friday, because he had a friend of his work over my carburetor for nothing.''

''Oh?''

''Well, Aggie's carburetor. In the Toyota.''

''Tell me about it.''

''Ain't much to tell. Cliff knew I was having trouble with it. Says, 'A friend of mine in the business owes me a favor.' So I go over to the guy's shop and he done something with it. Runs good now.''

''Who is the guy? What kind of shop are you talking about?''

''Name's Elliott. Big dude. Bigger than Cliff. Kind of a hole-in-the-wall repair shop up on the boulevard.''

Dowling tried not to appear eager. ''Is Elliott a first or last name?''

''I don't know, Sarge. You said never ask a question, so I didn't.''

''Ah, did you happen to notice what color eyes he's got?'' Dowling was instantly sorry he'd asked. He had to guard against saying anything that would provide a clue as to his area of interest. Baby Blue might try too hard to please if he had someone to focus on.

''Aw, Sarge. I don't go around looking at eyes unless a girl's wearing 'em. He's got black hair. Shaggy like.''

Within an hour Dowling had telephoned the Department of Motor Vehicles in Sacramento and the city business licensing office. When he hung up, he had more data to chalk onto the blackboard:

Elliott Krause   never arrested in Calif.
28 years old   owned shop 6 months
big guy

"So Elliott Krause could be our killer," he told his team. "I have a good feeling."

"What now, Sarge?" Speedy asked.

"Now we wait. We wait and see where this is going to take us. Maybe our luck is changing."

Through both official and confidential sources, Dowling added more data to his yellow sheets. Krause and Edwards both had meager amounts in their bank accounts. Neither had obtained credit ratings. Neither owned real property.

"All that's okay," he told Bones over a pitcher of beer. "My guts tell me we're onto something good. It's exciting. Sitting in this chair, knowing that if we wanted to, we could walk into some chicken-shit little garage and stand face-to-face with a mechanic who may like ski masks and sawed-off shotguns. Damn, Bones." He took a swallow. "Just think. We even get paid for doing this."

One of his immediate concerns was how to lie without really lying to Tom Stacy. He had been avoiding Stacy, and was buried in a stack of dreaded paper work at his desk. Initialing payroll rosters, dictating budget memos, absorbing new insurance-coverage information and interpreting and distributing updated department-policy bulletins went with his sergeant's job, and he was deeply into it when he saw Stacy approach. Dowling made it as far as the doorway, but Stacy caught him.

"Drop in and see me, Vince. I need an update. Where in hell have you been lately?"

Dowling hurried away and called over his shoulder, "Been busy, Tom. I'll be in soon."

"The four hundred bucks you drew. Anything?" Stacy yelled.

"I'll keep in touch, Tom." Dowling yelled back, almost out of sight around a corner.

The next night he sat at his dining-room table, fingering his gold medallion. He had told Stacy and Stephanie Mayfield and his team and his children. He reached for a sheet of writing paper, jerked a ball-point pen from a pencil jar and wrote, "Dear Dad."

*   *   *

Four hours later the ringing telephone woke Dowling, and he was certain it was a call-out.

"It's me, Sarge. I got to see you. Soon as I shake loose."

Dowling recognized the panic in Baby Blue's voice. "What is it? Shake loose from what? Are you in trouble?"

"I don't think so. Not now. It's that Elliott dude. He's crazy, Sarge."

"Tell me."

"I can't now. We're at a restaurant. He's in the crapper. I got to see you."

Dowling flicked on the light. "I'm heading for the office. Call me there as soon as you can. Do you need help?"

"Not right now. He's crazy, though."

When the toaster clicked Dowling yanked out the slice of wheat bread and spread it with peanut butter. The toast was in his hand as he started the car, backed out of his driveway and turned toward downtown. By 2:00 A.M. he was at his desk.

Exactly one hour later he was standing in the bushes on a hillside three hundred yards north of the empty parking lot at San Diego Jack Murphy Stadium. The moist air cut through his thin windbreaker, and he shivered. Scanning the expanse of blacktop with binoculars, he focused on the main entrance off Mission Village Drive.

Baby Blue had phoned the office, and Dowling, fearful of a trap, had said crisply, "Give me fifteen minutes, then drive directly to the stadium parking lot and wait in the car for exactly twenty minutes. I won't be meeting you there. After twenty minutes, drive to the Spanish Village landing on Harbor Drive, north of the airport. If it's safe, I'll meet you there. Just do as I say. And listen, in case Elliott or anybody else approaches you at the stadium, shine 'em on. You're waiting to meet a married woman, or something."

If Cliff Edwards or Elliott Krause or anyone else was

tailing Baby Blue, Vincent Dowling would not be found
with him. When Dowling spotted the Toyota entering
the lot, he watched the roadways until he was satisfied
no surveillance was being conducted. The Toyota
waited, and when it left, so did Dowling.

"He's crazy, Sarge. Big and tough and crazy."

They were parked next to each other, driver's door to
driver's door, talking through their open windows. The
moonlight made the water look like glass.

"Cliff told me Elliott wanted to look at my carburetor
again, so I go over there, and he takes a peek at it, and
we end up drinking a warm beer in the shop, and he
wants to go get a hamburger, and he wants to drive
and—" Baby Blue paused for breath. "Drives crazier
than a loon, Sarge. All around corners and up alleys,
and I'm asking what's going on, and Elliott, he acts like
I ain't even with him. Looking behind him, and all, and
finally he pulls up on this dark street, and next thing,
Sarge, I got a .45 stuck in my face."

Baby Blue stuck a stiff forefinger on the tip of his
nose. "Right there, Sarge. Then he cocks the thing, and
it sounds like a sledgehammer hitting a hunk of rock.
Says to me, 'Okay motherfucker, get your shirt off.' He
ain't foolin', Sarge. I take my shirt off, and he looks me
over and runs his hand all over my shirt. I figure he's
looking for a wire. He says, says, 'Get your pants off.'
He looks me all over. Goes through my wallet, Sarge."
Baby Blue's eyes were big, and he was talking with his
hands. "So I'm sitting there naked—I don't wear
shorts—and I says to him, says, 'I don't know what's
going on, Elliott, but you may as well go ahead and
shoot me, because if you don't, I'm going to kill you
for this.' Elliott starts laughing, Sarge, and puts the gun
away."

"Then what?" Dowling asked.

"Then it gets more scary, 'cause he's still laughing,
and I don't know whether to put my clothes on or run
or what. Can't jump him, 'cause he's too big and I'm
too sick."

"Go on."

"Then Elliott, he's still laughing, he pats me on the shoulder and says, 'You're OK, Baby Blue. You're my kind of dude. Put your clothes back on.' Then he sticks a fifty-dollar bill in my shirt pocket."

"Didn't he tell you anything else?" Dowling asked.

"Sure. He says, 'Let's go get that hamburger. I'm hungry.' That dude's crazy, Sarge."

℀ Twenty-three

Vincent Dowling was in a splendid mood. The conversation with Baby Blue had left him brimming with confidence. Renewed confidence. Sorely needed confidence. Elliott Krause was his killer, all right, and he spent portions of the morning congratulating himself on resolving at least that much. Then he reminded himself that a great deal of work remained before a celebration could be held. He lectured his team that the complexion of the investigation had changed drastically when Baby Blue had gone on the payroll. No longer was Dowling determining the direction of their thrusts, because Cliff Edwards and Elliott Krause had unwittingly placed him in the position of being a responder. He had taken great pains to impress upon Baby Blue the importance of going along with whatever Krause suggested.

"He's up to something, I guess," Dowling told him. "I have no idea what it might be. Stick with him for a while. Let him know you like taking money for doing nothing."

Baby Blue listened intently, particularly when Dowling tutored him about Aggie Pride.

"You say she's getting nosy about where you got the four hundred bucks and where you're spending your time? Let her *be* nosy. Tell her you're not stealing it. Tell her anything. Just sure as hell don't tell her about our deal."

"My mom must think Aggie is all right, Sarge. She invited her for Thanksgiving."

"Thanksgiving? When is it?"

"Next week."

"Jeez, I've got to get busy. Three pies."

"What?"

"Nothing." He handed Baby Blue another four hundred dollars.

"What do *you* think they're pulling, Sarge?"

"Who knows?"

What Dowling did know was that five weeks had elapsed since the blood of Rita Martinez had splattered the pavement of Sea World. He wondered if Edwards and Krause were being especially cautious since the night of his fiasco with Cookie.

"I've worked a hodgepodge of cases in my time," he told Larry Shea. "But I've never had one like this. This is a damn cat-and-mouse game. I know he's pulling the jobs, and he *knows* I know. It's like Sherlock Holmes and that professor. Or Batman and the Joker. Damn. Dowling and Edwards."

He no longer cared about his cardinal rule against becoming personally involved with his suspects. He *was* involved, and only the slamming of the jailhouse door would have restored his sense of balance. He wondered why they had taken the trouble to search Baby Blue for the wire. If they were that suspicious it would have been easy to ignore him. Perhaps they needed to feel in control. Perhaps Edwards was as personally involved as Dowling. Or . . . perhaps they needed Baby Blue.

⚒ Twenty-four

"We're not driving in that car, Baby Blue. Some cop will sure as hell stop us for that windshield being busted. You better get that fixed. Pull it over against that wall." Elliott Krause pointed to the side of his garage, where greasy engine parts were heaped on a tarpaulin. "We'll take my car. I want to drive anyhow."

Krause took huge strides toward the late-model Buick. He was several inches over six feet, with a thick, muscular physique. Black hair flapped over his ears. The face was large and square, and formed a backdrop for a too-small nose, which had been broken more than once.

"You'll never see old Elliott Krause driving something like a Toyota again," he said, pulling out onto the busy boulevard. "I had a big Mercedes lined up to buy the other day, but Cliff made me hold off. Where's your doctor's office at?"

"In Mission Valley. One of them big buildings near Texas Street. Closes in half an hour."

"We'll make it. Hey. Look at them whores. Peddling it right on the street corner."

"Yeah, brother. Remember when you never saw them this side of Broadway. Them and gangs."

Krause said nothing. They stopped for a red light.

"Who's in that blue car behind us? Next lane over."

"Just some old lady, Elliott."

"That old lady could be a policewoman. Watch her."

"Wow. Are you that hot?"

Krause snickered. "We're pretty hot, but we're pretty slick." He made a right turn at the intersection, then a U-turn, then a left turn, and pulled quickly to the curb. He looked in the side mirror.

"Thing is, Baby Blue, it doesn't matter how much they're on us. Because when we make our move, we make damn sure we've lost them." He began moving forward slowly, then accelerated rapidly. "Just takes a little longer getting from point A to point B this way." He laughed again.

Baby Blue put his hand to his mouth and coughed twice.

"You got a bad smoking cough. Dirty habit." Krause cut across a supermarket parking lot, then sped through an alley. "Do you use dope?"

"Not anymore."

"Good."

Krause eased the car into traffic on Interstate 8 while his eyes darted constantly to the rearview mirror. "What did you think when I was roughing you up the other night?"

"I figured you was crazy."

Krause glanced at the new hotel construction next to the freeway. "Me and Cliff, we're a team. His job is to check you out to see if you're who you say you are. Then, after he does that, I handle the rest. We were just being careful."

"Well, I never thought anybody would give me fifty bucks for stripping, brother."

Krause slowed drastically and jerked the Buick into the slow lane of traffic. "Something else, Baby Blue. Stay out of Luckie's."

"Huh?"

"Don't go into Luckie's anymore. Ever. You want to shoot a game, go to one of the other joints. Understand?" Before an answer could be given, Krause shouted, "Watch that motor home. That Winnebago. Cops!"

"Where?"

"Right next to you, but don't look now."

"How do you know it's cops?"

"Because Cliff says they use those motor homes all
the time. Think they're slick bastards." He passed the
Winnebago, then pulled a .45 automatic from under his
shirt and put it between his legs. "The bastards try and
take Elliott Krause, I'll take a couple with me," he
snarled. "Fix those pigs so they're lying flat, with a
fuckin' apple in their mouth."

Baby Blue shook his head. "I don't know, Elliott. I'm
on parole. I just got grass under my feet, and I'm liking
it pretty good. Messin' with cops is—"

"*You want out?*" Krause pulled the car toward an off
ramp. "I'll pull this thing on over and you get out.
Chicken-shit cock bite." He turned onto the frontage
road bordering the freeway.

"Aw, brother." Baby Blue waved at him. "You got
a short fuse. I didn't mean I want out. I just move slow,
is all." He coughed again.

Krause glared at him. "You're sure?"

"I'm sure."

As they pulled into the parking lot of a tall commercial building, Krause said, "Tomorrow night. I want you
over at my garage at six sharp."

"We going to fix a car, brother?"

"Nah. We won't be working on any car. We'll have
one in there with the hood up, though, to make it look
good. Then I'll be leaving for an hour or so. Around
seven. If anybody ever asks you, I was out on an emergency repair job somewhere. You got it?"

"I got it."

"Me and Cliff will be taking care of business. We're
a little behind schedule." Krause fingered the pistol.
"You seen *The Fugitive* yet?"

"No, brother."

"Well, everybody else in town must be seeing it, from
the look of the lines at the box office." He smiled
slightly. "But me and Cliff . . . we aren't going to be
staying for the whole show."

                    *   *   *

"So that's the gig, Sarge. They're going to take down the Cinema 21 theater a little after seven. That's where the movie's playing. I got the newspaper right here. Looked it up," he said proudly.

"Humph." Dowling played with the door of the phone booth.

"So I did pretty good, huh?"

"Yeah, pretty good."

"After you bust them at the theater, will you come by Elliott's garage and pick me up?"

"Baby Blue, if we arrest anybody you'll be the first to know. Go home and get some rest. And stay real loose tomorrow night."

At 5:00 P.M. the next evening, Dowling and his team circled his desk in the squad room. A portable police radio squawked softly. It was tuned to a frequency used by patrol cars in the area of the theater.

"If we're not going to cover the theater, who is?" Speedy asked.

"Nobody," Dowling answered.

"Nobody?" They said it almost in unison.

Dowling inhaled deeply on a cigarette, then flicked off the ash, which fell into the ashtray and on his desk top. "I'm sticking my neck out. I'm gambling there won't be a robbery."

"But . . ." Bones stammered, "Elliott said they were going—"

"Damn it, Bones, I know what Elliott said. I was up half the night thinking about what Elliott said. My guts are all churned up. Jeez, what a way to make a living." He puffed on the cigarette again. "I think it may be a ruse."

"Why a ruse?" Shea asked.

"A test, Larry. A test for Baby Blue. I don't know. It came quickly. Too quickly. Elliott didn't have to drop the hint about what picture was playing. A few nights ago they were searching him at gunpoint, and now they're telling him secrets?"

"But we could stake it out, Sarge. Just in case. No harm there," Speedy said.

"The hell there's no harm," Dowling shot back. "If it is a ruse, Cliff Edwards, or somebody, will be down there sniffing around. Looking for a stakeout. He's got a good nose, and he'd spot us. With our luck, patrol would come rolling in on some kind of a disturbance call, or something, and it would be all over for Baby Blue. All over for us."

"If you're wrong, boss," Bones said softly, "if you're wrong and somebody gets shot. Killed . . ."

Dowling looked at the ceiling and paused before answering. "Then by this time tomorrow, my badge will be on Stacy's desk."

⚡ Twenty-five

At 7:30 P.M., Baby Blue stood in front of the garage and watched Elliott Krause drive toward him. He hurried to the side of the car.

"What happened, Elliott? You've only been gone half an hour. Nobody came by here."

Krause slid from behind the wheel and shrugged. "There's been a change of plans." He looked toward the nearby sidewalks and buildings. "Come here a minute." He walked to a small, enclosed storage area inside the garage. When Baby Blue stood next to him, Krause took a few steps back, then put his right hand around the grip of the .45 in his waistband. A city bus passed, spewing fumes into the darkness. Krause sneered.

"It's striptease time again, Baby Blue. Take your fuckin' clothes off."

Baby Blue's back was up against a wall, and he shook his head. Smoke from a cigarette between his lips drifted into his eyes. His voice trembled.

"You're a big man, Elliott. And you got a gun. And I'm scared, brother. Scared silly." He fumbled with the buttons of his shirt. "You know what else, Elliott? You're crazy. Bad crazy." He yanked a button loose. "You ought to be on the end of a damn leash." He was breathing heavily. "And this is the last time—"

Krause was pointing the gun at chest level, holding the weapon with both hands. "Just do what I say, Baby Blue. This is the last time, one way or the other." His

voice quieted. "Just take your duds off. If you check
clean, you're one of us. If you got a wire on . . . you're
a fuckin' duster. Keep going."

Baby Blue hesitated, then began removing his shirt.
His knees shook. "No, I ain't one of you." He threw
his shirt on the ground at the other man's feet. "I figure
you for a big-mouth, crazy punk." He stared at Krause,
had trouble unfastening his belt buckle. "You don't
show me nothing, and neither does your buddy." The
buckle came loose. "You go around talking big and running scared. And all that other clown is good for is rack-
ing up billiard balls." He supported himself with one
hand on the wall and stepped out of the denim pants. "I
don't think you ever pulled a job in your whole life. I
think you're a fag, and you get your gun looking at my
peter." He kicked the pants toward Krause's feet, turned
around and bent over. "Here, fag. You want to look up
my butt hole too?"

Elliott Krause put the gun in his waistband and went
through the clothing with both hands. Then he wadded
them together, tossed them to Baby Blue and grinned.

"Like I said, this is the last time."

"You bet it's the last time," Baby Blue said, dressing.
He did not bother to button the shirt, and started to walk
by Krause. "I can get my own gigs. Old Baby Blue
takes care of himself."

Krause put a large hand on Baby Blue's chest and
shoved him gently.

"I know you can. Cliff and I know a lot about you.
Here, let's have a drink." He took a pint of Chivas Regal from his jacket pocket and unscrewed the cap.
"Come on. Have a belt. This was a setup tonight. Cliff
said he was pretty sure you weren't a snitch, but he went
down and checked that theater out real good a while ago.
Checked it for cops." Krause took a drink of scotch.
"Cliff said you'd have a wire on if you were working
for the cops." He took another drink. "See, you ought
to look at it this way. If we're cool enough to check you
out so good, then we know what we're doing. We're

good guys to hook up with." He held the bottle in front of him. "Come on. Have a drink."

Baby Blue sat on the crate behind him, looked at Krause and reached for the bottle.

"I should have my head examined. You put a gun on me twice. Then you hand me a jug, and here I am, thinking about having a drink with you." He took a long pull from the bottle. "Maybe I'm as crazy as you are, Elliott."

Krause pulled his shirt down to conceal the weapon, then sat next to Baby Blue. He took another swig, then wiped his mouth with the back of his hand. "We got a class operation. A class operation, and a place in it for you."

"I don't know, Elliott." He shook his head. "Give me another rip of that booze." After he drank he held the bottle to the light. "Darn near a dead soldier. Let's go across the street and get another one. This is pretty good stuff."

The second pint was nearly gone when Krause got unsteadily to his feet. "Got to take a piss."

Baby Blue struggled to a standing position and walked beside him to the small parking lot in the rear. When they were in a dark corner Krause said, "You been wondering why you never see me at Luckie's?"

"Elliott. I've been wondering about you since the first time you stuck that gun in my face."

Krause laughed loudly. He looked pleased. "I used to be around that pool hall all the time. Drifted in there when I first hit town. But after we started . . . that is . . . after a while Cliff says we shouldn't be seen together. Says that's admissible evidence." His words were slurred.

"Admissible evidence?"

"Sure. Cliff says it's only a fragment; that's what he called it, a fragment. But it puts us together." Urine spraying on the blacktop splashed both of their shoes.

"Maybe he's smarter than I thought, Elliott." Baby Blue unzipped his pants, clenched his penis and shot a yellow stream toward the ground.

When they were back inside, he watched Krause drain the bottle, then said, "Maybe I'm just drunk, Elliott, but you're going to be an OK dude, I think."

"You stick with me and Cliff, we'll have you farting through silk." He belched. "Chivas Regal and big cars and first-class pussy and—hey, Baby Blue." He was almost whispering. "You've been on a lot of jobs. You ever get . . . you know . . . sexed up when you're on a job?"

"Sexed up? Naw, Elliott. When I'm on a job it's like I'm getting a shot of something, but I'm sure not thinking about sex. Why?"

Krause plopped himself back down on the wooden crate and flipped the empty bottle toward a trash can. "Because when I'm on a job, I get a hard-on most of the time. Sometimes my shorts get wet and I don't even know it's happening. Even if there's no broads around. I don't understand it."

"Wow. That's heavy. I never heard of a dude getting a stiff pecker on a caper."

"One time, one time I was on a job and I raped some little chick while her mama and papa watched. Had them all tied up." Krause started laughing again, and his eyes flashed. "I almost blew my goddamn wad before I got her pants pulled off. Fact is, I think I did. And then"— he laughed harder—"I kept bumping my head on the refrigerator while I was throwing it to her."

He held out his hands and simulated holding the girl's hips. "I must have split her wide open but good when I got my big wanger in that little peehole. But you know what I bet?" He looked right at Baby Blue. "I'll bet the little bitch has something to tell her cherry girl friends about, huh?"

"I don't know, Elliott. Don't you ever worry about getting caught? About doing time?"

Krause sat back down next to him and put his arm around his shoulder. "Baby Blue. Me and Cliff have pulled eight jobs. Eight fuckin' jobs. And we are good, man. We are good. You'll see how good we are. Over eighty grand in pocket. And the whole damn San Diego Police Department and all of the damn sheriffs and Scotland fuckin' Yard, Baby Blue, not a one of them is ever going to take us down. Not today. Not tomorrow. Not ever.''

⚉ Twenty-six

Dowling turned the corner carefully. His vision to the rear was blocked, but he slowly brought the borrowed pickup truck to a halt in front of the house. He honked, and Matt and Jenny trotted out to the front porch.

"Come on. Give me a hand with this."

"Daddy. What a surprise," Jenny shouted.

The love seat was a traditional design, with maple legs, and had a rich blue-and-brick-red fabric. They carried it into the living room.

"Over there," he ordered. "In that corner." They struggled with it. "Your mother always said a love seat would go good in this corner."

After his children had left for a movie, Dowling sprawled on the new piece of furniture, with an arm thrown over one end and both legs dangling over the other. He felt good. Exhilarated. The tide was shifting, and he lay quietly and reflected on bits and pieces of conversations with Baby Blue.

"I've been spending a lot of time around you, and something just dawned on me. You almost never swear, do you?"

"Naw, Sarge. My mother raised me better than that."

"Tomorrow, you tell this Elliott Krause you won't be seeing him for a few days. Tell him you're going to L.A. to look at something." He handed him a thousand dollars in small denominations. "Tell Krause you're going to L.A. by yourself."

Baby Blue nodded and smiled. "You're pretty slick, Sarge."

"Then you and Aggie get out of San Diego and take a motel for a couple of days. Palm Springs, maybe. Buy her a couple of nice dinners. Use this dough." He gave him three hundred dollars he had drawn from Stacy. "When you get back into town, go into Elliott's garage and flash the big roll. But don't give him any details about how you scored in L.A. Show him you're tight-lipped. Got it?"

"Got it, Sarge. It's cool. Real cool."

"And don't let anything happen to that grand. It won't be so cool if I don't get it back into my savings account. Another thing. When you get back from wherever you're going, I want you to be driving your mother's car. Tell him Aggie is using the Toyota."

"Sure. Why?"

"Because I'm going to have the intelligence detail put a wire in the car. And you're going to get him to say on tape the things you say he's been talking to you about."

"I can't, Sarge. I can't have a wire. If he finds it, I'm dead."

"He'll never look for one in your mother's car. Trust me."

Baby Blue did not answer for a long time. "Okay, Sarge. But promise me one thing. If I do this, you'll never ask me to put a wire on my body. Promise?"

"I promise."

"I did a little too much talking in the garage the other night, Baby Blue. Not that I can't trust you. But Cliff would be pissed if he knew I opened up, you understand?"

"Not to worry, brother. I ain't going to be talking to Cliff anyway, from what you say."

"The way it's supposed to work is, even if you do run into Cliff, you can't say anything about jobs. That's the way Cliff wants it. *Hey.*" Krause pulled sharply to the curb and stopped. "See if that white Honda comes past us. He's been behind us for three blocks."

They watched the car go by; then Krause made a U-turn. "Your old lady's car turns pretty tight." They drove in silence while Krause maneuvered in and out of traffic, through alleys and across parking lots. He reached under his shirt and handed Baby Blue a .38-caliber revolver with a four-inch barrel.

"It's loaded. From now on, we'll both be healed."

Baby Blue looked at the Colt trademark on the brown walnut grip. "You know I'm on parole, Elliott."

"What I know is, you're in the big time now. You're either in or out. Name it."

Baby Blue put the weapon in his waistband and pulled his shirt over it. Patting the slight bulge, he said, "You got yourselves a new partner."

They stopped for a beer and a sandwich at a deli near San Diego State University. Krause selected a small table at the rear. Salami and mustard oozed from the corner of his mouth as he spoke.

"I'm going to give you a name, and I want you to remember it. The name is 'Dowling.'"

"Dowling?" Baby Blue let a kosher pickle drop from his hand to the plate.

"Yeah. Vincent fucking Dowling. A homicide sergeant. Red-haired guy about fifty years old."

"Elliott, Dowling busted me for murder."

Krause's face tightened. "He did?"

"Sure. What's he got to do with anything?"

A woman student with a tattered knapsack sat down near them, and Krause looked her over, then lowered his voice. "He knows Cliff is pulling jobs."

Baby Blue pushed his chair away from the table.

"Then it's bye-bye, blackbird for me, Elliott. That guy's one of the best. He put a piece of pie on a table once and I took a bite and woke up in Folsom."

Krause grunted and took another look at the woman. "Watch her close. I don't trust her." He turned his chair slightly. "Don't worry. Cliff says this Dowling used to be dangerous. Used to be a bulldog. Get his teeth in something and never let go. But Cliff says he ain't shit anymore." Krause jammed a giant scoop of potato salad into his mouth and talked while he chewed.

"Cliff is driving this Dowling crazy, because Dowling can't prove anything. Doesn't know who Cliff is working with." Krause pointed to himself. "Doesn't even know I'm alive."

"I don't know, Elliott. Dowling still knows me."

Krause drained his bottle of beer and went for another. He surveyed the restaurant as he sat back down.

"This Dowling's in charge of a team. There's a tall, skinny prick they call Bones. And a fat fuck named Shea. And a Mexican name of Montoya. Speedy Montoya. Remember those names too."

When they were back in the car, Krause said, "I told Cliff I'd kill this Dowling for him. Just to be sure. I went and looked at him once, but I didn't tell Cliff. He isn't much. Belly sort of hangs over his belt. I sat right across the street from the police station once and watched him. It would've been easy. I had the shotgun. Could have clipped him right there on the parking lot. Right at the pig station."

"Why won't Cliff let you?"

"Says it'll bring too much heat. But I think that's bullshit. Know what I think?"

"What?"

"I think Cliff just wants to drive that son of a bitch nuts. Beat him into the ground, for some reason."

As they neared the garage Krause told Baby Blue, "If I ever phone you and tell you to go out and buy curtain rods, it means I want you to buy ski masks. Get it? Curtain rods mean ski masks."

"Got it."

Krause drove around the block twice, rather than pulling up in front of the garage. "Let's check out that van down the street, Baby Blue. Could be cops."

He stopped on a residential side street, and they walked casually to the middle of the block. The occupants of the truck turned out to be teenagers necking. The door opened of the house they were standing in front of. An elderly lady wearing a light-colored housecoat leaned down in the doorway. She held a gray-and-yellow cat in her arms. They watched her bend down, put it on the doormat, mutter something and close the door. When they walked away, the cat slinked after them. Krause stopped and crouched.

"Here, kitty, kitty. Come here, little kitty," he said, brushing his fingers against his pant leg. The animal started toward him, hesitated, then continued coming. Krause picked the cat up as it started to rub against his shoe top. "Nice kitty." He cradled it in his arms and began walking slowly. Baby Blue followed, but his attention was diverted when a sports car sped past them. The screech startled him, and when he turned, Elliott Krause was wringing the animal's neck. The legs lurched once, twice, then the body hung limp, suspended only by Krause's hand around its throat.

"What in the devil are you doing, Elliott?"

Krause flung the cat through the air, and it landed with a thud on the doorstep.

"I hope the old cunt has a heart attack when she opens her door in the morning," he said, and walked away.

Dowling entered the men's bathroom near the homicide office. He had consumed several cups of coffee, and it was his second trip in less than thirty minutes. The instructions he had given Baby Blue about the gun were scribbled on notepaper in his pocket and would go into the file.

"A person has to have intent to commit a criminal act. Do you intend to violate the law by carrying that gun in your waistband?"

"Huh?"

"Are you intending to break the law?"

"I don't think so. Elliott gave me—"

"I know that. You are carrying that gun in order to act as an undercover operative, aren't you? To further this investigation, which is a felonious one. Right?"

"Yeah. Further it."

"Good. Then you're not breaking the law."

One urinal was not being used. Dowling hurried to it, and took his position. Before he finished, two Bunco squad detectives entered and stood behind him.

"Come on, Dowling. Quit playing with it and get out of there," one said.

He listened as they talked about a case they were working, known in the trade as a 'pigeon drop.' The name itself riled him, and he was sure his blood pressure surged. He wanted to strangle pigeon-drop suspects. They capitalized on the senility of the elderly to bilk them out of their savings. The suspects came in all ages, sizes, genders and colors. Smooth-talking scum bags in fancy suits and coiffed hair, scum bags in dirty Levis and scum bags in nice dresses. The scum bags changed, but the scenario never did. He winced as he pictured the suspects, randomly casing a bank and picking a victim, allowing her a half-block lead before they rushed to catch up.

"Pardon me, lady."

"Yes, young man."

"I just found this envelope on the sidewalk. It has ten thousand dollars in it. I don't know what to do."

"Oh, my."

"My friend is a lawyer, lady. He'll know what to do. Will you stand here and wait in case the person who dropped it comes back? I'll use that pay phone right there to call my lawyer friend."

"Why, yes, young man. I'll wait right here."

The scum bag would be sure his victim watched him leave the phone booth.

"We may be in luck, lady. My lawyer friend says if nobody claims the money in three days, you and I can split it."

"We can? How lucky."

"All we have to do is deposit good-faith money with the court."

"Good-faith money?"

"Yes. To show we're honest. How much do you have in your savings account?"

"Why, I have . . . Let me see . . . My book is right

here. Six thousand dollars. Is that enough?''

"That's just right, lady. Go get it. I'll wait here for you. Then we'll go to my lawyer friend, and then the judge will hold it for us.''

Dowling finished urinating, then almost caught himself in the zipper when he heard the words "Toyota with a shattered windshield.'' He turned on the water tap while one of the detectives took the urinal he had vacated.

"What kind of case do you have?'' Dowling asked.

"Typical. Victim's a sweet little widow. Eighty-two years young. Ophelia Matthews. Living on a railroader's pension. Happened two hours ago.''

"Got a suspect?'' Dowling soaped his hands.

"Got a physical. White guy. Twenty-eight to thirty. On the lean side.''

"Can Ophelia identify him?'' He rinsed his hands.

"Ophelia couldn't ID him if he took her out to dinner tonight. She just remembers his baby-blue peepers.''

"What about the Toyota?''

"Ophelia didn't see the Toyota. But we got a break. A guy who knows her saw her talking to the suspect. Got a little leery and watched him go to the car. Didn't get a license number but noticed the windshield. Now all we have to do is find it and put Blue Eyes behind the wheel.''

"Good luck,'' Dowling said. His hands were still wet when he left the bathroom and hurried down the hallway.

✂ Twenty-seven

Dowling's hands were still not dry when he jumped into the undercover car and sped to the street on which Aggie Pride lived. Driving past the house, he was glad the Toyota was not in the driveway. Gambling that Baby Blue would come along the street to the north, he turned the corner, pulled to the curb and watched dusk settle in. He had only been there a few minutes when he spied the Toyota coming toward him. The windshield was still shattered, as he'd feared it would be. When he was certain there was only one occupant he got out of his car and flagged it down.

"Follow me. Right now. Got an emergency."

"What is it, Sarge?"

"It's something about Elliott. I'll lead till we get somewhere we can talk."

"I have to go in the house for a minute first."

"No, right now," Dowling ordered.

"I have to take a dump."

"You can take one where we're going. Can't lose a minute. Now, shut up and follow me."

Dowling envisioned his case going up in smoke as he turned into Balboa Park. The Toyota was directly behind him as he drove through the parking lot surrounded by the municipal gymnasium and the Starlight Bowl. When he found no one parked behind the Aerospace Historical Center, he stopped.

"Where were you three hours ago, Baby Blue?"

"Huh?"

"You heard me. Where were you?"

"Home, Sarge. What's the matter?"

Dowling saw the look in Baby Blue's eyes he'd hoped he would not see.

"No, you weren't. I called you at home," he lied.

"Well, I was gone for a few minutes, is all. What's going on about Elliott?"

"Get out of the car. Where did you get the leather jacket?" He felt the smooth, rich sleeve of the tan garment.

"I bought it, Sarge."

"When?"

"I don't know. Yesterday."

It was all coming apart in a hurry, and his anger rose.

"Today. You bought that jacket today, didn't you? Just now."

Baby Blue did not answer. Dowling went through the jacket pockets and Baby Blue's pants pockets and found nothing. Then he threw open the door of the Toyota and frantically searched under the seats and in the glove compartment.

"Give me the keys."

"What?"

"Give me the goddamn keys." Jerking them out of Baby Blue's hand, he popped open the trunk and found the money. It was under an old blanket in the spare-tire well. Dowling flipped through it. It made a large bulge when he stuffed it into his pants pocket. He kept his back to Baby Blue and watched the glow from the downtown skyline. Taking several deep breaths, he could not help but detect the scent of eucalyptus trees.

He wheeled and kicked the fender of the Toyota as hard as he could. Pain shot into his foot like a bolt of lightning. Hobbling, he tried to walk it off.

Making several small circles before he stood in front of Baby Blue, Dowling put everything he had into the punch. The strength of his right shoulder went into the follow-through, and he came out of the arc with closed fists and a fighting stance. The force of the blow sent Baby Blue sprawling to the blacktop.

He was on his back, dazed, bleeding from the mouth, when Dowling grabbed the lapels of his jacket with both hands. Bending over, he sent the next punch in a straight line downward, and he saw Baby Blue's head snap back when it landed.

"You cock sucker. You gutless cock sucker." He hit him twice more. Pulling the limp form off the ground, he hurled it to the front of the Toyota, so that the torso bowed over the hood. Dowling grabbed Baby Blue's lapels again.

"She was *eighty-two years old.* You took her life's savings." He hit him again, uncertain whether Baby Blue was conscious or not. "*You didn't care about her. You piece of shit.*"

As he threw him to the ground, the leather jacket caught on the bumper and ripped. Baby Blue brought his knees up to the fetal position and covered his head with his hands and arms. His sobbing was louder than the hum of traffic on the freeway below them.

"You can quit crying. I'm not going to hit you anymore," Dowling shouted. He looked at his knuckles where skin had peeled. "I'm sorry I ever got mixed up with you. You're a dirt bag. You've always been a dirt bag. Always will be." He walked toward him again and looked down.

"Big, brave man in prison. Hah. I ought to throw you out on the freeway and do the world a favor."

Baby Blue removed his hands from his face. He was sobbing and spitting blood. A car with six-packs of beer on the dashboard and several teenagers in it approached slowly, and the driver stopped.

"Police business. Move on," Dowling growled, flashing his badge. The car sped off.

Dowling walked back to his view of the skyline and lit a Camel. He tried to accept the brutal prospect of continuing the liaison with the cowering figure in the leather jacket. Baby Blue was still sitting on the ground, working his jaw back and forth in his hands.

They had enough to arrest Elliott Krause. The conversation with Baby Blue when the car had been wired was damaging, and Dowling was thankful that California courts allowed surreptitious recordings. Yesterday his team had corroborated Krause's statements about the rape of the sixteen-year-old girl. Krause had told Baby Blue that he'd kept bumping his head against the refrigerator. Bones and Shea had revisited the crime scene and taken measurements, and the physical facts verified Krause's account of the assault. Elliott Krause was bought and paid for, but Cliff Edwards was another story.

Dowling ground his cigarette out on the pavement and lit another. Evidence-wise, they had nothing of substance on Edwards. He had insulated himself expertly, and was continuing to do so. Elliott Krause was going inside on the jobs, and Elliott Krause was the one shooting his mouth off to Baby Blue. Dowling pictured the responses of Edwards, were he confronted with Krause's statements.

"Krause? Krause? Oh, yeah. Big, mean psycho. He used to hang around the pool hall, but I threw him out. Probably got it in for me. He's bad news."

Even with Baby Blue to back up Krause, there was nothing that would hold together for very long. Edwards's attorney would attack the informant with gusto and would dig up old trial transcripts in which Baby Blue had perjured his ass, trying to save himself. The attorney would use the transcripts to impeach the present testimony, and it would all crumble on the floor of superior court.

Even if Krause rolled over and turned state's evidence, Edwards would still look good. Laws about the admissibility of coconspirators' statements severely hampered the District Attorney, and Edwards's lawyer would be granted a motion to sever, would obtain a separate trial for his client.

Dowling crushed out his second cigarette. He was convinced that they would never be able to follow Edwards and Krause to a crime scene, never catch them in the act. Airplane surveillance at night was tricky. Possible under some conditions, but not when the targets drove like rats in a maze.

He forced himself to look at Baby Blue again. He was all Dowling had left to work with.

"Well, what do you want to do?" Dowling asked as they stood next to the car. "Call it quits because you got your nose bloodied, or go back to work? I don't give a shit either way."

"No use quitting now," Baby Blue said quietly. He opened the car door to rest on the seat. "We're in this thing together. Even though you're paying me, we ... well, we're kind of pals, and—"

"No, we're not pals. We're business partners. I have something you need. Money. And you can get something I need."

"I thought there was more than that between us, Sarge."

"I made the mistake of thinking that too. But you and I are on different channels. Let's not either of us forget it. Now, go on home and do something with yourself. You look like you walked into an airplane propeller." Then he remembered. "Hey, wait a minute. How much money did you get from that old lady?"

"Six thousand, four hundred and fifty bucks."

"How much did you spend?"

"A hundred-ninety on the jacket. Ten for gas." He started to grin slightly. "You didn't give me much time, Sarge."

Dowling left the park and drove directly to the Fashion Valley Mall. At a stationery store he found a demonstration typewriter and, using the two-fingered method, typed: "Here's your money back. Couldn't live with myself. Sorry."

A few minutes later he stood at his bank's ATM machine and withdrew two hundred dollars. He winced at the account balance. Then he went to the records division and quietly obtained the home address of Ophelia Matthews.

*   *   *

"What in hell happened to you?" Elliott Krause said. They were in the repair shop, and Krause wiped grease from his forearm.

"Bunch of gang types jumped me. Did a job on me, but they didn't get my wallet." He patted his pocket.

"Why didn't you drill them?"

"I'd left my piece in the car. Ain't thinking right. I'm tired, and my darn chest hurts, because I ain't sleeping enough, I guess."

Krause used cleaner on his hands, then walked to his car. "Here. Three hundred bucks. Go buy two curtain rods. Then stash them good."

"They ain't a hundred fifty bucks each, brother."

"Keep the rest. Take your babe out of town. Get some rest. Buy those curtain rods out of town, too."

"Thanks. I'd like to get away."

"Me and Cliff are going to Vegas for a few days. We do that before a job. Nobody knows us there." He dried his hands on a stained towel. "Nice and relaxing. We bring a couple of party girls with big hooters and shoot dice and . . . It's a good life, Baby Blue. It's a big world out there, and you have to take what you want from it. When you want it." He grinned. "Check you later."

Dowling tried to cover up his notes as Stacy approached the desk, then realized he looked foolish and began scraping up all of the paper work as if to file it.

"You're onto something, aren't you, Dowling?"

"No, sir. Not really. Trying to get a jump on all of this staff work you keep throwing my way."

"Damn it, I haven't had a straight answer from you in weeks. What have you got?"

"Nothing worth talking about, Tom. Sifting through some leads."

Stacy pointed a finger at him. "If you're sandbagging me, I'll sift you back to Management Services, and you can reopen that toilet-paper caper."

Dowling pawed through telephone messages.

"Another thing, Sergeant. I can't hold off much longer on the task-force thing. They're starting to put names on the list.'' Dowling sneered, and Stacy continued. ''We're trying to defuse media heat on the series you're not solving. The chief is lining up a press conference, and you're going to be there.''

''Task forces. Press conferences. You're full of good news, aren't you? Try to hold off for a few more days on the task force. Please.''

They sat in comfortable leather swivel chairs on one side of the cocktail lounge, their empty dinner plates on the oak table in front of them. Elliott Krause had ordered brandies, and he sniffed his tumbler before lighting a huge cigar.

''What lawn did you pick that up off of, Elliott?''

''You got no class, Baby Blue. That is a fine Cuban 'ceegar' from Caesar's Palace.'' He tapped the ash off gingerly.

''How was Vegas, brother?''

''Fuck Vegas. We lost our ass. And me and Cliff almost went to fist city.''

''What?''

''Aw, I got my snoot in the Chivas again. See, we were on a job once, and Cliff wasn't where he was supposed to be afterward, and, well, I had a tight time for a few minutes, was all. Anyway, I brought it up, and one thing led to another.'' He waved his hand. ''That's history.'' He sipped brandy and puffed on his cigar; then he leaned forward and said, ''Monday night. A job. You're on it with us.''

''I'm ready, brother. I'm ready. What kind of gig?''

''What do you care? It'll be a big payday. After we knock off this brandy, you and I won't be seeing each other until the day of the job. That's the way Cliff wants it.''

A television set droned from a platform on the wall by the bar.

''Whatever you say, Elliott.''

''Bring your balls with you, Baby Blue. We may have to kill somebody on this one.'' Krause started to get up.

"*Hey.* There's that red-haired prick. Look." He pointed to the television set and sat back down.

Baby Blue swiveled, and saw Dowling seated next to a gray-haired cop. A battery of news people were seated. Both put their snifters down and stared at the picture.

"Is this the toughest case you've ever worked, Sergeant?"

"It's right up there."

"Do you think you will solve it, Sergeant Dowling?"

"I hope so. What do you people think? You cover a lot of these things."

"What the sergeant means . . ." It was Stacy talking. "He looks to the community for input. For help."

"Have you determined the make of the murder weapon? The shotgun?"

"That's one of the things I can't talk about," Dowling said.

"The dumb motherfucker can't talk about it because he doesn't know," Krause whispered.

"Do you assume they are local suspects, Sergeant?"

"I don't deal in assumptions. I deal in facts."

The camera zoomed in to a close-up of Dowling's face.

"Was the case handled differently because the mayor's brother was a murder victim?"

"Not by me, it wasn't." He squinted into the lights.

"By others, then?"

"You'd have to talk to 'others,' whoever they are."

"A final question, Sergeant Dowling. Are you telling us you have no suspects?"

Dowling's eyes searched out the reporter who'd asked the question.

"If I had evidence that somebody was doing these jobs, I'd go out and arrest him. I wouldn't be sitting here talking to you people."

The rest of the segment utilized film clips of the various scenes, interviews with witnesses, with voice-overs. Sea World was shown from a helicopter, and the cameraman had shot the Captain's Table restaurant so that whitecaps flapped atop the blue waters of the bay.

"Hey, Elliott. Just one thing. How do you know there's safes in all them houses?"

Krause leaned back in his seat, relit his cigar and made sure no one was within hearing range.

"Hah. You'll like this. Lean over here closer." Then he told him.

⚜ Twenty-eight

Dowling was wide awake when his telephone rang at 3:00 A.M. He had not slept at all, and half of the bed covers were draped on the floor. A sense of helplessness had prevented his eyes from closing. His conscience would not have allowed him to let the crime occur on Monday night, but it tortured him to consider arresting Elliott Krause and watching Cliff Edwards make a mockery of the system. He let the phone ring several times, fearful that they had tricked him again and were sorting fresh loot at that very moment.

"Hello," he said feebly.

"It's me. I got terrible trouble, and it ain't Elliott this time. It's Aggie."

Dowling could hear a woman shouting in the background, and he felt relief and anger at the same time.

"What's the matter now?"

"I had to tell her you beat me up. She's been pestering me all week about it, and just now it, you know, it all came out, and I told her."

"This is worth a phone call at three in the morning, huh?"

"Well, she wouldn't let it lay, and I ended up telling her, like, everything."

"Everything, meaning . . . ?"

"Working for you, and working Elliott and Cliff and—"

"Jesus H. Christ," Dowling said moaning.

"Aggie's so hot about it, she's going to go down to the pool hall as soon as it opens and tell Cliff Edwards and . . . She's sore as hell at me and sore as hell at you, Sarge. What'll I do?"

Dowling leaped out of bed. "What you do is, you get her in that car right now and meet me behind that building in the park. You know which one. I don't give a shit if you have to stuff her in the trunk. You get her there right now."

Dowling arrived behind the Aerospace building and smoked cigarettes and wished. He wished he had stayed in the Navy and never seen the inside of the San Diego Police Department. He was still wishing it when the Toyota drove into the lot and he saw Aggie Pride leap out of the passenger side before the car came to a halt.

"You son of a bitch." She was screaming it while she ran to Dowling. "So he works for you? That's where he's been half the day and night for six weeks." She was wearing a man's white dress shirt and brown corduroys, and her breasts were heaving. Baby Blue loitered a few yards away, looked at Dowling and shook his head.

"Is this how you treat all of your employees? Beat the holy crap out of them?" When he did not answer she screamed, *"Do you?"*

He stood passively, with his arms folded, and tried to think.

"Why did you beat him up, you son of a bitch? Answer me."

Dowling turned toward Baby Blue, who put his head down and remained silent.

"We had a misunderstanding," Dowling said.

"Oh, my God. A misunderstanding. What would you do if you really got angry at him? Throw him off the bridge? I almost took him to the hospital as it was." She crowded him. "I knew the day I met you in the hospital you were up to something. Remember? I asked you?" She mimicked Dowling. " 'What's the matter, can't a person just be nice to someone?' You use people. That's your game." She spun around and pointed at Baby Blue.

"And you. You're a rotten liar. Like all men are rotten liars. And cheats."

She was not through with Dowling. "This man was critically wounded in state prison. He was brutally stabbed because he had the guts to think of someone besides himself. And you—you treat him like this. You make a . . . a no-good informant out of him. Take away his self-respect. Degrade him. Beat him bloody." She hissed at Dowling, "You're worse than he ever was, because you're a cop and . . . God, I hate you." She started crying. "Tomorrow I'm going to see this Elliott Edwards, or whatever his name is, and . . . God, I hate you." She ran to the car and got into it.

"Well," Dowling said to Baby Blue.

"Well," Baby Blue said back.

Dowling walked slowly to the passenger side of the Toyota.

"I can't do anything about your hating me, but please listen to something."

She turned away from him.

"If you run to the pool hall, you'll blow our case out of the water, all right, but there's more. Baby Blue will be a dead man. The witness-protection program and the First Marine Division couldn't protect him from those two. They've got marvelous reasons to shut him up."

"I don't care about him either anymore," she said, the back of her head still turned to Dowling. She dabbed at her eyes.

"I know how you feel about me. And let's say I believe you when you say you don't care about him." He motioned toward Baby Blue, then wet his lips and took a deep breath.

"But how do you feel about Rita Martinez?"

"I don't know any Rita Martinez."

"I know," Dowling said. "Rita Martinez made the mistake of going to work one night. Rita Martinez wouldn't have hurt a fly. She was just trying to make a buck and take it to college with her, because nobody in her family had ever been to college, and she wanted to make her mother and father proud of her. Her father was waiting out in the parking lot for her the night it happened.'' Dowling stopped talking.

''The night what happened?'' She looked at him apprehensively.

''The night Cliff Edwards and his friend Elliott Krause blew her off the face of the fucking earth because they didn't want to work for their money.''

Dowling watched her face carefully.

''I get weary sometimes, Aggie. I get weary of looking at dead bodies and blood and gore and seeing people cry who are left behind. I get frustrated trying to make things like that stop happening. Sometimes I get so weary and so frustrated, I make mistakes.'' He sighed. ''When I get that way and I need to motivate myself, I carry a picture in my pocket to remind me what I'm here for.''

He reached into his jacket pocket.

''Here, Aggie. Here's a picture of Rita Martinez that was taken the night I met her.''

He put the photo in front of her face and flicked the dome light on.

''That hole is where her breast used to be, but she's a cute kid, don't you think?''

When she had finished crying, Aggie said, ''You win, you bastard. But you can still go to hell.''

When she had driven out of sight, Dowling ushered Baby Blue to a bench, and they sat down. The early-morning moisture soaked their pants, but Dowling did not care.

''I don't want to talk about Aggie,'' Dowling said.

They lit cigarettes and watched tree branches wave in the darkness. He knew the grass had been cut the day before because of its unmistakable smell, and he reached down and let clippings fall through his fingers.

''It's pretty here this time of the morning,'' he said. Then neither spoke for many minutes.

''By the way,'' Dowling said finally. ''You're going to put on a body wire.''

''Oh, no, Sarge.'' Baby Blue's head snapped up. ''They'll kill me. I can't do that. I won't.''

"Yes, you will," Dowling said, smiling.

"You promised, Sarge. You gave me your word you'd never ask me to wear a wire. You promised."

"I did, at that, didn't I? No matter. You're going to put the wire on and drop into Luckie's and have a little chat with Mr. Edwards."

Baby Blue got up. "You can't make me do that."

Dowling let his feet extend as far as he could and looked at the gray-black sky.

"Oh, I'm not going to hold you down while they hook the wire up. I'm not going to have to. You see, you and I are going to do a little trade-off. You've been in this cops-and-robbers business awhile. You understand all about trade-offs."

"What kind of trade?" Baby Blue asked cautiously.

"A two-by-two trade. We're each going to do two things. First of all, you're going to put that wire on and I'm not going to tell Aggie that you bilked that eighty-two-year-old widow out of her dough."

Baby Blue was shaking his head.

"Then, once we've done that, we're going to do one more nice thing for each other. I'm not going to tell your P.O. about the old lady."

Baby Blue sat down again.

"What am I going to do for you? To make up for that?"

Dowling smiled again, only the smile was wider.

"You're going out front in this case."

"Oh, no, Sarge. I can't go out front. I just give you info so you can work your case and . . . heck, no."

"Oh, you'll do it, Baby Blue. You are going to do just what good citizens are expected to do. Get involved. Do your civic duty. One for all and all for one. Take that oath in front of the judge and, for the first time in your life, tell the truth on the witness stand."

Baby Blue sank lower on the bench.

"You'll tell the court all about your conversations with Elliott Krause and all about the two wire searches at gunpoint, and I don't think you'll change your mind and try to lie on the stand. Because the judge will have a pretty good idea of which one of us is telling the truth. Judges are good at that.'' Dowling stretched.

''And when all the crappola is tossed into the courtroom stew pot and a bunch of D.A.'s and lawyers and witnesses get through stirring it around, Krause and Edwards will be on their way to your old address.''

He put his arm around Baby Blue.

''We make quite a team, don't we? Let's go find someplace we can drink a beer at four in the morning.''

≋ Twenty-nine

There were no pedestrians on the sidewalk in front of Luckie's pool hall. Baby Blue sat across the street in the Toyota and wondered if he was going to throw up again. His stomach knotted, and he hoped Cliff Edwards had taken the night off. He wondered if Edwards carried a gun, and he was glad that Krause had given him the Colt revolver. His chest hurt, and he was glad Dowling had affixed the body recorder around his crotch, instead of his upper torso. Dowling had used adhesive tape and ace bandages to secure the three-inch metal box to the inside of his upper thigh, and it was beginning to irritate his left testicle.

The box containing the strange-looking oval cassette and the wires leading from the box ended with two miniature microphones, which had been taped to the inside of his waistband. The microphones were in front, one on each side, and Dowling had cautioned him against unnecessary rubbing in that area, because the static would drown out any conversation.

"If you can, hook your thumbs in your waistband while you're talking," Dowling told him. "The mikes are hidden enough not to be seen, and you get a better recording that way."

The on-off switch was in the waistband also, in the back, and he turned it on when he began walking toward the pool hall.

When he entered he did not see Cliff Edwards, and

he breathed a sigh of relief. He decided to check the rest room, in case Dowling had someone watching him. Baby Blue almost collided with Edwards, who was pushing the door open from the inside.

"What the hell are you doing here?" Edwards said quietly, looking down at him. He carried a pool cue, and chalk dusted the lapel of his dark green velour shirt.

"I couldn't sleep, Cliff. Something's bothering me. Figured I better come by and talk to you about it."

Edwards eyed him suspiciously. "Man, I hardly know you. What have you and I got to talk about?"

"Nothing if you don't want to. I just got a problem about something a friend of ours told me. And you're the only dude that can straighten it out."

Edwards looked around and walked slowly to a table with no players. Baby Blue hesitated, then followed him. "What kind of problem?" Edwards asked.

"About tomorrow night."

"Tomorrow night? I don't know what the hell you're talking about. I'm busy. Got a business to run here." He didn't walk away, but stared at Baby Blue instead.

"Look brother, I can understand why you don't want to talk to me. I get the picture. Thing is, if I don't get something cleared up . . . then I'm going to be busy tomorrow night. Ain't going to be able to come out and play with you and your friend."

Edwards said nothing. Baby Blue started walking toward the front door, stopped, then returned to Edwards.

"I learned a long time ago not to do business with people unless I was sure I could trust them. And I got some big doubts about you. See you around."

He was almost to the sidewalk when Edwards called to him. "Wait a minute, man." Edwards had laid the pool cue down and was coming toward him. "Maybe we ought to talk, Baby Blue. Let's go out in the alley."

✂ Thirty

Across town, Dowling was serving dessert to his children, but his mind was on Baby Blue. Matt's voice drew him back.

"Dad, this is good orange meringue pie," Matt said. "Almost as good as the package stuff I get from the lunch wagon at work."

"Jenny, remind me to put the package stuff in Bob Hope's lunch bag from now on, will you?"

Jenny laughed. "It's nice to sit around the kitchen table again, Daddy." She eyed her brother. "Matt, have you told him yet?"

"Told me what?"

"I'd like to start Redlands next term, Dad."

"You would? This is a nice surprise. I thought you'd written college off."

"I guess I had. But I've been thinking a lot lately. And my boss was really encouraging about it. Said he could fit me in over summer and semester breaks."

"He's been shooting baskets at Muni gym, too, Dad. Getting ready. Three seconds in the key, and all of that jock-strap stuff."

"Jenny, ladies don't talk about jock straps," Dowling muttered.

She and Matt laughed.

"You're so funny," she said.

"What do you mean?"

"You just are." She smiled, keeping her lips pursed

286

together. Then she looked down and began tapping the bottoms of the glass salt and pepper shakers together. "Remember at the Chicken Pie Shop when we were talking and Matt said how he was thinking of Mom and kept pumping too much gas?"

"Sure, I remember."

"Something like that kind of happened to me a few days ago."

"Like what, Jenny?" Dowling took a drink of coffee.

"I went through a red light. And got a ticket."

"You got a traffic ticket? My daughter?"

"It's my first one."

"You shouldn't have been written up. That is, you should have stopped at the light. Didn't you tell him I was a cop?"

"No, I was too embarrassed."

"Embarrassed your father is a policeman?"

"No. Embarrassed I ran the light. Anyway, we have to go to court in two weeks."

"Who's we?"

"You and I. Silly as it is, since I'm a juvenile, I have to have a parent with me."

"You can't just mail it in?"

"Daddy. You're a policeman. You're supposed to know these things."

Dowling shook his head. "You have a great sense of timing, Jenny. You get a ticket and reduce the heat by telling me right on the heels of good news from Matt. I can't believe you got a ticket."

Jenny frowned. "Daddy?" she said. "Does drinking run in families? Heavy drinking like Mom's? Somebody at school said it did."

He looked into her big eyes, and her soft face reminded him of Helene's.

"It can," he said. "It does in some families."

When she looked distressed, he added, "It depends on human beings, Jenny. Not on genetics. We're only products of our environment to a point. A lot of people from what they call 'the wrong side of the tracks,' they stay on that side forever. Others get inspired. Cross over.

Get a vision. So with drinking, the trick is to get your life to have enough meaning so you don't need to drink. Don't need to look for escape routes.''

"Was Mom looking for escape routes?" Matt asked.

"Yes," he answered. "She wanted to escape so badly she . . . surrendered." He felt their stares.

"But by God, she gave the three of us a second chance. Her dying is why we're sitting here now, talking about the things we are instead of running off in separate directions. We're a family. Do you believe that, Matt?"

"I do now, Dad."

"How about you, Jenny?"

"I think I do."

"But you're not sure?"

"I'm scared."

He saw moisture in her eyes, and he moved closer to her. "What are you scared about?"

"Are you sure you want to know?"

"I've never been more sure," he said. "Tell me. Please.''

Jenny picked up two spoons and tapped them together. She wiped her eyes and put her head down.

"I'm scared 'cause I just turned sixteen, and I'm growing up without a mother. I'm scared because Mom killed herself. I'm scared because she was a . . . a drunk. I'm scared because Matt is leaving for college, and he and I are closer now than we ever were before, and now he's going." She was trying not to cry. "I'm working real hard, Daddy, at trying to understand why you lied to us about Mom's committing suicide. But I'm doing better, I think. And I better tell you this. . . . The last couple of years I wondered how much you loved me. But now I think I know, and I keep telling myself that when Matt leaves, you and I will do all right. Do you think we will?"

"I know we will," Dowling said. "I'm beginning to know a lot of things. Someone reminded me it's never too late to begin to know."

He got up and walked to the window and looked at

the hedgerow of Eugenias that he and Helene had planted.

"Remember what's written on the medallion that Grandpa sent me? 'Be ashamed to die until you have won some victory for humanity.' " He turned to them and folded his arms across his chest. "That's been going around in my head like a new tune."

"What does it mean, Dad? A victory for humanity." Matt tried to answer the question himself. "Like walking on the moon and discovering the polio vaccine, things like that?"

"It means different things to different people," Dowling said. "What it means to me is being the best person you can be. In your day-to-day life, trying to serve humanity in some way. Promoting peace in the world, maybe. Not standing around winking at bigotry and poverty. Treating people with dignity. I haven't got it all figured out yet."

"Did Mom die before she won a victory?" Jenny asked.

"Are you kidding? Two of her greatest victories are sitting right in front of me." He smiled. "Your mother made us take a hard look at our lives and try to improve them. What a great gift."

They both nodded.

"Daddy, Mrs. Mayfield called me. She wanted to know if I'd like help with French. Remember how she and Mom spoke it all the time? I do need help, so I told her yes." Jenny put her arm around him. "The other thing is, could I start taking piano lessons?"

The bank-account balance flashed through his mind, and just as quickly he thought of an offer he had received from the community-college district to teach one night a week in the criminal-justice program. He had tentatively turned it down, believing it would be too time-consuming when added on to family life and murders.

"You can start banging that keyboard tomorrow, Jenny. We'll line up a good teacher. And by the way, I'm going to be instructing at Grossmont from now on.

How do you like that? Your old man's gonna be a 'per-
fesser.' ''

After he'd rinsed the plates and replaced the pie in a
plastic container, Dowling went to the dresser in the bedroom and opened the bottom drawer. He found what he
was looking for under two of his old uniform shirts. It
was the oak picture frame with the paper napkin from
Angelo's. He looked at it and grinned, then carried it to
the hallway. The hook was still on the wall, and he put
up the frame and straightened it.

As soon as the phone rang, he knew it was the call
he had been waiting for.

"It's me. I've got a tape."

"Did he say something good?"

"You'll see. Come listen to it, Sarge."

They sat in Dowling's car at the rear of a dark church
parking lot in the Bay Park area. Baby Blue's smile covered half of his face. Dowling took a deep breath and
turned the recorder on. Like two statues, they sat in the
cool of the December night and listened.

"Now, what in the hell is your problem, Baby
Blue?"

"Just that . . . well, Elliott told me you and him
had a beef in Vegas. Something that went wrong
once. You weren't where you were supposed to be
on a job. And that bothered me some."

"Humph."

"Then he told me you were a cop, and he and
I about became ex-friends real fast."

"Used to be. I used to be a cop."

"Was. Are. Used to be. What's the difference?
A cop's a cop."

"Makes you nervous, huh?"

"Let's put it this way. I been pickin' my own

friends for twenty-eight years, and cops ain't high on the list.''

''They're not even on my list anymore. I was smart to get out when I did. Crap way to make a living. Bunch of little tin soldiers hassling people. Elliott tell you why I left?''

''No.''

''I got into an argument with a couple of supervisors. They didn't know their ass about real police work. So I took a hike.''

''Look, Cliff. I don't like this. I'm about to . . . to do business with you and Elliott, and I just find out you were a stinking cop. For all I know, you're a snitch. That's why I came over here. To size you up. See if I can trust you.''

''Humph.''

''On the way over here, I got thinking, I should have asked Elliott. To hear him tell it, he's running the show.''

''Him running the show? He has trouble finding his way home. He's got a big mouth. And he's dumb.''

''Well, he seems kind of dumb to me, too. I couldn't figure it.''

''One time, I tell him, 'Elliott, you have to come out the side door of the restaurant. The side door. You come out the back door, and some cop driving by has a chance of seeing you.' What does he do? Comes out the back door. He's dumb.''

''He's crazy too, Cliff. He wrung some cat's neck. For nothing. Just wrung its neck.''

''That's Elliott. Shit, he blew away some little broad at Sea World and he didn't have to. She surprised him. Came into the counting room. He had it under control. Had all the people down on the floor. But he had to shoot her.''

"That's cold, Cliff."

"Well, I don't give a damn about killing her. But it brings more heat. Shows how dumb he is."

"That clears things up some for me. Hearing your side of it."

"Another thing, Baby Blue. That crap about my not being where I was supposed to be that time. That was Elliott's fault, not mine. See, he goes in and I wait in a car with a police-scanner radio monitoring calls. I go to a pay phone and call him while he's inside. Make sure everything is cool. Then we time it from that point on. Anyway, that night I make the call, then I wait and I wait and I wait. No Elliott. I figure maybe the victim got loose and got to Elliott, or something. So I switch locations, get a little farther away, just in case. Come to find out Elliott's dick got hard and he's raping some little broad."

"Wow, Cliff. You think of everything."

"That's not all. I tell him exactly where to dump the victim's car. Then I pick him up and we're history. Those fuckin' cops are getting the radio call and we're counting our money and sorting out the jewelry. I always let it cool for a while before I deal it off. Always out of town. Phoenix. Frisco. I got all the right connections."

"That makes me feel better about everything. I run into a lot of dudes at Folsom and Q but I never run into anybody with your kind of smarts."

"When you have my kind of smarts, you don't end up in Folsom or Q."

"The announcer on TV said you guys pulled about eight jobs."

"Well, maybe after tomorrow we won't need old Elliott anymore. He's getting to be kind of a liability. Maybe it'll just be me and old Baby Blue. What do you think?"

"I think I'll go along with whatever you say, Cliff. Thing is, I'm starting to get a good edge on about tomorrow night. I like working my way up to an edge before a job."

"Good. I got a couple of reasons for wanting you along tomorrow night. It's a big job. You've been around a lot longer then Elliott, and I don't want him messing anything up. Like always, he'll be the inside man. You'll be outside, but not with me. I'll lay it all out for you tomorrow just before we leave the motel."

"The motel?"

"Yeah. We'll all three take a room and relax and go over everything. We all stay together. Nobody makes any phone calls, or anything. Nice and safe."

"I'm with you, Cliff. With you all the way. It's an . . . an honor to be working with someone like you."

"They're going to be talking about tomorrow's job for a long time, Baby Blue. That lousy police department and that lousy Dow—this detective. They're going to go crazy, because there will be so much heat put on them."

"Heat from where, Cliff?"

"Hah. Heat from the news media. Heat from the city. And lots of heat from the Chargers."

"The Chargers? We going to rob a football team?"

"Football team, hell. We're going to knock off San Diego Jack Murphy Stadium."

"San Diego Stadium?"

"Yep. Big money. After tomorrow night, Baby Blue, our lives are really going to change."

"I hope you're right, Cliff. I hope you're right."

🎗 Thirty-one

The next morning and afternoon were hellish, but at dinnertime Dowling made a quick trip home with a pizza for Matt and Jenny. He removed his prized raspberry tortes from the freezer for their dessert.

"What's the occasion, Dad?" Matt asked.

"No occasion." He grabbed his jacket. "I'll be late tonight. Wrapping up a case."

"Will it be dangerous, Daddy?"

"We stack the odds our way, Jenny."

"I love both of you guys," he said when he reached the door.

Speedy Montoya held the receiver between his cheek and shoulder as he fumbled for more change on the shelf of the telephone booth. He made the three phone calls in rapid succession:

"I love you, sweet girl. Talk to you tomorrow."

"I love you, sweet girl. Talk to you tomorr— What? Hell, no. I don't talk like this to anyone but you."

"I love you, sweet girl. Working late tonight. How about leaving the key out? I'll be cold and tired."

✹ Thirty-two

The alcove Dowling was hiding in on the third deck of the stadium was tiny. If he extended his arms fully, he could touch the coolness of the smooth concrete walls. There was a drinking fountain, which he had used three times in the fifteen minutes he had been there, and a dirty, sixteen-ounce paper cup lay on its side near his foot. Stale beer had dribbled out and was running in rivulets alongside his other foot. The corridor ran from the press box to the counting room. It was not possible to get to the counting room without walking past Dowling's hiding place.

He fingered the cold steel of the Remington 12-gauge shotgun leaning in the corner. At the same time, he wondered what Elliott Krause would do when they challenged him. Actually, Krause would be looking down the barrels of two shotguns, because Speedy Montoya was in an identical alcove directly across from Dowling. Three steps separated them.

Dowling had carefully cased the area and settled on the two alcoves because a few inches of their heads were the only parts that would be exposed when they confronted Krause. The wall would shield their bodies. At Dowling's request, the lights above them had been turned off. Krause would be looking into a black blur, but he would be perfectly silhouetted for the detectives.

Dowling had no idea where Krause was hiding, or how he had smuggled the sawed-off shotgun into the stadium. There were any number of places to hide, and he decided it was folly to try to flush the man out. Bones and Shea were waiting in the counting room, but the money had been quietly transferred to an off-site location. Four detectives were secreted in the press box at the end of the corridor, to cut Krause off if he chose to turn and run.

Ironically, only that morning had they been able to find an arrest history on Krause. They had been disadvantaged in their search, because they'd had no fingerprint records to submit. After Dowling had tried a string of combinations, Colorado had tumbled to him under his true name, Harold Elliott Krause. He had been released from the penitentiary at Canon City a few months before he'd drifted to San Diego.

Larry Shea had spoken with the Denver detective who had arrested him.

"Just one nasty, psycho son of a bitch. A burglar who liked to beat up women if they were in the house. But he went like a pussycat when we took him down. Keep him in California for a while, will you?"

The information had not surprised Dowling. Krause behaved the way tough guys reacted when they did not like the odds, he told Speedy. Their idea of a good time was kicking an old lady across the room or getting the drop on six guys around a poker table. When crazy cops were pointing shotguns at them, it was a different story.

Dowling slouched against the alcove wall to take some weight off his knees. Both legs were beginning to hurt. He wished he were ten years younger, because his eyes would have been ten years better and his reflexes ten years faster, and he wanted to rely on Vincent Dowling, and not Speedy Montoya or anyone else, when he squared off against Elliott Krause. The way he had relied on himself when he'd taken on all of the other vicious sociopaths he had waited for in alcoves and bushes and closets and on rooftops and . . .

He remembered the time he'd waited on his stomach for nine hours under a piano in a dark saloon, and when he'd finally made his move, the suspect had shot himself in the head. Stakeouts were a younger man's game. Stacy had reminded him of that and something else a few hours prior.

"You bastard, Dowling. I knew you were holding out on me."

"I was just trying to wrap this thing up, Tom"—he smiled—"and stall that damnable task force."

It was Stacy's turn to smile. "There was never any consideration given to a task force."

"But you told me—"

"Oh, I made all of that up."

"You didn't."

"Yeah. The chief's trying to modernize us old warhorses. That comes under 'motivational methods,' or something like that."

Dowling became irritated when he saw Speedy poking his head out of the alcove. Waving emphatically, he motioned for him to be more cautious.

Most of the day had been spent at his desk, planning. Search warrants had been obtained for the pool hall and the homes of Edwards and Krause. After the arrests the warrants would be executed, but Dowling had little confidence that anything incriminating would be found. Krause would be as good as convicted when they caught him, shotgun in hand, advancing on the counting room. Edwards was another matter, and Dowling had toyed with numerous plans throughout the afternoon.

It was highly unlikely Edwards would enter the stadium parking lot; doubtful he would be within a mile of the perimeter roads. His history was to insulate himself, and Dowling figured Edwards would head for the security of home when Krause and Baby Blue failed to appear at whatever spot had been designated. The plan then was for Baby Blue to telephone Edwards with a frantic message. A carefully rehearsed frantic message.

"Cliff. Something went sour. I can't talk now. Meet us right away. Parking lot. Fifty-fourth and University."

Then a patrol car staked out a few blocks from his house would stop him and transport him to the police station. Arresting him at home would be convenient, but family and neighbors had a habit of notifying attorneys, who sometimes beat the client to the station. Dowling held next to no hope that Edwards would waive his Miranda rights and talk to them, but at least they wouldn't have a lawyer in their face.

"No wonder we couldn't figure out how they knew those homes had safes," Dowling told his team. "If Krause hadn't told Baby Blue we still wouldn't know."

A small local business selling exterior security bars had purchased a customer list from safe manufacturers. Edwards had stumbled into a contact at the company, and the rest had been easy.

Dowling had taken color photographs of Baby Blue holding the ski mask he'd purchased, hoping to impress a jury. Afterward he brought home a pizza, then left for the stadium and watched sixty-one thousand Monday-night football fans file out of the Chargers-Raiders game. Finally, he'd gone to the alcove to keep his appointment with Elliott Krause.

When it happened, it was sudden. Dowling was certain he'd seen a figure in the corridor, some twenty steps away. Obviously, Speedy had seen it also. Picking up the shotgun, Dowling dropped to a semicrouch. When he looked again, an instant later, the figure had disappeared. He caught Speedy's eye and shrugged. Staring down the corridor he still saw nothing, then almost went limp when Speedy left his alcove and started across to him. Speedy was not carrying his shotgun, and by the time Dowling tried to motion him to go back, he was in the middle of no-man's land. Speedy had not seen the figure. Dowling heard Krause's voice at the same time that he was able to distinguish the ski mask in the darkness.

"Freeze," Krause shouted.

Dowling peeked. Krause was ten steps away, shotgun at waist level, aimed at the motionless Speedy Montoya. Dowling quickly calculated the risk. Speedy would be a dead man if Krause fired. If either of them fired. Taking a deep breath, he quietly laid his shotgun down, picked up the empty beer cup and staggered out of the alcove toward Speedy. He did not allow himself to look in Krause's direction, gambling on the darkness to conceal his identity. Weaving from side to side, he called to Speedy in a loud, drunken voice.

"I love you, you macho stud. Come suck my peter again."

He embraced Speedy and pushed him gradually toward Speedy's alcove.

"I love you," Dowling cried again. Krause was moving toward them.

"Get out of here, you fag bastards. Come this way."

Dowling fell to his knees, letting his arms slide down Speedy's legs. His heart was pounding.

"I'll suck your peter," he said loudly.

His fingers closed around the barrel of Speedy's shotgun. Speedy was safely in the alcove when Dowling, still on his knees, whirled. Falling flat onto the corridor floor, he pointed the shotgun and yelled, "Police, Elliott. Drop the fuckin' gun."

Dowling saw the red explosion and heard pellets splatter the wall near his head as he pulled the trigger. His brain was in the process of telling his finger to pull it a second time, when the masked figure lurched backward, shotgun clanging on the concrete. A flurry of activity at the end of the corridor caught his attention, and he recognized detectives running toward them, guns in hand.

"Suspect is down," Dowling shouted. "Be careful. He may have a .45."

Dowling got to his feet and advanced cautiously, aiming his shotgun at the form on the ground. Overhead lights came on, and he saw blood streaming from Krause's chest.

"Handcuff him first," Dowling ordered.

A detective with a walkie-talkie advised Tom Stacy that the suspect was in custody, then requested an ambulance. Dowling handed the shotgun to Speedy, then knelt. The torso was heaving, and the head jerked when Dowling reached for the bottom of the blue-and-yellow ski mask. When he lifted it he looked into the face of

Elliott Krause. Into the face of certain death.

They stared at each other. Krause's lips moved, but Dowling saw the blue eyes glaze as he shone his flashlight on them. They were still staring at each other seconds later, when Elliott Krause died.

"I'm sorry, Sarge. I'm really sorry. I was coming over to ask you if you thought—"

"I'll talk to you later, Speedy. We were lucky. And put your damn hands in your pocket. We're at a shooting scene."

"I'm a lucky guy. You saved my life."

Dowling saw Bones and Shea running toward them from the counting room.

"I don't know how you ever thought of that, Sarge. But I sure thank you," Speedy said.

Dowling looked at him. "I wasn't the one who thought of it. Some old retired cop taught me that one. You called him a slob. Remember? You know where he lives. You ought to go thank him."

"I haven't done anything. I don't even know what I'm down here for," Cliff Edwards said, grinning. He was seated at a table in the interrogation room, across from Dowling and Larry Shea. Dowling felt fresh and alert, and it surprised him. Only an hour and a half before, he had been at the stadium.

Edwards yawned, covering his mouth with his hand. Then he stretched. "It's one-thirty in the morning, Sarge. You keep lousy hours."

"Yeah. That's part of the price you pay when your luck changes," Dowling said.

"What do you mean?"

"Last time I saw you, you said, 'Better luck next time.' Remember?"

"I remember. You ought to have 'em flush this place out. It stinks." He wrinkled his nose.

"It's home to us, pal," Larry Shea said. "And you're down here because we've been investigating some robbery-murders."

"You must be pretty desperate. 'Course, I know you

got problems. I saw Sherlock Holmes, here, on the tube the other night.'' He gestured toward Dowling.

"I did have some problems the other night, Cliff. Tonight we're looking better.''

He was positive that playing on Edwards's curiosity was the only chance he had of getting him to waive Miranda. Leaning forward in his chair, he added, "You see, we were pretty desperate. Lot of heat from city hall and from the newsies and from the chief's office. Jeez, heat everywhere, Cliff.'' He lit a Camel. "So we found out that Elliott Krause had been in your pool hall a few times. And . . . He's a big sucker with blue eyes. Same build and same color eyes as the guy with the ski mask.''

"So?''

"So then we got to thinking,'' Larry Shea said. "You were a cop. You'd know how to plan these jobs. And you'd know how to get rid of the loot. And you'd know to have the guy wear gloves and a mask. Keep the lab from picking up prints, and witnesses from identifying him.''

"Sure,'' Dowling interjected. "We put two and two together and came up with you and Krause.''

"That's it. That's your case?''

"That's what we've got on you. We figure we may be able to convince the D.A. to charge you,'' Dowling said.

Cliff Edwards started to laugh. "You guys are funny. The D.A. will think so, too.'' He could not stop laughing. "I suppose you want to interrogate me, Sarge.''

"We would like to.''

"Well, let's get on with it, then, if I can stop laughing. Give me my rights.''

When Dowling had finished reciting them, he asked, "Do you understand your rights as I have explained them to you?''

"Sure, I do. Must have given them to people myself a hundred times.''

"Having in mind and understanding your rights, are you willing to talk with us?'' Dowling looked away from him.

Edwards hesitated slightly. "Sure. For a couple of minutes."

"Couple of minutes is all I feel like talking," Shea said. "I'm beat."

"Where's Krause now, Sarge? Did you pinch him too?"

"Yeah," Dowling said. "but he's not saying anything." He took his notebook from his pocket and wrote the time and the date on the top of the page. "What did you do tonight, Cliff? Be truthful, now."

"I pretty much stayed at home tonight. Then, a little while ago, I'm in bed, asleep, and I get a call from some punk who wants to see me about something, so I get out of bed and jump in the car, and some patrol car pulls me over and takes me down here. Hell, that's a violation of my civil rights. I may sue, come to think of it."

"Who's the punk who phoned you?" Shea asked.

"Oh, some guy who used to hang around the pool hall. I forget his name. Something Blue. Little Blue. Old Blue. I don't know."

Dowling turned in his chair and looked at Larry Shea. The two of them ignored Cliff Edwards.

"Blue, Blue, Blue. Jeez, Shea. Do you think it could be?"

"Who are you thinking of, Sarge? Baby Blue?"

"Yeah," Dowling said, looking mystified. He and Shea were still looking at each other. "Baby Blue. The police informant. The one who's been in Cliff and Elliott's back pocket for the last six weeks."

Cliff Edwards's face tightened; then his jaw dropped. His knuckles whitened as he gripped the edge of the table. Dowling faced him and put his face near Edwards's.

"Baby Blue, the police informant who wears his little tape recorder wrapped around his balls. Not all the time, huh, Cliff? But sometimes. Like last night. He had the tape recorder wrapped around his balls when you and he were bullshitting in the alley behind the pool hall." Dowling reached into his coat pocket and pulled out a cassette and let the tiny microphone and wires dangle from it.

"When you told him how all of the jobs had gone down. How Elliott came out of the back door of one joint, when you'd told him to use the side door. How you always make the phone call to him while he's on the job. How, quote, 'those fuckin' cops are getting the radio call and we're counting our money and sorting out the jewelry,' end quote, and how you're going to knock off the stadium and . . . ah, hell. My memory isn't as good as it used to be. Play the tape for Cliff, will you, Larry?"

Later, after Edwards had confessed, Dowling sat at his desk alone. The squad room was deserted. It was 6:00 A.M., and he was exhausted. The interview by Internal Affairs investigators had lasted longer than the interrogation of Edwards. Dowling had detailed for them the sequence of events.

The investigators, both lieutenants, had tape-recorded the conversation and nodded grimly. Dowling was not offended by the detailed line of questioning. He considered himself a company man, and knew the department would have looked bad if the lieutenants had conducted anything short of an open, honest and intense investigation.

Bones and Shea had been sent home after executing the search warrants. A matchbook from the Captain's Table restaurant had been found in a suit-coat pocket in Krause's closet. Nothing else connected to the crime series had been located. The same I.A. lieutenants who had questioned Dowling were now interviewing Speedy Montoya.

Dowling called home, softly explaining to Matt and Jenny what had occurred. He did not want them learning of the shooting from the TV or radio. The stack of reports on his desk had grown higher, but he decided it would wait another day.

Shea had called for a patrol car to transport Edwards to the county jail on murder and robbery charges. What

occurred next was an event that Dowling placed in his
"rocking-chair memories" file.

The patrol officer strolled into the squad room, and
Dowling was sure he had never seen a longer neck than
the one between the brown uniform collar and the an-
gular chin. But it was the dialogue that caught him off
balance.

"Remember me?" the officer asked Cliff Edwards.

"Sure," Edwards grunted. "How you doing, Ichabod?"

"I made it through my probation, no thanks to you."

"I guess anybody can make it, these days."

"By the way, that handle you hung on me stuck. All
the cops call me Ichabod now."

Dowling was a step from the door when he heard the
officer add, "Oh, well. I've known since I was in third
grade that I had a long neck. One thing, though. Long
as it is, it isn't as long as yours is going to be when
those cons stretch it. I hear they don't care much for
cops in the joint. Now, turn around and put your hands
behind your back while I snap the bracelets on."

꧁ Thirty-three

Dowling's team members worked hard the following week, but they enjoyed regular hours, and Dowling found himself sleeping better than he had in years. Everyone spent his time compiling voluminous reports covering all phases of the investigation.

"There's no such thing as a slam-dunk case anymore, Dowling. But this is pretty close," the Chief Deputy District Attorney told him with a smile. "You guys did a hell of a job."

Most days he left work promptly at 5:00 P.M. and went directly home or browsed in the stores, mingling with other Christmas shoppers. It had been a long time since he had done that.

When he took the time to calculate his finances he was pleasantly surprised. He was being paid well, his house payments were ridiculously low in an era of sky-rocketing San Diego mortgages and Helene had, he discovered, been stashing money in tax-sheltered annuities.

He had not seen Baby Blue since December third, the night of the arrests. He had spoken with him twice on the phone, chatting aimlessly in a manner Dowling intended would lead to phasing out the relationship. He had made it clear that he was not interested in cultivating an association with a full-time informant.

"What you need is a job, and I'll be making a few calls. But I'm not your rabbi. You have to get off your butt and start hitting the bricks. Don't you and Aggie ever talk about the future?''

"Aw, Sarge. I'm always tired. Can't get enough shut-eye.''

"I can tell by your coughing, you're getting enough cigarettes.''

He took Matt and Jenny to Palm Springs for a long weekend. They lounged beside a kidney-shaped swimming pool in eighty-degree weather and ate Mexican food every night. They never heard the ringing of a telephone.

"Matt and I went to the cemetery last week, Daddy. Neither of us had been there since the funeral. I'm glad we went. I haven't cried in a bunch of days.''

"I've been feeling pretty darn good,'' Matt volunteered. "Jenny and I have been having a lot of talks lately. She's pretty smart, for a kid sister.''

Bones, Shea and Speedy also took time off. Fourteen days before Christmas, Dowling boarded a plane for Indiana. Lesson plans and a course outline he had drafted for his class were the only work he had permitted himself to stuff in his attaché kit.

It amazed Dowling how little South Bend had changed. A tremendous field house had been added to the Notre Dame campus, and he and his father stood for a few moments, bundled against the cold, in the end zone of a deserted stadium. They toured the old St. Joseph county courthouse; then Dowling dropped into the police homicide office and frittered away three hours.

"It was just like being in the squad room at home,'' he told his father. "Cops are the greatest people in the world to be around.''

When he said good-bye at the airport, it was with a sense of sadness. His father was eighty years old, and he wondered when they would hug each other again. *If* they would hug each other again.

The day after he returned, he was in the dentist's chair, when his pager went off, and the hygienist dialed the communications division for him.

"Some lady called, Sergeant. Her son just got taken to the hospital. Unconscious. She thinks he may be dead. She wanted you to be called right away."

"Who is the guy? What lady?"

"She said you call him Baby Blue."

Dowling ran from the hospital parking lot to the emergency room. "Baby Blue. I'm looking for Baby Blue," he yelled to figures in green scrubs, who stared at him. A nurse, older, gray-haired, went to him.

"Who are you here for?"

"His name is Jimmie Bench. I call him Baby Blue."

"And you are?"

"Dowling. Vincent Dowling. I'm a friend of his."

"I'm sorry," she said. "There was nothing we could do. The doctor will talk to you in a moment. The decedent's mother and another woman are waiting in the chapel."

Dowling propped himself against a wall. Baby Blue could not be gone. Could not be dead.

"Of course he's dead," the doctor said. "For God's sake, he had a strangulated hernia. Are you the homicide sergeant?"

"Yes."

"His fiancée told me about you. The patient should have been resting frequently. Not smoking. Certainly not running around town, involved with robbers and—"

"But how did he die from it?"

"The intestines came back up and knocked off his blood supply. If you had taken him to a physician he would have found out he had an infection. There were symptoms. The coughing. Fatigue."

"And that's it? Just like that?" Dowling asked.

"His fiancée said he had made a mistake once, paid his debt and had completely straightened himself out. She said you used him . . . hired him. Caused him to abuse his health. Such a loss."

"Thanks for being so understanding, Doc."

He entered the hallway and saw Aggie Pride being consoled by two nurses. When she spied Dowling, she headed for him.

"You son of a—"

"So long, lady. This is where I came in," he yelled, and broke into a run toward the parking lot. He could not tell if she was following. When he turned the corner he knocked down an orderly pushing a cart of supplies. Dowling could not remember where he had parked, and began trotting in tiny circles across the asphalt. A man, a woman and a little girl were standing at the edge of the lot. They looked at one another when the red-haired man in the rumpled brown suit cupped his hands to his mouth and yelled at nobody: "*Come get him, Charon, you whoremonger. You were going to get him all along.*"

When he'd located his car he started it and drove rapidly across the lot. Instead of continuing into the street, he braked abruptly, put the gearshift in park and looked up at the gray skies. He tried to push everything from his mind, and was still trying when the rain began tapping on the roof of the car. Dowling gripped the steering wheel tightly, took a deep breath and looked skyward again.

He remembered from his patrol days how to get to the dirt maintenance road at the rear of the cemetery. The chain between the two metal posts was still not padlocked, and he left the engine running while he removed it. When he walked down the hillside he stepped gingerly on the wet grass, passing grave markers he had not seen for eleven months.

At hers, he folded his hands in front of him and spoke out loud as the soft rain washed over him. "I decided to come in the back way. Don't have the faintest idea why. You left in a hurry. There were so many things I wish I'd said. Isn't that always the way?

"I'm coming to terms with a lot of things about myself. And about what's left to be done. It's raining now, and it rained the last time we were here. Come to think of it, it rained on our first date. That was the happiest night of my life.

"The kids are doing all right, I think. I finally got around to telling them the truth. Fortunately, they seem

to have inherited your good sense, and we're working
our way through this.

"Jeez, you used to tell me to open up and quit keeping things in. Look at me now.

"A little while ago, some guy I was doing business
with died. He'd done a lot of time. He did a good job
for me. At first I thought he was doing it for the dough.
Then he kind of got caught up in it. Like cops do. Now
I don't know what to think about him."

The rain came harder, and his hair matted on his forehead. "Don't ever be ashamed of how you stepped out.
You had more goodness in your little finger than
most. . . ."

He wiped his eyes and forced a smile. "I'll be back
to see you from time to time. I loved you, Helene. I still
do."

Dowling drove slowly to the boardwalk at the foot of
Hawthorn Street. The Old Man was there, on the seawall, bundled in the green sweater. The rain had stopped,
and Dowling walked to his side. Whitecaps crested on
the bay.

"I listened to what you said, and it helped. Everything
is going to work out."

A gull swooped onto the piling nearest them. The bird
seemed to be looking at them. A tuna boat drifted from
its mooring.

"I have to ask you something. How do you know the
difference? Are you an ornithologist? How can you tell
one of those mangy things from the other?"

The Old Man turned toward him. "That bothers you,
doesn't it?"

"Yes, it does. It's frustrating. I study them and study
them. I'm a detective. I like to think I'm able to notice
the little things. But I can't tell one of those damn gulls
from the other."

The Old Man grinned. It was the first time Dowling
had ever seen him smile. Ever. The ancient black eyes
twinkled.

"The truth is, sonny, I can't tell one from the other
either."

Dowling glared at him. His jaw jutted out and his eyes narrowed. The Old Man's grin disappeared. Dowling whirled, took several steps and halted. With his back to the Old Man he looked into the harbor for a full minute. When he finally turned around tears were running down his cheeks. He smiled, then started to laugh. The Old Man looked at him. They laughed together.

Dowling was still laughing when he turned north on Harbor Drive. A cluster of marshmallow clouds was visible from the northwest. He glanced at the service station on the right-hand side of the street, hesitated, then swung into the parking lot between the telephone booth and the trash dumpster. Where the young attendant had been shot to death by the stickup man seven years before. Dowling got out of his car and looked at the dumpster. The suspect had fired, then run toward the side street. A pedestrian had gotten a good look at him, but the case had gone unsolved. Looking down, he paced off the distance from the phone booth to the dumpster. His hands were in his pockets.